THE LAST MAN

ROBERT MCNEIL

BLOODHOUND
BOOKS

First published in 2021 by Bloodhound Books.

www.bloodhoundbooks.com

Print ISBN 978-1-913942-35-9

ALSO BY ROBERT MCNEIL

The Fifth Suspect

1

DCI Alex Fleming was sitting in Superintendent Liz Temple's office. 'Why does Eathan Younger want to see us both, ma'am?'

Temple frowned. 'No idea, but he's been on my back ever since he took up post. My guess is he's probably not going to say anything that'll improve my view of him.'

Fleming was aware there was no love lost between Temple and the assistant chief constable for crime and criminal justice. She'd told him she'd had a run in with Younger some time ago and had described him as a buck-passer, an ambitious workaholic, and a dangerous bastard. Fleming had to admit he'd never liked Younger either, and Temple's advice to tread carefully around him had stuck in Fleming's mind.

'You think this might be anything to do with Upson?'

Fleming also knew that Cecil Daubney, the police and crime commissioner, was after the chief constable's blood because he held him responsible for the high number of unsolved murder cases in Thames Valley. Temple had predicted that Matthew Upson's tenure as chief constable was tenuous.

'Who knows? Daubney wants something done about detection rates on cold cases, and he doesn't think Upson is the man to do it. If Daubney does push Upson out, word has it Younger will be in prime position to take over. He's Daubney's blue-eyed boy apparently.'

'I'm now even more curious why he wants to see us.'

'Let's go find out then, shall we?'

Younger's office was on the top floor of the covert building at Long Hanborough near Oxford. Fleming felt as though he'd walked into a sterile room. The blue carpet showed no sign it had ever seen dust. There was no clutter. Younger's desk was clear apart from a computer screen and keyboard, an open file placed squarely in front of him, and three stacked wire-basket trays holding a few papers, all neatly arranged. Light poured in from a large window behind the desk. A photograph of a tall slim Younger hung on the wall over on the left, showing him receiving some sort of award from Upson. He wore his uniform like an army officer on parade, the epaulettes on his shoulder signifying high rank. Not a hair of his short grey hair was out of place. *A man who likes things to be neat and tidy*, Fleming thought.

Younger didn't get out of his seat. 'Pull up a couple of chairs,' he said without taking his eyes from the file he was studying. He closed it, pulled off his large brown-framed glasses and peered through the lenses to make sure they were clean. 'Just wanted a quick word with you both.'

'Something wrong, sir?' Temple asked.

Younger ignored Temple and looked closely at Fleming. 'Glad you're back at work, Fleming. How's the shoulder? Fully recovered?'

The question didn't seem to Fleming to carry any real sense of concern, despite Fleming having been shot. It was like someone greeting you and asking how you were without really giving a fuck. 'I'm fine, thanks.'

'And raring to get stuck into work again, eh?'

Fleming wondered what was coming next. 'Yes, sir.'

'Good man.' Younger looked at Temple. 'You're probably wondering why I asked to see you both.'

'The thought had crossed my mind,' Temple agreed with a hint of sarcasm.

'I have a little job I want Fleming to take on, working directly to me.'

'Isn't that unusual?' Temple asked. 'DCI Fleming normally reports to me.'

'I know, but I've decided to put him in charge of a cold case review–'

'Excuse me,' Temple cut in, 'DCI Miller heads the cold case review team. Shouldn't he be doing it?'

'Please don't interrupt me, Liz.'

'What's wrong with Jeff Miller and his team looking at it?' Temple persisted, glaring at Younger.

Fleming noticed a twitch starting in Younger's right eyelid. *Don't push your luck, ma'am.*

Younger put the palms of his hands down on his desk and sucked in air through his teeth. 'I have my reasons.'

'But–'

Younger cut Temple off curtly. 'Decision's been made, Temple!'

Fleming noted he'd dropped the use of her first name.

'Miller won't be happy,' Temple persisted.

The twitch in Younger's eyelid had morphed into a spasm in his cheek. 'I'll deal with it!' He tapped the file in front of him. 'William Stroud, worked at the AWE... the Atomic Weapons Establishment in Aldermaston.'

Temple raised an eyebrow. 'We do know what the AWE is.'

'Yes... well... Stroud was shot dead five years ago. No one was arrested and the investigation went cold.' Younger looked at

Fleming. 'I want you to review the case. Familiarise yourself with it and come and see me when you have.'

Temple looked as though she was about to protest again, but didn't get the chance.

'That's all,' Younger said. 'Shut the door behind you.'

Temple closed the door loudly. 'Fucking man!'

Fleming had looked at the case files and was sitting in front of Younger again the next day, on his own this time.

Younger took off his glasses perched high on his hooked nose and polished them with a small blue microfibre cleaning cloth. 'You've studied the files?'

'Yes. I was curious though why you picked this case. Any particular reason?'

'Upson wants quick results. I think the previous investigation was flawed and it's not too old. I think it stands a good chance of a speedy outcome.'

'What makes you think it was flawed, sir?'

'Chap called Frank Ingham was the former SIO. Had a drink problem, wasn't the most efficient officer and, to be fair, he was overloaded. He took medical retirement soon after Upson put the enquiry into mothballs.'

'I see.'

Younger smiled weakly and his right eyelid twitched as he examined his manicured fingernails. 'There's more to it. This is strictly between you and me, understood?'

'Of course.'

'Ingham was convinced a man called Garry Croft was the killer. Croft had moved to Australia a few months after Stroud's murder. Ingham had interviewed him, but there was little or no evidence to justify his arrest. All Ingham had to go on was there was a big row between Stroud and Croft. Something to do with a strike at the time which became a bit heated. You'll have seen it all in the case files.'

'Why is it so sensitive?'

'Because Upson refused to allow Ingham to get Croft traced in Australia on the basis that, even if he found him, there wasn't enough evidence to justify a trip out there to question him again.'

'I see.'

'If your investigation comes to the same conclusion, we may have a similar problem with Upson.'

Fleming smiled. 'So you'd rather I come up with a different suspect?'

The attempt at humour didn't go down well with Younger. His eyelid convulsed again. 'Just solve the case, Fleming. I want an arrest and conviction, and pretty damned quick. And I want you to ensure I'm regularly informed. I'm keeping close to this one, understood?'

Fleming felt duly chastised. 'One final thing, sir. Liz Temple did raise a valid point.'

'She did?'

'Yes. Why get me to take this on and not Jeff Miller?'

'Again, between you and me... there could be a conflict of interest.'

'Oh?'

'Jeff Miller and Ingham were close friends.'

'I'm not sure–'

'That's all, Fleming,' Younger cut him off. 'Keep me informed.'

Back in his own office, Fleming thought about what Younger had been saying and wondered if there was more to refusing to put Jeff Miller on the case than a perceived conflict of interest. *And why is Younger wanting to keep a close eye on this?*

2

There was no sign on the door to say what was inside the small ground-floor office at the back of Thames House. There was only room for two desks, set back to back against one wall. This is was what remained of MI5's subversion unit.

MI5 would never admit such a section existed. Checking up on trade unions, pressure groups, or people in positions of power was something they would rather the public had no idea they were doing. And they no longer saw disruption to key industries as a real threat. The risk, they thought, was now small. There were more pressing things to deal with, the director general claimed. Budgets were tight, and he'd assigned most scarce resources to more vital areas of work.

Toby Omoko sat at one of the two desks. He'd joined straight from university and his boss, Quentin Vere, had put him in the subversion unit. Vere, an assistant director general of dubious repute, had told Omoko the section was as good a place as any to gain experience. Something Omoko soon began to regret. The occupant of the other desk was on long-term sick leave. *Hardly surprising*, Omoko thought, wiping sweat from his forehead.

Health and safety would be an issue anywhere else in the building, but no one cared much about a unit the DG was thinking of closing down.

Sucking in what little cool air there was in the room, Omoko walked over to open the tiny window looking out over a small patio area at the back of the building. It didn't offer much by way of natural light and airflow wasn't a lot better. Omoko cursed and kicked the wall when the window refused to budge more than a couple of inches. He yanked off his tie, took a swig from his water bottle, and looked at the pile of newspapers on his desk.

Omoko dreamed of the day when the DG would see sense and close the unit. Maybe put him on more important work like counter-terrorism. But for now, he doubled up as an analyst and agent handler. The title was a farce. It seemed to imply he handled agents, but in fact he had only one. His agent was not an employee as such, but someone who Vere had recruited from outside to spy on certain people and provide intelligence in select areas.

It was hard, boring work sifting through the papers. His job was to see if there might be anything of interest to MI5. Despite the daily grind, Omoko was thorough, and he scanned every article with a keen eye. Taking off his large gold-framed glasses, he wiped the sweat beginning to run down his forehead into his eyes. He took another swig of water before putting his glasses back on. Then something caught his eye.

A reporter, Zoe Dunbar, had spoken to Eathan Younger, an assistant chief constable at Thames Valley Police. He'd told her they wanted to reduce the number of unsolved murder cases on their files. The bit drawing Omoko's attention was that Younger had asked a DCI Fleming to review a particular case, the murder of William Stroud. He'd been shot five years earlier while he was working at the AWE. No one had ever been arrested for the crime.

Omoko's eyes lit up. *This is interesting*. The problem was he would have to go and see Vere. Face-to-face meetings with him were something he tried to avoid. He sighed, picked up his phone and dialled Vere's number.

'Yes?' Vere's authoritarian voice boomed.

'It's Omoko, sir. I've found something I think you'll be interested in.'

'And what makes you think so, Omoko? It's not often you find anything of value.'

Why is he always such a prick?

'I think you'll find this is, sir.'

'If you think so, come up and see me... but it better be good. I've an important meeting in fifteen minutes.'

Vere's office was on the second floor at the front of the building. He was sitting behind an old antique desk, empty apart from a computer screen and keyboard on one corner. Behind him was a large window looking out over the River Thames. He was polishing a pair of horn-rimmed glasses as Omoko entered. He looked up and squinted at Omoko through watery brown eyes. Omoko thought the man looked ill. His pasty face, heavy jowls and bald head glistened with sweat.

'All right, Omoko, don't just stand there, tell me what you've found.' He put his glasses back on before adding, 'And keep it brief. I'm busy.'

Omoko noted the empty desk and doubted it. 'It's a newspaper article written by a journalist... Zoe Dunbar.'

Vere raised an eyebrow. 'Oh?'

'She had an interview with an assistant chief constable from Thames Valley Police who told her he'd put a DCI Fleming in charge of a cold case.'

'And?'

'He's to look into the murder of William Stroud.'

'Is that so?' Vere's attitude suddenly changed.

'Yes. You may recall he was shot five years ago after the strike at the AW–'

'I don't need reminding, Omoko!' Vere cut in. 'I'm perfectly aware of what happened to Stroud.'

'Sorry. There's also talk of another strike looming at Aldermaston.'

'Really?' Vere stroked his chin. 'In that case I think you'd best keep an eye on things there, and on this Fleming chap. See if he gets anywhere with his enquiries.'

'Yes, sir.'

'And get onto your agent, Falcon. We need to keep abreast of this.'

'Okay.'

'And make damned sure you keep a low profile. We don't want anyone to find out we have an interest, understand?'

'Of course.'

'All right. Keep me informed, and close the door as you go out, there's a good chap.'

Omoko turned to leave.

'By the way, Omoko, I think you should do something about your appearance.'

Omoko couldn't see the smirk on Vere's face, but he knew what he was talking about. It wasn't because he'd removed his tie or because he came to work in casual clothes. Vere had on more than one occasion commented on his curly-top haircut, pencil moustache and the short beard round his jawline.

You're a bigoted arsehole, Omoko thought as he closed Vere's door behind him.

~

Back in his office, Omoko picked up the phone.

Falcon answered after two rings. 'Yes?'

'I've just been to see Vere,' Omoko said. 'There's something you need to keep an eye on.'

3

Fleming pushed the door open to the spare office DS Harry Logan had managed to acquire for storing all the old files on the Stroud case. Logan was already there with DC Naomi Anderson.

'You seen this lot, sir?' Logan asked, looking up from an open box on the floor. 'Cardboard boxes full of files, reports, documents, case notes, witness statements, photos and God knows what else.'

'Keep you busy, Sarge,' Anderson quipped.

Logan closed the lid on the box he'd been handling. 'Oh yeah? Guess who's going to have to sort this lot out and make an inventory, Naomi. Every single piece of evidence, mind you. But before you start, I think coffees would be good.'

'Thought you'd never ask, Sarge,' Anderson retorted.

'You're so witty today, Naomi.'

Fleming smiled at the two of them. Logan: in his fifties, receding grey hair, ex-army, rugged weather-beaten face, acted like a father figure to Anderson. Naomi: young, still in her twenties, tall slim and attractive, Jamaican roots. Logan was deeply protective of her and she had developed a keen fondness for him. They ribbed each other at every opportunity but the bond between them was evident.

'By the way, boss, how's the shoulder?' Logan asked.

'Fine, Harry, thanks.'

Anderson made to go and put the kettle on. 'Suppose you'll want some of those chocolate biscuits I brought in, Sarge?'

Logan's eyes lit up. 'Naomi, what would we ever do without you?'

'Huh.'

'Oh, by the way, boss,' Logan said, 'Jeff Miller popped in earlier. Seems he's not a happy bunny. Heads the cold case review team, doesn't he?'

Fleming had been expecting a visit from Miller. 'He does.'

'So why is he not taking charge of this?'

'You're not the first person to ask why, believe me. But Eathan Younger has his reasons.'

Logan shrugged. 'Okay.'

The pair continued in silence to look through the boxes until Anderson returned with three coffees and a plate full of chocolate biscuits.

'Service with a smile,' Logan announced.

'They're for three, not just you,' Anderson reminded him.

Logan grabbed a biscuit and a mug. 'Speaking of Eathan Younger, boss, how come he's taking such an interest in this particular case? Unusual, isn't it?'

'Maybe. Not exactly sure why he's got a thing about this. But it doesn't really matter. It's down to us, and Younger's made it clear he wants an arrest and conviction and, to use his words, pretty damned quick.'

'No pressure then?' Logan groaned.

Fleming looked at the piles of boxes and documents littering the desk, sitting on filing cabinet tops, and all over the floor. 'No pressure.'

'Where on earth do we start, sir?' Anderson asked.

Fleming took a sip of his coffee and looked for a space on the desk to put his mug. 'We need to get some sort of order out of all this chaos. Let's start by listing all the material we have.'

'And then?' Logan asked.

'And then we create a spreadsheet–'

'Ah,' Logan exclaimed, cutting in, 'sounds like a job for you, Naomi. You're good at that sort of thing.'

Anderson smiled. 'Some of us *are* familiar with the use of technology, Sarge.'

Logan pointed to the computer screen perched on the end of the desk. 'Your computer awaits you...'

'All right. Naomi can set it up and do the typing, but you and I will have to get on with the sorting, Harry,' Fleming said.

Anderson smiled. 'I'm more than happy to do the spreadsheet. Pity there's a lot of dust on those boxes,' she added, looking at Logan.

'Hmm, trust you to end up with the clean job,' Logan complained.

'Your idea, Sarge.'

'Okay, boss,' Logan said, looking at Fleming, 'how do we do this?'

'We sift through everything. Naomi logs it all in date order by type of data or information received during the original investigation. And we need to list the names of everyone interviewed, by whom and when.'

'Ah, okay,' Logan said. 'I get it. We end up with lists in sequential order of the steps taken on the original investigation.'

'You've got it, Harry.'

'Then what, boss?'

'We create a to-do list of things that need to be done, by whom and in what order, and that gives us our investigative strategy.'

'You make it sound simple, boss.'

'It is. The difficult part is going to be finding the killer. Something the original investigation failed to do.'

'Do you want all this information on one spreadsheet, sir? Or do you want a separate to-do list spreadsheet?' Anderson asked.

'Keep it all on one if you can, Naomi.'

'Okay, no problem.'

'I told you she was good at that sort of thing,' Logan quipped.

Fleming smiled. 'The first thing I need to do is report back to Younger on how we're going to go about this. Then I want to go and talk to the HR manager at the AWE... see if we can get somewhere there to set up as a base for interviewing staff.'

'Anything you want me and Naomi to make a start on once we've finished logging everything?' Logan asked.

Fleming recalled Younger's words. *Chap called Frank Ingham was the original SIO. Had a drink problem, wasn't the most efficient officer and, to be fair, he was overloaded.* 'Might be a good idea to search for any strands of the investigation that may have been overlooked or not followed through.'

'Any reason for thinking things were missed?' Logan asked.

Fleming didn't want to repeat what Younger had told him. 'No, but if you check through all the records you may find someone was asked to do something that didn't get done.'

'You mean due to lack of time or resources?' Anderson asked.

'Or incompetence?' Logan offered.

'Always worth checking,' Fleming said. 'Then you can start to review the records of Stroud's last days: who did he see, where and when was he killed, why was he there, any forensic information, any DNA found at or near the murder scene.'

'Okay, boss. What's your plan?' Logan asked.

'I want to go and have a word with Frank Ingham.'

Logan frowned. 'Who's he?'

'He was the investigating officer. Now retired.'

At home later, Fleming was swirling some of his favourite Laphroaig single malt whisky round a glass, wondering if Younger had passed him a poisoned chalice. He wasn't convinced Jeff Miller's old friendship with Ingham would have prevented him reviewing the Stroud case impartially. *Maybe there's more to this than meets the eye. And why does Younger want me to report direct to him?*

4

The house Dan Rimmer was watching was halfway down a row of terraced houses in a residential area south of Reading town centre. He'd been sitting in his black Volvo V40 for the best part of an hour waiting for a sign of the target. Not wanting to get too near to the house, he'd parked his car where he found a space a few cars back from the man's silver Vauxhall Astra, making sure he was facing the same direction.

Rimmer's left leg was aching, and he was wondering if Astra Man was going to appear. He rubbed his thigh where a large piece of shrapnel had pierced his leg while serving in Afghanistan. Leaving the army after ten years, he'd joined his uncle, Phil Wyatt, as a private investigator. Rimmer was making to switch the radio on when his mobile vibrated and a James Bond theme ringtone indicated an incoming call. He glanced at the screen: *Phil.*

Rimmer tapped the answer icon. 'Hi mate.'

'Any joy?'

'Not yet.'

'Think he'll show this week?'

'Hmm. Not sure. Doesn't look like it. Might give it a few more minutes.'

'Okay. I'll see you in the office la–'

'Got to go.' Rimmer cut in. 'I have eyes on the target. He's leaving the house now.'

Rimmer watched the man climb into his Astra and a few seconds later it was pulling out behind a passing car. He tapped the palms of his hands on the steering wheel as he had to wait for three other vehicles to pass before he could pull out to follow. His target was heading in a southerly direction. Rimmer was catching up a few cars behind, but then cursed as the car in front indicated to turn right and had to wait for oncoming vehicles before it could turn. Rimmer sighed and ran a hand through his dark-brown tousled hair. The Astra was now some distance in front, but still in sight.

The car in front finally managed to make the turn and Rimmer put his foot down to try to close the gap on the Astra. He was two cars behind and began to relax, but not for long. There was a pedestrian crossing up ahead and a woman with a young child stepped out onto the road. Rimmer braked sharply. 'Fuck!'

The woman smiled sweetly and held a hand up as a gesture of thanks. The child dropped a doll on the ground and the mother paused to pick it up. She looked at Rimmer and mouthed, *sorry*. Rimmer returned the smile through his thick beard while he waited. The Astra was now going left. Once the road was clear, Rimmer put his foot down again and took the same turning as the Astra, but there was no sign of it. He stopped the car and thumped the steering wheel with both hands.

Rimmer called his uncle. 'Lost him.'

'Where are you?'

Rimmer gave him the name of the street.

'Hang on.' There was a short delay before his uncle was back on the phone. 'There's a recreation ground there with just a small entrance to a driveway leading to a parking area. It's about halfway along the street.'

'On it,' Rimmer confirmed, putting his car into gear.

He saw the entrance a few hundred yards further up the road and turned into the driveway. There was a large parking area on the verge of playing fields with several football pitches. He spotted the empty Astra, parked a few cars away facing the pitches. *Result!*

After a few minutes, football players streamed out from a single-storey building housing the changing rooms. One of the last men out was Astra Man. Rimmer watched as the players did their warming up exercises and kicked a few balls about.

Once the referee had checked everything was in order, the game started. Astra Man was playing in goal. *Perfect*, Rimmer thought. He picked up his camcorder and eased his long frame out of the car. Astra Man was soon in action, making diving saves and jumping to punch high balls clear. It was during the fourth session of recording when Astra Man spotted Rimmer.

'Oi, you! What the fuck d'you think you're doing?'

Rimmer had what he wanted and turned to leave as Astra Man left his goal and ran across the pitch towards him. The other players and referee watched with jaws dropped in surprise. Rimmer reached his car, reversed quickly and looked in his rear-view mirror as he pulled away to see Astra Man throw his gloves on the ground and stick a finger up in the air.

Rimmer smiled and threw a wave back over his shoulder.

The small office of Wyatt Investigations sat between two retail outlets in a row of shops just out of Reading town centre. Phil Wyatt lived in a flat above the office. He'd served with the military police for ten years and joined a firm of private investigators in London after leaving the army. His wife died in a car accident eight years later. He'd moved to Reading and set up his own private investigator company.

Wyatt had his feet up on a cluttered desk, his favourite handmade wooden pipe in one hand and a cup of black coffee in the other. 'So, young Dan, it looks like your fraud investigation is going to plan, eh?'

Rimmer smiled. He loved his uncle's good humour and cheery Welsh sing-song voice which belied the man's tough, resilient nature. 'I'm not that young, Phil. I am thirty-five, you know.'

'Ah, I know, Dan. But compared to a bald fifty-something-year-old man like me you're still young. Anyway, looks like your surveillance has paid off.'

'Yep, got the subject on camcorder, full of energy and no sign of any injury. It's case closed, and a big fat pay cheque on the way for us. A hundred grand fraudulent claim for compensation for an alleged injury at work will probably get him a custodial sentence. Video footage proves his claim he was hardly able to walk a load of crap.'

'Good job,' Phil said. He puffed on his pipe and blew a stream of smoke up in the air. 'By the way, have you seen this?' Pulling his feet off the desk, he threw a newspaper over for Rimmer to see. It was Zoe Dunbar's article on William Stroud.

Rimmer frowned. 'No.'

'Looks like this chap, DCI Fleming, has been asked to have a fresh look at the case.' Wyatt thought for a moment and rubbed a hand over his stubble beard. 'Best keep an eye on him and this

Dunbar reporter, eh? Might throw up some clues on Garry Croft. Speaking of which, have you heard anything lately?'

'No. Still in Australia by all accounts. His mother's in a care home in High Wycombe. The manager's promised to let me know if he comes back to see her.'

'Think she'll remember?'

'Maybe not. That's why I have something else in mind.'

5

Fleming was back in his office after a briefing meeting with Younger and Temple. It had been a relatively painless affair. Younger had been impressed with Fleming's methodical approach, but had once more made it clear he wanted rapid progress.

Fleming wasn't sure where Younger stood. Did he think Frank Ingham was right about Garry Croft? If so, was he prepared to approve funding for Fleming to pursue Croft in Australia? Or, did he think Ingham had missed something and someone else was the killer? What was clear was Younger wasn't prepared to offer a steer. Fleming recalled what Temple had told him. *The man's a buck-passer.*

The tension between Temple and Younger had been apparent again. Fleming wasn't sure what it was all about, but sometimes people didn't get on with each other. Temple had drawn Fleming to one side after they'd left Younger's office. 'Remember, be careful. I don't know why Younger's taking a personal interest in the Stroud affair and why he wants you to report progress direct to him.'

Fleming couldn't think why either.

'I want to know in advance what information you intend to pass on to him,' Temple had added.

Fleming pushed his thoughts to one side when there was a sharp knock on his door. Jeff Miller strode in without waiting. 'Got a minute, Fleming?'

Fleming noted the Welsh accent. He hadn't met Miller before but recognised him from the organisation chart photographs. Probably in his fifties, he was a tall, imposing looking man with short grey hair and the merest hint of stubble on his chin. 'Sure, DCI Miller, isn't it? Or do I call you Jeff?'

'Jeff is fine,' he replied in a hoarse voice.

He's either got a cold, or he's a heavy smoker, Fleming thought. 'What can I do for you, Jeff?'

Miller ignored the question. 'What part of Scotland do you hail from, Fleming?'

'Edinburgh. And you can call me Alex.'

'Thought so. I used to know someone from Edinburgh and the accent sounded familiar.'

Fleming smiled. 'I'm assuming you didn't come only to find out where I was born.'

'Ah, no, just making small talk.'

Fleming knew why Miller was there but asked anyway. 'So, what did you want to see me about?'

'Mind if I sit down, take the weight off my legs?'

'Help yourself.'

Miller pulled a chair over and sat astride it backwards, folding his arms over the top bar. 'Can I ask why Eathan Younger has asked you to look into the old Stroud case?'

'Liz Temple asked him why. She said you should be taking it on, but he told her he'd made the decision. I asked him again later when I was on my own with him and he suggested there might be a conflict of interest.'

'Ah, I get it. He told you Frank Ingham and I were friends?'

'He did.'

'Typical of Younger. He's never seen eye to eye with me... or Liz Temple for that matter. Fucking man doesn't think I've got the integrity to put friendship to one side and do a professional job.'

'Why do you say Younger never got on with you or Liz Temple?'

'Long story, but basically he fucked things up on an old murder enquiry and blamed Temple and me for it. Then, when we finally arrested the culprit and got a conviction, he took all the credit. Stabbed us in the back. Bloody buck-passer.'

So that's why there's no love lost between Temple and Younger, Fleming realised. 'Care to tell me how he fucked things up?'

'Temple was a DCI at the time and I was a DI. We were working together on a murder enquiry and felt we had enough evidence to arrest a man. Younger disagreed. Told us he wanted us to get more conclusive evidence before we made an arrest. He thought there wasn't enough to secure a conviction.'

'So what happened?'

'We held off making an arrest while we looked for more evidence. Frankly, we didn't think we needed any. We were convinced we had enough. Then the killer commits another murder and Younger goes public in a press conference to say how sorry he is. He says two detectives had let him down by not arresting the man sooner. Said he wanted the man arrested and claimed Temple and I delayed thinking we needed more evidence.'

'You didn't challenge him about that?'

'Temple tried to, but he told her it might affect her promotion if she opened her mouth. Told her it was our word against his and guess who the chief constable would believe.'

'So you both kept quiet.'

'Didn't have much choice, mate. We took the blame for Younger's cock-up. Bastard!'

Fleming was beginning to see Younger in a new light. *Tread carefully around him*, he recalled Temple saying. 'Listen, Jeff, I understand how you're hacked off with the way things are, but I can't refuse to carry out a direct order.'

'Don't worry, not your fault. This all confirms my suspicions. Younger wants to replace me as head of the cold case review team. Maybe he plans for you to take over.'

'I sincerely hope not. For your sake... and mine. I'd much prefer to stay where I am in the major crime unit. As far as I'm concerned, this is a one-off.'

Miller got up to leave. 'You know what makes it worse? The fucking man didn't even have the decency to tell me face to face he was getting you to look at the Stroud case. I found out when I saw the Zoe Dunbar article about it.'

'Sorry.'

'Not your fault, Alex. Best of luck. I think you'll need it.'

Fleming watched the door close behind Miller and was beginning to feel distinctly uneasy.

6

The trip down to Aldermaston had been uneventful, apart from the usual light-hearted banter between Logan and Anderson. Fleming had, in the main, remained silent. He had a lot on his mind.

Logan had booked a car out from the pool and was driving. The previous few days of hot, sunny weather had given way to thunderstorms. Logan had switched the wipers to full speed as bursts of rain hit the windscreen. They'd made good progress down the A34 despite the weather and heavy traffic.

'Rain and too many cars on the road,' Logan had muttered. 'Rather be back at the ranch with a nice cup of coffee and a few biscuits.'

'If you're in luck, Sarge, Ursula Nieve might supply some when we get to Aldermaston,' Anderson had retorted.

Nieve was the HR manager at the AWE. Fleming had phoned her the day before to arrange a meeting, explaining they had reopened the Stroud murder case. They'd arrived, had passed through security and were waiting in a reception area outside Nieve's office. A secretary had told them Nieve would be with them shortly and asked if they would like tea or coffee. They gratefully accepted the latter.

After a few minutes, the secretary's internal phone buzzed. She picked it up and listened. 'Okay, I'll send them in.' The secretary smiled. 'Ursula will see you now. Sorry for the delay. She had a conference call.'

Nieve rose from her desk, hand outstretched to greet them as they entered her office. Fleming shook her hand and noted the grip was firm and confident. She was tall, slim, had high cheekbones and looked every part the smart, efficient executive. Her jet-black hair was swept tightly back and pinned into a sleek low bun. He guessed she was in her forties. A pure white blouse contrasted with a neat suit matching the colour of her hair. 'DCI Fleming, I presume?' she whispered in a husky voice.

'Yes. DS Logan and DC Anderson,' Fleming said, pointing to his two colleagues.

'Pleased to meet you,' Nieve said, shaking hands with both of them. She waved a hand towards a small round table with four chairs. 'Take a seat. Can I get you a drink?'

Logan was about to say something, but Anderson spoke first. 'That's very kind but your secretary's already given us coffee.'

'Good.' Nieve looked at Fleming. 'You told me on the phone you were reopening the Stroud murder enquiry. Any particular reason?'

'The chief constable is under pressure to reduce the number of unsolved murders in Thames Valley. Because Stroud's murder is relatively recent, people who were interviewed at the time might still be around and be able to recollect things.'

'I see. I wasn't here then. The previous HR manager had some sort of breakdown after Stroud's death and took early retirement. I was recruited to replace him.'

'Can you let us have contact details for him? We'll need to talk to him.'

'I'm afraid you won't be able to. He died soon after taking retirement.'

Fleming thought for a moment. 'Any family we can speak to? It would be good to get some perspective of what was going on here at the time from people who knew him.'

'I think his wife is still alive. I'll get my secretary to email you her address.'

'Thank you.'

'As for what was going on at the time, there was a strike and Stroud was a prominent union member.'

'Yes, I was aware of that from the old casework files.'

Nieve frowned. 'Your files obviously had something missing.'

Fleming raised an eyebrow.

'You weren't aware Nat Horne was dead.'

'Who?'

'Nat Horne was the HR manager,' Nieve explained.

'Thanks for pointing it out.' Fleming couldn't remember seeing anything in the case notes to suggest anyone had ever interviewed the HR manager. *First oversight by Ingham?* He made a mental note to get Logan and Anderson to check the files again.

'By the way, you may have seen on the news we've got another strike looming. Same issue. It's all about pay and pensions again. Chap called Kauffman is the union boss. He's a bit of a militant. Meetings between management and the union have been somewhat acrimonious to say the least.'

'Was he the union leader during the last strike at the time of Stroud's death?' Fleming asked.

'Yes, as a matter of fact he was, though Stroud was killed some months after the strike had ended.'

'Okay, we'll need to speak to him, which brings me to why my two colleagues are here. We'll want to interview all the staff who worked here at the time of Stroud's murder and who are still employed by you. From a practical point of view, it would be great if you could find a small room where DS Logan and DC Anderson could carry out those interviews. We'll want to talk to those who were close to Stroud and all union members in particular.'

'Not a problem. I'll get something arranged. When do you want to start?'

'As soon as you have space available. Anderson can let you have a list of all the people the police interviewed before. It would be good if you could let her know how many of them still work here. Oh, and if any have since left, their forwarding addresses.'

'Sure, no problem.' Nieve hesitated for a second. 'You'll let me know how things are going?'

'Sure.' Fleming assumed she meant with the staff interviews. *Or does she have a wider interest.*

7

Rimmer had gone to see Yvette Boudreaux, the manager of the Ridgeway Manor Care Home on the outskirts of High Wycombe. He'd first been to see her a few years earlier when setting out to trace Garry Croft. The only clue he had was that his mother was resident in the care home. Boudreaux had promised to get in touch with Rimmer if Croft ever came to visit his mother or left any details of how she could contact him. He never did, but he sent a few letters to his mother and phoned every few months from a public payphone in Australia to see how his mother was. It was clear Croft didn't want anyone, including his mother, to know exactly where he was.

Boudreaux had nothing new to tell Rimmer, but on his way out, he bumped into a woman smoking a cigarette by the main entrance. 'Visits always a bit traumatic, eh?'

'No... I work here.' She paused for a moment and smiled. 'But working here can be stressful at times.'

'I bet.' Rimmer pulled out a pack of cigarettes. 'Mind if I join you?' He'd taken an instant liking to the woman. Maybe it was her smile and friendly face. She was short and had long dark hair which was neatly braided. Technically, she was obese, but it was kinder to look on her as being of solid build. Dark brown eyes peered through horn-rimmed glasses.

'Not at all. Have you been visiting?'

'Just been to see the manager.' Rimmer offered a smile of his own. 'Name's Rimmer, by the way, Dan Rimmer.'

'Makena Kibet.' The woman took a deep drag of her cigarette and blew smoke up into the air. She shifted her weight from one foot to the other. 'Have you a relative you want to find a place for here? That why you've been to see the manager?'

Rimmer saw an opportunity. 'No. I'm a private investigator and I'm trying to find a man who now lives in Australia. His mother's a resident here.'

'Really, who?'

'Ethel Croft.'

'Ah, yes, I spend a lot of my time with her. She's a dear old lady. It's a tragedy about her son. He hardly gets in touch with her and won't give her his address or phone number. It's awful for her.'

Rimmer took a chance. 'Maybe you can help me find him.'

Makena frowned. 'How?'

'You could keep your eyes and ears open and let me know if Mrs Croft hears from her son? Or maybe if you hear the manager saying anything if she gets a call from him. I'd be happy to pay you for any information you can supply that might help me trace him.'

'I don't know...'

Rimmer stubbed out his cigarette and made to leave. 'Think about it. Meet me at half five in Annie's café in Wycombe if you'd like to help. Mrs Croft might be grateful.'

Rimmer left, crossed his fingers and hoped she would come.

It was late afternoon and still hot. Rimmer was sitting in Annie's café waiting for Makena. A few wasps buzzed around cream cakes by the till and the smell of cooking wafted through from the kitchen. Settling for a black coffee, he found a spare table with two seats at the rear of the café. Rimmer sat with his back to the wall so he could see out onto the street through the large front window.

Makena was late. Rimmer was beginning to think she wasn't going to appear. Then he saw her, pushing her way through the door. He got up to greet her. 'Glad you came. What can I get you?'

'Coffee please, and could I have one of those cream cakes as well?'

Rimmer smiled. 'Sure, of course.' He placed the order and indicated to where he'd been sitting.

Makena was slightly out of breath as she settled herself at the table. 'Sorry, I'm a bit late. Didn't get away right on time.'

'No problem. I'm sure they keep you busy. Pleased you could make it though.'

'Been thinking about that. You told me you'd been to see Yvette and I was curious why you thought I might be able to help you any more than she could.'

'I saw her some years ago when I started trying to trace Mr Croft. The only lead I had was his mother in the care home. Mrs Boudreaux said she would let me know if he ever arranged to visit his mother or if she found any way to get in touch with him. I've checked with her a few times since but she had nothing. Today was yet another wasted trip... until I met you.'

'So how do you think I might be able to help?'

'Mrs Boudreaux is the manager and must have other more important things on her mind. You're on the front line, so to speak. You said you spend a lot of your time with Mrs Croft. You also seemed to know a bit about her and the fact her son hasn't given her any contact details. I'll pay you well for anything you can find out.'

Makena paused to thank the waitress who had brought her coffee and cake. 'Not sure how that'll help you though,' Makena mumbled through a full mouth after taking a sizeable bite.

'You would know if Mrs Croft did receive a letter or phone call. You could show interest in her son – maybe ask her what he says in his letters or what he tells her over the phone if he rings.'

'But he still won't leave her any way of contacting him.'

'This is where you could practice your detective skills.'

Makena tilted her head. 'How?'

'Ask her what her son has been doing. Has he visited anywhere? Has he given any clues as to where he might be living? Maybe he's been to see a concert, been to a theatre, show or football match. I could then check where that would have been in Australia. A general location would be a start. Get the idea?'

Makena hesitated. 'I... I think so. All a bit cloak and dagger though. It must be very important if you've been trying to trace Ethel's son for years.'

Rimmer felt he owed Makena an explanation. 'A client of mine wants to find him because Mr Croft's been left a large sum of money.'

'Did you tell Yvette about it? Surely she would have told Mr Croft on one of his phone calls?'

'I believe she did, but he'd told her there must be a mistake because he didn't know anyone with a lot of money.'

Makena nodded her understanding. 'Okay, I'll see what I can do.'

Rimmer was having a nightmare and woke in a cold sweat. His leg was aching and he was reliving the moment when the IED had exploded and he'd felt the searing pain as shrapnel slammed into his thigh. He went to the kitchen and pulled a can of beer from the fridge, took a deep swig and slouched into a chair, thinking about his meeting with Makena. *It really would be a result if she was able to find out something.*

8

Logan and Anderson were at the AWE with the list of all employees who Frank Ingham's team had previously interviewed. Ursula Nieve had ticked off those who still worked there. Quite a few had since left – some had forwarding addresses, some did not. Logan had decided the quickest way forward was to interview those who still worked at the AWE first. Afterwards, they would pick up the ones Nieve had contact details for who had left. Tracing those who had left and for whom there were no contact details would be last on the list.

'I hope this is okay for you,' Nieve said, opening the door to the temporary office she'd found for the two detectives. 'I'm afraid it's a bit small. We sometimes use it for appraisal interviews and when dealing with personal staff issues. I'm down the corridor. Give my secretary a shout if you need anything.'

Logan cast his eyes over the room. It was tiny, but big enough to accommodate three people. It did have a window which was a plus point. There was a small table with two chairs on one side and one on the other. *Just like a police interview room*, Logan mused. He smiled and looked into Nieve's brown eyes. 'It'll be fine, Mrs Nieve.'

Nieve turned to go. 'Once you're settled in, let my secretary know who you want to interview and she'll get them for you.'

'Great,' Logan said. 'We'll have to do it one by one though rather than give her a list with times. You never know how long interviews like this will take. Depends on how much people still remember.'

'I understand. Well, I'll leave you to it. I need to go. I've an important meeting with the union. Gloves could be off. Anyway, do let me know how you're getting on.'

As the door closed behind her, Anderson spoke. 'Have you noticed something, Sarge?'

'Being a good detective, I observe a lot of things, Naomi. Was there something in particular I'm supposed to have noticed?'

'That Mrs Nieve seems very keen to find out how we're doing.'

Logan shrugged. 'Natural curiosity – or polite enquiry?'

'Hmm, not so sure. She asked DCI Fleming to let her know how things were going as well. She also asked him if there was any particular reason for us looking into the Stroud case again.'

'You're getting paranoid. You'll be coming out with some conspiracy theory next. But well done for noticing things. Just keep your razor-sharp mind focused on the interviews. You might notice something important,' Logan quipped.

'Humph! And – she's only asked us again to let her know how we get on.'

Logan smiled and shook his head. He tapped a finger on the list of names and sighed. 'We've got our work cut out here.'

'With you on that one, Sarge. I still wonder why they've got us looking into this and not Jeff Miller and his cold case review team.'

'Your mind's working overtime. You need to focus on the interviews instead of driving yourself nuts with questions.'

'You're so full of wisdom, Sarge. Must make your brain hurt at times.'

Logan wagged a finger at Anderson. 'I'll make your brain hurt in a minute if you're not careful.'

Anderson smiled and held up her hands. 'You win, Sarge.'

'Okay, before we start, to recap – we have William Stroud, a union man working at the AWE. Murdered five years ago shortly after the end of a strike. The killer shot Stroud four times in the head at close range as he was leaving a pub with a friend. He'd pulled up next to the kerb on a large motorbike, fired the shots, and then sped off before anyone realised what was happening. Forensics reckoned the murder weapon was a Browning nine-millimetre handgun. No other forensic or DNA evidence was found at the scene pointing to the killer.'

'So, the first person to interview is the man who was with Stroud when he was shot?'

Logan thought for a moment. 'No,' he finally decided, 'because he'd said the man – assuming it was a man – was in full leather protective clothing and wore a dark visor helmet. He couldn't provide a description and had no idea who would want to kill Stroud.'

'Okay, according to the files, DCI Ingham was convinced the killer was Garry Croft who later moved to Australia. There was a big row between Stroud and Croft so maybe we should see the man who first reported that.'

Logan could see a plan of action forming. 'Good idea, Naomi. Then we see the union leader, Kauffman.'

'Followed by?'

'We move on to all those who knew Stroud well, then all the other union members.'

'This is going to take some time, Sarge – and that's before we have to start tracing people who've left and we have no contact details for.'

'Afraid so, Naomi, and there's no other resources working on this. It's only the boss and us two.'

'Going to be lots of overtime forms to sign off, by the looks of it.'

Logan grinned. 'Oh, yes! Extra cash is always welcome even if the additional hours aren't.'

~

Logan and Anderson had worked late into the afternoon. They'd seen ten people including the union leader, Bill Kauffman. 'What do you think of it so far, Naomi?' Logan asked.

'Not much has come up that we didn't already know from the old case files. Memories have faded. But maybe we have a clearer picture. Stroud seemed to be militant, but some thought it was a bit contrived. Croft was apparently a nasty piece of work, and Kauffman was certainly an extremist, but clever, and shrewd.'

'About sums it up,' Logan agreed.

'One thing though. I know you'll think I'm obsessed with this, but when I went to tell Mrs Nieve's secretary we were done for the day, Mrs Nieve's office door was open. I heard her on the phone to someone. She was telling them she'd arranged a room for us and was keeping an eye on progress – just saying.'

9

Fleming parked his old Porsche on Frank Ingham's rough flagstone driveway. Weeds were sprouting between and through cracks in the flagstones. The house was semi-detached on a little plot situated in a cul-de-sac less than a mile from Woodstock town centre and, from the look of the front garden, Ingham was no gardener.

Fleming rang the doorbell and waited. It was a minute before an out of breath Frank Ingham opened the door. He'd been a tall man when younger and fitter, but now he was overweight with a stooped posture. He was bald on top but had thick, untidy grey hair on the sides that merged into a short grey beard. A cigarette was hanging out of his mouth and he leaned heavily on a walking stick. The faded blue jeans, vest and cream cardigan he was wearing did nothing to enhance his appearance.

How to keep yourself looking good, Fleming mused.

'Been expecting you. DCI Fleming, isn't it? You'd better come in.'

Ingham showed Fleming into a rectangular, sparsely furnished sitting room. 'Take a seat.'

Fleming decided on the two-seater sofa and sank down on springs that had long since gone.

'I'll get that replaced at some stage.' Ingham laughed. 'You're looking at the old Stroud case I gather?'

'That's right. I'd like to ask you about the original investigation, if that's okay?'

Ingham took a last drag of his cigarette and stubbed it out in an ashtray next to a near-empty whisky glass on a coffee table by his side. 'Younger got you on this then instead of my old mate, Jeff Miller?' There was a hint of bitterness in his voice.

'Maybe it's because you were old mates,' Fleming suggested.

'I was being sarcastic. It won't be anything to do with the fact we were friends.'

'Oh?'

'There are things you obviously don't know, Fleming.'

'Go on.'

'Did Younger tell you I was sure I knew who the killer was?'

'He did. You thought it was Garry Croft, a union man who worked at the AWE – moved to Australia a few months after Stroud was murdered.'

'That's right. He and Stroud had a big bust-up over something to do with a strike at the time. I'd interviewed Croft and saw him as a prime suspect. Not enough hard evidence to arrest him though. Then he disappears off to Australia. That clinched it for me.'

'I heard that the chief constable put a hold on extending the investigation to Australia because he felt there wasn't enough evidence to justify the cost. Is that right?'

'That's what Younger told you, no doubt. But he was the one behind it, mark my words. It was all about budgets five years ago – saving money. I think he went crawling to Upson to say he could save money by putting a hold on the Stroud investigation. He tells him I was sure we had identified the killer and that there were no other suspects. Not worth getting the Australian police to trace Croft, send someone out to interview him when they find him, and then go through a long extradition process.'

'Hang on, so why would he now be chomping at the bit to have the case reopened?'

'Because things have changed. It's no longer about budgets – it's to do with clear-up rates now that the police and crime commissioner's on Upson's back to reduce the number of unsolved murder cases.'

'Still doesn't answer why Younger picked this case, especially if he was the one behind it being shelved five years ago.'

'Because he knows that I was right about Croft. He's sure he'll get a quick result with a bit more evidence, which he no doubt thinks you'll find. Cost is no longer an issue. It's all results driven now.'

Fleming frowned. 'So why not get Jeff Miller to deal with it?'

'That's what I was getting round to. Bugger all to do with us being friends. He doesn't like Jeff – doesn't rate him. Younger wants to get rid of him. There's a bit of history there. Blames Jeff for the poor results on cold cases.'

'He didn't think Jeff was up to it, is that what you're saying?'

'The opposite. He's obviously afraid Jeff would get a quick result based on my original investigation. That would hardly help his case for getting rid of him.'

'That's quite some claim, Frank.'

'There's more. It was soon after the case was shelved that Younger tried to persuade me to take early retirement on health grounds. Didn't want me around telling tales.'

'And you didn't have health issues?'

'Yes, I did but half of that was the stress caused by that prick, Younger. He was promoted to assistant chief constable just before the Stroud case and wanted to make a name for himself by saving money.' Ingham picked up the whisky glass, gulped down the remaining contents and placed the empty glass on the coffee table. 'He's now after Upson's job, you know.'

'So I hear.' Fleming remembered Temple's words, *he's a workaholic and ruthlessly ambitious. Tread carefully around him.*

Ingham sighed. 'I was glad to leave in the end.'

'How did you find out that Croft had gone to Australia?'

'I went to his flat and he wasn't there. Spoke to the landlady who told me that he'd gone to live in Australia and how awful it was that he'd left a frail old mother in a care home.'

'Where was that?'

'The Ridgeway Manor Care Home on the outskirts of High Wycombe. I saw the manager there and she had no way of contacting Croft. He left no forwarding address or contact details with anyone – not even with his own mother, for God's sake! Made me even more convinced he'd done a runner.'

'Okay, Frank, thanks for all that. Anything else I should know?'

'An investigative reporter came to see me – name of Dunbar, Zoe Dunbar. She was asking me about the case. Odd, isn't it? Suddenly all this interest in the Stroud case.'

Odd indeed, Fleming thought as he closed Ingham's front door behind him.

10

On his way to the Ridgeway Manor Care Home, Fleming was thinking about his meeting with Frank Ingham. The man had let himself go and Fleming thought how easy it would have been for him to do the same. Fleming's thirty-year-old wife, Trish, had died over six years earlier, and he'd been seeing a counsellor over flashbacks he still had of the night he witnessed Jimmy Calder killing his mother. Fleming was only twelve at the time. Still, he was over the pain of losing his wife and had recently attained closure on the Calder business.

The care home was on the outskirts of High Wycombe and Fleming found it easily. He parked the car and made his way to reception where a young woman was working on a computer. She looked up at Fleming. 'Hello, can I help you?'

'DCI Fleming. I'm here to see Yvette Boudreaux.'

'Oh, yes, she's expecting you. Come this way please.'

Yvette Boudreaux was a tall striking woman with long dark hair. She rose from her desk and came to greet Fleming. 'Hello, Yvette Boudreaux. DCI Fleming, I presume?' she said in a soft French accent.

'Yes. Thank you for seeing me.'

'I believe you're making enquiries about Ethel Croft's son?'

'Yes. I need to trace him in connection with a case I'm working on.'

'I'm afraid I don't have any contact details for him. It's all a bit of a mystery. He writes to his mother once in a while but never leaves any way of contacting him or says where he is. He phones to ask how his mother is occasionally but always rings from a public payphone in Australia. Is he in some sort of trouble?'

'I need to speak to him. It's very important.'

'Must be. You're the third person who's been to see me about him.'

'Oh?'

'Yes, a reporter by the name of Zoe Dunbar came to see me only a few days ago. She was investigating an incident that took place at the AWE a few years ago.'

'Ah, I saw an article by her. Seems she's interested in the same thing as I am.'

'Really?'

Fleming ignored the query. 'Who was the other person who came to see you?'

'It was a private investigator, Dan Rimmer. He came to see me a while back and came again the other day.'

'Did he say why he was looking for Mr Croft?'

'Yes. He told me he had a client who wanted to trace him because he'd been left a large sum of money by an uncle.'

'Did Mr Rimmer tell you that when you first saw him?'

'Yes.'

'And you told Mr Croft about it when he next phoned?'

'I did, but he told me there must be some mistake because he didn't have an uncle with lots of money.'

'What did Rimmer want when he came to see you the other day?'

'He wanted to know if Mr Croft had been in touch lately, and to remind me to call him if he arranged to come and see his mother.'

'And had he?'

'No.'

'Do you have phone numbers for the reporter and Dan Rimmer?' Fleming asked.

'Yes.' Boudreaux pulled an address book from her desk drawer and scribbled the details down for Fleming.

'Is it possible to see Mrs Croft?'

'Yes, but I have to warn you she's not entirely with it. I doubt she will be able to help you. She has dementia.'

'A few words maybe?'

'Okay, I'll take you to her room. You'll have more privacy there.'

'Thank you. I don't want to put you to any trouble.'

'No trouble at all. Ethel might be glad to see a visitor.'

Ethel Croft's room had a single bed, two white bedside drawers with oak-coloured tops, and a large armchair with high sides. A wardrobe stood in one corner and a large window looked out over a garden area. Makena Kibet was propping up Ethel's pillows, making her comfortable.

'Makena, this is DCI Fleming who's come to have a quick word with Ethel,' Boudreaux said.

Makena turned and smiled at Fleming. 'Oh, hello. Ethel's just had her medication so may be a bit confused. I'll take her back to the lounge when you're done, Yvette.'

'Thanks, Makena.'

Boudreaux went over to Ethel and held her hand. 'Ethel, this gentleman wants to have a quick word with you.' She pointed to the armchair. 'Why don't you sit next to her, Mr Fleming?'

Fleming took a seat and pulled the chair nearer to Ethel's bed.

'Hello, may I call you Ethel?'

Ethel looked at Fleming through confused watery eyes. 'Is that you, Garry? You didn't say you were coming.'

'No, I need to find Garry.'

Ethel peered at Fleming and her lips quivered. 'Is he hiding again?'

'Yes.'

'Under the bed... that's where he always hides.'

'I think he's hiding in Australia.'

'Australia? Why would he be there?'

'He lives there now – remember?'

'Does he?'

Fleming decided to change tack. 'Has Garry ever mentioned Melbourne or Sydney?' He watched Ethel's eyes to see if there was any glimmer of recognition.

Nothing.

'Maybe Brisbane, Perth or Adelaide?'

Nothing. Then Ethel suddenly blurted out, 'Is it tea time yet?'

Fleming looked at Boudreaux and shook his head.

'I'll get Makena to come and take you through to the lounge for tea, Ethel.' Boudreaux smiled weakly at Fleming. 'Sorry you've had a wasted trip.'

'No worries. You'll let me know if Mr Croft does arrange to visit or leaves any indication where he might be living?'

'Of course.'

As he left, Fleming was thinking Frank Ingham might have been right about Garry Croft. He was certainly taking steps to ensure no one knew exactly where he was.

11

Logan and Anderson were on their way to Aldermaston in a marked police car. Ursula Nieve had phoned to warn them that a twenty-four-hour strike had started and there was a picket line at the main entrance.

Anderson threw the newspaper she'd been reading onto the back seat. 'Don't know why I bother reading the papers. Full of bad news.'

Logan smiled. 'Thing is, Naomi, bad news sells better than good news. Easier to sensationalise. And what do editors want most of all?'

'Sales and profits?'

'Right. So don't believe anything it says in there about the strike. Just ask Mrs Nieve.'

'But the papers still have to report the facts, Sarge, don't they?'

'Sure, but they sometimes get things wrong. Like we do at times. Speaking of which, did you get a chance to check over the files and case notes to see if anyone did interview the last HR manager, Nat Horne?'

'Yes, and no one did.'

'Looks like that's one strand of the original investigation overlooked by Ingham's team.'

'Maybe it wasn't. Maybe Ingham thought it wasn't necessary because he was convinced Garry Croft was the killer?'

'Your faith in other people never ceases to amaze me, Naomi.'

'Some of us are not quite so cynical, Sarge.'

Logan was about to respond with another jovial remark when they arrived at the main gates to the AWE. About twenty men wearing yellow safety vests lined the pavement. Logan turned into the entrance to find a man standing there indicating for him to stop. Logan pulled over and slid his window down.

The man stood a respectful two feet away from the car. 'Why are you here? There's no trouble. This is a legitimate industrial action.'

'No worries, mate. Nothing to do with the strike. We've come on other business.'

It then dawned on the man. 'Ah, of course, the Stroud investigation. Should have known. Mrs Nieve told us the police would want to speak to people. Good luck with that today. In you go.'

~

'Okay to start straight away with interviews?' Logan asked.

'Of course,' Nieve replied. 'Go ahead. How are you getting on?'

'Ploughing through them.'

'Uncovered anything new?'

Anderson shot a knowing glance at Logan.

Logan paused. *Naomi definitely has a thing about Nieve being so keen to find out how we're doing.* 'Not so far.'

Nieve smiled. 'Ah, well, early days yet, eh? Best let you get on with it.'

They left Nieve's office and spent all day speaking to people, but no new information had surfaced. It was beginning to look like a wasted exercise.

'Let's get the last one in, then call it a day,' Logan said wearily.

Anderson looked up from her notes. 'Name's Seth Emerson. He's one of the foremen.'

'Okay, bring him in.'

Emerson was a sturdy looking man with tattoos adorning both forearms. 'Not sure I can help you much,' he said taking a seat.

'Not out on strike?' Logan asked. 'Or did they pull you in for this?'

'I was working.'

Logan looked at a document in front of him. 'It says here you were employed about ten years ago. So you were here during the last walkout and when William Stroud was killed?'

'I was, but I didn't know the man. I had nothing to do with him. I just knew of him.'

'What did you know of him?'

Emerson lifted his shoulders and pursed his lips. 'Not a lot. It was more what other people were saying.'

'What did other people say?'

'He was likeable enough. Kept pretty much to himself. Secretive sort of character, if truth be known.'

'How do you mean?'

'He arrived here a few months before the strike. Not much of a socialiser. Made out he was a left-wing radical, but people seemed to think it was a bit contrived.'

'Contrived? How do you mean?'

'Those who got to know him reckoned he wanted to give the

impression he was militant, but the fact he had a major fall out with someone who was definitely a left-wing extremist seemed to fly in the face of it.'

'Who was that?'

'Garry Croft.'

'This fall out was at the time of the industrial action?' Logan asked.

'Yes.'

'Did you witness it?'

'Yes, I wasn't with Stroud, but I saw him in a pub after work one night with Croft. I didn't notice them at first, but then their voices rose and things became heated.'

'They were arguing?'

'Yes.'

'Do you know what it was about?'

'Not really. It was something to do with the strike. It was noisy in the pub and I wasn't paying much attention.'

'You said it was a major row. What you've described sounds like a heated argument fuelled by drink.'

'There was a big commotion outside the pub later and I heard the argument had turned into a fight. Not surprising. Croft was a nasty piece of work.'

'In what way?'

'He was a bully... aggressive. That's all I know.'

'Okay, I think that's it for now, Mr Emerson. Thank you for talking to us,' Logan said.

Emerson left and Logan looked expectantly at Anderson. 'What do you make of it, Naomi?'

'Confirms what we knew. Major row between Stroud and Croft at the time of the strike. Stroud ends up dead and Croft disappears off to Australia leaving no way for anyone to contact him. And... Croft was a nasty piece of work.'

12

Fleming was about to get into his car when he heard a voice from behind. 'DCI Fleming?'

He turned to see a slim woman with shoulder-length auburn hair approaching him across the office car park. Fleming didn't recognise her, but the blue shirt, black jacket and trousers suggested a professional or executive.

'Zoe Dunbar, I'm an investigative reporter. May I have a word?'

Fleming met the steely gaze of her green eyes. He usually preferred to avoid conversations with reporters, but was curious about Dunbar. Yvette Boudreaux had given him Dunbar's phone number, and he'd intended to contact her. 'Five minutes? I was about to leave.'

'I was wondering why Eathan Younger asked you to look into the old William Stroud case?'

'Are you asking why he asked me in particular, or why that case?'

'The latter, but now you mention it, why not Jeff Miller? He heads the cold case review team, doesn't he?'

'You're remarkably well informed.'

'That's my job.'

'You'll need to ask Eathan Younger on both counts.'

'Are you always evasive?'

'That's my job.'

Dunbar smiled. 'Would I be right in thinking Younger picked this case for review because it's not too old – or maybe because it's to do with the AWE? An issue of national security maybe?'

Dunbar was fishing.

'Speak to Younger.'

'I have. He told me clearing up old unsolved murder enquiries was one of the aims of the police and crime plan.'

'So that's your answer.'

'I guess you've had a good look at the old files.'

'I have.'

'Any initial thoughts?'

Fleming ignored the question. 'Why are you interested in this?'

'I'm an investigative reporter. It's what I do.'

'Out of interest, how do you decide what to investigate?'

'I fish around and see what comes up.'

'And you saw a copy of the police and crime plan and went fishing to Eathan Younger?'

'Yes. And the William Stroud affair came up.'

'Has your investigation so far led you to believe there might be an issue of national security?'

'I aim to find out.'

'You've been to see Frank Ingham, I believe.'

'He told you?'

'Yes. What did he tell you?'

'Same as he told you probably.'

'Which was?'

Dunbar hesitated for a moment. 'About Garry Croft and the

care home where his mother is.' There was another brief pause. 'Ingham thought Garry Croft was the killer. What do you think?'

Fleming thought for a second. 'It's too early to say. We've just started our enquiries. I'm keeping an open mind.'

'Are you in touch with MI5 on this?'

'Why would I need to be?'

'Because William Stroud worked at the AWE.'

'You really think it was a national security issue?'

'I'm also keeping an open mind.'

'You went to the care home.'

'Ah, Yvette Boudreaux told you.'

'Did you speak to Mrs Croft when you went there?'

'Yes, briefly. She's a bit confused. Couldn't tell me anything.'

'So is your investigation going to take you to Australia looking for Garry Croft?'

'Big place. Wouldn't know where to start. How about you?'

'I have no immediate plans.'

'Are you going to ask the Australian police to look for him?' Dunbar pressed.

'We haven't so far.'

'But you might?'

'As I said before, we've just started our enquiries.'

'But you haven't ruled it out?'

'I haven't ruled out anything yet.'

'So you might?'

'Let's wait and see how the investigation unfolds, shall we?'

'You evaded my question about MI5 earlier. Any particular reason?' Dunbar suddenly asked.

'I did?'

'Maybe I could run a story saying a police spokesman declined to say whether they're in touch with MI5 over this.'

'I'm not, so you can't.'

'Thanks.'

Fleming thought for a second. 'Has anyone from MI5 been speaking to you?'

Dunbar smiled. 'If they had, I wouldn't tell you.'

'Glad we're having a frank exchange of information,' Fleming said, deciding he'd had enough of the verbal sparring. 'Sorry, I've got to be somewhere else.'

'To see Dan Rimmer?' Dunbar asked as Fleming was getting into his car.

Fleming paused for a second. *Yvette Boudreaux must have told her about him.*

13

Rimmer had a feeling someone was following him. He walked up the street stopping every so often to look in shop windows, thinking he might see a reflection of his imagined stalker walking past behind him. Nothing. Continuing on beyond Annie's café to the end of the road, he quickly turned back on himself. If anyone was following him, he'd be able to spot the furtive look of a tail trying to avoid his gaze. Again, there was nothing. *Either I'm getting paranoid, or they're professional.*

Satisfied no one was following him, he went into Annie's café, ordered a coffee and sat in the same seat he'd occupied when he last saw Makena Kibet. It was early morning, a good hour before Makena was due to start work. The enticing smell of frying bacon wafted through from the kitchen. Giving in to the temptation, Rimmer ordered a bacon roll. Makena was late again. Rimmer glanced at his watch and drummed his fingers on the table. She had asked to meet him so ought to be here. *Where is she?*

She appeared suddenly. Rimmer saw her through the café window, pushing her way past two women with children's push buggies who were blocking the pavement while engrossed in conversation. Makena entered the café and saw Rimmer. She waved and headed for the counter. 'Had breakfast yet?' Rimmer asked, joining her.

'Just a quick bite. I was running a bit late.'

'No problem. Can I get you something?'

'Could I have a tea and one of those?' she asked, pointing at Rimmer's roll.

'Sure.' Rimmer placed the order.

'Sorry to keep you waiting again,' Makena said as they settled into their seats.

'At least you're here. You have some news for me?'

Makena looked anxiously around the café as though making sure no one could overhear what she was going to say. It wouldn't do if someone heard her talking about residents at the care home. You never knew who was listening. It wasn't a big café. There were eight tables set in two single rows of four either side of a central aisle leading to the counter. Only four tables were occupied, but no one was sitting within earshot, providing you kept your voice down.

Makena was about to speak when two elderly women came into the café. One went to the counter and the other sat at the table next to Rimmer and Makena. Makena glared at the woman's back and leaned across the table to whisper to Rimmer. 'Yes, it's Ethel. She's been taken ill.'

Before Rimmer could say anything, his mobile rang. He glanced at the screen: *Phil.* He declined the call.

'Not important?' Makena asked.

'My uncle. I'll call him back.'

'Nice ringtone. Are you a James Bond fan?'

'Watched all the films. You said Ethel has taken ill?'

'Yes, she caught a cold and it's gone on to her chest.'

'And?'

'She's very poorly. Doctor says we need to keep a close eye on her due to the fact she was already frail.'

'Do you know if Mrs Boudreaux has been able to talk to Garry?'

'No, she has no way of contacting him. She has to wait for him to phone.'

'And do you know if he has since we last met?'

'No. I would have known if he had. And I'd have let you know like I promised.'

'Okay I–'

A sudden bang outside interrupted what Rimmer was about to say. He grasped the edge of the table and jumped to his feet. His eyes flashed in the direction of the front window. His whole body tensed up.

Makena's brow creased with concern. 'It's just a car backfiring I think.'

Rimmer relaxed and slumped into his seat.

'Are you okay?' Makena asked.

'Yeah, fine. Served in the army in Afghanistan and got injured by an IED. Loud bangs put me on edge.'

Makena's eyes glistened. 'I'm so sorry.'

'It's not a big deal,' Rimmer said. But inwardly he knew it was.

'Bloody wars. Nothing but tragedy and useless waste of life, that's what I say.'

'Sometimes it's necessary. But back to Ethel, have you tried prompting her about what they spoke of when her son last visited or phoned?'

'Yes, she's very vague. I don't think Ethel can remember much of the conversation they had, and she's no idea where he is exactly.'

'Have you seen any of the letters he sent her.'

'Good God, no. They're personal. I'd never ask to see them.'

'You could offer to read them back to her. Ask her if she would like that.'

'Oh... I don't know.'

'You'd be doing her a favour.'

'Okay, I'll try.'

'Good girl.'

'By the way, a detective called Fleming came to the care home to speak to Yvette and Ethel about Mr Croft.'

'Oh?'

'You told me Croft was left some money.'

'Yes.'

'So why would this detective want to speak to him?'

'I've no idea.' Rimmer laughed. 'Maybe the money he was left is stolen.' He saw the look in Makena's eyes. 'Only joking. Your guess is as good as mine.'

'Hmm.'

'Makes your daily grind more interesting though, eh?'

'There was one other thing.'

'Yes?'

'A reporter came to see Yvette asking about Mr Croft as well.'

'Really? Get her name?'

'I think it was Dunbar... yes, Zoe Dunbar.' Makena frowned. 'This is getting very mysterious indeed.'

'Just keep your eyes and ears open and let me know if there's any new developments.'

Makena left, leaving Rimmer pensive. *Interesting that both a detective and a reporter have been to the care home asking about Croft.*

14

The clouds darkened and thunder rumbled in the distance as Fleming was driving towards Reading. He'd decided to go on his own, leaving Logan and Anderson to carry on with the interviews at the AWE.

He found a car park near the office of Wyatt Investigations and walked the rest of the way. The front door opened into a tiny hallway. A narrow staircase was straight in front of him and a door to the left had a window with a sign for Wyatt Investigations hanging inside. The office was fairly small with a single desk, coffee table, two chairs and three metal filing cabinets. As Fleming entered, Dan Rimmer rose from behind the desk to greet him.

'I guess you must be DCI Fleming?'

Fleming thought Rimmer looked more like a guerrilla fighter than a private investigator. He wore a blue shirt and jeans and was over six foot, muscular, with tousled dark brown hair and beard. 'I am, and you're Dan Rimmer?'

'Yes, Phil Wyatt's my uncle. I came to work for him when I left the army.'

'Ah. Thank you for seeing me. I guessed it would be best to phone to make sure you would be here.'

'No problem.' Rimmer went to sit back behind the desk and pointed to a chair by the coffee table. 'Pull up a seat. What can I help you with?'

'I'm investigating an old unsolved murder case.'

'Oh?'

'Guy called William Stroud. Used to work at the AWE some years ago.'

'And you wanted to speak to me because...?'

'It seems we have a common interest.'

'We do?'

'Croft, a Mr Garry Croft.'

There was recognition in Rimmer's face. 'Ah! Garry Croft.'

'You told Yvette Boudreaux some years ago you had a client who wanted to contact Mr Croft because an uncle had left him some money, is that right?'

'It is.'

'Only Yvette Boudreaux told Mr Croft about it the next time he phoned to ask after his mother and he told her there had to be some mistake because he didn't have an uncle with a lot of money.'

'I don't doubt it.'

'Sorry, you're confusing me. Why are you still looking for him if you don't believe an uncle left him some money?'

'I didn't tell Yvette Boudreaux why I really wanted to get in touch with Garry Croft – for obvious reasons.'

'Which are?'

'My client wanted to try to flush him out with a cash incentive which clearly didn't work.'

'And?'

'He wanted to find him because he'd loaned Croft fifty grand. Croft didn't pay him back. Did a runner to Australia instead. My client wants his money. I couldn't tell Mrs Boudreaux because there's no way Croft would have revealed his whereabouts.'

'I see.' Fleming was beginning to wonder if Croft went to Australia to avoid paying back the loan. Maybe he didn't kill Stroud. Perhaps the row developed into a fight and was no more than a heat-of-the-moment thing fuelled by drink. It was possible Ingham hadn't known anything about the loan and had drawn the wrong conclusion when Croft fled to Australia. Fifty thousand pounds might explain why Croft was nervous about revealing his location. 'So who is this client?'

'He's a bit of a mystery.'

'How so?'

'All I have is a name, Liam Doherty.'

'No address – telephone number?'

'Afraid not.'

Fleming frowned. 'So how did you meet this client?'

'I didn't. Doherty phoned me from a public payphone and asked if I could find Croft for him. He explained why and offered to pay me a grand up front and another grand if I was able to find him.'

'How did he pay you the thousand pounds?'

'He put cash in an envelope and posted it through the office letter box.'

'So you never actually saw him?'

'No.'

'I'm struggling with the logistics here,' Fleming admitted. 'How were you supposed to contact Doherty, assuming that's his right name, if you found Croft?'

'Bit cloak and dagger, I must admit, but I was to stick a red card in the office window. When Doherty saw it, he was going to get in touch with me to get the details and would pay me the balance once he'd made contact with Croft.'

Fleming rubbed at the dark stubble on his chin. 'So has this Doherty ever been in touch with you since he paid you a thousand pounds? Seems a long time to be waiting for a result. Hasn't he been getting impatient?'

'He's phoned a few times. And yes, he has. I offered to go to Australia looking for Croft, but he didn't want to ramp up expenses. Fair enough I suppose. I'm his only option for now.'

'Doesn't it strike you as odd that Doherty wants to remain completely anonymous? Why the secrecy?'

'Believe me, you'd be surprised how much secrecy there is in my business.'

'You're a private investigator, have you attempted to trace him out of curiosity?'

'I tried 1471 and traced the calls to public payphones, never the same one. I couldn't find him on the electoral role, or any record in Companies House, Land Registry or social media. Loads of Liam Dohertys but no way to check who it is I'm working for.'

'Your client is definitely keen to stay anonymous, but I do need to find him if for no other reason but to eliminate him from our enquiries.' Fleming got up to leave and pushed a business card across the desk. 'Get in touch if you do get any leads on Croft. And, I'd like you to put a red card in your window. It appears it's the only way to get your Doherty to show his face. Have you got CCTV here?'

'Sorry.' Rimmer paused. 'Can I ask, is Croft a potential witness or a suspect?'

'Could be either.'

Fleming left making a mental note to check if there was a CCTV camera covering the street.

15

Fleming wasn't looking forward to his briefing meeting with Eathan Younger. Apart from feeling uneasy due to the fact Temple and Miller didn't have a kind word to say about him, Fleming had nothing much to report, and that was not going to go down well.

Temple had made it clear to Fleming that she expected him to see her first before he reported anything to Younger on the Stroud enquiry. 'He won't be happy,' she'd said when Fleming told her there wasn't a great deal to report. Fleming now had a better understanding why there was tension and mistrust between Temple and Younger after speaking to Jeff Miller. He also realised why Temple had told him to tread carefully around Younger. Internal politics and infighting were not new to Fleming, but he'd rather such matters didn't get in the way of his enquiry.

Fleming recalled Temple's words as he swallowed hard and entered the lion's den. *The man's a buck-passer*, she'd said. It reminded Fleming he'd have to watch his back.

'Ah, Fleming, come in. Take a seat.' Younger's desk was clear as always, apart from one piece of paper. 'I have here,' he said, looking over the top of his glasses, 'a copy of an internal memo from Cecil Daubney to the chief constable. I don't need to read it to you, but you should know he holds Upson responsible for the number of unsolved murder cases.'

'Sounds like pressure,' Fleming said.

Younger took his glasses off and placed them on the desk, adjusting their position with his fingers until the arms sat absolutely square with the edge of internal memo. 'It is. Upson is therefore putting me under pressure so I need the Stroud case wrapped up, for which *you* are responsible. Have you made any progress so far?'

'I'm not sure you would call it progress in terms of finding the killer, but we are making headway with the investigative strategy, sir.'

'Hmm. All well and good, Fleming, but I want to be able to say I'm confident you'll solve the case.'

It's pretty clear he's lining me up to be the fall guy if I don't succeed, Fleming thought. 'I think you can say you're confident in the approach. I'll do my best, sir.'

'You'd damned well better, Fleming. I need a result on this, so tell me where you are.'

'Jeff Miller came to see me. He wasn't happy you didn't put him on the case.'

'I've told you why. He'll get over it.' Younger hesitated for a second. 'Let me tell you something in confidence. It's not just the conflict of interest issue that made me decide not to put Miller on this. He and I do not see eye to eye. I don't rate him. There was an incident some time back – Miller and Temple were involved. I lost confidence in them. You did a damned good job on the Nielson case and I wanted someone I could trust to handle the Stroud enquiry. I asked you to report direct to me because I didn't want Temple involved.'

Fleming raised an eyebrow. 'I see.'

'Strictly between you and me, understood?'

'Yes, sir.' Fleming looked at Younger and saw the merest hint of a tremor in his right eyelid. 'I went to see Frank Ingham. He's still convinced Garry Croft was the killer. The HR manager at the AWE has set up an office for Logan and Anderson to conduct staff interviews. They've been working hard on them, but they've not yet uncovered anything new, except–'

'They've found a new lead?' Younger cut in. He was sitting forward in his chair, looking as though he was about to hear positive news.

'It would appear the row between Stroud and Croft was more than a quarrel. Turned out they exchange blows outside a pub following a heated argument inside.'

'Ingham's reports missed that out. Knew he wasn't the most efficient officer.'

'There's more. It seems a private investigator called Dan Rimmer is interested in finding Croft. Says he has a client who wants to find him because Croft owes him fifty thousand pounds. He gave Croft a loan which he failed to repay and then disappeared off to Australia.'

'Rimmer? Ingham made no mention of him either.'

'I've asked Ingham and he confirmed he knew nothing of Rimmer or this loan.'

'Bloody hell! What next?'

'The thing is, sir, Ingham could have reached the wrong conclusion about Croft–'

'Hang on, are you saying he may not be the number one suspect after all this?'

'Not at this stage, no. But it is possible the reason Croft fled to Australia without telling anyone where he was staying was because he either couldn't, or didn't, intend to repay the loan.'

'I don't believe this!' Younger slammed a fist on his desk. His eyelid was twitching angrily. 'Have you been to see this client of Rimmer's?'

'Seems he's a bit of a mystery man. Rimmer doesn't have any contact details for him.'

'What! This is ridiculous! How can you have a customer and not be able to contact them, for God's sake!'

'Rimmer waits for the man to phone him, which he only does from public payphones. I've got things in motion to try to flush him out.'

'Well, see you do, Fleming.'

'We've also discovered that Nat Horne, who was HR manager for the AWE at the time was never interviewed.'

'Unbelievable! I thought Ingham wasn't the most efficient officer. He was bloody incompetent! Probably the worse for wear with drink half the time. Never mind medical retirement – should have sacked the man.' Younger took a few seconds to regain his composure. 'You've seen him now though?'

'I can't, he's dead.'

Younger sighed. 'His wife? Was he married?'

'Yes. Ursula Nieve gave me her address.'

'Who's she?'

'The HR manager at the AWE.'

'So you'll speak to Horne's wife?'

'Yes.'

'Anything else?'

'There's quite a bit of press coverage on this. Maybe someone who didn't come forward before for whatever reason will do so now.'

'Bit hopeful aren't you, Fleming?'

'You never know. These things do sometimes happen.'

'Is that it then?'

Fleming thought for a moment. 'Have MI5 been in touch about this?'

Younger hesitated long enough to make Fleming wonder. 'MI5? Why on earth would they be interested?'

'The reporter you spoke to, Zoe Dunbar – she came to see me. Asked the same question.'

'Really?'

'Seemed to have a bee in her bonnet over it. Thought the whole thing might have been an issue of national security, sir.' Fleming raised an eyebrow, waiting for a response.

'I'm only interested in facts, Fleming – not idle speculation by a reporter.'

Fleming left Younger's office wondering if it was unfounded speculation.

16

Toby Omoko was having a bad day, and it was about to get worse. His colleague was still off ill. The office they shared in Thames House wasn't the healthiest of places. It was cramped, stuffy, didn't have much natural light from only one small window. Maybe it was sick building syndrome his colleague was suffering from. Omoko had come to work feeling fine, but by mid-morning had developed a headache and was tired. Definitely sick building syndrome, he concluded.

He was going through the daily grind, looking through the papers. There was very little of interest, but he did come across one article covering the dispute at the AWE. The union leader, Bill Kauffman, was claiming workers were being penalised due to the company putting in a low bid to win the contract to run the AWE. They were paying off personnel, and safety standards were slipping as a result. The old issue of pay and pensions had surfaced once more. With talks getting nowhere, the union had no option but to strike, Kauffman was claiming. It struck Omoko he didn't really need Falcon. The agent wasn't giving him much that he didn't get from the papers.

Omoko looked at his watch. It was almost time to make the

dreaded trip up to the second floor. Quentin Vere had asked to see him. He wanted to know how things were going on the Stroud case. His day was not about to improve as he didn't have much to report. The headache suddenly felt worse as he trudged up the stone staircase.

Omoko knocked on Vere's door and entered. Vere was standing, looking out the window at a barge ploughing its way up river against the ebbing tide. He turned as Omoko came into his office. 'Where have you been? You're two minutes late.'

'Sorry, sir. Met someone on the staircase who wanted something.'

'And that was more important than getting to my office on time?'

'No, sir... I–'

'Oh, never mind, you're here now.' Vere sat behind his polished desk and took off his horn-rimmed glasses to clean them with a handkerchief. 'What have you got for me?'

'I'm afraid there's not much. The first twenty-four-hour strike's taken place and there are more scheduled. Kauffman and the union are ramping things up and it's getting serious.'

'I can read the bloody papers, Omoko. What can you tell me that isn't in the news?'

Omoko shifted his weight uneasily from one foot to the other. 'Sorry... I–'

'Oh, for God's sake!' Vere cut in. 'What about Falcon? Anything?'

'Fleming's team have an office at the AWE where they're conducting interviews. But so far they haven't come up with anything new.'

'Is that all you've got?'

'Nat Horne, who was the HR manager at the time of Stroud's death, wasn't interviewed, by all accounts. He died soon after the Stroud affair. Fleming's going to speak to Horne's wife.'

'You need to get a grip of Falcon. We need better intelligence than this, Omoko.'

'Yes, sir.' Omoko was beginning to see the prospect of a move to a more exciting and important area of the office fading fast. This subversion business was getting him nowhere. His best hope was that Vere would retire. Omoko had thought the man looked ill last time he saw him. He was overweight and his chubby face with double chin was always sweaty and pallid. With a bit of luck, Vere would take medical retirement. It was Vere who had recruited Falcon who had failed to deliver any useful intelligence to date, but he was clearly going to hold Omoko to account for the lack of information.

'You disappoint me, Omoko. I had hoped you would show some promise when you joined us. So far, you haven't managed to deliver anything worthwhile.'

'Sorry, sir. But I–'

'No bloody excuses!' Vere cut in. 'To be inexperienced is okay, but to be incompetent is unforgivable.'

Omoko bit his tongue, wanting to tell Vere where to stick his fucking job. He'd show him how competent he could be. He'd forget Falcon and do his own unofficial field work unknown to Vere. But right now, he had no idea what he could do. The first thing was to get it clearer in his mind what the priorities were.

Vere calmed down. 'Are you okay? You don't look too good.'

'Bit of a headache, sir. I'm fine.'

'Don't be going off sick as well as that bloody useless colleague of yours. Just keep a close eye on things. There's a good chap.'

'Of course, sir. To be absolutely clear though, should we be concentrating more on who might have killed Stroud, or whether there are subversive elements within the AWE that aim to disrupt things there.'

'We shouldn't lose sight of the fact Stroud could have been

killed as a result of subversive activity. We also need to find out if there are attempts to destabilise essential work at the AWE through this current strike.'

Doesn't answer my question, Omoko thought. He tried again. 'So the priority is Stroud or what's currently going on at the AWE?'

'They could be linked.'

It was clear Vere was not going to give Omoko a steer. Maybe it didn't matter. Vere could be right. There might be something connecting the two things, in which case one thing shouldn't take priority over the other.

'Of course. I'll bear that in mind, sir.'

'Please do – and on your way out, ask my secretary to bring me some coffee.'

Omoko left and passed on the message to the secretary who smiled and raised her eyes to the ceiling.

Back in his own dingy office, Omoko thought about what he might be able to do. Waiting for information which wasn't exactly forthcoming was getting him nowhere. And he knew, whatever he did, he had to keep a low profile. It was important no one knew MI5 had an interest in the Stroud case, or indeed union activity at the AWE.

17

Fleming found Emma Horne's house in Fisherman's Lane on the edge of Aldermaston village. It was a modern three-bedroom house of red brick with a small gravel driveway.

He parked the car and rang the doorbell. No one appeared. Waiting a minute, he tried again. A woman next door came out to get in her car and saw Fleming standing at Emma's door. 'Hello there,' she said. 'She is in. I saw her earlier. Could be out the back. She's a keen gardener.'

Fleming smiled. 'Thank you. I'll have a look.'

He followed a path round the house and saw Emma Horne on her knees weeding a flower border filled with scented roses. 'Hello. Mrs Horne?'

Emma turned with a gasp. 'Oh! I didn't hear you coming. You startled me. I'm sure my hearing isn't what it used to be.'

'Sorry, I'm DCI Fleming. We spoke on the phone.'

'Yes. I was expecting you.' Emma rose rather unsteadily to her feet. 'Not so fit these days. Arthritis in the knees. Swollen knuckles on my hands as well. I suppose it's one of those things you have to put up with as you get older. Would you like to come in?'

The living room was clean and tidy and a copy of *The Times* was lying on a coffee table in front of a two-seater settee. There were two other armchairs with covers on each arm. A large-screen television was in one corner, and on the top of a small bookcase there was a photograph of Emma with a man Fleming guessed was her late husband.

'Nice place you have here, Mrs Horne,' Fleming observed.

'Thank you. Please, call me Emma. Mrs Horne sounds awfully formal.' Emma paused for a moment. 'I decided to stay here after Nat died. I did think of moving, but friends advised me not to make any hasty decisions. Anyway, I like it here. Nice and quiet, and I love the garden, especially in the summer when the roses are in full bloom.'

'Yes, I can see you look after it.'

'Tea? Can I get you some?'

'No, thank you. I won't take up much of your time.'

'Please, do have a seat.'

Fleming chose one of the armchairs and Emma sat on the settee.

'I'm investigating an old murder case from five years ago. William Stroud, who worked at the AWE,' Fleming said.

'I remember it well, dreadful business.'

'I believe your late husband was the HR manager there at the time?'

'Yes, poor old Nat. He used to enjoy working there...'

'There was a strike at the time. Is that when he stopped enjoying it?'

'Everything seemed to change. Nat seemed to withdraw into himself...'

'Oh?'

'He became quiet. Used to pour himself a stiff whisky when he got home.'

'Was he a drinker?'

'Oh, no. But let's be fair – we did enjoy a glass or two of wine with dinner of an evening.'

'Your husband was presumably under pressure at the time.'

'He was, poor man. Never spoke about work much. A lot of what goes on there is secret you see.'

'I understand. But maybe he talked about colleagues he got on with, or didn't get on with?'

'Maybe sometimes he would say he'd had a bad day because someone had given him a hard time.'

'Mention anyone in particular?'

'It was the union mostly. And that dreadful man, Kauffman. He's at it again I see.' Emma nodded toward *The Times*.

'Do you know if he ever dealt with Kauffman on a one-to-one basis, or was it usually in meetings with management and the union?'

'He never said. All he would say when I asked about the strike was it was getting a bit fraught.'

'In what way?'

'You know. Tempers rising. Things getting out of control.'

'Did he ever elaborate?'

'I can't say he did. It was general stuff. He was always a bit vague when talking about work.'

'Did he ever mention Stroud?'

'Only when he was murdered. He probably did know of him, Nat being HR manager.'

'I suppose so. Did he ever mention Garry Croft?'

'No, but I heard of him afterwards. It was in the papers about how he was a suspect and that he'd fled to Australia.'

'Nat was HR manager. Would he have known where in Australia Croft had gone to?'

'No, Nat took early retirement soon after Stroud was killed and Croft fled to Australia a few months after Nat had left.'

'So Nat's replacement would maybe know?'

Emma shrugged. 'I... I suppose so.'

Fleming made a mental note to check with Ursula Nieve.

'Are you sure I can't get you something to drink?' Emma asked again.

'No really, I'm fine. I won't keep you much longer. Your husband had some sort of breakdown shortly after Stroud's death?'

'Yes. He didn't say anything, but I could tell he was under pressure. Everything seemed to change. He was quiet, couldn't sleep.'

'And he took early retirement?'

'Yes. But he was never the same man.'

'Nat didn't improve after retiring?'

'No. There were obviously things going on there Nat wouldn't talk about. I was worried about him.'

'Did anyone come to visit him at home while all this was going on?'

'No.'

'And after he retired?'

'No. He died of a heart attack soon after.'

'I'm so sorry, Emma. Look, I won't take up any more of your time. You've been most helpful. Thank you.'

Emma showed Fleming out and as he got into his car he began to wonder. *Could Horne have killed Stroud? But what would his motive have been?*

18

Logan and Anderson were on their way to the AWE in an unmarked car to conduct more interviews. Logan was driving. 'What do you make of all this, Naomi?'

'You mean why are we involved and not Jeff Miller? Or the actual investigation?'

'Ah, you're getting like a politician – answering a question with another one.'

'You need to make it clear what you're after if you want a clear answer, Sarge. Thought with your experience you'd know that.'

'You're getting far too clever.' Logan laughed. 'I was looking for a response to both your queries.'

'You're making this up as you go along, Sarge. As to Jeff Miller, I still find it all a bit odd. Eathan Younger must have his reasons, but I've no idea what they might be.'

'The boss reckons Younger thought there might be a conflict of interest. Miller and Ingham were friends.'

'Really? As to where we are with the investigation, I'd say we've not made any progress over where Frank Ingham got to.'

'I think you're right. I'm beginning to regret being landed with this one. Give me a nice juicy current murder case any day.'

'Sarge! You sound as though you want another one to take place.'

'Just saying – they're much easier to solve. These old cases are a nightmare. Cold trails, fading memories, some witnesses no longer around. I'd say our chances of finding Stroud's killer are pretty remote.'

'That's what I like about you, Sarge, forever the optimist.'

'Said it yourself, Naomi, we're no further forward.'

'I'm curious over what the boss told us about this reporter, Zoe Dunbar. She seems to have a keen interest in the case.'

'Even more so is the private investigator the boss spoke to,' Logan added.

'Dan Rimmer?'

'Yeah, some story about a client of his who Garry Croft owed money to. What's interesting is Croft may have done a runner to Australia because of the money and not because he killed Stroud.'

'In which case we need to be looking for another–'

The sudden wail of sirens cut Anderson short.

Logan pulled the car over to the side to let two police cars speed by. 'I'll bet they're going to the AWE. There's been trouble with staff not on strike trying to cross picket lines.'

Sure enough, when they reached the main gates the two cars were parked with blue lights still flashing. There was a lot of shouting amongst chaotic scenes. Twenty or thirty men wearing yellow safety vests had surrounded four harassed-looking uniformed police officers. They'd tried to split the crowd up to question people separately, but without much success.

Logan parked the car and got out with Anderson.

'Cavalry's arrived!' Kauffman shouted. He'd recognised Logan.

Logan showed his warrant card as one of the policemen turned to challenge him. 'DS Logan. What's going on here?'

'We got a call from a member of the public who witnessed an assault on the picket line,' one of the policemen said. 'We're trying to get to the bottom of it.'

'Okay everyone. I want you all over there,' Logan shouted, pointing to the pavement to the right of the main entrance. 'Now!'

His ex-army sergeant's booming voice had the desired effect. The men slowly dispersed and shuffled across to where Logan had pointed. He looked at Anderson. 'Get the uniforms over there, split the men up and start questioning them individually. And keep Kauffman apart. I want to speak to him myself.'

'Okay, Sarge.' Anderson was impressed how one man could have the authority and command to instantly control an angry crowd.

'Anyone who doesn't co-operate will be arrested and taken to the local station for questioning. Up to you,' Logan added.

When the men had dispersed, Logan could see a man with a bloodied face leaning against a car parked at an angle across the entrance. The car windscreen was smashed in and there were scratches all the way down the paintwork on the driver's side. The man pushed himself away from the car to go and join the other men. Then Logan recognised him. 'Not you,' he said. It was Emerson, the man who hadn't been on strike when he and Anderson had interviewed him the other day. 'You okay?' Logan asked.

Emerson dabbed a handkerchief on his nose. 'Yeah, sure. Bastards!'

'Your car I take it?'

Emerson nodded.

'What happened?'

'I tried to drive into work but Kauffman waved me down with a stupid grin on his face.'

'You stopped?'

'Didn't have much choice – he was blocking the road with five other men.'

'What did you do?'

'I wound the window down and one of the men was screaming obscenities at me. A fist appeared from nowhere and punched me in the face.'

'Can you point out who it was?'

'It all happened so fast. I didn't see who did it.'

'And the damage to your car?'

'I was livid. Pushed the car door open to get out and a brick or something hit the windscreen.'

'And you didn't see who threw it?'

'No.'

'I lost my temper and lashed out at whoever was in striking distance. Might have been Kauffman. Someone thumped me from behind and I went down. I was dazed for a few seconds and heard sharp scraping. Someone pulled me to my feet and I saw all the scratch marks across the paintwork.'

'Let me guess. You don't know who did it.'

'No. Look, everything was happening so fast. Why don't you arrest the whole fucking lot of them?'

'We could do that, but then there's the problem of you lashing out at Kauffman. He could claim you assaulted him.'

Emerson spat out some blood. 'Unbelievable.'

'Better get yourself inside and find your first-aider if you have one. And ring your insurance company to get your car sorted out. We'll be in touch to let you know what's happening with all this lot.'

Emerson glowered across at the union men and shuffled off down the driveway.

Logan signalled for Anderson to bring Kauffman across to him.

The first time Logan had seen Kauffman's face he'd thought of Rasputin the mad monk. Kauffman was tall, in his fifties and of solid build with thick black hair. He'd dyed his hair which was showing signs of grey round the sides. The large dark beard completed the image. Logan noticed something he hadn't seen before. When he and Anderson had interviewed Kauffman he'd been wearing a tight-fitting black polo-neck jumper. Today, he had on a T-shirt beneath his yellow safety vest, and a hammer and sickle tattoo on his neck was plain to see.

'Like to explain what went on here?' Logan asked.

'This is a legitimate picket line,' Kauffman growled in a rasping voice. 'We were trying to persuade Emerson not to cross it like he did before. People who carry on working are undermining our position. Just what the fucking management want.'

'He says you blocked the road and he had to stop.'

'I tried to wave him down to speak to him, but he put his foot down and nearly drove into one of the men. He had no option but to pull over.'

'What happened then?'

'He got out of the car screaming abuse at me and threw a punch.'

'So how come Emerson is the one with the bloody face?'

'I think someone must have punched him when he attacked me. I'd turned away from his blows and didn't see.'

'Hmm. What about the damage to Emerson's car?'

'I heard a crash. Someone must have hit his windscreen with something. He almost ran someone over, for fuck's sake!' Kauffman's lips twisted in a smarmy smile. 'Heat of the moment. No wonder someone got angry.'

'And this justified someone scratching the paintwork on his car and smashing his windscreen?'

'The car's a bloody wreck anyway, for fuck's sake.' Kauffman belched and spat on the ground. 'Wouldn't waste police time on this, mate. I'll get the union to pay for his car if that'll keep you happy.' Kauffman glared at Logan with dark brown menacing eyes as though to challenge him.

Logan stared back. 'Let's get one thing straight – I'm not your mate. And I'll decide whether to make any arrests once we have all the written statements – yours included.'

A few minutes later, Logan and Anderson were ready to go into their temporary office inside. 'You'll be in real shit if there's any more trouble out here,' Logan told Kauffman who stood smirking with his hands in his pockets.

19

Rimmer's uncle, Phil Wyatt, had found the address and telephone number for the reporter Zoe Dunbar. Rimmer had been mulling over what to do with the information. Phil had suggested he get in touch with her to see what she knew about Garry Croft. As it happened, Dunbar made the decision for Rimmer. She phoned to ask if she could meet him.

The pub was in Colindale, quite near Dunbar's apartment. Rimmer had thought of taking the car but in the end decided to take the train. It was direct, leaving a few minutes after six. He arrived at Paddington twenty-five minutes later. From there he took the Bakerloo Line to Charing Cross and it was then he knew he'd made the wrong decision. It was a warm summer's evening and commuters were making their way home after a grim day in the office. Sullen, straight-faced passengers crammed into every square inch of the carriage. Sweat was trickling down Rimmer's back and legs. It reminded him of the confined space in the Mastiff patrol vehicle he used to share with seven other troopers in Afghanistan.

The train screeched to a halt at Charing Cross and Rimmer felt his muscles tense. The doors slid open and Rimmer was relieved to step out onto the platform. People pushed and shoved their way past each other as they dashed to get to the exit. *What a fucking existence*, Rimmer thought, wondering whether he should get the hell out of there and get a taxi the rest of the way up to Colindale. In the end he decided to stick with it and, pushing his way through the crowds, followed the signs for the Northern Line.

It took about twenty minutes to get to Colindale and Rimmer took the time to get clear in his mind what he hoped to achieve by agreeing to see Dunbar. The main thing he wanted to find out was why she was interested in the AWE and the Stroud case, how she came to know about him, and what she knew about Garry Croft.

The walk from the underground station to the pub only took a few minutes. It had a few tables and chairs next to the windows. A mixed clientele of people stood sipping at their drinks and chatting. Some in casual clothes, others more smartly dressed, looking as though they might have come out of nearby offices for a well-earned drink before setting off home. Dunbar had told Rimmer he would recognise her from her shoulder-length auburn hair and would be wearing jeans and a blue shirt. She wasn't in the pub as far as Rimmer could see. He ordered a pint of beer and retreated to one of the unoccupied tables.

A few minutes later he saw Dunbar arrive. She picked her way past groups of drinkers and ordered a glass of white wine. While waiting, she looked around for Rimmer. She gave a casual wave and smiled when she saw him, collected her drink and made her way across to where he was sitting. 'Mr Rimmer, I guess?'

'Dan – and, if I'm not mistaken, you must be Zoe Dunbar.'

Dunbar smiled again and took a chair next to Rimmer. 'Thanks for agreeing to meet me.'

Rimmer thought Dunbar looked attractive, but noticed her green eyes had a cold steely gaze. The hardened look of an investigative reporter. 'I was curious. You told me on the phone you wanted to talk about Garry Croft. How did you know I was interested in him and how did you find me?'

'Yvette Boudreaux, the Ridgeway Manor Care Home manager, told me you'd been to see her. She had your phone number.'

'Ah.' Rimmer didn't let on that Makena Kibet from the home had told him about Dunbar. 'How come you were at the care home to see Yvette Boudreaux?'

'Garry Croft's mother is a resident there. Mrs Boudreaux told me it was strange three people had been to see her about Croft.'

'Three?'

'You, me, and a DCI Fleming. I know what Fleming's interest is. What's yours?'

'It's a private matter.'

'Anything to do with the fact Croft was suspected of killing William Stroud?'

'Who?'

'William Stroud. He worked at the AWE and someone murdered him about five years ago.'

Rimmer thought for a moment while taking a sip of his beer. 'Of course, now you mention it, I recall seeing about it in the papers.'

'And Garry Croft was the prime suspect. He buggered off to Australia without telling anyone exactly where he was.'

'Ah, yes.'

'It took you a while to remember about Stroud so would I be right in assuming your interest in Croft isn't connected to the murder case?'

'I have a client who wants to find him,' was all Rimmer said.

'Why does your client want to find him?'

'As I said, it's a private matter.'

'Fleming's been to the care home. I'm sure Yvette Boudreaux must have told him about you. Has he been to see you?'

Rimmer saw no point in denying it. 'Yes, he has.'

'My guess is Fleming wouldn't accept your interest in Croft was a matter only between you and your client.'

'He didn't.'

'So you told him why your client wants to find Croft?'

'Yes.'

'I could run a story saying Dan Rimmer, a private investigator, has been interviewed in connection with the missing Garry Croft who was suspected of killing William Stroud, and he refused to divulge why he was looking for Croft.'

'Bloody persistent, aren't you?'

'That's my job.'

Rimmer sighed. 'My client wants to find Croft because Croft owes him some money.'

'And you told Fleming who this client is?'

'I couldn't. I have no way of contacting him, just a name – Liam Doherty.' Rimmer went on to explain why he had no contact details for his client.

'And that's it?'

'Yep. Can I ask why *you* are interested in Garry Croft and the Stroud case?'

'I spoke to an assistant chief constable for Thames Valley Police who told me they were looking into cold cases. Top of the list was the Stroud case. I decided it would be a good thing to investigate since it involves the AWE.'

'And where has your investigation led you so far?'

'Garry Croft. Seems three of us would like to know where he is in Australia. Two of us for the same reason and you for a different one.'

And none of us are any nearer to finding him, Rimmer thought.

20

Fleming was in his office at Long Hanborough waiting for Logan and Anderson to arrive. He'd asked them to call in first thing before they set off for Aldermaston to carry on with the interviews. Eathan Younger wanted to see him in an hour, and he wasn't sure he had any more to tell him since his last briefing meeting.

The office door was open and Jeff Miller appeared.

'Any progress, Alex?'

'Not a lot.'

'Garry Croft still the number one suspect?'

Fleming wasn't going to tell him Croft might have had another reason for fleeing to Australia. Nor was he inclined to tell him about his chat with Nat Horne's widow and that Horne himself, who Ingham's team hadn't interviewed, could be a suspect. Before he could answer, Logan and Anderson appeared in the doorway.

It was Logan who spoke. 'Okay to come in, boss?'

Miller turned. 'You've got company so I'll leave you to it.'

Fleming got up from behind his desk and sat on an edge where there was some space. Logan pulled up a chair and settled himself astride it with his arms folded over the back. Anderson took another spare seat, notebook at the ready.

'I've got a meeting with Younger in an hour, so I need to get an update on where we are,' Fleming said, looking at Logan. 'How are the interviews going?'

Logan sighed. 'We're ploughing through them. About done with all those who knew Stroud reasonably well, and we're working through all the other union members and staff. Next stage is to start tracing all those who have since left the company.'

'Any new information?'

'No. Had a chat with Bill Kauffman, the union leader. He's a bit of a character. Rude, uncouth, and quite obviously a left-wing extremist, bu–'

'But shrewd with it,' Anderson cut in.

'Thank you, Naomi,' Logan said. 'I was about to say that.'

Anderson smiled and tapped her pen against the notebook. 'Made a note of it here, Sarge.'

'Good to see you're taking notes.'

'But apart from his personality, he had nothing new to offer?' Fleming prompted.

Logan shook his head. 'Afraid not. But remember the foreman we told you about, Emerson?'

'The guy who told you the row between Stroud and Croft turned into a fight outside a pub?'

'That's him. There was an incident on the picket line the other day at the main gates of the AWE. Emerson was trying to get into work and it turned into a brawl with Kauffman. Emerson ended up with a bloodied face and his car was trashed.'

'You saw this?' Fleming asked.

'No. Someone rang the police and Naomi and I turned up after them. I questioned Emerson and Kauffman. All a bit inconclusive. Emerson claimed someone punched him in the face, but he didn't see who. He admits to lashing out at Kauffman, but didn't see who damaged his car. Kauffman told me it was Emerson who threw the first punch and said the union would pay for the car. Might be a matter of issuing warnings all round and no charges.'

'Hmm, looks like we're not making much progress with the case itself,' Fleming mused.

'Stroud had a girlfriend apparently,' Anderson suddenly chipped in. 'So far we only have people telling us they thought he might have. No one knows who she was though. He was pretty secretive about his personal life.'

'Do you know if she worked at the AWE?' Fleming asked.

'We're trying to find out,' Logan said.

Fleming nodded. 'I'd like to speak to her when you find her.'

Anderson jotted something down in her notebook and looked across at Logan. 'Are you going to tell the boss what I thought about Nieve.'

Logan laughed. 'Naomi's paranoid. Thinks there's something fishy about Nieve being keen to find out how we're getting on.'

'Yes, but I heard her on the phone to someone saying she was keeping an eye on us. Why would she want to do that, and who was she speaking to?' Anderson frowned. 'And wouldn't you like to know who she's speaking to about us, Sarge?'

Fleming remembered he'd also wondered if Nieve was only interested in how well the interviews were going, or whether she had a wider interest. 'Keep any information you give her to the minimum,' was all Fleming could think of saying.

'What about you, boss?' Logan asked. 'Anything new?'

Fleming shook his head. 'Not much. The reporter I told you about, Zoe Dunbar, she thinks the Stroud case might have something to do with national security.'

Logan whistled. 'Really?'

'She asked me an interesting question. Wanted to know whether MI5 had approached us.'

'I wonder why,' Logan said.

'Just fishing I think,' Fleming replied. 'I did ask Younger about it though. Didn't get a straight answer.'

'Gets more and more intriguing all the time,' Logan mused.

'Speaking of which,' Fleming said, 'I went to see Nat Horne's widow, Emma Horne.'

'Don't tell me, boss, she couldn't throw any light on matters,' Logan guessed.

Fleming hesitated. 'Maybe...'

Logan raised an eyebrow.

'She told me her husband had withdrawn into himself. He told her things were getting out of control. He was never the same after he retired, she told me. Thought there were things going on at the AWE Horne wouldn't talk about.'

'Interesting.' Logan thought for a second. 'You're not thinking he might have killed Stroud, are you?'

Fleming raised his hands as though in surrender. 'Let's keep an open mind. Oh, by the way, there are a couple of things I need you both to do. Can you ask Ursula Nieve if she has the forwarding address in Australia for Croft and if Frank Ingham had asked her for it? She'd taken over as HR manager before Croft left.'

'Okay,' Logan confirmed as Anderson scribbled another note in her book. 'You said a couple of things?'

'Yes. Can you see if there's any CCTV coverage on the street where Wyatt Investigations office is? I'm looking for a man who may have walked by regularly to look in the window.'

21

Fleming had used his old Porsche to drive down to Aldermaston. Logan and Anderson had left earlier to start interviews. He popped in to see them briefly before going to see Ursula Nieve who was about to go to a meeting. She had a few minutes spare and had offered to let Fleming use her office to speak to Kauffman.

'Let my secretary know when you've finished and she'll lock up,' Nieve said.

'Thanks, I shouldn't be too long. Logan and Anderson have seen Mr Kauffman, but I'd like a quick chat.'

'Any particular reason?'

'No, not really. There's one or two things I wanted to double-check.'

'How are your enquiries going? It must be painstaking work to have to go over everything that was gone over five years ago.'

'It is. You joined the company shortly after Stroud was killed, didn't you? After Nat Horne took early retirement.'

'Yes, I did.'

'Enquiries must still have been going on then.'

'Yes, they were.'

'And Garry Croft went to Australia after Stroud's murder.'

'Yes.'

Fleming realised he'd asked Logan to check this with Nieve, but thought he might as well ask while he was there. 'Would you happen to know where in Australia Croft went to stay?'

'DS Logan asked me this morning when he arrived.'

'Ah, sorry.'

'The only address I had was the one he was staying at in England. I'd no idea at the time he was going to Australia. As far as I know he didn't tell anyone. I gave the UK address to DCI Ingham. Look, I have to rush. I'm going to be late for my meeting.'

Fleming was sitting behind Nieve's desk when Kauffman appeared at the open door. He knocked anyway, one sharp rap on the door. 'You wanted a word?' The voice was deep and hoarse.

Logan had described Kauffman, so Fleming wasn't surprised at the size of the man. He was tall, well built, verging on overweight. The full, thick beard and menacing brown eyes gave him a sinister look. He was wearing jeans and a tight-fitting grey T-shirt with no collar and buttons at the neck.

'Yes, come in, Mr Kauffman. Take a seat.'

Kauffman pulled up a chair and slouched back in it with a smug look on his face. 'A bit like an interview, isn't it? I mean... you sitting there looking all official, and me on the other side of the desk. Is this supposed to unnerve me?'

Fleming took an instant dislike to the man. He could well imagine how he would rub management up the wrong way. 'Any reason why you should feel unnerved?'

Kauffman looked up at the ceiling as though bored. 'Not at all. Why should I be?'

'I just want to ask you a few questions. Shouldn't take long.'

'Take as long as you like.' Kauffman crossed his arms and glared at Fleming. 'But I've spoken to your colleagues. They forget to ask me something?'

'Only routine, Mr Kauffman. I'd like to get some background.'

'It's because I'm the union boss, isn't it? That why you lot want to grill me twice?' Kauffman growled.

'Not at all, Mr Kauffman. I just want to clarify a few things.'

'Fine. If it keeps you happy. Fire away.'

'When did you start work here?'

'About twenty-four years ago.'

'And when did you become the union leader?'

'What the fuck has that got to do with your investigation?'

'I'd like to fill in some background... okay?'

Kauffman shrugged. 'About nine years ago.'

'So you were the union leader at the time of the last dispute and William Stroud's murder?'

Kauffman's eyes narrowed. 'Yes,' he answered cautiously.

'What was the strike over?'

'Pay, pensions, health and safety.'

'Would it be fair to say tensions were running high at the time – tempers getting frayed?'

'It was an industrial dispute. We didn't agree with management, if that's what you mean. Conflict is a natural consequence.'

'How well did you know Stroud?'

Kauffman gazed steadily at Fleming. 'Not very well.'

'Was he involved in the conflict you mention?'

'We all were.'

'People have said he was a bit secretive, kept pretty much to himself. Is that how you saw him?'

'I've told you – I didn't know him very well.'

'Do you know who his girlfriend was?'

Kauffman flashed a quick look at Fleming. 'Didn't know he had one.'

'Stroud had a serious fall out with Garry Croft – in fact it came to blows outside a pub. Did you know about that?'

Kauffman hesitated. 'Yes. It was fairly common knowledge.'

'So you weren't at the pub when this happened?'

'No.'

'How well did you know Croft?'

'Quite well.'

'Did he tell you about the fight he had with Stroud and what it was about?'

'No, union men don't go around telling tales. What went on between them was nothing to do with anyone else.'

'Did Croft tell you he was going to Australia?'

'No. He left the company and I never saw him again.'

'He's never been in touch since?'

'Not with me, no. Look, are you about done?'

'Not quite. Did you have much to do with Nat Horne?'

'He was the HR manager.'

'Doesn't answer my question.'

'He was at all the meetings we had with management.'

'Was Stroud at any of those meetings?'

'Yes.'

'Did he and Horne cross swords?'

'Horne crossed swords with a lot of people.'

'Horne was apparently a troubled man after the dispute. His widow thought there were things going on her husband wouldn't talk about.'

'Really? I wouldn't know anything about that.'

'He took early retirement and died soon after.'

'Shame. Are you done now?'

'One more question. How do you get on with the foreman, Emerson?'

Kauffman scowled at Fleming. 'I don't. Fucking man refused to strike. He's trying to undermine our position.'

'Was that the reason for the incident on the picket line you and Emerson were involved in?'

'Are you going to cross-examine me about that as well, for fuck's sake? I've already provided a statement.'

'Any other reason you and Emerson don't get on?'

'As I said, conflict usually goes with industrial disputes.'

'You think Stroud was murdered because of the spat he had with Croft?'

'How would I know?'

Fleming had no more questions for Kauffman and ended the interview. He somehow had the feeling Kauffman had something to hide. And his personnel file was in Nieve's in tray.

22

Fleming had finished questioning Kauffman and had gone along to look in on Logan and Anderson. They had someone with them so he didn't interrupt.

On his way out he bumped into Nieve coming back from her meeting. 'Ah, there you are. I'm finished with Kauffman. Thanks for the use of your office. Any reason you had his file on your desk.'

'Been looking in my in tray?' she asked with a smile.

'It was sitting on top. Couldn't help but see it.'

'Just checking up on something.'

'Anything important?'

'Not really. I wanted to check when he joined us.'

'Twenty-three, maybe twenty-four years ago.'

'You looked in his file?' Nieve asked with raised eyebrows.

'No – I asked him,' Fleming said with a grin as he made to leave.

It was a nice sunny day outside and Fleming was mulling things over in his head as he made his way to the visitors' car park. He was beginning to think they were going round in circles. All they seemed to be doing was confirming what Ingham's team had found five years earlier. But then Younger had thought the original investigation was flawed. Ingham had been convinced Garry Croft was the killer so did Younger not agree? Fleming recalled Ingham saying he thought it was Younger and not the chief constable who had put a hold on funding for him to pursue the case with the Australian police. Younger had told Fleming the reason was the chief constable thought the expense couldn't be justified because there wasn't enough evidence against Croft. Maybe it *was* Younger who had withheld funds, but he'd done so believing Ingham was wrong about Croft. Fleming had thought Croft had another reason to flee to Australia when he discovered Ingham didn't know about Rimmer and the money his client reckoned Croft owed him. But Younger hadn't known about that, so why had he thought the case was flawed? Maybe he didn't think so, and it was all about budgets as Ingham had claimed. Then there was Nat Horne – and Kauffman who seemed as though he had something to hide.

Fleming's thoughts were brought abruptly to a halt as he reached his car.

'Nice car,' a familiar voice said.

Fleming turned to see Zoe Dunbar standing there. *What's she doing here?* 'I take it you're here to see someone other than me.'

'I am. Who have you been speaking to?'

'Nothing like getting straight to the point, eh? I happen to be investigating a murder, remember? And you?'

'I'm an investigative reporter, remember?'

Fleming was beginning to think they were about to engage

in another bout of verbal sparring as they had done in their first meeting. 'So what precisely brings you here?'

'Thought I'd have a chat with Ursula Nieve.'

'Any particular reason?'

'I want to get her take on what this current strike is all about and whether there's work going on here someone might want to disrupt.'

'You're still thinking this is to do with national security?'

'Subversive activity is always a possibility in a place like this, don't you think?'

'Possibly, but I'm investigating a murder that took place five years ago. What makes you think Stroud might somehow be connected?'

'There was a strike then as well.'

'And?'

'Just following up on every angle.'

Fleming smiled. 'Tenacious, aren't you?'

'That's what I do. How did your meeting with Dan Rimmer go?'

'You're assuming I went to see him.'

'You did. He told me.'

'How did you know about him?'

'Yvette Boudreaux at the care home told me.'

'And did Rimmer have anything to tell you?'

'Probably the same as he told you.'

'And that would have been...?'

Dunbar thought for a moment. 'At first he wouldn't tell me what his interest in Croft was. He told me it was a private matter between him and some client. I suggested you wouldn't take that for an answer and he would have been obliged to tell you.'

'And?'

'I threatened to run a story saying he'd been questioned in

connection with Garry Croft, the prime suspect in the William Stroud case, and he'd refused to answer questions.'

'Why doesn't that surprise me.'

'So he told me about the mystery client who wants to find Croft because Croft owes him a lot of money.'

'I see.'

'I take it you're looking for this mystery client?'

'I am.'

'But you haven't found him so far?'

'Not yet, but we will.'

'Will you let me know if you do?' Dunbar asked hopefully.

'Tell you what,' Fleming said, 'I'll give you a heads-up if you do something for me.'

'What?' Dunbar asked suspiciously.

'Run a story saying police are following up new leads in the Stroud enquiry and are hopeful someone who didn't come forward with information before may now feel safe to do so.'

'Bit hopeful, isn't it? Is this an indication you're not getting very far?'

'So you'll do it?'

'Okay.'

Dunbar turned and strode across the car park towards her car. She waved a hand over her head. 'Don't forget – I'm doing you a favour. You owe me one.'

Fleming shook his head. *And I'm sure she will want something in return.*

23

The Railwayman pub was in urgent need of refurbishment. But it was within walking distance of the office and handy for Rimmer and his uncle when they decided to finish the day off with a pint. A few high stools sat in front of a long bar covered in wet beer towels. Wooden beams ran across the white ceiling, stained yellow from the days when smoking was allowed in pubs, hinting at when it had last seen a lick of paint. The faded blue carpet did little to lift the décor. Old photographs and dull paintings adorned the walls, completing the picture of a sadly neglected establishment. Tables and chairs sat against the wall opposite the bar, mostly unoccupied. In fact, the place was virtually empty apart from a few men drinking.

Rimmer ordered two pints of Doom Bar and took them over to where his uncle was sitting. Rimmer stretched his left leg out and rubbed his thigh.

'Playing up again?'

'Nah, a bit stiff, that's all.'

Wyatt raised his glass and took a sip of his pint. 'Ah well, here's to another unsuccessful day. Seems a long time ago now when I could sit here puffing away on my pipe. Never see anyone with one now, do you?'

'I knew a captain when I was in Afghanistan. He smoked a pipe… indoors as well. Didn't give a toss.'

Wyatt laughed. 'Man after my own heart.'

They sipped at their beers and fell silent for a while. 'Ever hear from Val?' Wyatt suddenly asked.

Valerie had been Rimmer's wife until they divorced five years earlier. The continual absence with the army had taken its toll. Rimmer shook his head. 'Past history, mate. No children, so no need to keep in touch.'

They fell silent again. Rimmer suspected his uncle was probably thinking of his wife who had died in a car accident seventeen years earlier. He'd never remarried. Rimmer decided to change the subject. 'Remember I told you I had something in mind regarding Garry Croft?' he whispered.

Wyatt raised an eyebrow. 'Yes?'

'I'd intended to try to find someone at the care home who was closer to his mother than the manager. Someone I could get to fish for information.'

'And?'

'I went to see Yvette Boudreaux, the manager, and bumped into someone outside having a fag – name of Makena Kibet. Turns out she has a lot to do with Mrs Croft. I asked her to keep her eyes and ears open and try to see if she could jog Mrs Croft's memory.'

'Anything?'

'Not much… except Mrs Croft's taken ill. She's quite poorly it seems.'

'Think her son might come back to see her?'

'It's possible. Makena will let me know.'

'Be a result if you did find him after all this time.' Wyatt sipped at his beer. 'Oh, as it happens, I had an interesting phone call earlier.'

Rimmer leaned across the table. 'To do with Croft?' he asked eagerly.

Wyatt downed the last of his pint and pointed to Rimmer's near empty glass. 'Another?'

'After you tell me about this phone call. How come you didn't mention it before?'

'You were out, remember? Just came back to me.'

'Okay, so tell me now.'

'After I get another pint, I'm parched.'

Wyatt pushed himself up from the table and took the empty glasses back to the bar. He exchanged a few pleasantries with the barman pulling the pints, then returned to an impatient Rimmer with the drinks and some crisps.

'In case you're feeling peckish.' Wyatt threw the crisps onto the table.

Rimmer ignored them, and the new pint. 'Come on, Phil, don't keep me in suspense. Who was on the phone?'

Wyatt took a long sip of his beer and sighed. 'Ah, that's good.'

'For fuck's sake, Phil, are you trying to wind me up?'

'Calm down, Dan. He said he knew you.'

'Who?'

Wyatt fished in his pocket and pulled out a scrap of paper.

'Emerson – Seth Emerson.'

Rimmer frowned. 'Never heard of him. What did he want?'

'Wanted you to ring him back. He'd like to come and see you.'

'Did he say why?'

Wyatt helped himself to a handful of crisps. 'No. But here's the thing – he works at the AWE.'

'How do you know?'

Wyatt finished crunching his way through a mouthful of

crisps and washed them down with a swig of beer. 'He reckoned you met him and some friends of his at a pub in Aldermaston about four years ago when you first started looking for Croft. He told me you'd asked them if they knew where Croft had gone. They didn't, but you left a business card and asked them to contact you if they should hear where Croft was.'

'Did he say he had some information?'

'He said he still had your card and wanted to see you.'

~

Seth Emerson sat facing Rimmer in the office of Wyatt Investigations looking somewhat anxious.

'When I returned your phone call you told me you didn't have any information about Garry Croft, but you wanted to speak to me about something else,' Rimmer prompted.

'Yes. Sorry if you thought I had something to tell you about Garry. I never heard from him again after he went to Australia. I knew from the papers the police wanted to talk to him in connection with Stroud's murder and it didn't look good that he'd buggered off.'

'So what was it you wanted to see me about?'

Emerson shifted uncomfortably in his chair. 'I... I think my wife is having an affair and I'd like to use your services to check whether she is.'

'What makes you suspect that?'

'She's been a bit distant lately. Always says she's tired, doesn't want to talk, goes out and says it's with friends. What made me even more suspicious was a few days ago when there was an incoming message on her mobile. She'd left it on the kitchen table while she was upstairs. I saw who it was from before she came back and snatched the phone away.'

'Someone you know?'

'It was from Bill Kauffman, the union boss at the AWE. I'd noticed the way he looked at her when we went to the pub.'

'Did you ask her why he was sending her a message?'

'Yes. She shrugged it off, claimed he'd obviously sent it to the wrong person because it didn't make sense. I asked what it was. She said it was something to do with work and deleted it.'

'Would there be any reason for him to have her number?'

'We all gave him next of kin numbers... in case anything happened at work.'

'So you want me to carry out surveillance on her?'

'Yes.'

'Okay, I'll see what I can do. Let me have a photograph of her, a car registration if she has one, and your address. And give me a ring if she says she's going out with friends.'

'How much will it cost?'

'Depends on how much time I have to spend on surveillance before I get the evidence you need. I charge forty-five pounds an hour.'

'Okay.'

Emerson left and Rimmer wondered why everything seemed to be revolving round the AWE and its workforce.

24

There was no trouble on the picket line as Fleming drove past into the main entrance of the AWE. Kauffman was nowhere in sight.

Fleming had called in to speak to Eathan Younger before he left the office to let him know he was going to see Logan and Anderson who had been looking through CCTV footage of the street outside Wyatt Investigations. Younger was keen to know if it threw any light on Rimmer's mystery client. Fleming was hoping it would, though he wasn't sure how finding out who Rimmer's client was would get him any closer to identifying Stroud's killer. But he had to follow up every lead even if they led to a dead end. There was a link to Croft who was a prime suspect, so it was promising. But was it connected to Stroud, or just coincidence someone else was looking for Croft?

Fleming parked his car and made his way to Ursula Nieve's office first. It was a courtesy call before he went to see Logan and Anderson. He knocked and looked round the open door. 'Busy?'

'Yes, but I have a few minutes to spare. Another meeting with Bill Kauffman and his men.'

'That's why I didn't see him outside. How's it going?'

'Not good. One-day strikes are starting to bite, but we're unable to reach agreement with the union so far.' Nieve paused for a moment before adding, 'I hear there was a bit of a scuffle the other day on the picket line between Kauffman and a foreman called Emerson. Are any charges being brought?'

'I don't think so. It's all a bit inconclusive. Neither man wants to press charges. The union has agreed to pay for Emerson's car. Local police are dealing with it. I think it's going to be a matter of warnings all round.'

'Might be as well. There's enough trouble with the strike without having a court case on top.'

Fleming thought for a moment. 'Any particular line of work going on here that someone might want to disrupt?'

'We carry out research, design and develop warheads for the UK's nuclear deterrent. There's always the threat of subversive activity.'

'Any reason to think this strike might be aimed at that?'

Nieve frowned. 'I had a reporter come to see me the other day asking the same question. Do the two of you know something I ought to know?'

'No. I bumped into her in the car park on her way to see you. She happens to be interested in the old Stroud murder enquiry and is probing randomly in the hope she'll discover something.'

'And have *you*? I thought you might have something new when you called to say you were coming over.'

'Maybe. I want to go through some CCTV footage with Logan and Anderson.'

Nieve narrowed her eyes. 'From five years ago?'

Fleming laughed. 'No, something came up recently I want to check.'

'Progress then?'

'Could be. There's a possible link to Garry Croft we didn't know about before.'

'That sounds like progress. Anyway, must dash. Hope you find what you're looking for. Let me know.'

~

Anderson was pulling a face at Logan who'd made some joke when Fleming entered the office Nieve had found for them to hold interviews. Logan looked up from an open laptop. 'Ah, boss, just in time.'

Fleming looked at Anderson. 'Seems like it. You two been at it again?'

'He's trying to be funny, sir, but without much success,' Anderson said, putting a reassuring hand on Logan's back. 'You try your best though, Sarge.'

'Only pointing out someone on the CCTV footage who looked like her and wondered if she was Rimmer's mystery client.'

'Yeah, with a name like Liam Doherty?'

'Obviously an alias,' Logan quipped.

'And a man's voice?'

Logan was about to speak, but Anderson cut in. 'Don't you dare say anything else, Sarge.'

Logan smiled. 'Okay, Naomi, fun over. Boss is here.'

Fleming shook his head. 'Anything to show me?'

'I'm afraid not, boss. We've scoured hours of CCTV footage of the street. There's a few familiar faces though the images are slightly grainy. None of them stopped to look in Rimmer's office window, or even glance in that direction. The faces we've seen more than once could be people who work nearby or go to the same place regularly for some reason.'

'It was a long shot,' Fleming said. 'I'm going to Reading next to see Rimmer. It'll be interesting if he says his client hasn't been in touch.'

'Maybe the man doesn't exist,' Anderson offered.

'Which then begs the question, why would Rimmer make him up?' Fleming mused.

'That is a very good point,' Logan said.

'Very helpful,' Anderson jibed.

'Rimmer's a private investigator. Wouldn't he have tried to trace his client?' Logan asked.

'He did. All the usual ways including social media and found lots of Liam Dohertys, but no way of checking whether any of them was the man he was looking for.'

'It's also possible that whoever was watching out for the red card wouldn't have to stare overtly in the office window,' Anderson said. 'He would be able to see by just walking past and casting his eyes sideways. After all, he clearly wants to remain anonymous and would be aware of CCTV. And... Liam Doherty is probably not even his real name.'

'I think we can be certain of that,' Fleming agreed.

'And, he might have been wearing a disguise,' Logan added with a laugh.

Fleming and Anderson glanced at each other and smiled.

25

Fleming parked his car and walked the rest of the way to the Wyatt Investigations office. Rimmer was expecting him. He'd said his uncle was out on a job so Rimmer was on his own in the office. A kettle was boiling on a small table as Fleming entered.

'About to have a coffee. Want one?' Rimmer asked.

It was a hot day and Fleming was thirsty after the drive up from the AWE. 'A glass of water would be fine.'

Fleming took in his surroundings while Rimmer disappeared into an adjoining kitchen area to get the water. Fleming's eyes settled on the desk where he saw a folder with Croft's name on it. 'Anything to add to that?' he said, pointing to the folder when Rimmer came back with the glass of water.

'Afraid not,' Rimmer replied, pouring himself a coffee.

'Did Liam Doherty get in touch after you put the red card in your window?'

'As it happens, yes he did.'

'And?'

'He wasn't best pleased when I told him I hadn't found Croft but you wanted to know who he was. He just said, no police, and hung up.'

'The thing is, there's nothing on the CCTV footage of the street showing anyone looking in your window.' Fleming waited with interest for Rimmer's response.

'Doesn't surprise me. The man is desperate to remain anonymous. He could have walked by without looking in directly. Or he could have driven past, or have been sitting in the café opposite. Who knows?'

'Interesting he hung up when you mentioned police, don't you think?'

'Yes, it is. It's not unusual for people to want their identity kept secret, but I have to admit it's not so good when they don't want police involved. Could be several explanations though.'

'Go on.'

'Could be he's embarrassed he loaned fifty thousand pounds to a man who was the prime suspect in a murder enquiry and doesn't want his name to be associated with him. Maybe he's an eccentric odd ball, or...' Rimmer paused as though deciding whether to say what he was going to say next. 'Or he didn't loan the money to Croft, but paid him to kill Stroud and wanted to find him first before he could implicate him. Now that *would* be a good reason for not wanting the police to get involved.'

'But if you knew that, and your client killed Croft, you could be charged with being an accessory to murder. Or, you could be accused of withholding information in the Stroud enquiry.'

'Okay, take your point, but I'm only guessing. Anyway, I can't afford to turn work away on the basis the client could have some ulterior motive. As it happens, I've taken on a job where a man wants me to carry out surveillance on his wife because he thinks she's having an affair. What if I can prove she is and he kills her, would I be an accessory?'

'Interesting point of law I guess. But you might be given a hard time by the police.'

'Maybe so, but as far as I'm concerned with Liam Doherty, I'm only trying to trace someone who owes him a lot of money. That's what he told me.'

'Okay. I'm no further forward at the moment to finding Liam Doherty, who may not have anything to do with the Stroud case. But if you get any information on him at all you need to contact me right away, understood?'

'Of course, no problem. I'll let you know.'

'And if you find out anything about Croft.'

'Likewise.'

On his way back to the car, Fleming wondered if he was chasing a phantom and whether he might be wasting time trying to find Liam Doherty. Did he have anything to do with Stroud? *No police*, the man had said.

26

A big BMW motorbike pulled up outside the terraced house in Tadley. The rider, kitted out in black leathers and matt black helmet, dismounted. It was seven in the evening and the sun still shone in a cloudless sky. Toby Omoko removed the helmet and took a deep breath of fresh air which carried the scent of sweet peas.

On the way over from London, Omoko had been thinking about his last meeting with Quentin Vere. He'd made a scathing comment about being able to read the information Omoko had given him in the papers. Something not in the news was what he wanted. *Fair enough*, Omoko had thought. His agent hadn't come up with much so far. The only thing Falcon had found out was that a private investigator called Rimmer had a mystery client who wanted to find Garry Croft. Police were going through CCTV footage to try to identify him. Vere wasn't happy, so Omoko had decided to take matters into his own hands. It was a risk. He was an analyst and had no field training. But it was one he was prepared to take because of Vere's bullying. And... he had a plan.

When going through his daily trawl of the papers, Omoko had seen an article covering the strike at the AWE and the brawl between Emerson and Kauffman on the picket line. He wasn't sure what he hoped to achieve by what he was doing, but he felt he had to do something. It didn't take long for the wheels within MI5 to find Emerson's address and phone number. Omoko had phoned Emerson and told him he was William Stroud's nephew. He'd told him he would like to speak to Emerson about the strike and Kauffman. Omoko had added to the lie that his father worked for a firm of solicitors who might be able to get Emerson compensation for the assault and damage to his car. He'd guessed the mention of Kauffman's name and legal assistance would arouse his curiosity. Emerson had indeed agreed to meet Omoko who had given the false name of Valac Sono.

'Came on the bike,' Omoko said, explaining the leather gear when Emerson answered the door. 'Seth Emerson?'

'Yes. Mr Sono?'

'Yes. It's good of you to see me. I won't take up too much of your time.'

Emerson showed Omoko through a tiny hallway into a small living room furnished with a two-seater sofa, two chairs, a coffee table and large-screen TV. A glass cabinet sat in one corner and on the top shelf Omoko noticed a photo of Emerson and an attractive blonde woman standing in front of a light aircraft. Probably late forties, Omoko guessed. 'Your wife?' He pointed at the photograph.

'Yes,' Emerson replied. 'She's out... with friends,' he added after a short pause.

Omoko thought he detected a look of anguish in the man's eyes when he spoke. 'Ah,' was all he uttered, as though registering understanding.

'Take a seat. Can I get you a drink?' Emerson asked awkwardly.

'No, I'm fine,' Omoko said, sitting in one of the single chairs.

'I'm curious how you knew about me and got my phone number.'

'I saw an article in a newspaper about the affray on the picket line outside the AWE and thought you might be a good person to speak to since you weren't on strike and had a confrontation with Bill Kauffman. I got your number from a helpful clerk in HR,' Omoko lied.

'Surprised they gave it to you.'

'I was a little persuasive I have to admit. I told them it wasn't a problem as I could ask the police who took statements from you and Kauffman on the basis I was working for a firm of solicitors.'

Emerson smiled. 'What exactly do you think I can help you with? And why the sudden interest in your uncle now?'

'I'd not given it much thought to be honest, but then I saw a recent newspaper article about my uncle's case being reopened. Then I read something about the strike and your spat with Bill Kauffman. I was curious when I saw his name.'

'Why?'

'I recall my mother telling me her brother... my uncle... had told her about Kauffman. There was something going on between them my uncle wouldn't talk about.' Omoko waited to see if there was any response to the lie.

'Are you saying you think it might have been him? I mean, that Kauffman killed your uncle and not Croft?'

'All I know is there was no love lost between them. Kauffman was the union leader during the first strike as well, wasn't he?'

'Yes. Kauffman is always at the heart of any disagreement with management.'

'Do you think he has an ulterior motive for calling these strikes?'

Emerson thought for a moment. 'Kauffman is a left-wing

extremist. He hates management, politicians – in fact, I think the man hates everything other than the sound of his own voice. He's power mad if you ask me.'

'Hate enough to kill?' Omoko prompted.

Emerson shrugged. 'Who knows. He obviously has a violent nature.'

'You worked at the AWE during the first strike, I take it.'

'Yes,' Emerson said guardedly.

'You remember Garry Croft? After he fled to Australia, he became the prime suspect for killing my uncle.'

'I do, yes.'

'How well did you know Croft?'

'Not well. He was volatile... quick tempered, I can tell you. He had a big row with your uncle and it turned into a fight outside a pub.'

'Really? Do you know what it was over?'

'Afraid not.'

'What about my uncle? Did you know him well?'

'No, I only knew of him. There was something odd though. He was in the union and made out he was militant, but somehow didn't seem to fit the bill.'

'How do you mean?'

'He went on strike, but there seemed to be a conflict between him and Croft... and even more so with Kauffman. Don't know what it was all about, but there was definitely friction between Kauffman and your uncle.'

Omoko felt he wasn't going to gain any more from this. In truth, he'd gained very little. He pulled himself up from his chair. 'Well, thank you for your time, Mr Emerson.'

'What about the possibility of me getting compensation?'

MI5 had a legend to cover this. They'd created a fictitious firm of solicitors which agents could say they worked for.

Omoko gave Emerson a false business card headed Kemp and Kemp. 'Give them a call.'

Of course, someone would answer if Emerson rang. But they would simply say they'd looked into his case and compensation would not be possible.

27

'She works in a pub!' Anderson had announced gleefully, much to Fleming's amusement.

'Aha, we could see this Pat Quigley, then decide to have a social break and have a pint. Might even do food if we're lucky,' Logan said.

'And you'll be having burger and chips if I'm not mistaken, Sarge,' Anderson joked.

'I think the three of us should go,' Fleming had suggested. 'I'll speak to Quigley while you two go and get yourselves a drink. We can have a quick meeting after to catch up on things.'

'There goes my plan for having a break off duty,' Logan grumbled.

'Don't worry, Harry, we can consider ourselves not to be at work. Drinks are on me.'

'Sounds like a good idea, boss. I like meetings like that.'

Logan and Anderson had finally found someone who knew about Stroud's girlfriend. One of the union men they'd interviewed had told them it was Pat Quigley who worked in a pub on the outskirts of Baughurst. Fleming had phoned to check she would be there and if she could spare a few minutes to answer some questions about a man who they thought was her boyfriend some years back. She'd confirmed it would be okay.

Logan had gone to Long Hanborough to get a pool car and then picked Fleming and Anderson up in Oxford. The journey down to Baughurst took less than an hour and it didn't take long to find The Rifleman.

Pat Quigley was busy clearing glasses from a table when the detectives entered. She looked alarmed when Fleming showed his warrant card. 'Oh, I wasn't expecting to see three people.'

'Don't worry,' Fleming said, 'my two colleagues are going to get a drink and go outside to enjoy the early evening sunshine. I just want a few minutes of your time if that's okay?'

Quigley checked with the landlord who nodded his agreement for her to take ten. She took Fleming over to an empty table at the far corner of the bar. 'So how can I help you?'

Fleming sat opposite Quigley. She was an attractive woman with long black hair tied back into a ponytail. Probably late thirties, Fleming guessed. 'I wanted to ask you a few questions about someone who was an old boyfriend of yours... William Stroud.'

Quigley raised her eyebrows. 'Gosh, that was a long time ago. How did you know? I mean... how did you know he was my boyfriend?'

'My two colleagues... they found someone at the AWE who knew about you.'

'Must have been one of William's friends. He used to come in here a lot. That's how we met.'

'How long ago?'

'Must be almost six years. He came into the pub one night... on his own. I hadn't seen him before. He ordered a pint and we got talking.'

'Remember what you talked about?'

'Oh, goodness.'

'I mean, was it idle talk about things like the weather? Did he tell you where he worked? Who started the conversation?'

'I think I did.' Quigley giggled. 'Bit of a chatterbox at times. Helps working behind a bar.'

'I guess it does,' Fleming agreed.

'I think I remember saying I hadn't seen him before and asked if he was just passing through.'

'And what did he say?'

'William told me he'd started work at the AWE about a year before and had recently moved into lodgings in Aldermaston.'

'So not married?'

Quigley blushed. 'I think I asked him how come an attractive man like him wasn't married. I was being flirtatious and assumed he wasn't when he told me he'd gone into lodgings.'

'So he wasn't?'

'No.'

'How did the relationship start?'

'He came in again a week later. We chatted. He asked me out. We went out regularly afterwards.'

'Did he stay where he was or did you live together?'

'He moved in with me.'

'Did he ever talk about work?'

'Not really. Kept things pretty close to his chest.'

'He never spoke about the strike?'

'No.'

'Ever mention Garry Croft?'

Quigley thought for a moment. 'Yes, once. William came home one night with bruises and a cut face. Told me he'd had a bit of a skirmish with Croft.'

'Not here?'

'No.'

'Did he say what it was about?'

'Something to do with a disagreement over the strike. I think that might have been the only time he mentioned it. I felt there was more to it than he was letting on. He became more serious, sullen... as though he was troubled over something.'

'But he didn't say what?'

Quigley shook her head.

'What about Bill Kauffman and Nat Horne – did he ever mention either of them?'

Another shake of the head.

'How long had you known William?'

'About a year, maybe less.'

'How did the relationship end?'

'I found out he was having an affair. It was with someone's wife from the AWE.'

'How did you find out?'

'William changed. Went out on his own a lot. Would come back late. One night I could smell perfume on him. We had a row and he admitted there was someone, but he wouldn't say who. Told me there was a reason he'd started seeing them, but there were things he couldn't tell me about. He apologised and left.'

'Did you ever see or speak to him again?'

'No. Then I saw in the papers he'd been murdered.'

Fleming nodded and said he needn't take up any more of her time. He thanked her and went in search of Logan and Anderson who had gone outside.

28

Tall bushes and trees lined three sides of the lawn behind the pub. Fleming found Logan and Anderson sitting at one of the tables under a parasol. It was early evening, but still warm. The chat with Quigley hadn't helped much. The only thing Fleming had learned that he didn't know before was Stroud had been having an affair with the wife of an employee at the AWE.

'Enjoying the evening sunshine?' Fleming asked.

'Still a bit warm, sir,' Anderson said. 'Had to put the parasol up.'

'Can I get you both a refill?' Fleming asked, pointing at their near empty glasses.

'Better be a half shandy for me, boss. I'm driving,' Logan said.

'No burger and chips?' Anderson queried, nudging Logan playfully in the side.

'Ah, yes! How could I forget? I'll get the grub if anyone else wants anything.'

'I'll have the fish and chips then,' Anderson enthused.

Fleming laughed. 'Don't worry, I'll get it all when I pay for the drinks. Supper's on me.'

He returned a few minutes later with a tray of drinks. 'Food won't be long.' Fleming propped a wooden spoon with the number ten on it against the parasol pole.

'How did the chat with Pat Quigley go, boss?' Logan asked.

'Nothing much to report I'm afraid. She confirmed she'd lived with Stroud for about a year, but then he had an affair and they split up.'

Logan raised an eyebrow. 'So it could have been the aggrieved husband who killed Stroud and not Croft.'

'It's possible. Quigley reckons the husband worked at the AWE. Said Stroud had told her there was a reason he'd started seeing this other woman, but he couldn't talk about it.'

'All very cloak and dagger,' Logan observed.

'We need to find out who it was Stroud was having the affair with. Have you two got anything new to report?' Fleming asked.

'Afraid not,' Logan said.

'What's happening about the scuffle between Kauffman and Emerson?' Fleming asked.

'All swept under the carpet. Local police aren't interested. Neither man wants to press charges. Warnings all round about future behaviour and that's it.'

'Food's here,' Anderson suddenly announced as one of the bar staff came out looking around for number ten.

The portions were enormous. Logan wasted no time in pouring ketchup on the side of his plate. 'Cheers, boss. Very kind of you. Can we have more briefing meetings like this?'

'Thanks, sir,' Anderson said, tucking into the fish.

'No new leads then?' Fleming asked hopefully, stabbing his fork into a chip.

'No, we're getting nowhere. All we're turning up is stuff Ingham had covered,' Logan complained.

'We did speak to Emerson before the brawl with Kauffman,'

Anderson said after swilling down a mouthful of fish with some beer. 'He seemed to think Stroud was a bit secretive – kept pretty much to himself.'

'How so?' Fleming asked.

'Emerson believed Stroud wanted people to think he was militant, but somehow didn't come across like that.'

'Oh?'

Anderson shrugged. 'It's what he told me.'

'How about you, boss? Are you getting anywhere?' Logan asked.

'Same as you. Not really. I bumped into Zoe Dunbar the other day. She was on her way to see Ursula Nieve to ask if there was any work going on at the AWE that someone might want to disrupt.'

'I thought she was only interested in the Stroud case. How come she's banging on about national security and how the current dispute might be due to some sort of subversive activity?' Logan queried.

'She had some notion Stroud's murder might have been connected with the strike at the time. Following up on every angle... to use her own words,' Fleming replied.

'So she's thinking someone else could be murdered because there's another dispute?' Logan said with a smile. 'Give her full marks for imagination.'

Fleming smiled back. 'I asked her to run a story saying police are following up on new leads in the Stroud case.'

'We are?' Logan asked, looking bemused.

'I was hoping Croft might see it in Australia and panic... make a mistake.'

'Bit of a long shot, boss,' Logan said.

'Maybe it will jolt memories and someone might come forward with information they didn't reveal at the time for whatever reason.'

'Clutching at straws, aren't we?' Logan suggested.

'Croft is still the prime suspect,' Fleming said, 'but we now have Stroud's affair and an aggrieved husband who might have killed him. And there's Nat Horne – a man who had withdrawn into himself and who told his wife things were getting out of control. Things were going on at the AWE that he couldn't talk about. He has a breakdown shortly after Stroud's murder and dies of a heart attack.'

'And there's Rimmer's mystery client who's looking for Croft,' Anderson added.

'Yes, but what we don't know is whether there's any connection to Stroud,' Fleming said, 'except that Croft could have been Stroud's killer.'

'Still not getting us much nearer to the truth. Just loads of unanswered questions,' Logan muttered.

Yes indeed, Fleming thought as they finished their supper then made to leave.

29

A silence had descended upon the office of Wyatt Investigations. Rimmer was twirling a pencil round in his fingers, deep in thought. His uncle was tapping away on a computer while puffing on his pipe. 'When I smoke,' Wyatt had often reminded Rimmer, 'this is not an office – technically, it's my home.' Despite his lack of respect for regulations, Wyatt had displayed a no-smoking sign on the door and did refrain from doing so when clients were present. Today, there were none present, so it was fine in Wyatt's book.

The phone rang, breaking the silence. Wyatt glanced up from his computer screen and picked the handset up. 'Wyatt here.' After listening for a few seconds, he looked across at Rimmer. 'He's here if you want a word.'

Rimmer reached across the desk and took the phone from his uncle. 'Dan Rimmer.'

It was Makena Kibet. 'Oh, hello, Dan. I have some news, but I'm at work and can't really speak. Can I see you later?'

'Of course. I'll wait for you in my car outside Ridgeway and drive you home. What time will you leave work?'

'About five o'clock.'

'Okay, I'll see you then.' Rimmer ended the call.

'Who was that?' Wyatt asked.

'Makena Kibet. She has some news for me.'

'Great. I was thinking of getting you to take some work off me since nothing much was happening on the Garry Croft front.'

'What did you have in mind?'

'I've got three busy cases on the go.'

'Which are?'

'I've got a missing person. Sixteen-year-old girl fell out with her parents and left home. They think she might have gone to London, and they haven't heard from her for over three months. They're desperate to find her.'

'Getting anywhere?'

'Not yet.'

'Second case?'

'A suspected insurance fraud.'

'And?'

Wyatt puffed on his pipe and blew a cloud of smoke up toward the ceiling. 'Making progress, but not enough proof.'

'Last one?'

'A company asked me to carry out background checks on a prospective employee who they're dubious about.'

'In what way?'

'They reckoned his CV was a bit suspicious... and he was vague about previous jobs and why he left them.'

'Can't they get a DBS check done?'

'They have, but they seem to want more than the Disclosure and Barring Service has given them.'

'Oh well, good luck with all that.'

'I'll see how I get on, but I might need you to help out with one of the cases.'

'Sure, no problem. Shout if you need me.'

Wyatt suddenly remembered something. 'What did the guy from the AWE want – the man who rang and wanted to see you?'

'He thinks his wife is having an affair with someone from the AWE and wants me to carry out surveillance on her.'

'All happening at the AWE,' Wyatt observed. 'Strikes, murder, and affairs.' Wyatt took another puff on his pipe and exhaled smoke slowly, looking as though he was deep in thought.

Rimmer set off in plenty of time. The last thing he wanted was to be late meeting Makena outside the care home after work. He was driving along the A404 near Marlow in his old Volvo V40 when he heard the familiar wail of a siren. Alarmed, he looked at his speedometer. He was slightly above the speed limit. 'Fuck,' he muttered. 'Can't be.' Glancing in his rear-view mirror he saw a police car closing in on him fast, blue light flashing. 'Fuck, fuck, fuck!'

Rimmer's hands tightened on the steering wheel. Beads of sweat formed on his brow. He was passing a car on the left as the blue lights closed in on him. Putting his foot down he overtook the car and pulled in. The police car shot past him and carried on up the road with siren blaring and blue light flashing. Seconds later, there were more sirens and blue lights, and two ambulances sped past.

Rimmer relaxed, but two miles further up the road the inside lane was blocked where there had been a serious accident. Traffic was at a standstill.

After what seemed an age, a uniformed officer waved traffic past on the outside lane. Rimmer looked at his watch. Just as well he'd left early. He might still get to the care home in time.

Makena was there on the side of the road outside the Ridgeway Manor Care Home, looking at her watch when Rimmer arrived. He pulled over and Makena climbed in. 'Thought you weren't coming,' she said.

'Sorry, got held up – accident on the A404.'

There was concern in Makena's voice. 'Nothing serious I hope.'

'Nah,' Rimmer lied, noting Makena's alarm. 'What's this news you have, Makena?'

'I was going to offer to read back some letters Mrs Croft had received from her son like you suggested – to see if I could get any idea where in Australia he is.'

'And?' Rimmer asked.

'She became too ill and it wasn't possible.'

'And that's your news? You said you couldn't speak on the phone and wanted to see me. It couldn't be just to tell me that surely?'

'Don't get ratty with me, Dan! I'm doing you a favour here. I was about to go on to tell you what happened.'

Rimmer felt suitably chastised. 'I'm sorry. I know you are, and I appreciate it, honestly.'

Makena smiled weakly. 'It's okay. What I wanted to tell you is Garry Croft rang to speak to his mother, but she was too ill to take the call. Mrs Boudreaux told him the doctor had advised it would be a good idea if he could come over to see her. She's very frail, you see.'

'Terminal?'

Tears welled up in Makena's eyes and she pulled a tissue out of her bag. 'I... I think so,' she said, sniffing.

'I'm sorry. You're obviously quite close to her.'

'I'm upset because that bastard–'

'Her son?'

'Yes. You won't believe it, but he told Mrs Boudreaux he didn't think he would be able to get over.'

'Unbelievable!' Makena probably mistook Rimmer's reaction as being one of disbelief that a son wouldn't find a way to come and see his dying mother, even if it meant travelling from Australia. The truth was Rimmer was incensed because a possible opportunity to find Croft had been lost.

'Yes,' Makena agreed, 'it's unreal, isn't it?'

'Listen, Makena, I'm very grateful for all your efforts to check things out for me.' Rimmer slipped her two twenty-pound notes. 'You'll let me know if anything changes, yeah?'

'Thanks, I'll do my best.'

'Lift home?'

'Yes, please.'

Rimmer drove Makena home and, on his way back to Reading, was thinking about what she'd told him. Beginning to think Croft was going to be a lost cause, he turned on the radio. Dire Straits were playing 'Brothers In Arms'. He turned the volume up and hoped Croft would change his mind.

30

The phone rang as Fleming was about to leave the office. He decided to let it ring, but then changed his mind and picked it up. It was a decision he instantly regretted.

'Got a minute, Fleming?' Younger asked.

'Sure.'

'Pop up and see me, will you?'

Fleming put the phone down and cursed. The last thing he needed was another grilling from Younger when he hadn't much more to offer by way of progress.

He climbed the stairs and saw Younger's office door was open. He knocked anyway and Younger waved him in.

'Glad I caught you. Any news since we last spoke?' Younger asked, polishing his glasses with a lint-free microfibre cleaning cloth.

'Not much I'm afraid. So far we're coming up with pretty much the same information Frank Ingham did.'

'What about this business about Croft owing someone a lot of money and your theory Croft may have fled to Australia because of that?'

'It's only a possibility. We've been unable to identify who this client of Rimmer's is.'

'This isn't going well, Fleming, is it?' Younger said, perching his glasses back on the end of his hooked nose. 'I was hoping you might have made more progress by now.'

Fleming saw Younger's right eyelid twitch – a sure sign he was getting agitated. 'There are two things I'm following up on that Ingham's team seem to have missed,' Fleming said with little enthusiasm.

'Yes?' Younger's eyelid had stopped trembling for a moment.

'I saw Nat Horne's widow and it seems he was a changed man after the strike – withdrawn, drank a lot, told his wife matters were getting out of control and there were issues at the AWE he couldn't talk about.'

'Are you saying he could be a suspect?'

'He started to behave differently. I need to keep an open mind.'

'Hmm, you said two things.'

'We found out Stroud had a girlfriend. I saw her and it appears she lived with Stroud for about a year. He had an affair and they split u–'

'And does that have any relevance,' Younger cut in.

'It was with someone whose husband worked at the AWE. She said Stroud had told her there was a reason why he was seeing this woman but he couldn't tell her why.'

'Great. What the hell is going on there?'

'It's a secretive place,' was all Fleming could offer.

'It's about time you unravel some of these secrets then, don't you think?'

Fleming took his leave, telling Younger he was going to see someone from the AWE who might have more information.

Emerson had asked Fleming to meet him in the car park of a golf course near Tadley. Fleming arrived first and parked his old Porsche where he could see any cars arriving. After fifteen minutes there was no sign of the three-year-old blue Ford Focus Emerson had told him he would be driving. Fleming had been curious about the call from Emerson and why he wanted to see him. He wouldn't say why over the phone – only he had some information. He'd asked to meet here so there was little chance anyone who knew him would see him with Fleming.

A few minutes later, Emerson's car arrived. He parked a few cars away from Fleming's Porsche. He locked his car and ambled over to Fleming who opened the passenger door for Emerson. Fleming took him to be in his fifties, and he could tell by the way he walked he was not a fit man. His frame suggested years of excess and the round, ruddy face hinted a possible liking for alcohol.

'Nice car,' Emerson observed as he climbed in. 'Had it long?'

'It's an old car,' Fleming replied, 'but I only got it about four years ago.'

'Good nick by the looks of it. Sorry I'm a bit late. I was up at High Wycombe to see how they were getting on with repairs to my Cessna.'

'You have a light aircraft?'

'Yes. It was my father's. He left it for me when he died. It's a Cessna 172 Skyhawk. He gave me flying lessons and I got my pilots licence before he passed away.'

'Wow, I'm impressed. But much as I'd like to ask you more about it, you said you had some information for me? I was curious why you didn't give it to DS Logan and DC Anderson when they spoke to you.'

'I wasn't sure whether I should, but something's happened since, and I saw the newspaper article saying you were following up new leads in the Stroud case. You were hoping someone might come forward who hadn't before.'

'I'm very grateful you have, Mr Emerson. What's made you decide to speak up now?'

'It's a bit delicate and I don't know if it has any bearing on the case, but after thinking about it I decided to call you.'

'Go ahead.'

'I think my wife might be having an affair. I had my suspicions before, but now I'm sure. I've hired a private detective to check up on her.'

Fleming recalled the conversation with Rimmer. 'It isn't by any chance Dan Rimmer?'

'How do you know?'

'I spoke to him about something recently and he told me he'd taken on a case for a man who thought his wife was having an affair. Seemed like too much of a coincidence. How did you come across him?'

'It goes back some time, but after Stroud was killed and Garry Croft disappeared off to Australia, Rimmer came to our local pub enquiring if any of us knew where in Australia Garry had gone. Said he was trying to trace him for a client. None of us knew exactly where he was so Rimmer left some business cards with a few of us asking anyone to get in touch should they find out. I still had his card and he's quite local, so I used him.'

Fleming wondered where this was going. 'And you think your wife's affair, if she is having one, might somehow have some bearing on the Stroud case?'

'No... not directly, but the man I think she's seeing might.'

'Go on.'

'This is all a bit vague, but I think it's Bill Kauffman.'

'And the connection?'

'Stroud was seeing Kauffman's wife before he was killed.'

Fleming tried to stay calm. 'How do you know?'

'Gwen, my wife, and I went out for a meal one night. It was to a pub that did food. I didn't see them while we were eating because the tables were in different areas, but when we walked through the pub to go home, I saw them. It was Stroud and Kauffman's wife. They were deep in conversation, holding hands across the table. They were so engrossed with each other they didn't see us.'

'Is that it? It could have been an innocent meeting. Kauffman's other half could have been upset about something and Stroud might have been trying to comfort her.'

'No, there's more. A few weeks later, Gwen went to a hen party. Kauffman's wife was there. She'd had a bit too much to drink and Gwen heard her boasting to a friend she was having a fling with Stroud. She told her friend she'd better keep quiet and giggled, saying if Kauffman found out he'd probably kill Stroud.'

'And you never thought to mention this when Stroud was killed? Why not?'

'The press reckoned the police saw Croft as the prime suspect because he'd had a serious bust up with Stroud then fled to Australia, not leaving any way for people to contact him. You wouldn't want to get on the wrong side of Kauffman or any of his union mates, so I kept quiet. There was no way I was going to get ostracised by the union by casting suspicion on Kauffman or start telling tales his wife was having a fling with Stroud. You have to work in that sort of environment to know why you keep your head down. Things can get pretty nasty if you fall out with the union.'

'Clearly.' Fleming was thinking of Stroud and his fight with Croft. 'So why are you now prepared to speak out?'

'I've had enough of the place, Kauffman and his cronies. I refused to strike and I'm already despised by the union.'

'Hence the recent brawl on the picket line?'

'Right, and because I'm convinced Kauffman is seeing Gwen. I'm handing my notice in, and if Rimmer proves Gwen is having an affair with Kauffman I'm going to move somewhere else wherever I can get another job.'

'I can understand that.' Fleming thanked Emerson for volunteering the info and told him he'd need to give a statement to Logan.

'Okay.'

'One more thing before you go… do you happen to know of a man called Liam Doherty?'

Emerson shook his head. 'Never heard of him.'

Emerson left and Fleming scribbled a reminder into his notebook to get Logan to take a statement from him. *Did Frank Ingham get it all wrong and should Bill Kauffman have been the prime suspect?*

31

Maggie Kauffman lived in a flat above a shop near the centre of Reading. Fleming had phoned and arranged to speak to her there. The place was as untidy as Maggie Kauffman. She was wearing scruffy jeans with tears in both knees and a loose-fitting blue sweater. Fleming guessed she was in her late forties which would have made her about forty-five when she had the alleged affair with Stroud. She placed her third cigarette of the night into the ashtray balanced on the side of her chair and brushed a strand of blonde hair from her eyes. The large glass of white wine in the other hand was her second of the night.

'Are you sure I can't get you something to drink?' she asked Fleming again.

'No, thanks. I'm fine.'

Maggie looked quizzically at Fleming. 'You wanted to speak to me about Bill. Any particular reason?'

'I want to get a bit of background into how things were at the time of the last strike. I gather you're separated?'

'Divorced.'

'When did you meet Bill?'

'About twenty-nine years ago. We were married two years after we met when I was twenty-two, Bill was twenty-eight.' Maggie took a large drag of her cigarette and blew smoke up to the ceiling. 'Oh, sorry, I should have asked. Do you smoke?'

'No.'

Maggie examined the glowing tip of her cigarette. 'Filthy habit. I've tried to give it up, but hey, if you enjoy it...' She paused for a moment. 'Do you mind me smoking while you're here?'

'It's your flat.'

Maggie took a large gulp of wine. 'Doesn't seem right somehow. Me sitting here drinking and puffing away while you have nothing.'

Fleming smiled. 'I'm on duty – you're at home relaxing.'

'That's all right then,' Maggie said, taking a last drag of the cigarette before stubbing it out in the ashtray.

'Where were you married?'

'Liverpool. We were both born there. We met each other through friends and started going out. Bill worked for a small engineering company. He was more relaxed then... good fun.'

'What changed?'

'The company paid him off two years after we were married. They told him they had to start getting rid of staff. Falling orders, increasing costs. You know... that sort of thing. Bill was angry. He had too much to drink one night and slagged off managers with their big salaries, expensive cars, foreign holidays, and lavish entertainment. They could afford those things, but not pay the staff a decent wage, he would complain. He used to harp on about the miners' strike in 1984 and how the workers were crushed and downtrodden by the government. He became militant. Blamed everything on the government and the rich.'

'What did he do when he was made redundant?'

'Threatened to burn down the fucking factory to teach them a lesson.'

'But he didn't, did he?'

'Of course not. It was all pent-up anger.' Maggie lit up another cigarette.

'So how did you manage?'

'Oh, I had a little job in a supermarket and did some cleaning. Bill did odds and ends for mates of his.'

'What exactly?'

'Labouring mostly. Did some gardening work. We didn't have much, but we got by.'

'When did Bill start at the AWE?'

'He was out of work for a year and we moved to Reading when he managed to get a job at the AWE. Must be twenty-three, twenty-four years ago. He joined the union and seemed to become even more militant.'

'What did Bill do to make you think that?'

'He went to union meetings, grumbled about management and how they were as bad as the engineering company. Claimed the consortium that won the contract to run the AWE cut costs by paying staff off and suppressing wages.'

'Anything else?'

'He became more active in union affairs. He's actually quite clever and shrewd. Can deliver a powerful and persuasive argument. Stood him in good stead. They made him union leader fifteen years after joining the company. Four years later he'd orchestrated a strike.'

'The strike after which William Stroud was murdered?' Fleming noticed Maggie stiffen when he mentioned Stroud's name.

Maggie took the last sip of her wine, put the glass down on a coffee table, and sucked in heavily on her cigarette before answering. 'Yes.' Smoke exhaled slowly from her mouth as she spoke.

'How close to your husband was Garry Croft?'

'They were thick as thieves, Croft, Stroud and two other men – can't remember their names. Bill used to call them his disciples.'

'Really? Did Bill ever tell you why two of them fell out and came to blows?'

'I heard about the fight.' Maggie took another deep drag of her cigarette and smoke drifted out of her nostrils. 'No idea what it was all about though.'

'Did you or Bill know Croft was going to Australia?'

'I didn't. Don't know about Bill.'

'If they were close Croft must surely have said something.'

'You'll need to ask Bill if he did.' Fleming didn't say he already had.

'When did you get divorced?'

'Five years ago.'

'The year Stroud was murdered?'

Maggie shot an anxious glance at Fleming. 'Why do you say that? You sound as though you think the two things are connected.' She stubbed her fourth cigarette out in the ashtray with more force than was necessary.

'Are they?'

'Of course not. What an absurd idea.'

'Why did you get divorced?'

'We grew apart. Bill was obsessed with the union. He became more and more agitated... aggressive. I think he lost interest in me.'

'And you?'

'What do you mean?'

'Did you lose interest in him?'

'I suppose so. Maybe I was starting to dislike who he'd become.'

'A changed man?'

'You could say so.'

'You said he became aggressive. Was he ever rough with you?'

'He didn't touch me if that's what you're getting at. But he did have a temper.'

'Did he behave differently after Stroud's death, do you think?'

'I don't think so, he'd started to change all the way back to when he was made redundant and was never the same since.'

'Did Bill ever mention Nat Horne?'

'He used to be the HR manager.'

'Did Bill ever talk about him?'

'Only that he was at the management meetings with the union. Bill thought Nat was weak, you know... a yes-man. Did anything the managers asked of him.'

'Did Bill ever say anything about Horne and Stroud clashing at these meetings?'

'Can't say he did, no.'

'Was Seth Emerson one of Bill's disciples?'

'God no. The two didn't get on. Emerson did join the last dispute, but is refusing to go on strike this time.'

'How do you know?'

'I'm seeing someone who works there.'

'You heard about the spat between Bill and Emerson on the picket line?'

'Yes.'

'Did Bill ever mention a man called Dan Rimmer?'

'I can't remember his name being mentioned.'

Fleming was fishing. 'Liam Doherty?'

'No.'

'You and Bill grew apart and you thought he'd lost interest in you. Is that why you were seeing William Stroud?'

Maggie froze. 'What?'

'You were seen having a meal with him in a pub, holding hands.'

'Who told you?'

'Were you?'

'I... I–'

'You were also overheard at a hen party boasting you were having an affair with Stroud.'

'I–'

'You said Bill would kill Stroud if he found out. Did he? I mean... did he find out?'

'Yes,' Maggie whispered and started to cry.

'Did he kill Stroud?'

'I... I don't know. I thought the police were sure Croft did it. You don't...?'

'Just exploring every lead.'

Fleming had what he wanted. Confirmation that it was Kauffman's wife Stroud was having an affair with. He thanked Maggie for her time and left her pouring out another glass of wine with shaking hands.

On his way home in the car, Fleming wondered if the focus of attention was shifting towards Kauffman.

32

Seth Emerson had been letting Rimmer know when his wife told him she was going out with friends. Rimmer had followed Gwen on several occasions, but most of the time she did indeed meet with female friends at a local pub. He'd seen her with Kauffman at the place, but they could have been chance meetings. There was nothing definite to suggest they were having an affair.

Emerson had phoned Rimmer two days earlier to let him know his wife had arranged a London trip to do some clothes shopping with a friend. She'd told her husband they might take in a show and stay overnight.

Now, sitting in his car along the street, Rimmer was keeping a watchful eye on the house. He'd left Reading early to drive to Tadley so he didn't miss Emerson's wife leaving home. After half an hour, Gwen Emerson appeared carrying a small bag. She opened her car door and threw it onto the passenger seat, climbed in and drove off. Rimmer followed her up to Reading where she parked in an NCP car park. Rimmer pulled into a space nearby, followed her to the ticket machine and saw her purchase a two-day ticket before walking to the station.

The early morning commuters travelling into London from Reading had gone. It was after ten and the station was busy, but not overcrowded. Rimmer was a safe distance from Emerson when a man with a backpack slung over one shoulder appeared from behind a small crowd of people and called out to Emerson. 'Gwen!' It was Kauffman. 'I've got the tickets.' He waved them above his head as he made his way over to Gwen. She turned, smiled at Kauffman and the two embraced.

Rimmer managed to get a couple of photos before glancing up at the departure boards to see all the next trains for London were going to Paddington. He looked for the nearest ticket machine and bought one, never letting Kauffman and Gwen out of his sight. Fortunately, Kauffman was a big man with a big beard and Gwen was wearing jeans and a bright red top so there was no way Rimmer was going to lose them.

Rimmer kept close as they made their way to the departure platform and watched which carriage they entered. He stepped into the same one and sat where he could keep an eye on them without getting too close.

It was about half an hour to Paddington where they got the tube to Charing Cross. Rimmer tailed the pair up onto the street where they headed west towards Trafalgar Square and then up to the Thistle hotel. He took several more photos of them walking hand in hand.

Rimmer watched them enter the hotel, got more photos, then waited twenty minutes to see if they reappeared. When they didn't, he walked into the reception and spotted a young receptionist who was free. He ambled over and she looked up expectantly. 'Hello,' Rimmer said, 'I wonder if you can help me. My wife and I are hoping to catch up with our friends later. They told us they would be staying here. Can you tell me if they've checked in? It's Mr and Mrs Kauffman.'

The receptionist looked at her computer screen. 'Yes,' she

announced, 'they have. Would you like me to call them to let them know you're here?'

'No,' Rimmer said, thinking on his feet. 'They don't know we're here in London as well. It's my friend's birthday and we thought we'd surprise them. They may already have arranged to go out somewhere so we might catch them later for a drink.'

'Ah.'

'Grateful if you didn't mention to them that I'd been here. Don't want to spoil the surprise. I'll call them later.'

'Of course.'

Rimmer thanked the receptionist, stepped outside, lit a cigarette and thought about what to do next. Kauffman and Gwen could stay in the place all afternoon, and night for that matter. Even if they left the hotel, Rimmer wasn't sure following them again would give him any more than he had. Surely the fact they'd checked in as Mrs and Mrs Kauffman was enough evidence for Emerson. What more did he need? No, Rimmer might as well get the train back to Reading. Job done.

He turned to make his way back to Charing Cross, taking one final glance inside the hotel. Then he saw him. Kauffman was heading for the exit – on his own.

Rimmer stubbed out his cigarette and stood on the kerb as though waiting to cross the road. Kauffman came out and strode back towards Trafalgar Square. Rimmer was curious Kauffman had come out on his own and seemed to know exactly where he was going. This was no aimless stroll. The private investigator instinct in Rimmer told him to follow Kauffman.

Kauffman carried on past Trafalgar Square, down Whitehall towards Westminster and past the House of Commons to Millbank where he turned left into Victoria Tower Gardens. He walked across the grass where some men were playing football. People had poured out of nearby offices to bask in the sunshine and enjoy their lunchtime snacks. Tourists wandered around studying maps and others stretched out on the grass sunbathing. Kauffman crossed the tree-lined walkway to lean against the wall, facing out over the Thames. He glanced at his watch then up and down the walkway.

Rimmer stopped in his tracks and held a hand up to shield his face from the glare of the sun. *If I'm not mistaken, he's meeting someone.* Rimmer sat on the grass as though taking a break and leaned back with both hands on the ground behind him. Then he saw him. A man in shirt sleeves and carrying a small leather briefcase was heading straight for Kauffman. The man looked furtively over his shoulder as though checking no one was following him. He glanced briefly across in Rimmer's direction, but Rimmer had turned his head to look at the men playing football.

The man stopped next to Kauffman and turned to lean against the wall beside him. There was an exchange of words, but Rimmer was too far away to hear what they were saying. The sound of wailing sirens in the background didn't make things any easier.

This is weird. Who the fuck is he? Rimmer casually pulled his smartphone from his pocket and took photos of his surroundings, making sure he captured Kauffman and the other man.

After a while the other man unclipped the briefcase, dipped a hand inside and pulled out a thick brown envelope which he passed deftly across to Kauffman who stuffed it into his shirt. There was another exchange of words. The man snapped his briefcase shut, shook hands with Kauffman and set off towards Westminster tube station.

Rimmer had captured images of the handover. There was no point in continuing to follow Kauffman. Rimmer's attention had switched to the other man. He got up and tailed him at a discreet distance up past the House of Commons where he crossed the road and headed for the QEII Centre. Rimmer followed him inside and watched him pick up a name badge and head off in the direction of signs pointing to the Russian Trade Delegation seminar. He took one last photograph and left in case anyone had seen him.

Rimmer strolled back to where Mystery Man had met Kauffman, but Kauffman had gone. He pulled out his smartphone and scrolled through his contacts until he found who he wanted. He tapped on the telephone icon and waited.

'Hello,' Zoe Dunbar said.

'Hi, it's Dan Rimmer.'

'Oh, hello. What can I do for you?'

'I think I might have something for you. Could be a rather interesting story involving the AWE.'

'Really? You have my attention.'

'Not over the phone. But so you know – I'd want to be paid for the information.'

'How much?'

'Depends on how much you think it's worth. Can we meet?'

They made arrangements and Rimmer wondered how much Dunbar would be prepared to pay. *Not a bad day's work.*

33

Rimmer had arranged to meet Zoe Dunbar the next day at the same pub in Colindale where they had met before. It was as good an excuse as any to stay overnight in London. He would put the expenses on Emerson's invoice. After all, he had followed Emerson's wife all the way to London and had watched her book into the Thistle with Kauffman. It would seem plausible Rimmer had stayed there as well to keep an eye on them.

The only thing concerning Rimmer was the conversation he'd had with the receptionist. What if she recognised him and thought it odd that he – and his fictitious wife – hadn't come to join their friends? She might say something to Kauffman. No, it would be too risky to stay there. The best bet was to check in somewhere else and take in the sights. He would tell Emerson he'd lost the hotel receipt should he ask to see it with his invoice.

Before looking for another hotel he called in to the Thistle again on the off chance he would get one more sight of Kauffman and Gwen Emerson. No luck, there was no sign of them in the restaurant or bar. Rimmer was about to leave when a smart-looking businessman dressed in a grey suit, blue shirt and bright red tie walked in and strode up to reception. 'Mr Theodore, I have a reservation for one night,' the man said.

Fortunately, it was a different receptionist to the one Rimmer had spoken to earlier. She checked the man in and Rimmer took the opportunity to have a quick word with her. 'What's the rate for one night please?'

The receptionist looked at Rimmer. 'I'm afraid we have no single rooms, but we have a twin room at a hundred and thirty pounds.'

'Ah. Okay,' Rimmer said, and left, leaving a bemused receptionist behind the counter. He could now tell Emerson he was sorry he didn't have a receipt, but he could always check with the hotel if he wanted to. He'd say he checked in as a Mr Theodore and give him the rate he'd paid.

Rimmer was satisfied he could do no more that night with regard to Kauffman and Gwen Emerson so decided to find a crowded pub to lose himself in. Not particularly hard in central London on a Saturday night. He'd go up to the Thistle in the morning to see if he could catch Kauffman and Emerson at breakfast – even snatch a sneaky photo if he was lucky.

It had been a successful day. Rimmer decided to celebrate after finding a hotel near Leicester Square with a room available. He called in at several pubs before finding one near his hotel. It was full of customers standing in groups, some sat at tables, and others stood at the bar waiting to be served. It was chaotic and loud. Rimmer eased his way past the crush of people and headed for one of the short side bars. It took a while to get through the throng, but eventually he reached the bar and ordered a pint of Doom Bar. He took his drink and retreated into the crowd where no one noticed him.

Next morning, Rimmer's head felt as though there was a shrinking leather band tightening round his head. He felt marginally better after a cooked breakfast and a few cups of coffee. It wasn't far to the Thistle so Rimmer made his way on foot to get some fresh air. Though central London was probably not the best place to find it.

Rimmer made his way casually to the restaurant and there, much to his amazement, were Kauffman and Gwen Emerson, deep in conversation and oblivious to everyone around them. 'Table for one?' a waiter asked, appearing from behind Rimmer.

'Er, no, it's all right. I'm looking for my friends.'

The waiter smiled and waltzed off to find someone else to help.

How the hell am I going to get a photo without being noticed? Rimmer pulled his smart phone out and wandered through the tables making his way towards Kauffman and Emerson with it held in front of his face as though reading a message. But in fact, he had it in photo mode and was snapping away getting as many shots of Kauffman and Gwen Emerson as he dared before someone saw what he was doing.

Rimmer went by their table and they didn't even look up – they only had eyes for each other. Rimmer froze as someone tapped him on the shoulder. 'Have you found your friends?' It was the waltzing waiter who had appeared suddenly from behind him.

Christ! The man's everywhere, Rimmer thought.

'No. My sight isn't as good as it used to be so I was walking around looking. As it happens, they're not here. Thanks for asking.' Rimmer left the waiter with his mouth open and made a hasty retreat out of the restaurant and out of the hotel.

Rimmer found somewhere to have a coffee before taking the tube up to Colindale to meet Zoe Dunbar. It was Sunday lunchtime and the streets were busy when he reached the pub. He pushed his way through the doors to find throngs of people milling around in groups. There was the constant sound of chatter, shouting and fits of laughing. One or two people propped up at the bar looked as though they'd already had their ration of booze for the day.

Dunbar was already there, sitting at a table by a window, drinking a glass of white wine. Rimmer noticed she had nearly finished her drink. He held his right hand up to his face as though about to drink from an imaginary glass. Dunbar signalled a yes by nodding.

Rimmer went to the bar and knew he really ought to order an orange juice or any other non-alcoholic drink after the previous night's over indulgence. 'A pint of Doom Bar,' he said, 'and a large glass of white wine please.'

'Any particular one?' the barman asked. Rimmer pointed to Dunbar sitting at the table over by the window. 'Whatever she had.'

The barman nodded. 'Pinot Grigio,' he muttered, and turned to pull a bottle out of the fridge.

Rimmer took the drinks over. 'Hi there,' he said, putting his pint and Dunbar's glass of wine on the table. He pulled up a chair. 'Glad you could come.'

'You told me you had something of interest for me... to do with the AWE?'

Rimmer took a sip of his beer and instantly wished he'd ordered an orange juice. 'Yes,' he replied, pulling a face.

'Not good?' Dunbar asked, pointing a finger at Rimmer's drink.

'Beer's fine. It's me that's not so good.'

'Let me guess – you had one or two last night?'

'You could say that.'

'So what have you got for me?'

Rimmer wasn't sure how to play this. He needed to reveal what he had so Dunbar could agree how much it might be worth, but he didn't want to give too much away until they'd struck a deal. 'I have something on Kauffman.'

'You need to be more specific.'

'I was keeping a client's wife under surveillance – he thinks she's having an affair with Kauffman.'

'Is that it? Newspapers won't be interested unless it involves royalty or a celebrity.'

'No, there's more. I followed them to London yesterday. They checked into a hotel and shortly afterwards Kauffman left on his own.'

'Get to the point, Rimmer. What's this information you think it's worth me paying for.'

'Kauffman met a man who handed him a thick brown envelope – the type that says cash.'

'What makes you think it was money?'

'An educated guess. The thing is, I followed this man out of curiosity after he passed the envelope to Kauffman. He went to the QEII Centre and walked into a Russian Trade Delegation seminar.'

Dunbar fell silent for a moment. 'And the story?' she pressed, as though she didn't know.

'There's a strike at the AWE where secret stuff goes on, and Kauffman's a militant socialist if ever there was one. I'm guessing the brown envelope he was handed was more than likely a payment by a man who has links to Russia. Incentive to disrupt any work going on there maybe? What more do you want?'

'Photos?'

'I have them, but we need to discuss money first.'

'How much are you thinking this is worth?' Dunbar asked.

'Two thousand?'

'I'm an independent. I'll have to find a newspaper interested in running the story and test how much they would be prepared to pay. Then I need to take my fee from whatever they agree. I doubt they'd hand out two thousand though.'

'Why don't you ask around and let me know? If it's worth it, I'll let you have the photos – deal?'

'I'll see what I can do.' Dunbar downed the rest of her wine and left.

34

Fleming had asked Kauffman to attend the police station at Reading voluntarily for an interview under caution. The interview room was small, no more than eight feet wide and ten feet long. The walls were bare and painted powder blue. It was sparsely furnished with a table and four chairs, but it was well lit and ventilated even though the door had no window. A digital recorder sat on the edge of the table next to the wall. The old cassette tape recorder had been dispensed with. Kauffman sat facing Fleming and Logan who had set up the recorder ready to start.

Fleming nodded at Logan who pressed the record button. 'This is being recorded,' Fleming said. 'This is an interview with...' Fleming looked across at Kauffman. 'State your full name please.'

Kauffman obliged confidently in a gruff voice.

Fleming went on to ask Kauffman to state his address and date of birth.

Kauffman stared steady at Fleming while he spoke.

'I am DCI Fleming. Also present is...'

Logan added his name and rank.

'There are no other people present,' Fleming said. He went on to confirm the date and time before adding, 'We are in interview room one at Reading police station.' He looked at Kauffman. 'You do not have to say anything. But it may harm your defence if you do not mention now something which you later rely on in court. Anything you do say may be given in evidence. You are not under arrest and you're not obliged to remain at the station so you can leave at any time. Free, independent legal advice is available if you want it.'

Kauffman glowered at Fleming. 'You think I need a lawyer?'

'Up to you.'

'I don't need one. I've done nothing wrong.'

'You've been asked to come here to answer questions pertinent to the murder of William Stroud five years ago.'

'So I was told.'

'You previously confirmed you were the union leader during the last strike and at the time of Stroud's murder.'

'I did, but I don't see what bearing that has on anything.'

'You told me conflict was a natural consequence of a strike. Was Stroud involved in any disagreement with anyone else other than Garry Croft?'

'If I recall correctly, I told you I didn't know Stroud well, so how would I know?'

'You would if it involved you.'

'True... I would remember if there was a clash between us, but there wasn't.'

'Your ex-wife told me you have an aggressive side to you.'

'Did she?'

'There was the incident involving Emerson on the picket line.'

'I've answered all the questions on that, and the matter's been dropped.'

'You're divorced?'

'Yes. Look, where the fuck is this all going? What's my marital status got to do with Stroud?' Kauffman leaned forward putting both hands on the edge of the table. His dark eyes bore into Fleming's.

'Would you like a break? Coffee maybe?' Fleming suddenly asked.

'I'd like a fag as well... if you don't mind.' There was no doubting the sarcasm in Kauffman's voice.

'To repeat – you're free to leave at any time so you can nip outside if you want. I would be grateful though if you did come back,' Fleming added. 'Interview suspended for a short break at ten a.m.'

Kauffman grunted and left the room. 'See you in a few minutes – and it's one sugar and milk in my coffee.'

Logan glanced sideways at Fleming. 'Was that a good idea? I mean to pause the interview?'

Fleming got up to stretch his legs. 'I could sense he was starting to get a bit touchy when I mentioned the divorce. There was a chance he might have got up and left right then. I thought it best to offer a break.'

'Okay, boss. Coffees all round?'

'Thanks, Harry.'

A few minutes later Kauffman returned. Logan hit the record button again and Fleming announced the time the interview had recommenced and reminded Kauffman he was still under caution and that he had the right to legal advice.

Kauffman sipped at the coffee Logan had put in front of him and grimaced. 'Not exactly the tastiest cup of coffee I've had.'

'Vending machine,' Logan said. 'Best I could do.'

'So why did you and your wife get divorced?' Fleming asked Kauffman, taking up from where he'd left off.

Kauffman shrugged.

'Was it because you were getting more involved with union activity? She got bored maybe?'

'What are you suggesting, Fleming?'

'I'm just asking how come you got divorced.'

'Shit happens,' was all Kauffman said.

'Maybe you were spending too much time with the disciples?'

Kauffman froze and shot Fleming the sort of look suggesting a mix of alarm and disbelief. 'What?'

'The disciples. I hear you had a close group of four union men – Stroud, Croft, and two others. Who were the other two?'

'I've no idea what you're talking about. Where the hell did this come from?'

'Your ex-wife. She told me all about them. She knew about Croft and Stroud but didn't know who the other two were.'

Kauffman sneered. His coffee remained untouched after the first sip. 'She's deluded. I don't know where the fuck she got that from – it's ridiculous.'

'You – she said she got it from you.'

'My ex-wife is capable of telling you anything. She's a compulsive liar.'

'Did she lie to you about having an affair with Stroud.'

Kauffman's eyes shot wide open and he glared at Fleming with a look of panic. It took him a few seconds to regain what composure he had left. 'What the fuck has she been telling you? There was no affair. We simply got fed up with each other.'

'She was seen with Stroud holding hands in a pub.'

Kauffman laughed. 'And that's it?'

'She was overheard at a hen party boasting she was having an affair with Stroud.'

'She was probably pissed out of her mind.'

'She admitted it to me,' Fleming pressed.

'I don't know what she's up to, but she's lying.'

'She said if you found out you would kill Stroud.'

Kauffman shook his head. 'Oh, that's what her game is, the bitch. She's trying to put my name in the frame for Stroud's murder. Unbelievable!'

'She claimed you did find out.'

'This is crazy!' Kauffman shouted.

'Where were you on the day Stroud was murdered?'

Kauffman looked in disbelief at Fleming. 'You've got to be fucking joking. Apart from the fact I don't know what day it was – how the hell would anyone remember what they were doing five years ago!'

'Okay, Mr Kauffman. Thank you for agreeing to speak to us. You're free to go.' Fleming looked towards the recorder. 'Interview terminated at ten thirty.'

Kauffman left leaving Fleming and Logan on their own. 'Before I forget, Harry, can you get a statement from Seth Emerson. He was the one who told me Stroud was having an affair with Kauffman's wife.'

'Beggars belief Frank Ingham missed all this,' Logan said. 'The thing is – where do we go from here? There was no DNA or other forensic evidence found at the scene of the crime.'

'We keep an eye on him. If he is guilty, he may panic and make a mistake.'

'Like?'

'Make a run for it?'

Logan's look told Fleming he wasn't convinced.

'Or maybe someone else knew and will come forward – you never know.'

'True,' Logan agreed, 'who knows what will turn up next.'

35

The trip from Oxford to the AWE had taken less than an hour. Fleming left his flat in Summertown early. Logan and Anderson had told him they would wait until after he arrived before their first interview of the day. There was no Zoe Dunbar to accost him in the visitors' car park. Fleming made his way up to Ursula Nieve's office and popped his head round the door to let her know he was there, but wanted a quick word with Logan and Anderson first.

The two detectives were waiting for him. 'Coffee?' Logan asked.

'That would be good,' Fleming replied.

Logan looked at Anderson and nodded towards the door.

'Universal sign language,' Anderson muttered as she was leaving to go and get Fleming's coffee. 'I suppose you'll be wanting one as well, Sarge?' she called over her shoulder.

'Yes, please,' Logan replied with emphasis on the please.

Anderson threw a wave over her head as she disappeared out the door.

'How's it going?' Fleming asked.

'Seen everyone who knew Stroud well. About done with all the rest who still work here. We'll need to start tracing people who've left the company next.'

'Good job. How's Naomi doing?'

'Great. I'm sure she'll go far. She's got a good brain on her, conscientious, thorough, and has a good sense of humour.'

Fleming grinned. 'She'd need to working with you, Harry.'

Logan was about to say something when Anderson returned.

Fleming pulled out his mobile. 'Just need to make a quick call,' he said, smiling his thanks to Anderson who'd handed him a mug.

Fleming looked up his contacts and tapped on the one he wanted.

Ingham picked up after a few rings. 'Hello, Frank Ingham speaking.'

'Hi, Frank. Alex Fleming. I just wanted to ask you a couple of things.'

'Go ahead.'

'Did you know Stroud had an affair with Bill Kauffman's wife?'

There was a long pause before Ingham answered, suggesting a certain degree of embarrassment. 'No... no I didn't,' he answered thoughtfully. 'Are you about to tell me Kauffman is a suspect?'

'Only a possibility. I'm keeping an open mind.'

'Well, I'll be–'

Fleming cut Ingham off. 'The other thing is – did you ever hear anyone talking about the disciples?'

'The who?'

'The disciples. That's what Kauffman called a close circle of union friends apparently.'

'Never heard of them. Where did you find out?'

'From his ex-wife, but Kauffman denies they existed. He claimed his wife was making it up. Reckoned she was a compulsive liar.'

'He may well be right on that count. All sounds a bit unlikely to me.'

'Okay, thanks for your time, Frank.' Fleming ended the call and sipped on his coffee. He turned to Logan. 'Can you ask around – see if anyone has heard of the disciples?'

'Sure. Oh, by the way, boss,' Logan suddenly remembered, 'I got the statement you wanted from Seth Emerson.'

'Thanks, Harry.' Fleming's mobile indicated an incoming call: *Yvette Boudreaux.*

'Hi, Yvette, what can I do for you?'

'It's about Croft – Garry Croft. He phoned from Australia. One of his rare calls to ask how his mother was. I told him she was terminally ill and he ought to come over.'

'And?'

'He told me it was impossible. There was no way he would be able to make it.'

Fleming frowned. Croft certainly didn't want to risk coming back to England. 'Okay, thanks for letting me know. You'll call me immediately if there's any change?'

'Of course,' Boudreaux confirmed and ended the call.

Logan looked quizzically at Fleming. 'Anything important?'

'Croft rang the care home. His mother's critically ill, but he says he can't get back to see her.'

~

Ursula Nieve was on the phone when Fleming knocked on her open office door. She looked furtive for a second, but waved him in and finished the call.

'Sorry to interrupt,' Fleming said. 'I could have waited.'

'No problem, it wasn't important. I'll ring them back. Come in and have a seat.'

'Thanks.'

'I saw Zoe Dunbar's newspaper article. She reported you were following up new leads.'

'We are.'

'May I ask?'

'What?' Fleming was being deliberately obtuse.

'What new leads you have.'

'I don't want to disclose anything at this stage which might compromise our enquiries.'

'You can trust me to be discreet.'

'I'm sure I can. But let's say I don't want to get too far ahead of myself.'

'I understand. You said on the phone you wanted to ask me something?'

'Did you ever hear anyone mention the disciples when you took over from Nat Horne?'

'The disciples? How curious. No... I can't say I did.'

'Do you have any records of an employee, or previous member of staff, by the name of Liam Doherty?'

'I'd need to check. Can I get back to you?'

'Sure. I'd be grateful if you would treat it as a priority.'

'Of course.'

'One final thing. Can you let me have the names and contact details of anyone who left the company after Stroud's death who were not on the list of those previously interviewed.'

'I guess you'll want them quickly as well?'

'Please.'

'Are all these questions to do with your new leads?'

'Just following up on every possible line of enquiry.'

Fleming left with a promise from Nieve to get back to him as soon as she could with the information he'd asked for. On the way out to his car Fleming couldn't help thinking Nieve's interest in the Stroud investigation bordered on more than mild curiosity.

36

The two-storey small apartment block was within a few hundred yards of St Kilda Pier in Melbourne. Garry Croft lived on the second floor and often wandered over to the kiosk at the end of the pier for a coffee.

He'd been there a few days earlier, enjoying the pleasantly warm midday sun outside the kiosk. He occasionally made the effort to call his mother in the care home. That day he'd called on impulse, but the manager had given him some bad news. His mother was terminally ill and the doctor had advised he ought to come over to see her. Garry was undecided what to do. As far as he knew, the police still saw him as a suspect in the Stroud murder case, but there was a good reason for him to see his mother. He'd stalled and told Yvette Boudreaux he wouldn't be able to come back.

After giving the matter further thought, he'd decided it was maybe worth the risk to return to England. Surely after five years the police wouldn't still be checking ports and airports. No, he'd convinced himself, he should take a chance. After all, he needed to make sure his mother hadn't changed her will which left everything to him. There were no other siblings and no other surviving relatives. The main asset was the house in London which had been rented out. The income from that, plus his mother's state and work pensions covered the cost of the care home. The surplus went into his mother's bank account. When his mother died, he would give the tenants notice to quit and then sell the house which he reckoned would be valued at least a million. Yes, definitely worth a gamble going back.

Croft had booked the return flight with Emirates and was sitting in the terminal two departure lounge when he had a sudden panic attack, wondering if he was doing the right thing after all. It was a calculated risk he was taking, but Croft did need to be sure about the will. Yes, he could have asked over the phone when his mother was still lucid, but he knew a physical presence was necessary in case his mother had changed the will, or had thought of doing so because he hadn't been visiting. She had to think Garry was the dutiful son.

He'd decided to tell her a cock and bull story that he couldn't come to see her over the years because the Australian intelligence service had recruited him as an agent to work undercover. That was why he couldn't give anyone his contact details and why he was so secretive over where he was. Much to his regret, he'd been unable to visit before now. Not very plausible, but that was the best he could come up with. He was sure his mother would believe him. After all, he was with her now, wasn't he?

Croft had reassured himself and the panic subsided. He had another look at the departure screen and saw gate number ten for London Heathrow was now open. He picked up his small cabin bag and made his way to the gate.

There was one stop at Dubai for an hour and a half before the final leg to Heathrow. The total journey time was over twenty-two hours. On arrival at Heathrow, Croft was feeling tired and exhausted as he queued up to go through passport control. Sweat was running down his back and he was breathing hard. Someone tapped him on the shoulder and he spun round in alarm, looking like a rabbit in headlights.

An older man was behind him. 'Sorry,' the man said, pointing in front, 'you can go through. There's a green arrow showing over there.'

Croft glowered at the man. 'Too tired. I didn't notice,' he grumbled.

'No worries,' the man said in a broad Aussie accent.

Croft ambled forward to the available automated gate. He opened his passport and placed it face down on the reader, but the gate didn't open. Panic was starting to set in and he glanced furtively over his shoulder. A uniformed officer came over towards him and Croft was trying to stop shaking. *I'm done for*, he thought.

The officer looked closely at Croft. 'Take your hat off, look straight at the camera and stand still until the green light shows.'

Croft nodded his understanding and did as the officer advised. *Thank fuck for that*, he thought when the green light came on. He removed his passport and left the gate quicker than he'd entered it. After collecting his bag from baggage reclaim, he was soon outside looking for a taxi.

'High Wycombe?' he asked the first available one.

The driver gave a thumbs up, got out of the car and put Croft's bag in the boot.

'Anywhere in particular in High Wycombe?' the driver asked on the way out of the airport.

'The train station will do fine.'

'Been somewhere nice?'

'Australia.'

'Holiday?'

'Yes,' Croft lied.

'Whereabouts? Never been there myself.'

One thing Croft hated was people asking questions. 'Travelling,' was all he offered by way of reply.

'Ah, big place. Which parts did you travel to? Did you go to… what do you call it… you know the rock?'

'Ayers Rock.'

'You went there?'

'No.' *He'll be asking where I work next, I'll bet,* Croft thought.

'What do you do then? I mean for work?'

Knew it!

'In between jobs.' Croft then folded his arms and closed his eyes hoping the driver would take the hint.

Half an hour later the taxi pulled in at High Wycombe Station.

Croft paid the driver without leaving a tip and found the nearby hotel he'd booked using a false name. The first thing he needed after checking in was a drink. He rang his most trusted old union friend while enjoying a pint. 'I'm back home to visit my mother in High Wycombe. If you can make it, we could meet up for a drink tomorrow night. Keep this to yourself though. Don't want the cops finding out I'm here, okay?'

He gave his friend the name of the pub he would be in and ended the call. Croft sipped on his pint and thought about what he would say to his mother the next day. He would see his old mate afterwards, then get the hell out of England before too many people found out he was there.

37

The Cessna 172 Skyhawk circled over Wycombe Air Park before coming in to land. It taxied along the runway to the parking area at the north side of the airfield where Emerson kept it in the summer months. Hanger facilities were more expensive and Emerson only tended to use them during the winter.

Rimmer had been viewing from the café and terrace beneath the control tower. He shielded his eyes from the glare of the sun and watched the propeller shudder to a halt as the engine spluttered and died. Emerson climbed out and made his way over to where Rimmer was sitting. They'd arranged to meet here. Emerson had wanted to check the Cessna out after the repair work on it, but also wanted to avoid any chance his wife might be at home if Rimmer went there. This meeting was strictly confidential.

'Nice landing,' Rimmer observed as Emerson approached.

'Thanks. Good to know everything's in working order. Had the engineers fix a few things.'

Rimmer smiled. 'Just as well, eh?'

'I've got every faith in the guys who work on it. Handles like a dream now.'

'How come you've got a light aircraft? Must have cost you a pretty penny.'

'It was my father's. There's no other family and he left it to me when he died.'

'Lucky you.'

'Yeah. I love it. It's a single engine, fixed-wing aircraft – quite old, but it still flies well. It's great coming here and taking off. I can spend two to three hours up there without having to land to refuel. Five hours tops. On a nice day I often fly up to the Lake District and back. The wings sit above the cockpit so you get a good view of the ground.'

'How many seats?'

'Four.' Emerson thought for a moment. 'I could take you up for a spin sometime if you like.'

'Really? I'd like to do that. Could fancy a Lake District trip.'

'I'm sure we could arrange something.' Emerson changed the subject. 'You said on the phone you had something for me?'

Rimmer felt as though he was about to burst Emerson's bubble. 'Sorry, mate, but you were right. Your wife *is* having an affair with Kauffman. Either that, or they're on very friendly terms.'

Emerson's head dropped and he looked at his feet. 'The London trip?'

'Afraid so. I followed your wife to the station in Reading. She met Kauffman there. I have photos of them embracing when she found him. They did go into London. They were walking hand in hand to a hotel near Trafalgar Square. They checked in as Mr and Mrs Kauffman. I have some more photos. I saw them again next morning at breakfast–'

'You stayed there as well?' Emerson broke in.

'Yes,' Rimmer lied. 'But I'm afraid I lost the receipt. You can always ring the hotel to check. I registered under a false name – Theodore.'

'That won't be necessary,' Emerson mumbled.

Rimmer felt sorry for Emerson and even more sorry he'd lied to him, albeit necessarily. 'Tell you what,' he said, trying to lift the mood, 'how about I delete the hotel stay from your invoice in return for you taking me for a spin in your plane up to the Lake District sometime?'

'Okay,' Emerson said without enthusiasm. 'Have you got the photos?'

Rimmer passed Emerson all the ones he'd taken of his wife and Kauffman. 'So what do you intend to do now?' he asked as Emerson glanced through them.

'Kill Kauffman?' Emerson joked.

'Wouldn't blame you if you did. Probably do the AWE a favour. Seriously though, what next?' Rimmer asked.

'I'll have it out with her and start divorce proceedings.'

'And then?'

'I'm thinking of leaving the AWE. I'll take off in my plane somewhere and look for another job. Maybe go to France.'

Rimmer put a hand on Emerson's shoulder. 'Good luck, mate. But don't you be jetting off before I get the trip you owe me, will you?' he joked.

'I won't,' Emerson promised, trying his best to smile.

'You take care,' Rimmer said, leaving Emerson looking dolefully across at his Cessna, the only thing left of value to him.

~

Rimmer's mobile indicated an incoming call: *Dunbar.* He answered it. 'Hello?'

'Hi, Dan?'

'Yes.'

'Zoe Dunbar. Just to let you know one of the tabloids have agreed to run the story. They're prepared to pay one and a half thousand for it. I'll go halves with you.'

'No way. I'm the one who got the story. All you have to do is write it. How hard can that be?'

The line went quiet for a moment. 'Zoe?'

'I'm still here – just thinking.'

'I'll settle for one thousand,' Rimmer said. 'You get five hundred – deal?'

Another long pause. 'Okay, send me the photos.'

38

Toby Omoko was back in his office in Thames House, his short foray into field work over. He was disappointed in his efforts. Thinking he could somehow find valuable information Falcon had so far missed showed his inexperience and naivety. He wondered why he thought he could magically conjure up something that would impress Quentin Vere. No, that hadn't worked at all. His confidence was low. It didn't need negative misgivings from Vere to lessen his moral.

He was still the sole occupant of the stuffy ground-floor office. Omoko wondered if his sick colleague would ever return. Maybe he'd had enough of the place. Possibly looking for medical retirement. Omoko wished more than ever he could get out of his current job. He wouldn't mind being an analyst in counter-intelligence or counter-terrorism – that would be exciting. But subversive activity? Nothing much happened these days, certainly not to warrant interest from MI5, until now.

Omoko had thought things were going to get interesting with the new focus on the William Stroud murder case and the current dispute at the AWE. But little had come to light. The one-day strikes were ongoing – no sign of a resolution. If anything, it seemed like it might head towards an all-out strike. A recent newspaper article had claimed the police were following new leads on the Stroud case, but hadn't specified what they were. Maybe that was a ploy. The police wouldn't want to show their hand, Omoko guessed. And Falcon had remained silent.

The shrill ring of his phone shook Omoko out of his thoughts. Most calls tended to be from Vere. He picked the handset up with dread. 'Omoko.'

'My office – now!'

Omoko grimaced. The tone of voice, and the economical use of words indicated Vere was in a bad mood. Not unusual. Rumour had it the director general and Vere had crossed swords. Vere had joined MI5 straight from Cambridge University and had worked his way up the ranks, upsetting most staff on the way. He had reached the dizzy heights of assistant director general for counter-intelligence where he eventually blotted his copybook. He was fifty-six at the time and the DG had farmed him off to the less onerous role in charge of subversion and insurrection where he could do no damage.

Omoko climbed the stairs in dread. He walked up to Vere's secretary in the outer office. She looked shaken and red-eyed. 'You okay?' he asked.

The secretary looked up. It was clear she'd been crying. She smiled weakly. 'I'm fine, thanks.'

Omoko turned to knock on Vere's door.

'He's in a foul mood,' the secretary added.

Omoko's hand stopped a few inches from Vere's door. He breathed deeply, then knocked.

'Come in!'

Omoko entered and immediately saw the problem. Vere had a newspaper on his otherwise-empty desk. Omoko could see the headline and the photograph. He'd seen Zoe Dunbar's article himself, but hadn't got round to alerting Vere to it.

Vere's face was red and beads of perspiration glistened on his forehead. 'Have you seen this, Omoko!' Vere thumped a chubby fist down on his desk.

'Yes... I–'

'Then why am I seeing this before you come and tell me, eh?' Vere cut in. He pulled off his glasses and threw them on the newspaper.

'Sorry, I was about to call you, sir.'

'Is that a fact. We pay you to keep on top of this and I find out before you tell me. It's not good enough, Omoko,' Vere said, his face twisted into a sneer.

'Sorry.'

Vere picked up his glasses and rammed them back on his head with shaking hands. He tapped a forefinger on the paper. 'This,' he said, spitting with venom, 'is unacceptable. A man handing Kauffman a package – no doubt cash – and then the man disappears into a bloody Russian Trade Delegation!'

'I... I–'

There was no stopping Vere's rant. He cut Omoko off again. 'He could be a Russian spy, for fuck's sake! And Kauffman, who's using a strike to disrupt work in the interests of the defence of the nation, is seen taking money from him.'

'We don't actually know–'

Vere was in no mood to let Omoko say anything. 'What's not good enough,' he cut in, 'is that this appears in the bloody press before we know about it! What the hell is Falcon doing?'

'I don't think Falcon was in a position to know about this. You recruited an agent to be eyes and ears only, not to carry out surveillance,' Omoko said, amazed he was able to finish a sentence at last.

'The DG will go mad. He'll want to know what you're doing. How the fuck did the press get this before us?'

Omoko noted Vere had said the DG would want to know what *he* was doing, not what *they* were doing. *Not that there's a blame culture here*, Omoko thought, *but he's setting me up to be the fall guy.* 'We had no resources to carry out surveillance on Kauffman. Our only source of information comes from the newspapers and Falcon, sir.'

'So I tell the DG we could have been ahead of the game if we had more resources?' Vere's eyes had narrowed and he mopped his brow with a handkerchief.

Omoko was gaining courage to speak out. 'I suppose so. Our unit isn't considered important enough these days.'

Vere stood and walked to the window, looking out over the Thames with his back to Omoko. He put his hands on his hips and remained silent. After a few moments he turned and faced Omoko. 'We won't get any more resources, so it's down to you.'

'Sir?'

'I want you to get in touch with Eathan Younger. Tell him the DG wants him to get DCI Fleming to go and see this reporter, Zoe Dunbar, and ask how the hell she got hold of this.'

'Yes, sir. What about Kauffman? Should we get Fleming to question him about the package?'

Vere thought for a moment, scratching his chin. 'No, let's see what Dunbar has to say first. And arrange a phone tap on Kauffman, get his bank account checked, and trace the man on the photo with him. I want to know who the fuck he is.'

Omoko was beginning to feel uncomfortable. This type of work was out of his normal remit. 'I'll give it a go, but this isn't–'

'Don't fuck this up, Omoko,' Vere cut him off once more, then sighed. 'Liaise with Thames Valley Police. Ask their force specialist operations people to put Kauffman under surveillance. Once you've done the groundwork, we'll hand it over to them to pull Kauffman in for questioning and charge him if there is a case against him.'

Omoko was feeling far from happy, but at least he had an opportunity to do more than analyst work and prove his worth. 'Okay, sir.'

'One last thing,' Vere said, 'we do not want the press knowing we have an interest in this.' He fixed Omoko with a steely glare. 'Understood?'

'Yes, sir.'

Omoko was relieved to escape Vere's office and return to the relative calm of his own workplace. *One day I'll hit the bastard*, he thought, picking up his phone to dial for an outside number.

39

The one-day strikes had failed to shift the company position and Kauffman had pulled everyone out indefinitely, claiming the management approach to negotiations was inflexible and aggressive. He said they were reneging on previous agreements over pay and pensions, and safety standards were at risk due to reduced staffing levels.

Fleming arrived to find a large gathering of men in yellow safety vests manning the picket line at the main entrance. Kauffman was there, scowling at Fleming as he eased his car past the pickets. Once through the throng, Fleming glanced in his rear-view mirror. Kauffman had walked into the middle of the road, arms folded as he stared at the back of Fleming's car.

Fleming parked and made his way to Nieve's office. She looked harassed. 'Bad time to call in?' he asked.

Nieve coughed and took a sip of something from a steaming mug. 'You could say so. Kauffman's changed tactics and the union's upping its game. We could cope to some extent with the one-day strikes, but an indefinite strike is a disaster.' Nieve's voice was huskier than normal.

'You don't sound too good.'

'Damned cold on top of everything else. Last thing I need right now.'

Fleming shot Nieve a sympathetic glance. 'Stressful time – immune system suffers.'

'Should have been a doctor.' Nieve tapped the newspaper on her desk. 'Have you seen this?'

Fleming leaned over her desk and turned the newspaper round. It was the photographs of Kauffman receiving a package from the man who went on to a Russian Trade Delegation seminar. 'Yes, I have. Has anyone spoken to Kauffman about it?'

'We had a management meeting with him and some other union men first thing this morning. Didn't make any progress on the strike, but we held Kauffman back after the meeting to question him.'

'What did he say?'

Nieve pulled out a handkerchief and blew her nose. 'Hope I don't give this to you.'

'Strange thing for him to say,' Fleming quipped.

'Very funny. Forget doctor – you should have been a comedian.'

'Sorry.'

'He claimed it was a fake photograph of him and that someone was obviously trying to set him up to discredit him and undermine the strike.'

'I suppose photographs can be fabricated. Fakes are not uncommon.'

'That's what he claimed. Reckoned someone had manipulated it with some clever camera tricks. He even accused us of being behind it.'

'But you weren't?'

Nieve gave Fleming a cold stare. 'Have you got many friends?'

Fleming held his hands up as though in surrender. 'What about the other man in the photo? How does he explain that?'

'He couldn't. Says the image of the package handover must have been manipulated with separate photos of him and the other man, or someone was made to look like him. Claims he's never seen the other man before.'

'You buying that?'

'I think we need to speak to this reporter.'

'As it happens, I'm going to see her next after I've had a word with Logan and Anderson. I'll let you know what she says.'

'Thanks.'

'You said the strike was now a disaster. Any special line of work being disrupted?'

Nieve thought for a moment before answering. 'Can't go into details, but we were working on some research and design stuff on components for a nuclear warhead. We're also in the middle of dismantling weapons retired from service.'

'So the strike is a threat to safety?'

'It could bring us to a standstill,' Nieve admitted.

'Serious stuff, eh?' Fleming looked pensive for a moment. 'What I really came for was to see if you'd had any luck finding a record of Liam Doherty.'

Nieve reached for her hankie again and blew a nose that was rather red. 'Afraid not,' came the nasal reply.

'What about people who left the company after Stroud's murder?' Fleming prompted.

Nieve opened a bottom desk drawer and pulled a folder out from a suspension file. 'There are names of twenty-six people in here. We had phone numbers and addresses for some, but not all of them.'

'Job for Logan and Anderson,' Fleming said with smile. 'I'll catch them on my way out.'

Fleming thanked Nieve for the information and confirmed

he would let her know what Zoe Dunbar had to say about her article. He left Nieve to her misery and popped along the corridor to drop the folder off with Logan and Anderson before going to see Dunbar. 'Bit of homework there,' he said. 'List of people who left the company after Stroud's murder. I need you to fill in the gaps where there are no contact details and then find and interview them all.'

'Just when we thought we'd done with interviews, boss.' Logan looked at Anderson with raised eyebrows. 'Want to make a start?'

'Anything you say, Sarge,' Anderson said with a loud sigh.

'Oh, by the way, boss, we haven't found anyone who admits to knowing anything about the disciples.'

'Right, thanks. I'll leave you both to it then.' Fleming left, wondering whether Dunbar would stand by her article and the integrity of the photographs.

~

It had come as a surprise to Fleming that Eathan Younger had called him up to his office to tell him to question Zoe Dunbar about the Kauffman article. Younger wanted to know how she had come across the story and how she got the shots. Did she take them, or did someone give them to her? Fleming guessed there was more to Younger's request than he was prepared to say and wondered why the sudden interest in the story. Fleming was sure someone had asked Younger to get the information, but who?

Fleming had already decided to question Dunbar about her article long before Younger had asked him to. Kauffman was now a possible suspect in the Stroud murder case and anything suspicious involving him was a matter of interest to Fleming.

Dunbar had agreed to meet Fleming at the Reading

westbound service station on the M4. The car park was filling up with travellers stopping off for a spot of lunch. Fleming had spotted Dunbar's car arriving about twenty minutes after him. They were sitting outside having a coffee. It was early September and humid. The downside was the traffic noise.

Dunbar took a sip of her drink and looked quizzically at Fleming. 'I think I can guess why you wanted to see me. It's my article on Kauffman, isn't it?'

'Right.'

'So what do you want to know?'

'Did you take the photographs?'

'No.'

'Are you sure they're genuine?'

'Yes.'

'Who gave them to you?'

'My source has asked to remain anonymous.'

Fleming's eyes shot skywards in disbelief. He'd had enough of sources and clients wanting to keep their identity a secret. 'Miss Dunbar, I hate to tell you this, but there's no such thing as staying anonymous in a murder enquiry.'

'Are you saying Kauffman is suspected of killing Stroud?'

'I'm just following up on every lead, and anything suspicious to do with the AWE or its employees is of potential interest. Now, are you going to tell me who gave you the photos or do I have to charge you with obstructing a police enquiry?'

'You're joking, right. You wouldn't... would you?'

'Believe me, I would.'

'Even though I did you a favour by running a story about police following new leads?'

'Even so.'

'Okay, how about we come to an agreement. I tell you where I got the photos from and you give me an exclusive on Kauffman and the Stroud case if he turns out to be the killer... so I get to run the story before anyone else.'

'You think you're in a position to bargain?'

'Yes,' came the confident reply.

Thunder rumbled in the distance and Fleming felt the first spot of rain. 'Might have to go indoors,' he suggested.

'Or my car?' Dunbar offered. 'It's over there.' She pointed to a two-year-old silver Audi A5.

'Reporting must be paying well,' Fleming observed.

'I get by.'

'Okay,' Fleming finally agreed. 'You give me the name and I give you a heads-up on any major developments. But let's be clear – I can only give you information which is about to become public knowledge.'

'Deal. It was Dan Rimmer.'

Fleming raised an eyebrow. 'Gets everywhere, doesn't he? Why did he come to you with the photos?'

'Money.'

'You paid him?'

'I came to an arrangement with the newspaper.'

'How do you know what he gave you was genuine and not fake?'

'I'm a journalist. I know a fake when I see one.'

The rain started in earnest and they both made a dash for their cars.

'Don't forget,' Dunbar shouted after Fleming, 'I get the heads-up first.'

40

The rain had turned to a downpour by the time Fleming reached his car. Streaks of lightning flashed across the darkened sky and thunder rumbled directly overhead. The rain drumming on the roof of the car sounded like a deluge of hailstones.

Fleming pulled out his mobile as he watched Dunbar's car ease out of the service station car park. He was close to Reading so it was worth a try. He searched for Rimmer's number and tapped the green telephone icon.

Rimmer straight away. 'Hello?'

'It's DCI Fleming. I'm near Reading and wondered if you were in the office.'

'I am, why?'

'Just wanted a quick word with you. I can be there in about twenty-five minutes.'

'Okay.'

'See you shortly.' Fleming ended the call and pulled out of the car park onto the M4 and headed west towards Theale. He left the motorway there and turned right along the Bath Road to Reading. Traffic was heavy in Reading and it took about forty minutes to get there and walk the short distance to Wyatt Investigations. Fleming was grateful the storm had passed and the rain had stopped by the time he parked his car.

Fleming could smell the smoke as soon as he stepped into the office. He pointed to the no-smoking sign and raised a questioning eyebrow at Rimmer.

Rimmer smiled. 'My uncle. He smokes a pipe. Reckons the office is his home when there's no one here. He's gone to see a client.'

'I don't suppose it's Liam Doherty?'

'Afraid not.'

'He's not been in touch again since you told him I wanted to speak to him?'

'Nope.'

'And what about Croft?'

Rimmer seemed to hesitate for a moment. 'Yvette Boudreaux rang me to say he'd phoned her,' he finally admitted. 'Seems his mother's terminally ill, but he told Boudreaux he couldn't get back from Australia to see her.'

'So I gather.'

'Boudreaux told you as well?'

Fleming nodded.

'Doesn't want to be found, does he?'

'Seems not,' Fleming agreed. 'Did you put another red card in your window for Doherty after Boudreaux rang you?'

'No, there seemed little point. I'd only be able to tell him Croft knew his mother was critically ill but couldn't come to see her. I didn't want to piss him off again.'

'What happens if he suddenly turns up?'

'Who, Croft or Doherty?'

'Hardly likely Doherty's going to turn up is it? I mean Croft.'

'I'll stick a card in the window and hope Doherty contacts me.'

'And you'll let me know straight away?'

'Of course.'

'Anyway, that's not what I wanted to talk to you about.'

'No?' Rimmer sat back in his chair, put his feet up on the desk, and rubbed his left leg.

'Cramp?' Fleming asked.

'Old war wound,' Rimmer said. 'Shrapnel injury in Afghanistan. Plays up sometimes.'

Fleming's face screwed up as though he felt the pain. He watched Rimmer closely as he spoke. 'I wanted to ask you about Zoe Dunbar's article on Bill Kauffman.'

'Oh?' Rimmer's eyes narrowed for a second.

'She told me she got the photographs from you.'

Rimmer stroked his beard thoughtfully and pulled his feet off the desk. 'I asked her to keep my name out of it.'

'She did tell me you didn't want your name mentioned.'

'But she told you anyway.'

Fleming smiled. 'You could say I was persuasive.'

'Let me guess, you threatened to charge her with obstructing a police enquiry?'

'I can be persistent.'

'Okay, so I gave her the photos.'

'How come you happened to be there at the precise time this package was handed to Kauffman? Or were you tailing him for some reason?'

'I had a woman under surveillance for a client who thought his wife was having an affair with Kauffman. I managed to catch Kauffman on his own.'

'Seth Emerson's wife the woman?'

'How did you know?'

'Emerson came to see me,' Fleming said. 'Told me he'd recruited you to check up on his wife because he thought she was having an affair with Kauffman.'

Rimmer nodded his understanding and got up from his chair to open the top drawer of a four-drawer filing cabinet. He pulled out two glasses with one hand and a bottle of whisky with the other. He waved the glasses at Fleming. 'Want one?'

'No, thanks. On duty and driving.'

'Ah, right.' Rimmer put one of the glasses back and poured a large measure for himself before rummaging in his desk drawer for some painkillers. He took two and knocked them back with a gulp of whisky. 'Best thing to kill the pain,' he said, lifting the glass as though in salute.

'How come you were following Kauffman if you were checking up on Emerson's wife?'

'I was following her and she met up with Kauffman. They went to London. He came out of the hotel they'd checked into and went for a walk on his own. I decided to follow him and the rest is history.'

'Kauffman is claiming the photos are fake.'

'I'd do the same if I were him.' Rimmer took another gulp of whisky and stared through the glass.

'But they're not?'

'Why the hell would I fake them, for fuck's sake?'

'To fabricate a story that you get paid for?' Fleming suggested.

'You really think I'd do such a thing? I'm not mercenary. Take it from me, Fleming – they're genuine.'

'Never doubted it for a minute.' Fleming thought for a second. 'So why did you then follow the other man if your only interest was in Emerson's wife?'

'Private investigator instinct I suppose. I knew what was going on at Aldermaston from the press and Kauffman was the union leader. I thought it odd when I saw him being handed a package furtively. There was no point in following him again, I knew where he was going – back to the hotel. I decided to follow the other man out of curiosity.'

'And you thought you could earn a bit on the side by selling the story.'

'That's about it, yes.'

'It didn't cross your mind to report what you'd seen?'

'Who to?'

'AWE?' Fleming suggested.

'Nah. In any case they found out when they read the article. Only difference is I got paid.'

Fleming smiled. 'And there was me believing you're not mercenary.'

Fleming arrived back at Long Hanborough after leaving Wyatt Investigations. He reported to Younger on what Rimmer had told him before sauntering down to the incident room.

He went over to the whiteboard Logan had attached to the wall, picked up a marker pen and scribbled notes. Stroud's name was first on the board, then Croft's, Kauffman's and Nat Horne's with lines and arrows connecting them to Stroud. Circling Stroud and Croft, he wrote disciples with a question mark and drew a dotted line from there to Kauffman. He drew another line from Kauffman to Emerson and tapped the pen against his chin before scribbling in another question mark. Fleming then circled Kauffman's name and scribbled in motive – wife's affair with Stroud. Studying what he'd written, Fleming sketched further lines from Croft to Rimmer and then on to Liam Doherty with a final question mark. As an afterthought, he put in a dotted line between Rimmer and Kauffman.

While staring at his handiwork, Jeff Miller appeared from

behind him. 'Looks like you're making a bit of progress there, Alex,' he said, looking carefully at the whiteboard.

Fleming tossed the marker pen into the mug Logan had provided as a pen holder. 'Not entirely sure, Jeff. Seem to have far more questions than answers at the moment.'

Miller patted Fleming on the back. 'Keep up the good work, Alex.' Before leaving the room, he called over his shoulder, 'See you haven't put a motive against Croft's name.'

Fleming thought for a moment and wondered why he hadn't.

41

Croft had waited to the last minute before going down for breakfast. He'd decided to lie-in as long as he could to try to recover from jet lag. He'd enjoyed a full English and was on his second cup of coffee, thinking what he was going to say to his mother. Would she recognise him? Would he be able to get any sense out of her?

His thoughts then turned to the friend he'd phoned yesterday. Was that a good idea? Could he rely on him to keep quiet about his return to England? *Too late now. It's done.* Croft finally convinced himself it would be okay. He intended to check out of the hotel after breakfast, go and see his mother, meet his friend at the pub later and then get the train back to London and on to Heathrow. *I'll be gone before anyone else finds out I'm here,* he told himself.

Croft checked out and asked if he could leave his bag there until later, then took a taxi to the Ridgeway Manor Care Home. He paid the driver and walked into the reception area. There wasn't anyone there so he waited, looking furtively around him. Eventually, Makena Kibet came through a door leading to a day room. 'Excuse me,' Croft said, 'I'm here to see my mother, Ethel Croft.'

Makena looked at Croft as though in amazement. He was tall, stocky and wearing jeans and a red polo shirt. Although in his fifties, Croft had his hair cut in a Mohican style. His head was shaved on the sides and a strip of brown – probably dyed – hair lined the top of his head. The brown goatee beard completed the image of a man who looked like someone you would not want to get on the wrong side of. But it wasn't Croft's appearance that made Makena's mouth drop open. It was the fact he'd turned up with no prior warning. He'd told Mrs Boudreaux he couldn't get back to see his mother.

'It's Garry – Garry Croft.'

'Yes... yes of course. It's just we weren't expecting you. I'll take you round to Mrs Boudreaux's office. I think she'll want to talk to you before you see your mother.'

Croft stuffed his hands in his pockets and shrugged. 'Okay, but if she's busy I'll go and see my mother if you show me where her room is.'

Makena led Croft past the day room and down a corridor to Boudreaux's office. The door was open as usual. Boudreaux liked to keep an open-door policy. Makena knocked anyway and Boudreaux looked up from her desk. 'Mr Croft has arrived to see his mother,' Makena announced. 'I thought you might like to see him first.'

Boudreaux looked as surprised as Makena had. No doubt it was the appearance as well as the fact that he was here despite saying he couldn't come. 'Mr Croft, I'm so glad you could make it after all,' she said, rising from her desk. 'You should have let us know you were coming. We could have pre-warned your mother.'

'Didn't know myself until the last minute,' Croft muttered, knowing full well he could have sent a text message on his way here. Only he didn't want anyone to have prior knowledge of his visit.

'At least you're here now,' Boudreaux said. 'Your mother is not at all well I'm afraid. The doctor says it's just a question of time.'

Croft stared hard at Boudreaux. 'How long?'

Boudreaux looked surprised by Croft's abruptness. No sign of any emotion. 'I don't really know. Soon I imagine. The doctor advised that we should let any relatives know so they could make arrangements to see her. As you're the only relative it's as well you phoned me when you did to see how she was.'

'How ill is she? I mean... is she conscious? Will she know I'm there?'

'I'll take you to her room. If she's asleep you can sit next to her – hold her hand and speak to her. She might be able to hear you.'

'What about personal papers – would they be here?'

'She only has a few letters – the ones you sent. Did you have something in particular in mind?'

Croft looked uncomfortable. 'The will maybe.'

Boudreaux looked disapprovingly at Croft. 'I'm afraid not. When she first came into the home, we made a record of what bank and savings accounts she had. She gave us the name and address of a solicitor who has her will.'

'I'll need the details,' Croft said tersely.

'Of course. I'll dig them out for you while you're with your mother. I'll take you along now.'

Makena had left Ethel's window wide open and sunlight poured into the room. A breeze wafted through the window and gently tugged at the curtains. Ethel was propped up in bed, but her eyes were closed. Her breathing was irregular and came in short gasps.

Boudreaux went over to Ethel and held her hand. 'Ethel, there's someone to see you. It's your son, Garry.'

No response.

Boudreaux looked at Croft. 'Why don't you sit and talk to her for a while. If she doesn't wake up, she may still sense your presence. Come and see me before you leave and I'll let you have the information you wanted.'

42

Boudreaux went back to her office and picked up the phone. She got through to an answering machine in Fleming's office. She left a message to say Croft had turned up unexpectedly then tried Fleming's mobile. He wasn't picking up on that either, so she left another message. Then she called Rimmer's number, unaware Makena had already phoned him.

'Hi, Dan Rimmer speaking.'

'Oh, hello, Mr Rimmer, it's Yvette Boudreaux here. I'm calling to let you know Garry Croft has turned up without warning. He's with his mother now.'

'Thanks for letting me know.'

Boudreaux hesitated. 'Shall I ask him to ring you or let him know you want to see him?'

'No need. I'll let my client know. He could be up there in about forty minutes. It'll be a nice surprise for Garry.'

'What if he leaves before your client gets here?'

'Get his mobile number or the address of where he's staying.' Rimmer ended the call and put a red card in the office window.

Just over an hour after Boudreaux had spoken to Rimmer her phone rang. She picked it up. 'Ridgeway Manor Care Home.'

'Hello, I'm after a Mr Garry Croft. Is he still there?' The voice sounded Irish.

'Who's this speaking?' Boudreaux asked.

'Doherty – Liam Doherty,' the voice answered.

'Are you Dan Rimmer's client?'

'I am.'

'Yes, Mr Croft is still here,' Boudreaux said hesitantly. 'Shall I get him for you, or get him to call you back?'

'No, don't do that. He owes me some money and I don't want him running off like he did before. I've been waiting for five years to catch up with him.'

Boudreaux was confused. 'Dan Rimmer said you wanted to contact Mr Croft because he'd been left a lot of money, not that he owed it.'

'Ah, you must excuse the slight deception. I didn't think he would respond if we told him I was trying to contact him to get what he owed me back, so I got Rimmer to tell you an uncle had left Croft some money. More chance he'd get in touch.'

It suddenly dawned on Boudreaux why Croft had said there must be some mistake because he didn't have an uncle with lots of money. 'Look, I understand why you want to see Mr Croft, but this is a care home – I don't want any trouble here.'

'Don't you worry. There won't be any. I'll get myself up there and catch him when he leaves.'

Boudreaux didn't like the sound of this at all, but she had left a message for Fleming. Maybe the police would get here first. *Not my problem*, she thought.

Garry Croft had no idea what to do. His mother was still dozing. He'd always been emotionless and detached. His ex-wife had called him a cold bastard.

All he needed to know was that his mother had still left everything to him in her will. He'd get the solicitor's details from Boudreaux, but thought he wouldn't be able to see the will until after his mother died. What if she'd changed it? How was he going to get it changed back? He really needed to know what was in it.

The last time he'd held anyone's hand was when he was married. That was before the rot had set in. Although finding it awkward, he took his mother's hand. 'Mum,' he whispered. 'Can you hear me?'

There was no response.

'It's me, Garry, your son.'

Was that a flicker of the eyes? The breathing came in gasps. 'Garry, is that you?'

Croft leaned closer. 'Yes... yes it's me. They told me you were ill so I finally managed to get away to come and see you.'

The eyes were open, staring straight ahead, watery and unseeing. 'Where have you been?'

'Australia, Mum. You remember? I went there a while back. I was working undercover for Australian intelligence. That's why I couldn't tell anyone where I was or leave any way of contacting me.' Croft knew it sounded ridiculous.

Ethel's breathing came in short gasps. 'Australia you say? I don't remember.'

'It's a long way away, Mum. Too far to be able to get to see you as often as I'd like.' He squeezed her hand. 'But I'm here now to make sure everything's okay.'

Ethel's eyes closed and for a moment Croft thought she'd died. But then her chest heaved and she sucked in air through an open mouth.

Croft didn't want to leave yet. He wanted to ask about the will and wondered how he was going to raise the subject. He sat there listening to the slow shallow breathing for what must have been at least thirty minutes.

Eventually, the eyes flickered open again. 'Garry?'

Croft squeezed his mother's hand again. 'Yes, I'm still here. Everything's going to be fine. I've taken care of everything. The solicitor's got your will. There's no need to worry about anything. It's all taken care of.'

'Will?'

'Yes, you had your solicitor draw up a will years ago leaving everything to me when you died. Not for a long time yet of course,' Croft added quickly.

'Oh, yes I think I did.'

Croft's pulse raced. He gripped his mother's hand tighter. 'But you haven't had a new one drawn up have you?'

'New will? Should I have done one?' The breathing became deeper and Ethel's eyes closed again.

'No... no, of course not. Just wanted to make sure all your affairs are in order.' Croft had what he came for. His mother was clearly not quite with it, but although he couldn't be certain, it didn't look like she had ever changed the will.

43

Croft didn't stay much longer with his mother. There seemed no point. He strolled round to Boudreaux's office, receiving a dark glance from Makena on the way. He picked up the details Boudreaux had pulled out for him, thanked her and was about to leave.

'How did you find you mother, Mr Croft?' Boudreaux asked, getting up from her desk.

'Sleepy,' was all Croft said.

Boudreaux went to the window and pushed it open a bit further. 'Yes, maybe the heat is getting to her.'

Croft shrugged.

'It must have been tiring coming all this way from Australia. I've been a couple of times. I have a sister there.'

'I am tired, yes,' Croft said curtly. He really didn't feel like starting a conversation with Boudreaux.

'Whereabouts in Australia do you live?'

'Perth,' Croft lied.

'Ah, never been there myself. My sister lives in Melbourne.'

Croft's eyes narrowed when Boudreaux mentioned the name.

'Do you know Melbourne?'

Croft began to wonder if Boudreaux was trying to hold him up. *Why would she want to? Maybe she saw in the papers years ago that I was a suspect in the Stroud killing and she's phoned the police.*

'Would you mind letting me have your phone number, you know... in case...' her voice trailed off.

'Got to go,' Croft said. 'I'll call you.' He left Boudreaux's office without another word, pulling his mobile out of his pocket as he left.

He looked up the taxi number and tapped the ring icon. It was an age before the phone was answered. 'Croft here. Can you pick me up at the Ridgeway Manor Care Home as soon as you can?'

'Fifteen minutes,' was the answer.

Fuck, thought Croft. He pulled a cigarette packet from his pocket, lit up and tossed the spent match onto the gravel driveway. He looked nervously towards the entrance to the home, expecting to see a police car turn up any minute. *Should never have chanced it.*

Then it happened. His worst nightmare. The sound of wailing sirens approaching. He looked anxiously around trying to work out where he could run, but then caught the sight of an ambulance speeding past the entrance. He sighed with relief. Sweat was running down his back. He took a deep drag of his cigarette and blew a cloud of smoke up in the air.

After what seemed like an eternity, the taxi turned up. The driver leaned through his window. 'Mr Croft?'

'Yeah.' Croft jumped in glancing once more in the direction of the entrance, oblivious to the fact someone had been watching him. 'Station,' was all Croft said to the driver.

Croft had no way of knowing a car was following not far behind. He sat in the back of the taxi wondering whether he ought to alter his plans. Hell no, he decided after a while, he could still see his old friend. All he needed was a slight change to the arrangement. He'd had a scare at the care home and was probably starting to get paranoid thinking Boudreaux had phoned for the police. She sounded foreign and may not even have been in England when his name had hit the press five years earlier. No one knew where he was staying in Wycombe and, in any case, he'd checked into the hotel using a false name.

The taxi pulled into the station a few minutes later. Croft paid the driver and walked to the hotel to pick up his bag, unaware someone was following him.

Standing outside, Croft threw down his bag, lit another cigarette and pulled out his mobile to ring the friend he'd arranged to meet for a drink. He didn't notice the man across the street looking in his direction.

His friend picked up straight away.

'Hi, Garry.'

'Listen, mate,' Croft said. 'I need to change plans slightly. Can you make it for a pint this lunchtime instead of tonight? I've decided to leave a bit earlier.'

'Problems?'

'Just being cautious.'

'Sorry, I can't make it for lunchtime. You sure you can't stay until tonight?'

Croft wondered whether to chance it, after all he couldn't bring forward his flight from Heathrow later that evening. No, he decided after a few moments, best to leave Wycombe early even though he'd have a few more hours to kill at Heathrow. 'It's a shame you can't make it. I'll just have a quick pint on my own then be on my way.'

'Okay, mate. Pity I won't get to see you. Catch up next time?'

Croft knew there wouldn't be a next time. 'Sure.' He ended the call, picked up his bag, and set off towards the station where it would be easy to grab a taxi for Heathrow. More expensive, but quicker and easier than a train to Marylebone, tube to Paddington and then Heathrow Express to the airport. It was only a five-minute walk to the station and he found a pub nearby. Croft pushed the door open and made his way to the crowded bar to order a pint, unaware there were eyes watching him.

44

Fleming woke suddenly. His alarm was ringing off the bedside table. He saw the empty glass and remembered. The previous day had been a long one and he'd sat down at home for some of his favourite Laphroaig single malt whisky. One glass had turned to two or three and he'd gone to bed with one more.

He didn't know whether it was the whisky or something else that sparked it off, but he'd had one of those recurring nightmares he thought he'd shrugged off for good. Watching as Jimmy Calder stabbed his mother to death. Calder looking at him with a mix of horror and rage. Chasing twelve-year-old Fleming down the street shouting for him to come back. Fear and adrenaline pumping through Fleming's body. Then the car, headlights, the shock of the impact, and darkness.

Fleming had agreed to counselling over the years and had recently put the memory behind him, or so he'd thought. He no longer went for the sessions. Didn't feel he needed them anymore. He groaned, pulled himself out of bed, showered and shaved. Breakfast was three cups of black coffee and a piece of toast.

Before driving in to the office, Fleming decided to call into a shop to get some food and a newspaper. Logan and Anderson had completed all the interviews of staff still working at the AWE. They had to tidy things up before coming back to Long Hanborough to start work on tracking down all those who had left the company since Stroud's murder. Fleming had arranged to meet them there for an update meeting at noon so he had plenty of time. He'd updated Younger yesterday on his conversation with Dan Rimmer over the Zoe Dunbar article so there was no need to see him today.

Logan and Anderson were already at their desks when Fleming arrived, realising he'd left his mobile phone at home. Anderson screwed up a piece of paper and threw it at Logan. Logan ducked and laughed. 'Just in time, boss. Anderson here has nothing better to do. Got anything useful to keep her occupied?'

Anderson looked a bit sheepish. 'He asked for a coffee and then had the nerve to complain because there wasn't enough sugar in it. Bloody cheek.'

'Your language is getting worse, Naomi,' Logan quipped.

'Learning the ropes from an old master. The emphasis being on old.'

Fleming interrupted the verbal sparring before Logan could respond, as he was sure to do. 'Anything new?'

'Not a lot, boss. Super says she wants to see you. She didn't look particularly happy, I have to say.'

That's all I need, Fleming thought. 'Okay, I'll nip along and see her first.' He paused, looking at Naomi. 'Dare I ask for a coffee when I get back?'

'For you, sir, not a problem.'

'And another for me – with plenty of sugar this time,' Logan joked.

Fleming could see Anderson screwing up another piece of

paper as he turned to head for Temple's office at the far end of the open-plan area. Her door was ajar, but he knocked anyway out of courtesy.

'Come in, Alex,' she said, the tone more formal than friendly. She'd done well to get to superintendent despite prejudice from certain quarters. Fleming suspected most of it came from Younger. She was in her forties and could go further up the ladder, assuming no more blocking by Younger. She was an attractive woman. Slim. The light olive-brown complexion and shoulder-length black hair perhaps suggesting eastern roots. Temple was wearing her customary white shirt and black suit. She didn't get up from behind her desk. Something told Fleming this was definitely going to be formal.

'Logan said you wanted to see me, ma'am.'

Temple didn't invite Fleming to sit. She took off her rimless reading glasses and placed them carefully on her desk. 'Yes, I do. Has your memory started to fade, Alex?'

Fleming was confused. 'Ma'am?'

'Do you recall me saying I wanted to know in advance whatever you were going to feed back to Eathan Younger?'

'Yes, I remember,' Fleming said, suddenly realising he had unintentionally left her out of the loop.

'Did he tell you to bypass me?' Temple demanded.

'No, ma'am, he did not. I–'

'So how come I find out you went to see him yesterday without telling me?' Temple cut in.

Fleming had been tired and forgot to tell Temple. 'I'm sorry, ma'am. It wasn't intentional. I'd had a long day and it slipped my mind.'

Temple then picked up a newspaper and waved it at Fleming. It was the Dunbar article. 'And how come you didn't tell me about this?'

'I didn't know about it either until I saw it in the papers.'

'What did you see Younger about?'

Fleming drew a deep breath. 'It was the article. I don't know why, but he told me to go and see the reporter to find out how she came across the story.'

'And?'

'She got the photographs from a private investigator called Dan Rimmer.'

'And you spoke to him as well?'

'Yes.'

'And that's what you reported back to Younger?'

'Yes.'

'And what did this Rimmer have to say?' Temple pressed.

'He had someone under surveillance for a client who thought his wife was having an affair with Kauffman and he happened to come across that,' Fleming said, pointing to the newspaper.

'Has it crossed your mind MI5 might have asked Younger to get you to delve into this?'

'It did cross my mind.' Fleming hesitated. 'Zoe Dunbar picked up an interest in the Stroud case after an interview with Younger and she seems to think MI5 might have a reason to be interested in this.'

'Really?'

'She asked me if they'd been in touch with us.'

'Please don't tell me they have and you hadn't bothered to let me know.'

'They haven't contacted me.'

'And Younger?'

Fleming was beginning to wonder himself. 'I don't know. He'd didn't say so.'

'While you're here, is there anything else that's slipped your mind to tell me?'

Fleming realised he'd made an error in not keeping Temple up to date with everything. 'Ma'am, I can assure you I had no intention to keep you out of the loop on developments,' he explained. 'In truth we're not making much progress. I know you're always busy and I didn't want to trouble you with every new piece of information.'

'Very thoughtful of you, Alex,' Temple said sarcastically, 'but from here on I want to know everything, understood?'

'Yes, ma'am.'

'So *is* there anything else? I saw the story by the same reporter which claimed you were following up new leads.'

'Not strictly true. I asked her to run the story. I was hoping whoever killed Stroud would panic and make a mistake, or someone who hadn't come forward before might do so.'

'I thought Croft was the prime suspect.'

Fleming thought before answering, realising this could upset Temple even more. 'We could have someone else.'

'What! For fuck's sake, Alex. Why do you always have a habit of springing surprises on me?' Temple breathed deeply. 'So who is this other suspect?'

'Kauffman's wife was having an affair with Stroud. Possible motive there, but no more.'

'Does Younger know this?'

Fleming realised he'd told Younger about Rimmer and the Kauffman photographs. He'd told him Stroud was having an affair with the wife of someone who worked at the AWE, but he hadn't yet told him he'd found out who.

'He knows Stroud was having a fling, but he doesn't know who with,' Fleming admitted.

Temple smiled for once. 'So you omitted to keep him fully informed as well?'

'Haven't got round to it.' Fleming wondered for a second

whether to tell Temple about Rimmer and his mystery client, Liam Doherty. He dismissed the idea. It didn't seem to have any direct bearing on the Stroud case. Rimmer's client was interested in Croft over a personal matter.

'All right, Alex. Just make sure you keep me in the loop from now. Do I make myself clear?'

'Yes, ma'am.'

Fleming walked back to Logan and Anderson. 'Any chance of a coffee, Naomi,' he asked. He sat chatting with Logan for a while until Anderson returned with the drinks.

'Six sugars in yours, Sarge,' Anderson joked. 'Trying to sweeten you up,' she added with a smile.

'Guess who's going to have to fill in all the overtime forms?' Logan retorted.

Fleming sipped on his coffee and made for his office. He opened the door and noticed the message light flashing on his telephone stand. Taking another sip from his mug, he pressed play. He listened intently for a few seconds then rushed out to Logan and Anderson who were still engaged in frivolous banter.

'Message from Yvette Boudreaux,' he gasped. 'Croft turned up without warning at the care home just over two hours ago.'

Anderson's eyes shot open.

'Bloody hell!' Logan exclaimed.

'Get on to Wycombe police and tell them to get a car round to the care home to pick him up – now! And put out an all-points bulletin in the Wycombe area.'

'On it, boss.' Logan reached for the phone.

'And in case they miss him, start checking for flights in from Australia. See if you can trace where he went to stay after landing – most likely in High Wycombe.'

Logan nodded, then punched numbers into the handset.

Fleming looked at Anderson. 'Best check for flights out to Australia. See if you can find if he's booked a return.'

Fleming cursed himself for forgetting his mobile and not coming into the office sooner. *Temple and Younger will go mad if we lose him.*

45

Constables Gale and Zaahid were on routine car patrol in High Wycombe when their radio crackled and burst into life at forty minutes past twelve. 'APB out on a Garry Croft. Wanted for questioning in relation to an old murder enquiry. Last seen at the Ridgeway Manor Care Home at ten hundred hours this morning. White male, fifties, no other description available,' the voice said.

Zaahid hit a button and the siren wailed into life. The car turned sharply and sped off in the direction of the care home with blue lights flashing. Traffic was heavy and Gale steered his way past cars which had pulled over, and others that had not. The car eased carefully through three sets of red lights, on through the town centre and into the outskirts of Wycombe.

Ten minutes later the patrol car was nearing the care home. Zaahid cut the siren, but left the blues on. The car swerved onto the gravel driveway and crunched to a halt outside the entrance. Gale and Zaahid jumped out and walked briskly into the home.

Makena Kibet appeared carrying an empty tray. She looked in alarm at the two policemen. 'Can I help you?' she asked nervously.

'Is there a Mr Garry Croft here?' Gale asked.

Makena frowned. 'He... he was. He left a short while ago.'

'What time?' Zaahid asked.

'I'm not sure. I'll take you along to see Mrs Boudreaux, she's the manager. I think Mr Croft went to see her after he'd seen his mother.'

'Can we see his mother please? We need to ask her if she knows where her son was going next.' It was Gale who spoke this time.

'I'm afraid Mrs Croft is terminally ill. She's barely conscious and isn't really aware of what's going on around her. She doesn't even know where her son lives.'

'We'd better speak to the manager then,' Gale said.

Yvette Boudreaux looked up from her desk when Makena showed the two uniformed officers in. 'Ah, you got the message?'

Gale looked confused. 'Message?'

'Yes, DCI Fleming asked me to let him know straight away if Mr Croft turned up here.'

'DCI Fleming?' Gale raised an enquiring eyebrow.

'I left a message for him shortly after Mr Croft arrived,' Boudreaux explained.

Gale realised what had happened. DCI Fleming, whoever he was, must have phoned Wycombe police who put out the APB. 'What time did Mr Croft leave?'

'It would be just before lunchtime.'

'Being what time exactly?' Gale prompted gently.

'Oh, sorry. A few minutes before twelve.'

'Your colleague thought Mrs Croft wouldn't be able to tell us where her son might be.' Gale had taken the lead.

'No... no she definitely wouldn't,' Boudreaux confirmed. 'She's not with it at all.'

'Have you got an address for Mr Croft.'

'I'm afraid not. I know he lives in Australia now, but he's

never left any contact details with us.'

'Isn't that a bit strange, due to his mother being here?' Zaahid asked.

'Yes, it is. I suppose there must be some reason why he's so secretive over his whereabouts.'

Gale looked at Zaahid who shook his head.

No, probably not necessary to tell her why they were looking for Croft, Gale thought.

'Do you know where he's staying while he's back here in England?' Gale asked, knowing what the answer was likely to be.

'No. I asked him, but he said he had to go and left quite suddenly saying he would call me.'

Gale grimaced. 'And he didn't say or let on where he might be going next?'

Boudreaux sighed. 'No. I'm not being very helpful, am I?'

'Don't worry. You can't tell us what you don't know.' Gale got out a notebook. 'But what you can do is describe him – what he was wearing.'

Boudreaux thought for a moment. 'Tall, maybe not quite six feet, stocky build. His hair style was... interesting. The sides of his head were shaved, and he had a strip of spiky dark hair on top. Oh, and he had a goatee beard.'

Gale had scribbled some notes. 'What was he wearing?'

'Blue jeans and a red polo shirt.'

Gale snapped shut his notebook. 'Thank you, Mrs Boudreaux. You've been most helpful.'

The two officers left and climbed back into the patrol car. 'What do you think?' Zaahid asked.

Gale gunned the engine. 'Get the blues and twos on. We're about an hour behind Croft. Let's head for the town centre and see if we spot him. Maybe try the station first.'

They arrived in the town centre and on to the station, but there was no sign of Croft.

46

Logan was driving Fleming to the care home from Long Hanborough. Oxford was on the way, so they called in to Fleming's flat to pick up his mobile phone. There were two messages on it. One at ten fifteen from Yvette Boudreaux, the other at twelve thirty from Rimmer. He'd left a message to say he'd put a red card in his window after getting a call from Yvette Boudreaux and that Doherty rang him about an hour later to tell him he was on his way to the home.

Anderson had stayed at Long Hanborough to liaise with the police in High Wycombe. Shortly after Fleming and Logan had gone, she phoned Fleming to say the uniforms had missed Croft by about an hour at the care home. They'd then rushed off to see if they could find Croft after questioning Boudreaux.

It took Fleming and Logan fifty minutes to get to the home. Yvette Boudreaux was in her office, looking bemused over what was taking place. Garry Croft turning up out of the blue after saying he couldn't get there. A phone call from someone who was after Croft because Croft owed him some money. Then uniformed police arriving, and now Fleming. Boudreaux had never known such drama.

Fleming introduced Logan who had taken out his notebook. 'What time did Croft arrive here?' Fleming asked.

'Must have been about ten this morning. I spoke to him briefly before taking him to see his mother. I then came back here to ring you, about fifteen minutes later. There was no answer on your office phone so I left a message, and another one on your mobile.'

Fleming squirmed at the thought he could have got the message quicker if he'd gone to Long Hanborough earlier and hadn't forgotten to pick up his mobile phone from home. 'What did you speak to Croft about?'

'I explained to him how unwell his mother was and that the doctor had said it was just a question of time. He asked if she was conscious and I told him that, even if she wasn't fully conscious, she might still realise he was there.'

'Anything else?'

'I was a bit shocked really. He showed no sign of emotion. All he seemed interested in was his mother's personal papers – her will and bank account details. He asked if the will was here.'

'Is it?' Fleming asked.

'No, it's with her solicitor.'

Logan was busy making notes.

'Did he say where he was staying while he was here?' Fleming asked.

'No. I did ask how I could get in touch with him, but he said he would call me and left straight away.'

Logan tapped his notebook with his pencil. 'Did he say how long he was in England for?'

'No. He came to see me after he'd been with his mother for a while. All he wanted was to pick up his mother's bank account and solicitor's details. He didn't say how long he was staying.'

Fleming scratched his head. 'What time did Croft leave?'

'A few minutes before twelve, but I think he waited outside for a taxi for a while.'

'And what time did the police arrive?' Fleming asked.

'About forty-five minutes later.'

Fleming cursed inwardly. *Forty-five bloody minutes!* 'Did they leave straight away?'

'No, they stayed for a while asking some questions. They wanted to know what he looked like and what he was wearing.'

Logan stopped scribbling in his notebook for a second. 'When did they leave?'

'About quarter past one I guess,' Boudreaux said.

'So by the time they'd gone they would be about an hour and a quarter behind Croft,' Logan pointed out, looking at Fleming.

I don't need reminding, Fleming thought. His mobile indicated an incoming call: *Anderson.* 'Hi Naomi, any news?'

'Not good, sir. The uniforms haven't found Croft.'

Fleming sighed. 'Great.'

'This is not going well, is it?' Logan said.

'Bloody nightmare,' Fleming confirmed.

'There was something else,' Boudreaux offered.

'Go on,' Fleming said.

'About an hour after I left a message for you, a man rang me. He told me his name was Liam Doherty.'

Fleming raised an eyebrow. 'Did you phone Dan Rimmer to let him know Croft was here?'

'Yes, I promised I would,' Boudreaux confirmed.

'What time?'

'Right after I'd sent a message to you.'

Logan looked sharply at Fleming. 'That would give an hour for Rimmer to put his red card in the window to alert Doherty and for Doherty to call. Possible?'

'Could be if this Doherty has a way of keeping a fairly constant eye on Wyatt Investigations office.'

'We don't know where this Doherty lives, but he could have had enough time to get here before Croft left,' Logan observed.

Boudreaux suddenly remembered. 'When I spoke to Mr Rimmer he told me his client could be at the home in forty minutes.'

'So he could have arrived about the time Croft was leaving,' Logan said.

'Did Doherty come in to see you when he arrived?' Fleming asked Boudreaux.

'No. He said something about Mr Croft owing him a lot of money so not to tell him he'd called. I told him I didn't want any trouble. Doherty told me not to worry, he'd catch up with him outside.'

'Think that's why the local uniforms couldn't find Croft. They turned up after Doherty who got to Croft first?' Logan wondered, looking at Fleming.

'This doesn't sound very good, does it?' Boudreaux said. 'You don't think this Doherty chap has done something to Mr Croft, do you?'

'I certainly hope not,' Fleming agreed. 'There're some questions we need to ask Croft, assuming we can find him.'

Fleming thanked Boudreaux for her help before he and Logan let themselves out.

As they were getting back into the car, Fleming wondered how he was going to explain to Temple and Younger how Croft had slipped through his fingers.

47

Seth Emerson was on his fourth bottle of beer when his wife came home. She looked flushed and was a little unsteady on her feet. 'Nice time with your friends?' he asked.

'Yes, lovely.' Gwen pulled off her coat and kicked her shoes across the floor on her way to the kitchen. She came back with a large glass of white wine and slumped down on the settee beside her husband's chair.

'Where did you go?' Seth asked casually, before taking a sip of his beer.

Gwen stretched her legs out full length on the settee. 'The local.'

'Who was with you?'

'Oh, there were only three of us.'

'See anyone else we know?'

'No. It was fairly quiet.'

'I think a couple of my mates were going to the pub tonight,' Seth lied. 'I'll have to ask them how you were behaving. Bet you were all a bit giggly.' He noticed Gwen stiffen.

'They would probably be in the bar. We were in the back lounge,' she said unconvincingly. 'They won't have seen us.'

'Ah, right.' Seth looked closely at the label on his bottle as though deep in thought. He took another sip of his beer. 'One of them the same friend you went to London with?'

'You're very inquisitive tonight, Seth. You don't normally show any interest in who my friends are or what I'm doing.'

Seth downed the last of his beer. 'Just making conversation.' He pushed himself up from his chair. 'Think I might have another of these.' He looked at Gwen's near empty glass. 'Top-up?'

'Don't mind if I do.'

Seth disappeared into the kitchen to get the drinks. *Let's make her squirm a bit more before I hit her with the proof.*

'You're usually very quiet these days,' Gwen said as Seth returned with the drinks. 'You never want to speak to me.'

Seth took a swig out of his fifth bottle of beer. 'Maybe I want to now.'

'Bloody drink talking,' Gwen spat out.

'So what did you and your friends talk about at the pub tonight?'

Gwen frowned. 'I've never known you to ask so many questions. Are you okay?'

'Fine,' Seth lied, and took another large gulp from the bottle. 'So, go on then, tell me what you gossip about when you see your friends.'

'Bloody hell, Seth. What's the matter with you?'

'Why won't you tell me?'

'This and that. The strike, what we've watched on TV, putting the world to rights. For fuck's sake! What's got into you?' Gwen took a large gulp of her wine, spilling some down her front.

'What about your London trip. Buy any nice clothes?'

'As it happens, I didn't.'

'What show did you see?'

'We didn't. Went to a pub instead.'

'What was your hotel like? Nice?'

'Give it a rest. Why all these questions all of a sudden?'

'Just curious. You always say I don't take any interest in you these days, so I'm trying to be a good attentive husband.'

'Humph, that'll be the day.'

'You're not happy with our marriage, are you?' Seth suddenly blurted out.

Gwen pulled her legs off the settee. 'I'm tired. Think I'll go to bed.'

'You want to avoid an awkward conversation, don't you?'

Gwen stared at the floor, cheeks beginning to burn. 'I'm not,' she whispered. 'You've had too much to drink. I'm going to bed.'

'You know the other day when a message came in on your phone? The one from Bill Kauffman?'

'What about it?'

'Why was he sending you a message?'

'For fuck's sake! I told you! He'd sent it to the wrong person.'

'Why did you delete it straight away?' Seth pressed.

'Why would I keep a message that wasn't meant for me, you idiot?'

'Maybe it was.'

Gwen glared at her husband. 'What are you saying? Come on, spit it out.'

Seth thumped his bottle down onto the coffee table. 'I've seen the way he looks at you. You think I'm a fool? I know what's going on.'

Gwen jumped to her feet, spilling wine on the settee. 'Is that why you had the spat with him on the picket line? You're jealous. You think he's got a crush on me and you're jealous.'

'Look me in the eye and tell me there's nothing going on between you.'

'There isn't,' Gwen lied.

'You're not going out with girlfriends, are you? It's him, Kauffman. You're seeing him.'

Gwen's face had reddened. 'You're crazy! What makes you think that?'

Seth got to his feet and glared at Gwen. He waved his bottle in front of her, swaying unsteadily on his feet. 'I hired a private investigator, you know.'

'You what!'

'You heard. He followed you. Oh yes, you went to London, but not with who you said you were.'

'You're making this up!' Gwen screamed, beginning to panic.

Seth was in full flow. 'He saw you meeting Kauffman at the station, all lovey-dovey and he took photos. Want to see them?'

'You bastard!' Gwen shouted and burst into tears.

'Followed you both up to your cosy little hotel hand in hand.'

'Enough!'

'Oh no it isn't. You checked in as Mr and Mrs Kauffman. I've got more photos of you having breakfast together.'

'Okay, so I am having an affair with Bill.'

Seth waved the bottle at Gwen again. 'Ah! It's Bill now.'

'You know what?' Gwen said. 'You're a selfish prick! I've had enough of you. Our marriage was dead ages ago.'

'Rich coming from you. Letting me provide for you, paying all the bills while you go off cavorting with Bill fucking Kauffman.'

'Don't speak about him like that!' Tears flowed down Gwen's face, staining her cheeks with black mascara.

Seth reached under the cushion on his chair and pulled out a brown envelope. He took out the photos and flung them in Gwen's face. 'There you are. Evidence of your infidelity.'

Gwen glared at Seth and tossed the rest of her wine in his face.

Seth raised his bottle above his head and threw it at the glass cabinet in the corner. The panes shattered and fell to the floor, sending shards of glass across the room. 'You know what you can do, don't you? You can pack your fucking bags and get out of here. Go off to your precious Kauffman!'

Gwen stared at her husband through narrowed eyes for a second, then kicked the coffee table over and ran out of the room.

'Don't take too long packing!' Seth shouted after her. He looked at the glass littering the floor, but decided cleaning it up could wait. Right now, he needed another drink.

Seth knocked the top off the bottle and remembered joking with Rimmer about killing Kauffman. *Wouldn't blame you if you did*, Rimmer had said.

48

'Might as well get back to Long Hanborough,' Fleming suggested to Logan. 'Leave it to the uniforms to keep looking for Croft. You can drive,' he said, climbing into the passenger seat.

They drove in silence for a while. Fleming was deep in thought, cursing the fact he'd missed the calls from Boudreaux, and that the local police had failed to catch Croft at the care home by less than sixty minutes.

'Penny for them,' Logan eventually said.

Fleming stretched his legs and looked out the side window at the countryside flashing by. Logan was putting his foot down on the M40. They needed to get back to base as soon as possible to start work on trying to trace Croft's movements from when he arrived at Heathrow, assuming that's where he landed. 'Just cursing we didn't get Croft. If I hadn't left my mobile at home, or had gone to the office sooner...'

'No good blaming yourself, boss. Bloody bad luck, that's all.'

'Not so sure Temple and Younger will see it like that.'

Logan grimaced. 'I must admit I don't envy you having to tell them. They're not the most sympathetic people. Especially

Eathan Younger,' he added after a few seconds. 'Wouldn't want to cross swords with him. Bit of a buck-passer I hear.'

Fleming had no doubt in his mind where the buck was going to stop if they didn't find Croft. 'So I gather.'

'Changing the subject, what do you make of this business about Doherty phoning Boudreaux?'

'Fits in with the fact Boudreaux had promised to call Rimmer if Croft turned up and that he would have put a red card in his window to alert Doherty.'

'Hmm. You think it's plausible Doherty could have been in touch with Rimmer within an hour?' Logan queried. 'Which he would have to have done to ring Boudreaux about sixty minutes after she left the message for Rimmer,' he added.

Fleming scratched his chin. 'You have a point there, Harry. The only explanation is Doherty had someone opposite or nearby who could keep a constant eye on Rimmer's office.' Fleming hit his forehead with the palm of his hand. 'Speaking of which, we should have done this before.'

'What?'

'We need to get all the addresses within sight of Wyatt Investigations office checked out for anyone who knows or has seen this Doherty. Something we can get Reading CID to do.'

'What about the timing?' Logan asked. 'If Boudreaux rang Rimmer around ten fifteen, Doherty must have called Boudreaux around quarter past eleven. She reckons Rimmer told her Doherty could be at the home in forty minutes. So Doherty could have arrived there as Croft was leaving.'

'Or maybe just before he left. Don't forget, Yvette Boudreaux said Croft may have waited outside for a taxi.'

'What do you think might have happened if Doherty did get there in time to catch up with Croft, because the uniforms couldn't find him?'

'Anybody's guess,' Fleming said.

'I'm not sure I want to guess.'

Fleming cast a sideways glance at Logan. 'I hope we don't end up finding a body.'

It wasn't long before they arrived back at Long Hanborough. Fleming left Logan to catch up with Anderson while he went to see Temple. As Fleming had expected, she was not impressed.

'You're going to see Younger to tell him this I take it?' Temple asked.

'Yes.'

'Then best of luck. But don't be surprised if he takes you off the case and blames everything on you. That's what he does.'

'Thanks, ma'am.' Fleming smiled. 'I'll let you know if I'm still around to take on something else.'

'I wouldn't joke about it if I were you. I told you to tread carefully around him. He's treacherous.'

'Could be that bad, eh?'

Temple nodded confirmation.

'Okay, well I'd better get it over with.'

Fleming left and found Younger on the phone when he knocked on his open door. Younger waved Fleming in with his free hand and ended the call. 'That was the chief constable wanting to know how things are going.' Younger smiled weakly and the corner of his mouth twitched. 'So I hope you bring good news for a change, Fleming.'

Fleming's wasn't relishing what he had to say. 'Good and bad, sir.'

'I don't like the sound of the latter. You'd better tell me the good bit first.'

'The good news is Croft has arrived back in England. He came back to see his terminally ill mother in a care home in High Wycombe.'

Younger leaned forward and gripped the side of his desk. 'You've got him?'

'No, sir.'

Younger glared hard at Fleming. 'Is that the bad news?'

'Afraid so, sir.'

'You'd better tell me how you failed to get him.'

'He'd left the home before the local police got there.'

'Because they were too slow?'

Fleming paused. 'It wasn't their fault.'

'Then whose?'

'I'd asked the care home manager to let me know if Croft arranged to come back to see his mother. She phoned me to say Croft had rung her to ask how his mother was. She'd told him she was critically ill, but he said he couldn't get back to England.'

'Christ, man, get to the point! So how come he ended up there?'

'She tried ringing me this morning and left a message to say Croft had turned up unexpectedly.'

'It wouldn't have taken more than a few minutes for the uniforms to get there. Croft couldn't have stayed long if they missed him.'

There was no point in delaying the truth any longer. 'I didn't get the message until too late.'

'Is that so?' Younger asked with a degree of sarcasm.

'The message was on my phone in the office, but I didn't get in until lunchtime.'

'Why not?'

'Logan and Anderson were finalising things at the AWE before coming back here and I'd arranged to meet them at twelve.'

'So why weren't you here before then?'

Fleming thought of saying he'd had to go into Oxford, but realised Younger would ask what for. Might as well say it as it was, he decided. 'I went to get some shopping.'

Younger looked incredulously at Fleming and his right eyelid twitched a bit more than usual. In fact, the whole right cheek looked in spasm. 'Christ! I don't believe it! What were you thinking of?'

Fleming winced. 'I didn't know there was a message.'

'Didn't the care home manager try to get you on your mobile when you didn't answer the office phone?'

This is beginning to sound like a sacking affair, Fleming thought. 'She did, but I forgot to take it with me.'

Younger slammed a fist down so hard on his desk Fleming thought it would split in half. 'Bloody hell! Give me one good reason why I shouldn't ask for your warrant card and send you home, pending a decision on your future!'

'I do have a bit of progress to report,' Fleming said weakly.

'It had better be good, Fleming. You're on a knife edge.'

'I've found out whose wife Stroud was having the affair with. It was Bill Kauffman's, so he could be a suspect.'

Younger sighed. 'You're in the last chance saloon, Fleming. You can redeem yourself if you find Croft and get this case wrapped up. No more fuck-ups, understand?'

'Perfectly, sir.'

'Then get the hell out of my office before I change my mind.'

Fleming left and took a deep breath before joining Logan and Anderson.

'Ah, boss, we have a result,' Logan said. 'Naomi's discovered which flight Croft came in on. We found him on CCTV going through passport control and baggage reclaim, then getting into a taxi. Naomi tracked the driver down who told her he took Croft to the station in High Wycombe. Croft's booked onto a return flight from Heathrow leaving at eleven thirty tonight.'

Fleming gave a sigh of relief. 'Good work, Naomi. Well done.' *I might just keep my job.*

49

The meetings with Temple and Younger had gone as well as Fleming could have hoped under the circumstances. It wasn't good, but it could have been much worse. Temple had told him not to be surprised if Younger took him off the case and had even questioned whether he would still be here. It had been close. Fleming's only hope was to find Croft and get the Stroud case wrapped up.

Logan and Anderson were at their desks. 'How did it go with Temple and Younger?' Logan asked Fleming.

'They weren't best pleased, for sure. Let's just say it's crucial we don't lose Croft.'

'And if we do? Not that there's any reason now why we shouldn't get him,' Logan quickly added.

'I could end up stacking shelves in a supermarket.'

'No way!' Anderson exclaimed. 'It's surely not that bad, is it? I mean suspects often slip through the fingers of the police. Can't be helped sometimes.'

'True, Naomi, but when lack of diligence is involved it's a different story.'

'I'm not with you, sir,' Anderson said.

'I didn't see the message on my mobile because I left it at home by mistake. Then I went to get some shopping before coming into the office and missed the call about Croft on my landline.'

'But you weren't to know there was a message on it, sir. You could have been out of the office interviewing someone. What difference does it make why you weren't here?'

Fleming was impressed with Anderson's attempt to defend him. 'The difference is that an interview would be official business – shopping is not.'

'Speaking of which,' Logan said, 'did you get more coffee and biscuits, Naomi?'

Anderson rolled her eyes. 'I might have guessed. That your idea of an answer to a crisis?'

'It is a disaster if we run out,' Logan complained.

Anderson shook her head. 'I don't know. Think you've got your priorities all wrong.'

'I believe someone once remarked that first we eat, then we do everything else,' Logan said.

'Sounds like your philosophy,' Anderson countered.

'Maybe we should start thinking about what we should do,' Fleming suggested with a laugh.

Logan ran a hand through his receding grey hair. 'We know Croft is on the half past eleven flight out from Heathrow tonight so check-in will open at half past nine. It's just past half three, so we have plenty of time to alert Heathrow.'

'I'd like to catch Croft before he even gets there,' Fleming said.

'Local uniforms in Wycombe haven't found him yet though,' Anderson reminded Fleming.

'No, but Croft was last seen there. It's unlikely he went

anywhere else because he's due to catch a plane tonight. He may already have left High Wycombe, so we need to alert Aviation Policing Command. If they don't find him before, they'll get him when he checks in.'

'Aviation Policing Command?' Anderson queried.

'It's a specialist operations unit of the Met,' Logan explained. 'They provide security and policing services at Heathrow.'

'We also need to get the Wycombe police to keep an eye on the station, all the taxi ranks in Wycombe and the bus station in case Croft hasn't left there yet.'

'It would be easier if we catch him there,' Logan agreed. 'We could hold him at Wycombe police station for questioning.'

'The problem we have,' Fleming said, 'is that the only evidence we have against Croft is he had a major row with Stroud over something, then fled to Australia after Stroud was murdered.'

'He might confess under close cross-examination,' Logan said hopefully.

'He might,' Fleming agreed, 'but if he doesn't, we'll either have to charge him within twenty-four hours or release him on bail.'

'Chances of getting a conviction on what little we have?' Logan queried.

'Not great,' Fleming admitted. 'We could apply for an extension to hold him in custody for up to thirty-six hours given the seriousness of the offence, but I'm not sure in that time we would get any more evidence.'

'I have to admit, boss, it is pretty flimsy even though Ingham seemed to be convinced Croft was the killer,' Logan said.

'What about the old HR manager, sir?' Anderson asked Fleming.

'Nat Horne? He died, remember, so not a priority. And it was just a thought I had after speaking to Mrs Horne. She reckoned her husband was under a lot of pressure and wouldn't talk about what went on at the AWE. He had a breakdown shortly after Stroud's murder and took early retirement. Could be coincidence, or the signs of a troubled man who had killed someone. Can't think of a motive though.'

'Kauffman?' Logan wondered.

'Again, all we have is that his wife had an affair with Stroud, and Stroud was allegedly one of four men Kauffman called his disciples. They're the only connections we have between Stroud and Kauffman.'

'That we know of,' Logan added.

'About sums it up.' Fleming paused for a moment then smiled. 'Tell you what, why don't I go and get the coffees and biscuits while you two get in touch with Aviation Policing Command and Wycombe police?'

'Then what, boss?' Logan asked.

'We sit and drink coffee, eat biscuits and watch the clock, waiting to hear from Wycombe police or Heathrow.'

~

By seven thirty they had heard nothing from Wycombe police. Nothing from Aviation Policing Command by half past nine.

They sat drinking more coffee and watched the minutes ticking by. Fleming was tapping the desk. Anderson stared at the clock with worried eyes, and Logan walked round the room to stretch his legs.

The time edged closer to eleven and there was no word about Croft.

'Check the flight hasn't been delayed,' Fleming said.

Logan checked and shook his head. 'On time.'

The second hand on the clock seemed to have slowed down, but eleven thirty came with no word about Croft.

'Check with Aviation Policing Command,' Fleming said, 'and confirm the plane took off.'

Five minutes later, Logan slammed the phone down. 'Croft didn't turn up and the plane took off on time.'

Fleming's shoulders drooped. *This is going from bad to worse.*

50

Toby Omoko's shared ownership apartment was a short ten-minute brisk walk from Highams Park. He caught a train from there to Walthamstow Central where he joined the Victoria Line. It was the usual rush-hour chaos of overcrowding and stifling air on the tube.

Commuters pushed their way through doors the driver was trying to close, then had to open once more to allow people to retrieve briefcases and bags jammed between them. Omoko was forced further back into the carriage as each new throng crammed in as though life itself depended on getting this train. No matter another one was right behind. After twenty-three minutes of hell, the train pulled in at Victoria Station.

After more pushing and jostling to get to the escalator, Omoko stood to one side to let impatient commuters run up on his left. Eventually reaching street level where traffic was heavy, he breathed in the polluted air and set off in the direction of Westminster and the Thames House HQ of MI5.

Ten minutes later he was walking up the steps and through to the main reception area. He picked up his pass and keys from the woman behind a screen and walked over to the glass security booths where he pressed his pass on a panel on the side of one of them. The door slid open and Omoko strode along a short corridor with offices on either side. All the doors were closed and there were no signs to say who or what was behind them. Everything in MI5 was on a need-to-know basis.

Omoko's door was locked. No sign of his sick colleague. *I'm sure I'll never see him again,* Omoko thought. He unlocked the door and entered the stuffy office. First job – open the bloody window as far as it would go, but it didn't budge. He hadn't been looking forward to today. In fact, he didn't look ahead to any day. There was a nine thirty meeting with Quentin Vere who wanted an update on the Kauffman photographs.

Omoko had a quick look on his computer for any emails and didn't find anything that couldn't wait. Upstairs, there was a man who definitely didn't like to be kept waiting. Omoko locked his door and made the dreaded climb up to Vere's office on the second floor.

Vere's secretary smiled at Omoko as he approached her desk. 'He's on the phone. You'll have to wait a minute.'

Omoko returned the smile. 'In a better mood today?' he asked hopefully, nodding towards Vere's door.

The secretary shrugged. 'Bit hard to tell. He's his usual arrogant self.'

'Right. Better brace myself then,' Omoko said.

The secretary's phone buzzed and Omoko cringed.

She put the phone down. 'He'll see you now. Good luck.'

Omoko knocked and entered.

Vere was sitting at his desk with a closed file in front of him. 'Come in, Omoko. What do you have for me?'

Omoko noticed the red confidential stamp on the top corner of the file with Kauffman's name in the middle as he approached Vere's desk. 'Eathan Younger rang me to say DCI Fleming had been to see the reporter, Zoe Dunbar.'

'And?'

'It would appear she got the photographs from a private investigator–'

'Name?' Vere cut in.

'Chap called Dan Rimmer. He works for his uncle at Wyatt Investigations.'

'Is that so?' Vere said thoughtfully. 'And how did he come by them?'

'Fleming went to ask him. It turns out he had a woman under surveillance for a client who believed his wife was having an affair with Kauffman. He saw Kauffman on his own in Lond–'

'I can tell from the bloody photos it was in London!' Vere cut in once again. 'When are you going to start telling me what I can't work out for myself, for God's sake!'

'Sorry, sir, I was going to add he saw him receiving a package.'

'All right. We're sure this Rimmer chap was really following the woman and not Kauffman for some reason?'

'Quite sure. Kauffman and the woman had checked into a hotel and Kauffman came out on his own shortly after. Rimmer followed him out of curiosity and he saw a package being handed over.'

'And everyone is assuming the envelope contained cash?'

'Nobody has actually said so. Zoe Dunbar wrote the article in a way which questioned what Kauffman was doing in London receiving a package from a man who then went into a Russian Trade Delegation seminar.'

'The inference being he was being paid by the Russians to disrupt work at the AWE?' Vere guessed.

'I think that's about it, sir. Only...'

'Only what, Omoko? It's perfectly clear the man's in the pocket of the Russians.'

Omoko wasn't sure how Vere would react to what he was

about to say next. 'The management at the AWE tackled Kauffman about the photos. He claimed it wasn't him in the photographs and that they were fakes. Reckoned someone was trying to discredit him and undermine the strike.'

'Rubbish!'

'I'm only telling you what we know, sir.'

Vere picked up the file and stabbed a finger at Kauffman's name. 'This bloody man is a militant socialist working for the Russians. You mark my words. The only thing that's fake is his explanation of events!'

'Yes, sir. But it is a fact that experts can fake photographs. Happens all the time apparently.'

Vere thumped a fist down on his desk. 'Listen, Omoko, I don't want to hear anymore of you trying to defend Kauffman. Is that clear?'

'I'm not defending him. Just pointing out we can neither prove nor disprove the photos are genuine.'

'Well, get the bloody things forensically examined by experts. They'll soon tell us if they're fakes or not.'

'Yes, sir.'

'What about the surveillance on Kauffman. I take it you did manage to arrange that?'

'I did, but to date there's no more evidence to suggest Kauffman is up to anything illegal.'

'Bank account?'

'Likewise.'

'Phone tap?'

'Nothing so far.'

Vere sighed, got up from his chair and put his hands on his ample hips. 'What about the Russian? Have you managed to trace him?'

'We don't know for sure he is Russian.'

'For fuck's sake, Omoko, are you serious!'

Omoko glared at Vere and his face reddened. 'I haven't been able to identify him yet. That's why I'm saying we don't know for certain he is Russian.'

'Then get the hell out of my office and find out who he is!' Vere ranted.

51

It was early morning on a warm day in September when Uri Zabair set off from home in his car with his Labrador, Bella. He drove a few miles along the minor road which wound its way through dense woodland to where he knew there was a place he could pull off the road and park.

Bella loved these woods as Zabair himself did. He'd been coming here regularly most days to walk the dog. He opened the boot and Bella jumped out, tail wagging furiously. Zabair set off along a narrow path with Bella running ahead. They hadn't gone far when a squirrel suddenly appeared and ran across in front of them. Bella stopped and stared, then bounded off after it into the undergrowth.

Zabair whistled, but Bella didn't come back.

'Bella!' Zabair called out, but still the dog didn't return. Odd. Bella usually came running back when he shouted for her. Then he heard her barking. He headed in the direction the noise was coming from and finally saw her, standing at the top of a small gully.

'Bella, what are you doing?' Zabair said as he approached. 'Come here!'

The dog ignored him and carried on barking.

Zabair reached the edge of the gully and was about to pull Bella away when he saw what had caught her attention. It was the body of a man lying at the bottom of the ditch. There was a neat bullet hole in the centre of the man's forehead and two lifeless eyes stared up at the sky.

'Oh my God!' Zabair exclaimed, retching and reaching for his mobile at the same time.

~

Liz Temple took the call from the local police in Marlow a little after ten thirty in the morning. She listened intently before speaking. 'Okay, I'll get someone over there straight away.'

Temple put the phone down thoughtfully. Fleming happened to be the on-call SIO, but Temple knew Younger would go mad if she asked Fleming to attend the scene. But procedures were what they were, and they dictated she sent the on-call SIO to the scene. *To hell with Younger.* Temple got up from her desk to go and look for Fleming.

She found him with Logan and Anderson in the small incident room they'd been using. 'I've just had a call from Marlow police,' Temple said, looking at Fleming. 'A man discovered a body in woods nearby. You'd better get over there now.'

Something told Fleming he knew who it was. Marlow was near High Wycombe and the local uniforms hadn't found Croft. Neither had he turned up at Heathrow to check in for his flight. It had to be too much of a coincidence.

Ten minutes later Fleming and Logan were on their way.

It took a little over an hour to reach the crime scene. Logan parked the car in the same place Uri Zabair had left his earlier. The entrance to the pathway leading into the woods was blocked off with blue and white tape and a uniformed constable stood guard to ensure no unauthorised people entered.

Fleming and Logan opened the boot of their car and donned the scene-of-crime kit of latex gloves, overalls and plastic shoes. Fleming nodded at the constable and showed his warrant card. 'DCI Fleming and DS Logan from the major crime unit.'

'Follow the path,' the constable said. 'It's not far.'

The two detectives ducked under the tape and set off until they reached the inner cordon about twenty yards away from the gully. The scene of crime team had erected a tent over the body to preserve the immediate area in case of rain. SOCOs in white overalls were at work, taking photographs and searching the surrounding area for any forensic evidence.

Fleming showed his warrant card again and a uniformed constable let them under the tape. The forensic pathologist, Dr Nathan Kumar, was talking to another man at the top of the gully.

'Ah, you must be DCI Fleming and DS Logan,' the other man said as Fleming and Logan approached. 'I'm DI Bent, local CID and this is–'

'Dr Nathan Kumar,' Fleming cut in to finish the sentence for him. 'Hello, Nathan, we meet again. How are things?'

'Busy as always, Alex,' Kumar said.

'You two obviously know each other,' Bent said.

'We have a habit of turning up at the same crime scene,' Fleming replied. He pointed down into the gully and looked at Bent. 'You've had a look?'

'Yes,' Bent confirmed. 'Only from a distance.' He looked at Kumar. 'We haven't touched the body. We were waiting for you.'

Fleming nodded. 'Okay, let's have a look, shall we?'

They all scrambled their way down and entered the tent. The body lay on its back and the cold unseeing eyes stared up at them.

'Who found the body?' Fleming asked Bent.

'Man by the name of Uri Zabair. Usual thing. He was walking his dog and it found the body.'

'Better get fingerprints and DNA from him as he's already contaminated the scene. We need to separate his details from any DNA the killer may have left on or near the body.'

'It's been arranged,' Bent confirmed. 'Mr Zabair was a bit shaken up, but he managed to give me a statement.'

'Send it over to me at Long Hanborough,' Fleming said. 'What time did he find him?'

Bent looked at his notebook. 'He called in at nine thirty this morning.'

Fleming crouched down and searched the man's pockets. He pulled out a passport, flicked it open and looked up at Logan. 'Had a feeling it might be him.'

'Garry Croft?' Logan guessed.

'Unless someone's planted a passport in his pocket, it's him,' Fleming confirmed.

Bent was scratching his head. 'How come you knew who it was?'

'Working on a cold case – a murder that took place about five years ago and Croft happened to be the main suspect. We were looking for him. He was last seen in High Wycombe yesterday and was booked on the flight to Australia last night, but didn't check in.'

Bent nodded his understanding and pointed to a clump of bushes. 'That explains the small bag found over there.'

'Has it been moved?'

'No, left it there for the SOCOs to examine.'

'Okay.' Fleming turned to Kumar. 'You can do your stuff now, Nathan.'

Logan had climbed back to the top of the gully looking pensive.

Fleming joined him. 'What are you thinking, Harry?'

'First thing – what was he doing here with his bag? Doesn't make sense, which means someone brought him here. The question is whether he was killed somewhere else and dumped down there,' Logan said, pointing down to where the body was, 'or whether he was shot here.'

'My guess would be the latter. It would be difficult to shoot a man in broad daylight in High Wycombe, if that's where Croft was at the time.'

'I think you might be right, boss,' Logan agreed.

'And the next thing?' Fleming prompted.

'Dan Rimmer's mystery client, Liam Doherty, had been looking for Croft for about five years and rang the care home while Croft was there. He told Yvette Boudreaux he would catch Croft outside. Maybe he did, brought him here and shot him.'

'What about the money Doherty was supposedly owed by Croft?'

'Killed him because Croft didn't have it and he'd wasted five years of his life trying to find him?' Logan offered.

Fleming thought for a moment. 'There is another possibility.'

'There is?'

'Kauffman's ex-wife reckoned Kauffman called Stroud and Croft his disciples. What if someone had a reason to kill the disciples, kills Stroud, and Croft flees to Australia fearing for his life, not because he killed Stroud.'

Logan whistled. 'You mean this Liam Doherty?'

'Yes. The story he gave Rimmer about being owed some money could have been a ploy and Liam Doherty is probably an alias.'

'If that's the case, we need to look for someone with a connection to Kauffman and his disciples,' Logan mused.

Fleming was about to respond when Kumar appeared out of

the tent. 'All done here. Single bullet wound to the head. There's also heavy bruising, a deep cut and swelling on the back of his head behind his right ear. Looks like his killer hit him with a blunt instrument from behind before shooting him. I'll get the body off to the local mortuary and let you have a detailed report as soon as I've completed a post-mortem.'

'Thanks, Nathan,' Fleming said, turning to leave.

'You were about to say something, boss,' Logan reminded Fleming.

'There were four disciples according to Kauffman's ex-wife. She couldn't remember the names of the other two. If my theory about someone having a reason to kill the disciples holds water, we might be looking at two more murders.'

52

On the way back to Long Hanborough, Fleming remembered he hadn't yet contacted Ursula Nieve to let her know what Zoe Dunbar had told him about the Kauffman photographs. He pulled out his mobile and rang her number.

After a few rings she answered. 'Hello, Ursula Nieve speaking.'

'Hi Ursula, it's DCI Fleming. I promised to let you know what Zoe Dunbar said about her article on Kauffman.'

'Oh, yes.'

'She got the photos from a private investigator called Dan Rimmer, and she's adamant they're genuine. I spoke to Rimmer as well, and he says the same.'

'How did he come by them?'

'It's a long story, but he had someone else under surveillance who happened to be with Kauffman and he went off on his own for a while. Rimmer followed him out of curiosity, and then tailed the man who slipped Kauffman the package.'

'I see. Thank you for letting me know. Very grateful.'

'What will you do about it now?' Fleming asked.

'Talk to the management and let them decide.'

'Right. Sorry it took so long to get back to you – been a bit busy.'

Fleming left Logan and Anderson carrying on with the work tracking down all the staff who had left the AWE after Stroud's murder while he went to see Temple. She'd just come back from Younger's office looking tight-lipped and her eyes were blazing.

'Is this a good time to tell you what we found at the crime scene and let you have a high-level investigative strategy, ma'am?' Fleming asked tentatively.

Temple sighed. 'Not in the best of moods after seeing Younger. I should warn you he's furious because I sent you out to the incident near Marlow. He asked me why I'd sent you and made it clear he expected you to be on the Stroud case full time.'

'Thanks for warning me. I need to go and see him next. It was Garry Croft's body that was found. Shot through the head.'

'Not sure how Younger will take that. On the one hand he'll be happier because the case is relevant to the Stroud enquiry, but on the other he'll not be best pleased you missed Croft and can't now question him.'

'The way things are going, there is a possibility Croft may not have killed Stroud.'

Temple frowned. 'You mean it could have been Kauffman because he found out his wife was having an affair with Stroud?'

'There is that chance, yes, but we still don't have any more evidence, and there's something–'

'Don't tell me you have another little surprise for me? Something else you forgot to mention?'

'I didn't tell you this before because it didn't seem to have any bearing on the Stroud case.'

'Alex! How many times do I have to tell you I wanted to be kept fully informed of what was going on?'

Fleming shifted uncomfortably and knew now he ought to have told Temple about Doherty. 'Dan Rimmer, the private investigator who took the photos of Kauffman, has a client called Liam Doherty who wanted to find Croft over a personal matter.'

'That being?'

'He reckoned Croft owed him a lot of money. Doherty found out Croft was at the care home, phoned to ask if he was still there, and told the manager he'd catch him outside.'

'You think this Doherty could have killed Croft?'

'It's looking like a distinct possibility.'

'So you're pulling him in?'

'It's not so simple. No one has ever met or seen him and there's no way of contacting him.'

'What! How the hell can this Rimmer have a client that he can't contact, for God's sake?'

'He phoned him from a payphone initially to ask Rimmer to find Croft for him. Paid an upfront payment with cash pushed through the letter box.'

'How was Rimmer supposed to get in touch with Doherty if he found Croft?'

'He was to put a red card in the window and if Doherty saw it, he would ring Rimmer.'

'Unbelievable!'

'There's one more thing – Kauffman allegedly called Stroud, Croft, and two other men his disciples. I'm beginning to wonder if this Doherty had a grudge against the disciples, killed Stroud, and Croft fled to Australia thinking he was going to be next. It would explain why Doherty, if that's his real name, wanted to remain anonymous.'

Temple shook her head. 'This is getting out of hand. You said there were four of these disciples. Are you saying you suspect this Doherty may strike two more times?'

'It's possible. There's always a chance he could already have done so.'

'How do you make that out?'

'I've got Logan and Anderson tracking down everyone who left the AWE after Stroud's murder. Some of them could have moved to areas covered by other police forces.'

'Worth getting a check on HOLMES 2 then?'

Fleming had used the Home Office Large Major Enquiry System before when working for the Met. 'I'll get Logan and Anderson to check it out.'

'So what's your immediate strategy, Alex?'

'Get Rimmer in for questioning, step up the search for those who left the company after Stroud's murder, see if we can establish if there's a link to Kauffman and his four disciples, and if there have been similar shootings once we get the post-mortem report. Oh, and check HOLMES 2.'

'Okay, Alex, but do try to keep me informed this time. Do I make myself clear?'

'Perfectly, ma'am.'

Fleming took his leave and made for Younger's office thinking he would have more time for investigating if he didn't have to spend so much time informing.

~

Fleming soon realised Temple had assessed Younger's mood accurately. He was stony-faced and red blotches on his neck contrasted sharply with the white of his shirt collar. His steel-grey eyes glowered at Fleming as he came through the door.

'I hear Temple had you down as the on-call SIO and sent

you out to an incident this morning. Not happy she did that,' Younger announced.

'We are a bit thin on the ground, sir. Work needs to be shared out.'

'Amongst everyone else maybe. But I wanted you to concentrate on the Stroud case only, which I have to say is not exactly progressing as quickly as I would like.'

'As it happens, the call-out this morning is connected to the Stroud enquiry.'

Younger's eyes narrowed. 'How come?'

'A dog walker found a body in woods near Marlow. It was Garry Croft. Shot through the head.'

'What! I don't believe this!'

'The good news is we don't have to find funding to go over to Australia looking for him.'

'Don't get flippant with me, Fleming! If you hadn't left your bloody mobile phone at home and gone shopping, we would have caught him before someone murdered him. Christ! This is turning into a nightmare.'

'Rimmer's client is a man who calls himself Liam Doherty. It's possible he found Croft at the home and could have abducted him.'

'Hang on, how the hell did Doherty find out Croft was there?'

'Through the private investigator, Dan Rimmer, who'd been alerted by the home.'

'Neat timing, wouldn't you say? I mean for all that to happen in what might have been Croft's short visit.'

'I've gone through all the timings and it's feasible.'

'So you think this Doherty abducted Croft in High Wycombe, took him to these woods near Marlow and shot him?'

'It's a line of enquiry I'm following.'

'Was Doherty seen at the care home?'

'No. He phoned the manager to ask if Croft was still there and told her he would meet him outside.'

'Unbelievable! So no one has ever seen Doherty?'

'No, but there could be a good reason why he wants to stay anonymous.'

'Do tell, Fleming. This is becoming a farce.'

'He could be the killer. Kauffman apparently called Stroud and Croft his disciples. It's possible Doherty set out to kill them both for an as yet unknown reason. He kills Stroud and Croft flees to Australia, hence Doherty employing a private investigator to find him.'

'So how do you propose locating this elusive ghost of a man?'

'I'm going to pull Dan Rimmer in for questioning.'

'And?'

'It seems Kauffman had four "disciples". I'm trying to trace everyone who left the AWE after Stroud's murder to see if I can establish who the other two men are. I need to trace them because they might know who Doherty really is.'

'Otherwise?'

'I might know what type of gun was used once I get the post-mortem report and I can run a check to see if there have been any other similar shootings. Then it's down to fingerprints and DNA checked against the database.'

Younger stayed silent for a moment and tapped his fingers on his desk. 'You're running out of time, Fleming, and I'm losing patience. I want the Stroud and Croft cases tied up in the next month.' He stared hard at Fleming. 'That's all.'

53

It was hot in interview room one at Reading police station. It was the same room Fleming and Logan had used to question Kauffman. Three glasses and a large jug of water were on the table next to the digital recorder. Fleming and Logan sat on one side of the table and Rimmer sat opposite.

Logan had switched on the recorder and Fleming had gone through all the usual preliminaries, stating who was present, the date, time and location. He'd cautioned Rimmer on the basis he'd had dealings with a man who was now the prime suspect in the Croft killing, but had stressed he was not under arrest and was free to leave at any time. Rimmer had declined to have a solicitor present saying he had nothing to hide.

Fleming looked across the table at Rimmer who seemed relaxed. 'Help yourself to water,' Fleming said.

'Rarely touch the stuff. Much prefer beer or whisky.'

Fleming smiled. 'Afraid these rooms don't provide such luxuries.'

'Should have done this at my place then. Any reason why not?'

'None at all. Seemed convenient here. Do you know why we asked you to come in?'

'No, I don't.'

'You heard the news this morning or saw the daily papers?'

'I try to avoid listening to the news... it's usually bad.'

Fleming looked for any sign of reaction in Rimmer. 'A body was found in woods near Marlow yesterday. A man was shot through the head.'

Rimmer raised an eyebrow. 'There you are. Bad news.'

'It was Garry Croft.'

Rimmer looked shocked. 'No way!'

'You took a call from Yvette Boudreaux on the morning Croft turned up at the care home.'

'I did, yes.'

'She told you Croft was there.'

'She did.'

'What did you do after she rang you?'

'Had a whisky.'

'I'd prefer if you treated this more seriously, Mr Rimmer,' Fleming said with a note of irritation.

'No, really, I did. After five years he turns up. That was worth a small celebration.'

'Okay, what did you do after you had your whisky?'

'I stuck a red card in the window as soon as I'd poured it.'

'You didn't think you should go up to the care home to catch Croft. He might have gone before Liam Doherty got in touch with you.'

'I did think of it, but I'd had a drink. Unfortunately, my measures were enough to put me over the legal limit for driving.'

Fleming narrowed his eyes. 'So why have a drink instead of dashing off to the care home?'

'All Doherty instructed me to do was let him know when I'd found where Croft was. It wasn't my problem he hadn't given me a phone number. I let him know by putting the red card in the window as he'd asked. I did tell Mrs Boudreaux to get Croft's mobile number and address before he went.'

'Doesn't sound very thorough given you spent five years trying to find Croft for Doherty,' Fleming suggested. 'There was always the chance you would lose him again.'

'True, but as I said, not my problem. If I'd gone racing off to the care home, he might already have left anyway... and, what would I have done when I got there? I don't have powers of arrest.'

Fleming thought Rimmer had a point. He couldn't restrain Croft, and Croft was unlikely to wait around for Doherty to arrive demanding his money. 'You could have followed him.'

'Right, and if I'd left the office, how was I supposed to contact Doherty?'

Another valid point, Fleming thought. 'So you waited for Doherty to get in touch with you?'

'While enjoying my drink, that's exactly what I did.'

'When did Doherty contact you?'

Rimmer scratched his beard. 'I guess about an hour after I put the card in the window.'

'How would Doherty see the card so quickly? Seems unlikely he would just happen to be walking past within sixty minutes of you putting it there?'

Rimmer shrugged. 'I'd always wondered about that and the only thing I can come up with is he used someone nearby who had fairly constant sight of the office window.'

'We got local police to check all the buildings within sight of your office. No one had ever heard of Liam Doherty, and no one admitted to someone asking them to keep an eye on your window for a red card.'

Rimmer sighed. 'Look, this guy has done everything to

remain anonymous. He most likely paid someone to keep quiet – maybe even threatened them if they ever let on.'

'What did you say to him when he rang you?'

'I told him Croft was at the care home.'

'What did he say?'

'He noted the address, said he was on his way there and hung up.'

'You promised to let me know if Doherty contacted you,' Fleming reminded him.

'I did. You weren't picking up so I left a message for you.'

'Doherty is now wanted for questioning in connection with Croft's murder. He'd been looking for him for five years. We have him setting off for the care home, Croft disappearing, then he's found shot dead the next day. Doherty has to be the prime suspect.'

'Bloody hell!' Rimmer exclaimed. 'Why would he kill him though? How was he supposed to get his money back?'

'Croft maybe told him he no longer had it. Could have used it to get to Australia and get himself set up there.'

'Is it worth killing someone for fifty grand?'

'I've known people kill for far less. Speaking of which, you're the only person we know of who's had contact with Doherty. You're a key witness so he may come after you.'

'Nah, I've never seen him so it's hardly likely.'

'You could recognise his voice though,' Fleming suggested.

Rimmer pursed his lips. 'Okay. Thanks for the warning. I'll watch my back.'

'Right, I think we're about done here. One more thing for the record. Where were you for the rest of the day after you took the call from the care home?'

'In the office with my uncle, drinking whisky.'

'Can anyone verify that?'

'My uncle.'

'Anyone else?'

'Afraid not. It was a quiet day.'

'Okay,' Fleming said. 'Interview terminated at eleven thirty am.'

Logan switched off the recorder.

54

Toby Omoko had been busy. He'd been in touch with the force intelligence and specialist operations section in Thames Valley Police. The cousins in MI6 across the river in Vauxhall had been helpful. And MI5's own D and H Branches had provided the final proof that Omoko needed. For once, he felt at ease treading the stairs up to Quentin Vere's office. At last he had something to report.

'Mood today?' Omoko asked Vere's secretary with a degree of trepidation.

'Oh dear, you always seem to catch him at his worst.'

'What's happened now?'

'He's just back from the director general's office. He walked past me without a word – not even the customary demand for coffee, and slammed his door shut so hard my cup rattled in its saucer.'

'Great.' Omoko sighed. 'That's all I need. Wish me luck.'

Omoko took a deep breath and knocked on Vere's door. There was no answer. He knocked again.

'All right! All right! Come in, dammit!'

Omoko braced himself and entered.

Vere was sitting behind his desk glaring at his computer screen. 'Better have something useful for once, Omoko, I'm not in the mood for bad news.'

'A lot has happened in the last couple of days, sir. Got some good news for you.'

'Better be. What is it?'

'The covert financial enquiries unit in H Branch have found two recent large cash deposits into Kauffman's bank account. They are out of the ordinary because there are no other similar deposits over the past twelve months.'

Vere squinted through the thick lenses of his horn-rimmed glasses. 'How much is large?'

'Five thousand pounds each time.'

'Well, why didn't you say so rather than say large, for God's sake?'

Omoko shrugged. 'That was how H Branch described it.'

'What was the timing of these deposits?'

'One just before the one-day strikes started.'

Vere slapped his desk with the palm of his right hand. 'And the second just before the indefinite strike started?'

'Yes, sir.'

'Anything else?'

'Yes. D Branch managed to get a warrant signed by the home secretary to initiate a tap on Kauffman's phone. They've been eavesdropping on recent calls, checking previous ones made, and they've also checked text messages and emails.'

'Did they find anything?'

'Kauffman received a couple of calls from a London payphone to set up meetings. The caller didn't identify himself by name. He did warn Kauffman never to use his landline, mobile or computer to make contact, always to use public payphone boxes.'

'And was one of those calls to arrange the meeting in

Victoria Tower Gardens?' Vere asked.

'It was.'

'What about the specialist operations people? Anything come up from their surveillance of Kauffman?'

Before Omoko could answer, there was a meek knock on Vere's door and his secretary came in with a tray. 'Your morning coffee and biscuits, sir,' she announced. Then, looking nervously at Omoko. 'Can I get you anything?'

Omoko was about to reply, but Vere answered for him. 'He doesn't need anything. He can get his own once we're finished here. Oh, and buzz the DG's secretary. I need to see him in half an hour if he's free. I have some good news for him.'

'Very well, sir,' the secretary said and left the office.

Omoko wondered why Vere's secretary put up with him. Vere was a pompous, arrogant bully. *Begs the question why I tolerate him.*

Vere dunked the corner of a biscuit carefully in his coffee and looked up at Omoko. 'Well?'

'Well, what, sir?'

'The bloody surveillance, man. For God's sake, do keep up.'

'Oh, yes, of course. Not much, but he did meet the same man he met at Victoria Tower Gardens again.'

'And dare I ask – have you managed to trace this man?'

'I checked with MI6. They were helpful, but they had no record of the man, suggesting he might be a low-key diplomat.'

'That's it?'

'No, sir. A clerk in the H Branch registry looked through all their records of Russian diplomats. Took some time, but she eventually found him. He came over from Russia a couple of months earlier to take up post in the embassy.'

'I knew it!' Vere shouted. 'A bloody Russian spy. Didn't I tell you, Omoko?'

'You did, sir. Oh, and I had the Kauffman photos examined

by forensic experts. There's no way they're fakes, they say.'

'Good man!'

Omoko was taken aback by the sudden praise from Vere. *Must be losing his marbles.*

'Right! We now have enough evidence to get Kauffman arrested on the basis he's in the pocket of the Russians who want to use the dispute at the AWE to disrupt the defence work being done there,' Vere concluded.

'There could be more to it.'

Vere took off his glasses and mopped his brow with a handkerchief. 'Oh?'

'What if the idea of an indefinite strike is not only to disrupt the work, but to make safety a real hazard.'

'You mean like a major accident?' Vere asked, eyes wide open.

Omoko nodded. 'You never know. It's possible.' He paused for a second. 'You may also be interested to know that Garry Croft, the man suspected of killing Stroud, has been murdered. Shot through the head.'

'When?'

'Yesterday.'

'All happening quite fast now, Omoko. Let's hand the Kauffman business over to the intelligence and specialist operations guys. Get them to arrest Kauffman and pull him in for questioning.'

When the police turned up at the AWE, Kauffman wasn't there. His union colleagues had been expecting to see him on the picket line, but he hadn't turned up. Ursula Nieve had no idea where he was. Neither was he found at his Reading flat. A warrant was issued for his arrest.

55

An incident room would normally be full of people working on the various strands of a case. But times were not normal and staff were in short supply. That was why only Fleming, Logan and Anderson were working on the Stroud case.

The room they were using was a small meeting room. The three detectives were sitting at a table going through what they'd found out so far. Fleming pulled himself up from his chair and went over to the whiteboard on the wall. He picked up a red marker pen and drew solid lines direct from Liam Doherty to Croft and Stroud.

'You still thinking Doherty killed Stroud and Croft, boss?' Logan asked.

'It's possible,' Fleming said.

'Interesting chat with Rimmer,' Logan said. 'Everything seems to point to Doherty being Croft's killer, but I can't quite get my head round the logistics of how he managed to get to the care home so fast.'

'We did think it possible that Rimmer's account of how Doherty found out so quickly that Croft was there would stand scrutiny,' Fleming reminded Logan.

Anderson tapped the table with her pencil and took a deep breath.

'Hang on, Naomi's about to amaze us with her powers of detection,' Logan teased.

Anderson glanced in Logan's direction. 'There is another angle on this. What if Croft did kill Stroud, and Doherty was a friend of Stroud's. He vows revenge and hires Rimmer to find Croft for him. It takes five years, but he finally gets him.'

'Bloody hell, boss, she's got a good point,' Logan admitted. He patted Anderson on the back. 'Good thinking, Naomi.'

Fleming rubbed his chin. 'Yes, indeed. Which would also mean Doherty might not be after the four disciples. Maybe he was just after Croft. Nothing to do with the disciples – in which case we may not be looking for another two murders.'

'On that happy note,' Logan said, 'shall we adjourn for a coffee break?'

'Tell you what,' Fleming said, 'I'll get the coffees if you two go through your notes and let me know how you're getting on with tracing and interviewing all those who left the AWE after Stroud's murder.'

Fleming left Logan and Anderson to it while he went to get the coffees. Anderson had made a valid point, but there were now so many possibilities regarding Croft and Stroud. Was there anything to connect the murders? It was all a tangled web of intrigue and they were making no real progress on solving the mystery. Doherty had to be the prime suspect for the Croft murder, but what about Stroud? It could have been Croft, Doherty, Kauffman, maybe even Nat Horne, or was there someone else whose name hadn't come to light yet?

Coffees done, Fleming returned to find Logan and Anderson poring over their notes. 'Maybe we should have a break from guessing about Doherty, Croft and Stroud,' Fleming said. 'How about your interviews with the people who'd left the AWE?'

'We've interviewed all those who didn't move house,' Logan said. 'Nothing new to report, except one man seemed to know about Kauffman's disciples.'

'Did he have names?' Fleming asked.

Logan took a sip of his coffee. 'He confirmed there were four as far as he could remember. He knew about Stroud and Croft and thought the other two were Owen Pearce and Vic Jackman.'

'You haven't mentioned them before. Were they among those who moved to different areas?' Fleming asked.

'Yes,' Logan confirmed. 'Of the twenty-six people on the list Ursula Nieve gave you, only four moved house.'

'You have contact details for Pearce and Jackman?' Fleming asked.

'Yes, both men left at pretty much the same time, one month after Stroud's murder.'

'Interesting,' Fleming said.

Logan looked at his notes, flicking through pages until he found what he was after. 'Pearce left and went to Birmingham where he got a job with a small engineering company. He's on the list to interview next.'

'And Jackman?' Fleming asked.

'He went back to his roots up in the north east. Got himself a job as a storeman at Durham Prison.'

'Something was nagging at the back of my mind when you told me they both left the AWE about a month after Stroud's murder,' Fleming said.

'What?' Logan asked.

'My theory about Doherty wanting to get even with the disciples.'

'You're losing me, boss,' Logan admitted.

'Think about it, Harry. If the disciples were Stroud, Croft, Pearce and Jackman...'

'Yes?'

'Stroud is murdered. A month later Pearce and Jackman leave the company and move out of the area altogether. Soon after, Croft leaves and flees to Australia without telling anyone where he was staying, not even his own mother.'

'So the four disciples...' Logan began to say.

Anderson suddenly chipped in, looking at Fleming. 'You're thinking they all knew someone wanted to kill them for some reason and they tried to run after Stroud was murdered?'

'That's right. And the second disciple has just been murdered – probably by Doherty who'd been looking for him for five years.'

'Making Pearce and Jackman at risk...' Logan's voice tailed off as he realised something.

'If Pearce and Jackman were still here in England, isn't it possible Doherty would have found them before he finally caught up with Croft?' Anderson asked.

'Exactly,' Logan agreed.

'I was going to get you both to check this next but I think you'd better do it right now,' Fleming said.

'HOLMES 2?' Logan guessed.

'Right, let's go back to the office so you can get into the system.'

Fleming and Anderson were looking over Logan's shoulder as he went through the security procedure to access the system. Once in, he looked for any details on Owen Pearce first. After a few clicks on the mouse he found it. Logan turned to Fleming. 'Owen Pearce, shot dead in Birmingham two months after Stroud.'

'I have a bad feeling about this,' Fleming said.

Logan continued his search and found Vic Jackman. 'Looks

like we're definitely looking for a serial killer. Jackman was murdered in Durham a month after Pearce, also shot dead.'

'Hmm. All four disciples shot dead. A serial killer with a gun,' Fleming whispered. *Find the link between the four disciples and we have the identity of Doherty.*

56

Fleming was in his office mulling things over. DI Bent had sent him over Uri Zabair's statement, but it only confirmed what Fleming already knew. The local uniforms had taken Zabair's fingerprints and a DNA sample to pass to forensics so they could disregard his details when looking at any other forensic evidence they found at the scene of the murder.

Logan and Anderson were outside Fleming's office in the open-plan area, busy phoning round everyone they'd interviewed to see if they could find anything to link Stroud, Croft, Pearce and Jackman. Next on Logan's list was to check HOLMES 2 again to look for all shootings recorded over the past five years or so. He wanted to see if there was a record of any suspects and what type of gun the killers used.

The shrill ring of Fleming's phone interrupted his thoughts. It was Nathan Kumar. 'Hi, Nathan. What have you got for me?'

'I'm sending over a full autopsy report, but thought I'd give you a call to give you a heads up on the main points.'

'Fire away.'

'Forensics recovered the bullet that killed Croft. The ballistics people can tell from the unique pattern of ridges and grooves around the bullet that the killer fired it from an old Browning nine-millimetre handgun.'

'Old army issue. They were replaced by the Glock 17,' Fleming said.

'I believe so,' Kumar agreed. 'From the abrasions surrounding the entrance wound I'd guess Croft was shot at quite close range. And from the angle of entry and exit wounds I'd say he was most likely standing erect when shot. I'd guess the killer was of a roughly similar height to Croft.'

'Time of death?'

'I'd say Croft had been there for up to twenty-four hours which would put the approximate time of death early afternoon the day before he was found.'

'Maybe a couple of hours or so after Croft left the care home. Anything else?'

'A bit of bruising round the ribs, and the bruising and cut on the back of his head I mentioned to you at the scene.'

Fleming thought for a moment. 'Croft was last seen in High Wycombe. Maybe the killer clubbed Croft from behind, manhandled him into the boot of a car, drove him to the woods and shot him there.'

'That might account for the bruising on his ribs,' Kumar agreed.

'Thanks, Nathan. Very helpful.'

Fleming ended the call and leaned out of his door to speak to Logan. 'Dr Kumar's been on the phone. Thinks the gun used on Croft was a Browning nine-millimetre handgun. Might help with your HOLMES 2 enquiries.'

Logan lifted a thumb. 'Cheers, boss.'

Fleming disappeared back into his office as his phone rang again. Younger this time.

'Ah, Fleming, glad I caught you in. Thought you'd want to know. I've just come out of a senior management meeting. The head of force intelligence and specialist ops was there. He was talking about the newspaper article on Kauffman and the incriminating photographs. MI5 had apparently asked to have Kauffman put under surveillance. I told him we were also interested in Kauffman as a possible suspect in an old murder case.'

'Anything come out of the surveillance?'

'There's a warrant out for Kauffman's arrest. He's suspected of subversive activity and industrial espionage within the AWE.'

'They haven't found him yet?'

'No. Thought you ought to know.' Younger rang off.

Fleming grabbed his coat, updated Logan and Anderson on the latest development and left the office.

Gwen Emerson was at home, which was at Kauffman's flat in Reading. Fleming showed his warrant card. 'DCI Fleming. Mind if I come in to ask a few questions?'

Gwen looked confused. 'The police have been here looking for Bill. He didn't come home last night. What's he done? Not another fight with my husband?'

'No. It would be better if I could speak to you inside.'

Gwen shrugged and stepped aside to let Fleming in.

The flat was untidy. Newspapers littered a coffee table, half burying an ashtray full of cigarette butts. Empty beer cans filled a wastepaper basket and a wine bottle sat on the floor beside the settee.

Gwen sat on the settee and pointed to a chair opposite. 'Have a seat,' she said. 'Sorry the place is a bit of a mess. I've been worried about Bill and didn't have the energy to clean.'

Fleming nodded. 'I take it you've left him? Your husband I mean.'

'Yes. We had a massive row. Seth found out I was having an affair with Bill and he threw me out. Bloody pleased to get out, I can tell you.'

'Sorry to hear that.'

'He had no time for me anymore. It was either work or that fucking plane of his. Always flying off somewhere. Never offered to take me anywhere. Mind you, I'm not sure I would have felt safe in the thing.'

'You're now living with Bill?'

'Yes.'

'Do you know why the police were looking for him?'

'No idea. They didn't say. Do you know what he's supposed to have done?'

'Did you see the newspaper article about Bill and the photographs of him receiving a package from someone?'

'Yes. But he's explained everything. Someone was trying to set him up. They were fake, he said.'

'Could be about that,' Fleming lied. He wasn't going to tell her there was a warrant out for his arrest.

'Three or four of them came though.'

'Really? Do you know where he is?'

'No. He left the flat yesterday morning. Told me he was going to the picket line and might call in at the pub afterwards.'

'What pub?'

'The local in Aldermaston.'

'Did you call the police when he didn't come home last night?'

'No, he took the car to drive to Aldermaston. I guessed he had too much to drink at the pub after spending the day on the picket line and stayed over with a friend.'

'He didn't call you to say what he was doing?'

'No, Bill isn't the sort who thinks he has to account for his every movement. Probably slipped his mind if he had one too many.'

'Did you try to ring him?'

'Yes, but he wasn't picking up.'

'Did he know Garry Croft was back in England?'

'Who?'

'He never mentioned the name?'

'No.'

'Did he ever speak about a man called Liam Doherty?'

'No, look, what's going on?'

Fleming ignored the question. 'Ever hear your husband or Bill talk about the disciples?'

'What? Who are they?'

'There's talk there were four men Bill called his disciples. William Stroud, Garry Croft, Owen Pearce and Vic Jackman.'

'Don't know anything about that.'

It was clear to Fleming that Gwen Emerson was not going to be able to throw any light on the disciples. 'Thank you for your time, Mrs Emerson. I'll let myself out,' he said, handing her a card. 'You'll let me know right away if Bill comes home or gets in touch?'

'Yes, of course. You don't... you don't think something's happened to him, do you?'

'Try not to worry, Mrs Emerson. Call me if you hear from him.'

'Okay.'

Fleming thanked her again and left, having found out nothing.

57

Fleming had left Logan and Anderson in the office. They were still busy phoning people they'd interviewed to see if anyone could throw any light on a possible link to the disciples that might lead them to Doherty. He'd also asked them to carry out further checks on HOLMES 2 for any crimes where a Browning nine-millimetre handgun had been used. Fleming told them he was going to speak to Maggie Kauffman again.

She wasn't at home in her flat. Fleming went back down the stairs, out onto the street and into the shop below the flat. A balding man in his fifties gave him a wary glance from behind the counter. He was wearing a brown shopkeeper's coat tightly buttoned over his ample stomach and had folded his arms as though in defiance. 'Before you say anything, I don't want whatever it is you're selling. I've had a bellyful of cold-call reps.'

'You'll be pleased to know I'm not a sales rep,' Fleming said. 'I'm looking for Maggie Kauffman. She's not in her flat upstairs.'

'Oh yeah? And who might you be?'

'I might be a health and safety inspector,' Fleming said, watching the shopkeeper's eyes widen, 'but I'm not,' he added with a smile as he pulled out his warrant card. 'DCI Fleming from Thames Valley Police. Any idea where she is?'

'Ah, sorry, she works in a small supermarket a couple of streets away.' The man gave Fleming directions. 'Always happy to help an officer of the law,' he said, wringing his hands together as Fleming left.

He found the supermarket without any trouble and spotted Maggie down an aisle stacking shelves. 'Hello there, Maggie. Could I have a quick word?'

Maggie looked nervously around her and saw a young floor manager looking her way. 'Let me check it's okay with him,' she said, pointing in the youth's direction. 'He's a control freak. Thinks he's top management. Gives me a hard time.'

Fleming watched as she approached Control Freak who looked as though he was just out of school. There was a hurried exchange of words. Maggie pointed down the aisle to Fleming who smiled. Control Freak nodded and Maggie waved Fleming up towards her.

The young manager had wandered off the other way looking self-conscious.

'He says it's okay. We can use the small office at the back of the store. There's no one in it at the moment. Ten minutes is all we have.'

Once in the office, Maggie turned and looked hard at Fleming. 'What's going on? I had police round at my flat first thing looking for Bill. What's he done? Is it to do with the newspaper article showing him receiving what everyone is claiming is cash?'

'I don't know,' Fleming lied. 'Do you know where he is, or might be?'

'We're divorced, remember? How the hell would I know where he is? Why don't you ask his latest live-in lover?'

'I have. She doesn't know.'

'Have you seen or spoken to Bill recently?'

'No.'

'When we last spoke, you told me Bill and four other men were thick as thieves. Garry Croft, William Stroud, and two other men whose names you couldn't remember. He called them his disciples you thought.'

'I did, yes.'

'I think I now know who the other two men were. Owen Pearce and Vic Jackman.'

Maggie screwed her face up and shook her head. 'I don't recall their names ever being mentioned.'

'A couple of days ago, Garry Croft was found dead in woods near Marlow.'

'What! I didn't see anything in the papers about that.'

'I've since discovered Pearce and Jackman left the AWE about a month after William Stroud was murdered. A few weeks later, Pearce was shot dead in Birmingham.'

Maggie's face went white.

'And shortly afterwards, Jackman was shot dead in Durham.'

Maggie shuddered. 'So the four men Bill called his disciples were all killed,' she whispered. 'Is that why the police are looking for Bill? They think he did it?'

Fleming left it to conjecture. 'Or, someone wanted to kill the four disciples and maybe Bill as well.'

'Oh my God!'

'You're absolutely sure you don't know where he might be?'

'No idea. We don't keep in touch.'

'It going back a bit now I know, but apart from the fall out between Stroud and Croft, did Stroud ever talk about anyone who might have had a grudge against him.'

'Not that I can think of, no.'

'He didn't mention the names of anyone else he might have fallen out with?'

'No.'

There was a knock on the office door and Control Freak popped his head in. 'Ten minutes are up, Maggie. If you want any more time, you'll have to take the rest of the day off on unpaid leave,' he said with a smirk.

Maggie threw an enquiring glance at Fleming and received a nod. 'It's okay... we're done,' she said.

Fleming turned to go. 'Call me if you hear anything.' Pushing his way past Control Freak he muttered, 'Let me give you a tip, son, you might earn some respect if you're nice to people.'

Walking back to his car, Fleming was frustrated he was no nearer to finding anyone who could provide a link to the four disciples – someone who could help identify the mysterious Liam Doherty.

He reached his old Porsche and kicked the front wheel. 'Fuck!'

Someone had slashed the tyre with a knife.

58

Schools had gone back a couple of weeks earlier, but the three boys had decided not to bother. They had other ideas. They'd planned the day before to bunk off school and cycle across town to a place where they knew there was a small corner shop which sold cans of beer. It was far enough away from home so there was no way the shopkeeper would recognise them.

Smithy, Jacco and Woody liked to think of themselves as the gang of three. Smithy was the youngest having just passed his thirteenth birthday. Woody was in the middle, one year older than Smithy. The undisputed leader was Jacco, the oldest by nine months. He was always the one who made the decisions.

'Okay, guys, this is the plan,' Jacco said. 'We go on our mountain bikes up side streets and back alleys. We stay clear of main roads. Don't want Smithy here causing an accident the way he rides his bike.'

'Hey, that's not fair! I can ride a bike as well as anyone,' Smithy complained.

Jacco gave him a playful nudge. 'Only joking.'

Woody laughed.

'Don't know what you're laughing at, Woody,' Jacco said. 'I've seen how often you fall off your bike trying to do tricks.'

'Ha, ha!'

'All right, let's stop pissing about,' Jacco said. 'We get ourselves up to the shop and park our bikes outside. We wait till there's no one else in the shop before we go in. Me and Woody will have open newspaper bags slung over our shoulders. I go to the counter and distract the shopkeeper asking if I can have something off the shelf behind him so he has to turn round.' Then to Smithy, 'Your job, Smithy, is to browse around the shop as though you're looking for something.'

'What am I looking for?' Smithy asked.

Woody giggled.

'Something you can knock over. Something that'll cause the biggest noise and chaos.'

'Then what, Jacco?' Smithy asked again.

'You hightail it out of the shop pronto and get ready to follow Woody and me at top speed. Okay?'

'What about me?' Woody asked.

'You grab as many cans of beer as you can while the shopkeeper's distracted, stuff them in your bag and get outside ready to hightail it.'

'What will you be doing?' Smithy asked.

'I'll be right behind you two after I grab some beers, but when I get outside, we ride off, fast! Shopkeeper's likely to be right behind me.'

'Where are we going?' Woody asked.

Jacco ran a hand through his long black hair, pulling it back behind his right ear. 'I know a place where we can hide out. Should only take us ten minutes max to get there.'

'Police will be everywhere looking for us by then,' Smithy complained.

'Don't believe it,' Jacco said. 'Police these days often don't even turn up at the scene of minor crimes. No manpower. You never see a policeman on the beat anywhere nowadays.'

'That's true,' Woody confirmed.

'Hardly the great bank robbery. Police won't give a toss about kids nicking some cans of beer. Trust me,' Jacco said.

Everything planned, the three boys set off.

~

The shop had been quiet. No one was in other than the sole shopkeeper and Jacco's plan had worked. They left the shop at speed on their bikes leaving an angry shopkeeper shouting after them. Jacco and Woody had bagged a dozen cans of beer between them. Laughing and yelling at each other, they pedalled furiously north, away from Reading town centre.

A few minutes later they found the place Jacco knew about. It was an old industrial site south of the river. 'Here it is,' Jacco said triumphantly, swinging his bike onto a potholed parking area in front of a boarded up two-storey building. He pedalled across and skidded to a halt in front of some double iron bar gates on the left-hand side of the building. 'Wait a minute!'

'What's the matter?' Woody asked.

Jacco was holding up the heavy chain with a padlock hanging off it. 'Someone's already broken in. Last time I was here I had to climb over the gates.'

'If the gates are open, we can park our bikes inside,' Smithy suggested.

Woody was getting nervous. 'What if there's somebody there,' he whispered.

'Only one way to find out.' Jacco pulled the chain through the bars and shoved one side of the gate open.

'I'm not so sure now,' Smithy said. 'What if Woody's right?'

Jacco laughed. 'You're a pair of wimps, you two. Stop moaning and let's get in.'

Smithy and Woody looked at each other. Woody shrugged. 'You lead the way then.'

There were some tall bushes screening the parking area from the road so they hid their bikes behind one and walked over to the building. All the windows on the front were boarded up.

'How'd you get in before, Jacco?' It was Woody speaking, having lost some of his nerves.

'There's a gate round the side we can climb over.'

'Then what?' Smithy asked, looking nervously back at the road.

'You go past the office block here at the front and there's a warehouse with a broken window at the back. We can climb in there,' Jacco said.

Woody nodded. 'Okay. Lead the way.'

Jacco climbed over the gate first, then Smithy. Woody followed last. His feet touched the ground and all three froze as the sound of wailing sirens came closer.

'Fuck! They've found us,' shouted Smithy, his eyes wide open.

'No way,' Jacco said. 'Must be something else.' He pulled himself up to peer over the gate. 'Christ!' he shouted, dropping back down to the ground.

'What is it?' Woody whispered urgently.

'Armed police. Three cars.'

'We're dead,' Smithy moaned.

Jacco grinned and nudged Smithy's shoulder. 'Had you both there, didn't I? Only joking. You really think the police knew where we were and would send armed officers? Idiots! It was two fire engines.'

'Wish you wouldn't joke like that. Nerves are all on edge,' Woody complained.

Jacco laughed. 'Come on, you two. Let's get inside and crack these beers open. I've got some fags.'

They climbed through the broken window without any further messing about. Inside was a large warehouse area with lines of thick steel uprights holding up a framework of metal joists and struts supporting the roof. Sunlight streamed in from four massive skylights and dust danced in shafts of light.

'We made it!' Smithy laughed hysterically. 'We bloody well did it!'

'No sign of anyone else here,' Woody observed.

'Probably a gang of drug dealers in the offices,' Jacco said with a straight face.

'You're joking again, right?' Smithy asked, looking at Jacco.

'Relax. Let's get the beers out.'

The three boys settled down on the floor with their backs against the steel uprights, drinking the beers and smoking.

Jacco sucked deeply on his cigarette and blew a cloud of smoke up in the air. 'Better than school any day, eh?' he said, tapping ash on the floor.

'Bank next?' Smithy suggested, getting light-headed from the smoke and effects of the beer.

Woody got up and wandered over to the far end of the warehouse. 'Some place this,' he called out over his shoulder. He reached the far wall and peered through a window in the large double metal doors. 'Wow! Come and look at this,' he shouted.

'What is it?' Jacco asked lazily.

'A burnt-out car outside.'

Jacco went over to see what Woody had found. 'Bloody hell. Let's get outside and have a look.'

The three boys climbed back through the window and walked down a narrow path by the side of the building.

'It's an old Volkswagen Golf hatchback.' Jacco peered inside. 'Nothing in there.'

Woody saw a long metal rod lying on the ground. 'Let's try the boot.'

Jacco simply pulled on the boot lid. 'No need for that,' he said, looking at Woody's improvised key.

The boot lid flew open. 'Fucking hell!' Jacco shouted, staggering back, retching. Inside the boot was the charred remains of a body. 'Let's get the hell out of here!'

Woody's rod clattered to the ground and Smithy gaped in horror.

'Come on!' Jacco urged. 'Let's go!'

59

With a recently fitted new tyre on the front wheel of the Porsche, Fleming was driving down towards Tadley to see Seth Emerson with Logan sitting in the passenger seat.

Logan was looking thoughtful. 'Bit of a day yesterday, eh? Trying to solve one old murder case and now we have two new ones. First Croft and now Kauffman.'

'I know. Younger wasn't best pleased Temple had sent me out to yet another crime scene, but was bemused by the fact that both the Croft and Kauffman murders may somehow be linked to Stroud.'

'I take it you've kept him and Temple fully up to date with things. Wouldn't want to see you get into more trouble with them.'

'Good to know you have my best interests at heart, Harry.'

'Just making sure, boss.' Logan was about to say something else when a car overtook them at speed on the brow of a hill. 'What's he doing?'

Fleming flashed his headlights at the car. 'He was a lucky man. Could have been messy if something had been coming the other way.'

'Not sure about lucky, he was a bloody lunatic. We should have got his registration number and paid him a visit. That would give the idiot a shock.'

'Got enough on my plate at the moment. Anyway, to answer your question, I told them both about the interview with Rimmer.'

'What did they think?'

'Doherty is the main suspect.'

'What about the disciples. Have you told them about Pearce and Jackman?'

'Yes. They agree the most important line of enquiry is to see if we can find a link between the four disciples and Kauffman – that may lead us to finding out who Doherty really is.'

Logan thought for a while before speaking again. 'You reckon it was kids who found Kauffman and rang for the police?'

'That's what the local uniforms say.'

'What would they be doing there?'

'They were bunking off school, drinking beer and having a smoke.'

'Are you guessing, boss?'

Fleming smiled. 'I know.'

'Logan shook his head. How the hell do you know?'

'Local police told me three kids went into a shop nearby and ran off with cans of beer. I found some empty cans and fag ends on the old warehouse floor. Must have been them.'

'Right. They know who these kids are?'

'No. The shopkeeper wasn't much use. He didn't know any of them and his powers of observation were such he might as well have been blindfolded. No CCTV either.'

'That good, eh?'

Fleming smiled again. 'I doubt the local uniforms will lose much sleep over three kids.'

Logan stretched his legs and yawned. 'What do you make of this Kauffman business, boss?'

'Nathan Kumar, the pathologist was there. His initial assessment is an assailant bludgeoned Kauffman to death from behind before dumping him in the boot of his own car and setting light to it.'

'Do you think it's Doherty again?' Logan asked.

'Could be. Looks like he could have killed the four disciples... and they're linked to Kauffman. There's just one thing about linking this to the disciple killings though,' Fleming scratched his head.

'Oh?'

'The four disciples were all shot. Kauffman wasn't.'

'Maybe the killer couldn't use a gun so used something like a hammer or heavy-duty pipe wrench instead.'

'I suppose so. If you want to kill someone you have to pick the best way at the time.'

'We're so close and yet so far,' Logan grumbled. 'We think we know the same man killed four, maybe five, men. But we've no idea who Doherty is, if it is him. Frustrating, isn't it?'

'We're getting close. The man who killed Kauffman knows Reading.'

'How do you know?'

'There's no apparent reason why Kauffman would have been at the old industrial site, and the padlock on the gates was broken. If Kauffman had arranged another of his clandestine meetings, he's hardly likely to break into somewhere for it.'

'So?'

'The killer probably broke in to hide the body after he killed Kauffman somewhere else. He must have known about the site and that it wasn't in use.'

'I'm with you so far, boss.'

'Kauffman left home to go to the picket line and that's the

last seen of him. His killer could have been lying in wait for him, so knew where Kauffman lived and knew how to get to the industrial site.'

Logan whistled. 'You think the killer saw Kauffman leave his flat and followed him to his car. No one else was around so he seizes his moment and hits him over the back of the head several times with a heavy instrument and bundles him into the boot.'

'It's a possibility. The killer then drives Kauffman's car to the industrial site, breaks in, takes the car round the back and sets light to it, having first made sure Kauffman is dead.'

'Okay, so the killer knows Reading. That leaves a hell of a lot of people to check,' Logan pointed out.

'Yes, but if that is what happened, the killer either parked close to Kauffman's flat and took a taxi or bus back after driving Kauffman's car to the industrial site. Or, he left his car near the site and took a taxi or bus to get to Kauffman's place. My guess is the former.'

'How does that help us, boss?'

'We get all the CCTV footage we can of the streets around Kauffman's flat and interview the owners of every car parked there on the morning Kauffman left home.'

'What if the killer did park close to the industrial site?'

'Same. Check all CCTV footage of the area. We also need to check all the taxi companies in Reading to see if anyone gave a lift to someone from near the site.'

Logan sighed. 'This is where the painstaking side of police work comes into play. I can see the overtime forms piling up.'

~

Ten minutes later they were knocking on Seth Emerson's door. He appeared after Fleming knocked a second time. Emerson's face was ashen and gaunt, and it was obvious he'd lost some weight since Fleming last saw him. The man looked ready to collapse as he stood there holding on to the door handle for support.

Fleming raised an eyebrow in surprise. 'It's good of you to see us at short notice.'

'It's okay,' Emerson whispered.

Fleming frowned. 'You don't look too good. Are you ill?'

Emerson smiled weakly. 'I've been off work for a few days with a stomach bug. I'm dehydrated and a bit frail, but I'm sure I'll survive. Come in.'

Fleming looked closely at Emerson. 'You should have said you weren't very well when I phoned. We could have come at another time.'

'No problem. I might not feel up to flying my plane or playing golf, but I'm sure I can answer a few questions.'

Emerson led them into the living room. 'Gwen's gone,' he muttered over his shoulder. 'We had a big row and she left.' He waved a hand at two chairs. 'Have a seat,' he said, slumping down on the settee.

'I'm sorry to hear that,' Fleming said. 'I saw her at Bill Kauffman's flat.'

Emerson shrugged. 'Best of luck to her now.'

'You know then... about Kauffman?'

'Yes, I heard it on the news this morning.'

'Must have come as a bit of a shock?'

Emerson peered at Fleming. 'I suppose it was, yes. But I can't pretend I'll lose any sleep over it.'

'You had a spat with Kauffman. Was there any more to your dislike of each other than the fact your wife was having an affair with him?'

'At the time of the incident on the picket line I only had a suspicion about it. Wasn't until later I got proof. My loathing of him was due to his bullying nature as union leader.'

'So how did you feel about him when you obtained proof of the affair?' Fleming asked.

'I know what you're thinking, but I hated my wife more than Kauffman.'

Fleming decided to change tack. 'How well do you know Reading?'

Emerson hesitated for a moment. 'Not that well. I know how to get to the centre and where the station is, but I'd struggle to find anywhere else.'

'I have to ask you this. Where were you on Monday morning, the day Kauffman was killed?'

'I set off for work, but didn't feel well so came back home. I called in at a chemist on the way to get something for my stomach. I've been at home since, reading and watching old films on TV.'

'Can anyone verify your whereabouts?'

Logan had been busy jotting down notes in his notebook and had his pen poised, waiting for the answer.

'My elderly neighbour saw me leave the house and come back. The chemist might remember me. Otherwise, I saw no one.'

'I'd like you to call into the police station in Reading to have your fingerprints and a DNA sample taken,' Fleming said.

'Are you arresting me?'

'No. But we do need to check out your story, and your fingerprints and DNA would be a great help.'

'Fine I'll go in as soon as I feel a bit better.'

Fleming thanked Emerson and left with Logan in tow. *I wonder how long he'll wait before calling in to the police station.*

60

The focus of attention had shifted towards finding who killed Croft and Kauffman in the hope it would help solve the Stroud case. It seemed almost certain there was a connection. A further link was the murders of Pearce and Jackman. Neither West Midlands Police nor Durham Police had identified the killers. Maybe another indication they were all looking for the same man.

Fleming had been to see Temple and Younger and returned to find Logan and Anderson at their desks. 'How are you getting on?'

'We've been checking social media for any signs of activity by either Croft or Kauffman. Nothing on Facebook, Twitter, Instagram or LinkedIn. Neither man used any of them. No mobile phone was found for Croft, and Kauffman's was destroyed in the fire.'

'Has Emerson provided fingerprints and a DNA sample yet?' Fleming asked.

'No,' Anderson said. 'But we have been checking his alibi.'

'And?'

'There are some inconsistencies.'

Fleming pulled up a chair and sat next to Anderson. 'Go on.'

Anderson flipped through her notes. 'Emerson's neighbour did confirm he saw him leave the house early in the morning, but he's no idea what time it was, and he didn't see Emerson coming back. He was a bit... vague,' she said, as if trying to avoid saying she thought the man was senile.

'But Emerson was quite adamant his neighbour did see him coming back to the house,' Logan pointed out.

'I checked with the chemist on the route to the AWE,' Anderson continued, 'and Emerson did call in there.'

'But,' Logan added, 'the timing doesn't make sense.'

Fleming frowned. 'Oh?'

Logan looked at his notes. 'The chemist reckons Emerson called in about mid-morning. It's a six-minute drive from Emerson's house in Tadley to the AWE. If he was setting off for work, he'd probably need to leave home before eight. So we wondered where he was till mid-morn–'

Fleming cut in suddenly. 'It's a half-hour drive from Tadley to Reading, give or take. If Emerson killed Kauffman in Reading, he would have to have left Tadley very early in the morning to make sure he didn't miss Kauffman before he set off for the AWE. It's possible he could have done that, killed Kauffman, and still have been back at the chemist by mid-morning.'

'Apart from the timing issue,' Anderson said, 'and the fact Emerson's neighbour didn't see him coming back, Emerson can't actually prove he was at home all morning.'

'I think we need to get him in and question him again under caution,' Fleming said.

'Done,' Logan confirmed. 'We went to see him and I asked why he hadn't been to get his fingerprints and DNA taken. He told us he still wasn't well enough. Also, I was about to say on the matter of the chemist timing, he changed his story and said he'd been confused. Said he went straight back home and went out again later to the chemist.'

'Convenient,' Fleming remarked.

'When I told Emerson his neighbour had said he didn't see him coming back he laughed,' Logan said. 'Claimed the man wasn't quite with it and couldn't remember what day of the week it was. He insisted he was at home all morning apart from the two short trips out. One aborted attempt to go to work, and one to go to the chemist. He offered to tell me chapter and verse what books he'd been reading and what recorded films he'd watched while at home on his own.'

'Okay, looks like we'll have to wait for him to get his fingerprints and DNA taken to see if there's any match at the crime scene,' Fleming said. 'We also need to crack on with checking CCTV footage on the streets around Kauffman's flat and at the industrial site. And check all the taxi companies on the off-chance one of them took a fare from near the site.'

'Should keep Naomi and me busy for a while,' Logan said. 'Speaking of which, we do have a bit of a result.'

'The search on HOLMES 2?' Fleming guessed.

Logan checked his notes again. 'There are thousands of crimes involving guns recorded over the last five years, so I decided to narrow my search down to specific reference to the Browning nine-millimetre handgun. We knew from Kumar it was the type of gun used to kill Croft. Details recorded for Stroud, Pearce and Jackman revealed the same type of weapon was used.'

'Confirms our suspicions about a serial killer,' Fleming said.

'How did you get on with Temple and Younger?' Logan asked.

'I've persuaded them to hold a press briefing to say we believe we are now looking for a serial killer. I want them to announce we think the deaths of Stroud, Croft, Pearce, and Jackman are all linked. Possibly Kauffman as well. We need to appeal for anyone who has any information regarding these men to come forward, and warn the public that the killer is armed and dangerous.'

'Think it'll jog any memories?' Logan asked.

'Right now, we're struggling. Anything is worth a try.' Fleming got up and grabbed his coat. 'See you both later. I need to go and see someone in Oxford.'

~

The Perch pub was a good place to meet. It was far enough away from the town centre to ensure there was less chance someone who knew Fleming would see him with Zoe Dunbar. It wasn't too busy either, and the pair sat at a table outside where they were well out of earshot of other people.

'Have you uncovered anything yet to suggest the Stroud case and the strike at the AWE is anything to do with national security?' Fleming asked.

Dunbar ignored the question. 'I thought you said you had something for me. I didn't come all the way up here for you to pump me for information.'

'Just curious.'

Dunbar gave him a look. 'Things are getting interesting. Croft finally turns up and gets himself shot, and now someone's murdered Kauffman. Any leads?'

'There's a possibility Dan Rimmer's mystery client, Liam Doherty, killed Croft.'

Dunbar thought for a second, taking a sip of her white wine. 'If Croft did kill Stroud, do you think Doherty could have been a friend of Stroud's and killed Croft in revenge? Is that why he was looking for Croft for all those years?'

'Could be. But there is another possible explanation which is why I asked to see you.'

Dunbar leaned forward over the table. 'Go on.'

'Have you come across anyone who mentioned the disciples?'

Dunbar frowned. 'No, why?'

'It would appear there were four men who Kauffman called his disciples.'

'Stroud and Croft were two of them?' Dunbar guessed.

'Yes. The other two were Owen Pearce and Vic Jackman. Both shot dead. Pearce in Birmingham, and Jackman in Durham. They were murdered two to three months after Stroud.'

'And you're telling me this off the record?'

'I promised to give you a heads-up on any major developments in return for you running the story about us following new leads and for giving me your source for the Kauffman photos.'

'Is that it? Two names, Pearce and Jackman?'

'Eathan Younger is about to hold a press briefing. He's going to say we're now looking for a serial killer and we believe the same man killed Stroud, Croft, Pearce and Jackman. The killer used the same type of gun in all four cases.'

'What about Kauffman?' Dunbar asked.

'He wasn't shot, so we're keeping an open mind.'

'You think this Liam Doherty killed the four disciples?'

'It's a distinct possibility, yes. I've given you the heads-up I promised on the basis this is all about to become public knowledge anyway, so you can get your story out first. I don't want you to mention Doherty's name though. It's confidential, understood? Just say we're looking for one man.'

'Any leads on finding him?'

'I've given you all I can.'

Dunbar studied Fleming's face. 'So there is more?'

'No.' He wasn't going to tell her about Emerson.

'Okay, thanks.' Dunbar sipped the last of her wine and left.

Fleming sat for a few minutes more, contemplating the orange juice he hadn't touched. *Maybe Younger's press briefing and the newspaper articles that'll follow will panic the killer into making a mistake.*

61

Ursula Nieve had shaken off her cold and was back to her usual brisk, efficient self. Fleming arrived having phoned to check she was free. They were sitting in Nieve's office at the small coffee table used for informal meetings. Her secretary had provided coffee.

'Dreadful business about Bill Kauffman,' Nieve said. 'The strike's in disarray. No one in the union seems to know what to do. Kauffman was the driving force. There's talk they may come back to work.'

'Some good coming out of bad, eh?' Fleming said putting his cup on his saucer.

'Please don't say things like that,' Nieve pleaded. 'People will think we had something to do with it.'

'But you didn't, did you?'

'You're joking, right?'

'Of course, bit tactless. We do have some theories about what might have taken place though.'

'Oh?'

'Can't say at the moment.'

Nieve took a sip of her coffee, looking thoughtful. 'You told me before you were checking some recent CCTV footage regarding Garry Croft. Did you find anything, because he's now dead as well?'

'Yes, I'm afraid the body count is mounting.'

'I saw Eathan Younger's press briefing. You're now looking for a serial killer I believe. All four men were in the union. And, of course, so was Kauffman. Do you think the same person killed him as well as the other four?'

Fleming finished his drink and sighed. 'I don't know. It's possible. We're looking for anything that might connect them all.'

'Isn't the AWE and the union the link?'

'Yes, but I want to find out if there's something else. Maybe someone who has a connection with all five men.'

'Can't help you on that one I'm afraid.'

'Which brings me back to why I phoned you. We already have a list of everyone who left the company after Stroud's death. Have you managed to dig out the names of everyone who left up to a year before that?'

Nieve rose from her chair and went over to her desk to pick up a sheet of paper from her out tray. 'You're in luck. We retain our personnel records for six years after people have left. There're ten people on the list,' she said, placing the paper in front of Fleming. 'And there's one name which may be of particular interest to you. According to the file he was made redundant after the strike.'

'Oh?' Fleming was scanning the list as she spoke. 'Rimmer,' he whispered.

Nieve had sat at the table again. 'I remembered when I saw the name that you'd mentioned it once before. It was the private investigator Dan Rimmer who Zoe Dunbar got the photos of Kauffman from, wasn't it?'

'It was, but the name on your list is Ian Rimmer.'

Nieve pursed her lips. 'There could be thousands of Rimmers in England, but it seems like too much of a coincidence, don't you think?'

Fleming reached for his phone. 'I'll soon find out.'

Logan answered after a few rings. 'Hi, boss.'

'Harry, an Ian Rimmer was made redundant after the strike at the AWE ended five years ago. It would be a few months before Stroud's murder. I've got a forwarding address, but the records are five years old. Can you check him out? See if he still lives there and if he's any relation to Dan Rimmer.'

'Okay, boss, will do. Are you coming back to the office?'

'Not yet. I want to go and see someone first.'

Fleming thanked Nieve for the list of names and took his leave. Back in his car, he frowned. *Is the same surname just a coincidence?* He pulled out his phone and rang Emma Horne.

Emma Horne was at home. She'd offered tea which Fleming declined. 'I won't take up much of your time,' he said. 'I know you told me your husband didn't speak about work much, but I need to ask you about something very important.'

Emma frowned. 'I answered all your questions last time you came.'

'Yes, I know, but something's come up I need to ask you about.'

A look of realisation crossed Emma's face. 'I read in the newspapers about Garry Croft and Bill Kauffman... and I saw the press briefing. Is it to do with that?'

'Possibly.'

Emma nodded. 'I'll do my best to help.'

'Thanks, I wanted to ask you in the off chance your late husband might have mentioned a name.'

'Oh, who?'

'Did he ever mention a man by the name of Ian Rimmer?'

Emma stiffened and her face went pale. Her hands were shaking.

'Are you okay?' Fleming asked.

'Yes, yes, it's just...'

Fleming waited for her to regain her composure.

Emma took a deep breath and continued. 'I'm sorry I didn't mention this before...'

'Go on, take your time,' Fleming said.

Tears welled up in Emma's eyes. 'I didn't say anything before because I didn't want Nat's name dragged through the mud. What took place was nothing to do with him.'

'What happened?' Fleming asked gently.

'There was a strike. Ian Rimmer refused to stop work because his wife was apparently seriously ill and he was the only income earner. There was talk of bullying, intimidation and harassment.'

'Of Ian Rimmer?'

'Yes. Nat told me there were four men in particular.'

Fleming's stomach was churning. *The disciples!* 'Did he name them?'

'No, he was under a lot of pressure as I told you before. The strike ended but the management told Nat to pay Ian Rimmer off. He said it was dreadful. Bill Kauffman had insisted a condition of them going back to work was they got rid of Rimmer.'

Fleming's mind was racing. *Is Ian Rimmer the killer? Is Dan Rimmer related?*

Emma's tears were flowing freely. 'Rimmer's wife died and soon after he took his own life.'

Fleming looked in pity at the distraught women and stayed

silent for a while. 'I'm sorry this has brought it all back. It must have been very distressing for you at the time.'

Emma sniffed and dabbed her eyes with a handkerchief. 'It's why Nat had to leave. They killed him, didn't they? The pressure and the stress of it all, and that poor man. No wonder Nat had a breakdown and died soon after.'

'Emma, you've been extremely helpful. I'm sorry to have dragged all this up. I can arrange counselling if you think it would help.'

Emma smiled. 'No, thanks, I'll be okay.' She blew her nose. 'He had a son, you know.'

'Who?'

'Ian Rimmer... he had a son who was in the army. He left soon after his father died. Dan, I think his name was.'

62

The phone was ringing, but no one was answering. Rimmer threw his pencil across the desk. 'Come on! Pick up, for fuck's sake!'

Rimmer had seen the press briefing and knew it was only a matter of time before Fleming worked out that he killed Stroud and the other three disciples. Fleming had already interviewed him under caution and had to see him as a suspect because he'd been looking for Croft, even though he'd seemed to buy the story about Doherty. *They'll be onto me in no time if Fleming finds out about my father*, Rimmer thought. He knew he had no time to waste.

After what seemed like an age, Emerson answered in a wary voice. 'Hello?'

'Seth, is that you?' Rimmer asked.

'Yes, who's this?'

'Dan... Dan Rimmer.'

'Oh, hi. Didn't recognise your voice, sorry.'

'Listen, Seth, I need to ask you a big favour.'

'Yes? What's that?'

'Remember you offered to take me for a spin in your plane?'

'Yes.' The long, drawn out emphasis on the word suggested the response was a cautious one.

Rimmer took a deep breath. He wasn't sure how to put this. 'I need to get over to France as soon as I can.'

'Something to do with one of your investigations?'

Rimmer wondered why he hadn't thought of it himself. 'Yeah,' he lied. 'Client's daughter left home. He suspects she's gone to France.'

'Right. Big place. Where exactly do you want to be?'

'There's an airfield at Le Touquet in northern France. I'd be grateful if you could get me there. My client thinks his daughter may have gone across from Dover to Calais. She has a friend she knows there.'

'Why not just get the ferry across to Calais?'

'Like I said. I need to get to France quickly in case she moves on somewhere else.' Rimmer was getting into the spirit of the lie.

There was a long pause on the other end of the phone. 'You're in luck. Remember I told you I was going to throw Gwen out, leave the AWE and maybe go to France?'

'I remember. You've decided to go?'

'Yeah. I can take you to Le Touquet if you like.'

Rimmer's eyes lit up. *Result!* 'Your trip's nothing to do with Kauffman, is it?' he teased. 'I thought you were joking when you said you would kill him.' He heard a sharp intake of breath.

'Sorry, only kidding.'

'It's no joke. DCI Fleming has questioned me. He knew about Gwen's affair with Kauffman. I don't have an alibi anyone can verify. I'm sure he sees me as a suspect. He's asked me to go in to have my fingerprints and DNA taken.'

'Is that a problem?'

Emerson didn't answer the question. After a short pause, he

spoke again. 'I saw the press briefing,' he whispered, 'about Croft and the other three men.'

'Yeah. I saw that too.'

'You were looking for Croft.'

'For a client, yes.'

A long silence and an uneasy bond had formed between the two men, each believing the other was guilty of something they weren't quite ready to admit.

Emerson eventually spoke. 'If you can get yourself to the airfield at Wycombe there's a caravan park just south of it where I have a static caravan, number thirty-six. If I'm not there, you'll find a key in a small safe box beside the door. Code's 1722. I'll meet you at the caravan later this afternoon. We'll leave today if there's enough daylight left.'

'Great. See you later,' Rimmer said. 'And Seth...'

'Yeah?'

'Thanks, mate. Owe you one.'

~

There was no time to lose. Rimmer's uncle was out working on a case. Dan would have preferred to say goodbye to Phil face to face, but that wasn't going to be possible. He left a note to say he had to leave, something they'd both known might be necessary one day. The day had come.

After leaving the note Rimmer rushed off to his nearby flat. Going straight to the bedroom, he pushed the bed to one side. Underneath was a rug which he tugged aside to reveal a square hatch he'd fitted into the floorboards. Lifting the cover, he pulled out a plastic bin bag. He ripped it open to find a large leather holdall.

Rimmer had planned for this meticulously and had left nothing to chance. He always kept clean clothes in the bag so he didn't have to waste time thinking about what to pack. A brown envelope contained ten thousand pounds in sterling and ten thousand in Euros. His passport was tucked into a separate side pocket.

Reaching a hand further back between the joists, Rimmer pulled out a cloth sack. Inside was a Browning nine-millimetre handgun. Checking there was a thirteen-round magazine loaded, he wrapped it back up in the sack and placed it at the bottom of his bag under his clothes. Last of all, he threw in a pair of dark sunglasses.

There were only two more things he had to do before he left.

63

Fleming's phone indicated an incoming call: *Logan*. 'Hi Harry, I was about to ring you.'

'Saved you the bother, boss. You go first.'

'I'm at Emma Horne's house. She told me all about Ian Rimmer who refused to strike five years ago and how four union men bullied and harassed him.'

'The disciples,' Logan guessed.

'Right. It seems Kauffman had whinged to the management and told them a condition of everyone going back to work was they had to pay Rimmer off. The directors put Nat Horne under pressure to find a way to make him redundant without people querying it. Rimmer's wife was ill and died. Shortly after Horne ended his employment, Rimmer took his own life.'

'Ah, that's what I was calling you about. I checked the address you gave me and found Rimmer was no longer there. A neighbour told me all about how tragic it was when Rimmer's wife died and how he committed suicide soon after the AWE paid him off.'

'Did the neighbour tell you about the son?'

'No.'

'Ian Rimmer had a son in the army. Dan. He left the army shortly after his father died.'

Fleming could sense Logan was absorbing this information. 'I didn't find out about Dan,' Logan said. 'So do we assume there is no Liam Doherty and it was Rimmer all along?'

'I think it's almost certain,' Fleming confirmed. 'The link between Stroud, Croft, Pearce and Jackman is Dan Rimmer. He obviously blamed his parents' death on the four men and left the army to exact his revenge.'

'Unless...'

'What?'

'Unless Rimmer hired someone to kill them all. Liam Doherty?' Logan suggested.

'Hmm, I think it's more likely he made him up to give us a reason for him wanting to find Croft.'

'Just a thought. What about Kauffman?'

'I'm reserving judgement on who might have killed him. It's possible Rimmer murdered him as well, though the others were all shot. Kauffman wasn't. Seth Emerson also had a motive and his alibi has some question marks over it. Speaking of which, has he been in to have his prints and DNA taken yet?'

'Not so far, no.'

'I think you should get on to him to remind him. Tell him if he doesn't go in soon, we'll arrest him and take him in to have it done.'

'Okay.'

'What about CCTV footage around Kauffman's house and the industrial site? Any luck?'

'Anderson's still ploughing through it all and she's checking all the cars which were parked on the street within walking distance of both locations. There must be over a hundred cars to check out.'

'Taxi companies? Anyone pick up a fare near the industrial site?'

'Still checking, boss.'

'Okay. Can you pop in and update Temple on the state of play? Ask her if she'll be kind enough to inform Younger.'

'Shall I get Reading police to pick Rimmer up?'

'I'm setting off for his office right now.'

'Bloody hell, boss. On your own? Rimmer's armed and dangerous, remember?'

'I don't think he's a threat to me.'

'Boss! What is it they say, nothing as dangerous as a cornered animal?'

'If it makes you happier, get the local uniforms to meet me at Wyatt Investigations office. I should be there in about twenty-five minutes.'

'I can be there in an hour. I'll see you there.' Logan ended the call.

Logan left Anderson with instructions to remind Emerson about prints and DNA and to ring Reading police while he went to update Temple.

'He's not gone there on his own, surely,' Temple said.

'You know the boss, ma'am. I did try to convince him it wasn't a good idea.'

'Yes, I know him only too well. Once he's made a decision, there's no stopping him.'

'Anderson's ringing Reading police now. They ought to get to Wyatt Investigations office before him. He said it would take him about twenty-five minutes to get there from Aldermaston.'

'What's he doing there?'

'He went to see Nat Horne's widow. That's where he found out about Dan Rimmer being Ian Rimmer's son.'

With nothing more to tell Temple, Logan left her office, grabbed his coat and set off for Reading.

There was no sign of any police at Wyatt Investigations office. Fleming couldn't wait for them. He walked in to find Phil Wyatt sitting behind his desk. 'Can I help you?' Wyatt asked.

'We haven't met before,' Fleming said, casting an eye round the office. 'I'm DCI Fleming.'

'Ah! Dan told me about you. What can I do for you?'

'I'm looking for Dan. He's not here?'

'No, he left a note to say he was out on a job. I don't know when he'll be back.'

'Did he say what it was?'

'No. Can I get him to ring you?'

Fleming doubted very much that he would. 'Yes, please. In the meantime, can you give me his home address. I'll check there.'

Wyatt was busy scribbling down the address when the sound of wailing sirens approached.

Here comes the cavalry, Fleming thought. *Bit late though if Dan Rimmer had been here.*

Wyatt looked up as six armed police burst through the door. 'What the fuck–'

'He's not here,' Fleming cut in, looking at the armed men. He held up his warrant card. 'DCI Fleming.' He nodded towards Wyatt. 'And this is Rimmer's uncle.'

The armed officers looked at each other as though embarrassed for their late arrival.

'Let's try his home address.' Fleming held out his hand for the piece of paper Wyatt had scribbled on.

Fleming glanced back at Wyatt as he was leaving the office. 'Don't you be going off anywhere. I'll want a word.'

64

Rimmer's heart was pounding as he went to work in the bathroom hacking at his beard with a pair of scissors. The last time he felt such a rush of adrenalin was in Afghanistan. He knew he was taking a risk staying in the flat longer than he had to, but there would be no time on the train to do this. Having trimmed his beard as close to his face as possible, he then went to work with his electric shaver.

Once done, he rubbed in some aftershave balm, scooped up all the hair and flushed it down the toilet. Making sure there was no trace of hair left anywhere, Rimmer went to the bedroom. Taking a false beard and moustache from his bedside cabinet, he applied some spirit gum to his face and stuck them on. Satisfied it looked an exact replica of what he'd shaved off, he threw some gum remover into his bag. Once he'd left a trail for CCTV, it was going to be much quicker to remove the fake beard on the train than to try to shave off the real one onboard.

There was one last precaution Rimmer had to take before leaving the flat for good. Glancing at his watch, he saw he still had plenty of time. It wouldn't take long to get to the station. Laying the false trial might take a bit of time, but he could still be at the airfield at Wycombe by afternoon. Pulling his laptop down from the top shelf of his wardrobe, he dropped it onto the bed and logged on. After permanently deleting all his contacts and emails, he uninstalled everything. As a fail-safe measure, he took the laptop to the cupboard in the hallway where he kept his tools. Taking off the back, he grabbed a hammer and demolished the hard drive.

The flat wasn't a problem. He'd taken care of that. Rimmer's uncle had suggested they should buy it in his name in case Rimmer ever had to go on the run. That way, his uncle would be able to sell up and send the proceeds to Rimmer once he'd set up an account wherever he fled to. Going to his bookcase in the living room, Rimmer pulled a book on relocating to Sydney forwards slightly from the other books. It was only a minor detail, but that final touch might lead police searching the place to believe he'd been reading up on it in preparation for moving there.

Satisfied he'd done everything he needed to, Rimmer grabbed a bright red anorak off a peg. *Time I was gone.* He closed the front door behind him and set off for the station.

The sky had darkened with ominous black clouds and a light drizzle was falling. At least the anorak wouldn't seem out of place. There was a bank on the way, so Rimmer used his debit card to draw out the maximum daily amount. It all added to the trail he was leaving.

After getting the cash, Rimmer quickened his pace. The station was five minutes away. He wondered whether he ought to call into the office to see if his uncle had returned, but then decided against it. He knew the police would pull Phil in for questioning and would put pressure on him to reveal where

Rimmer was going. They would threaten to charge him as an accomplice. No, it was better his uncle had no idea where he was going to try to escape to. And best he didn't delay his departure any longer than necessary. For all he knew, he may already have run out of time.

Rimmer's pulse raced when he saw a police car cruising down the street. Trying to avoid looking self-conscious, he stopped and gazed into a shop window. The anorak was beginning to make him sweat, and Rimmer could feel his shirt sticking to his back. Looking at the reflection in the window, he watched as the police car drove slowly by. The two officers in the car paid no attention to him.

Rimmer drew several deep breaths and could feel the muscles in his neck and shoulders tighten. He turned and continued at an even brisker pace. Not far now.

The station was still busy even though the early morning rush had gone. Rimmer's eyes darted around looking for any sign of extra police activity. He could see only two uniformed constables, but they were walking away from him and merged into the crowd. Rimmer's breathing was short and shallow. Glancing up at the departure boards, he saw the next train for London Paddington was in ten minutes. Feeling light-headed, he joined the queue for tickets. Taking deep breaths, he was looking at his watch when he felt a tap on his shoulder. His whole body tensed as he spun round expecting to see a policeman.

'There's a free ticket booth at the end,' an elderly man pointed out, his tone making clear his irritation at someone delaying him.

Rimmer didn't take kindly to the tap on the shoulder. 'So there is,' he snapped, shooting a glance at the man through narrowed eyes.

The man stepped back in alarm and stuttered, 'Sorry, I... I thought you hadn't noticed.'

'As it happens, I hadn't. I was busy looking at my watch. Sorry if a few seconds hold-up annoyed you.'

The man's face reddened.

'But very kind of you to let me know,' Rimmer added sarcastically.

The man kept a safe distance behind while Rimmer bought his ticket and strode off to the departure gate, trying to spot where the CCTV cameras were. He wanted to make sure the cameras picked him up getting on a train to London.

65

The armed response unit sped towards Rimmer's flat in three squad cars with blue lights flashing and sirens wailing. Fleming followed behind. Logan had not yet arrived from Long Hanborough.

The light drizzle had turned to a steady downpour and the car tyres hissed on the wet road as they threw up spray over bemused bystanders. They skidded to a halt in the parking area in front of a four-storey block of flats. Six armed officers wearing helmets, black uniforms and bulletproof vests flung the doors open and climbed out armed with Glock 17 pistols and Heckler & Koch MP5 semi-automatic carbines. Another man carried a battering ram – otherwise known as the enforcer or the big red key.

They ran to the entrance and up three flights of stairs to Rimmer's flat, with Fleming following behind. The officer Fleming took to be in charge of the unit knocked heavily on the door and shouted, 'Police! Open up!'

There was no reply so he nodded at the man with the enforcer and stood back. The first blow was about to be unleashed against the door when a neighbour suddenly appeared. 'He's not there,' the man said, looking uneasily at the armed men.

'Know where he's gone?' Fleming asked while signalling to the officer with the enforcer to carry on.

'No idea,' the man admitted. 'I saw him leave with a bag. Seemed to be in a rush,' he added inanely, given what was happening outside Rimmer's door.

'What time?' Fleming prompted.

The man shrugged. 'Couple of hours ago maybe.'

'What was he wearing?'

'A red anorak and jeans, I think. He was carrying a smart leather bag.'

Fleming pulled out his phone and called Logan. No answer. He was probably on his way to Reading. He tried Anderson. She was in the office. 'Naomi, it's Fleming. I've been to Wyatt Investigations office and I'm now at Rimmer's flat. He's gone. I'm going in to search the place. Can you update the PNC to mark Rimmer as wanted in connection with a number of murders – and make sure an alert is circulated to forces at all UK ports and airports. He was last seen wearing a red anorak and jeans and carrying a leather bag.'

'Okay, sir. Right away.'

'Can you also see if you can get hold of CCTV footage on the streets around Rimmer's flat and the station and see if we can pick him up. Tall order, but we could do with getting footage at all main London stations to see if he's picked up there, particularly St Pancras in case he tries to get on the Eurostar.'

'Okay, sir.'

'Better let Temple know – and see if you can get in touch with Logan, or leave him a text. Tell him where I am.' Fleming gave Anderson the address and ended the call.

Rimmer's door was hanging off its hinges and the armed officers, taking no chances, had fanned out through the flat, semi-automatics trained in front of them. They never took what someone told them at the scene of an incident as being a hundred per cent accurate.

The officer who seemed to be in charge took off his helmet. 'All clear,' he told Fleming.

'Thanks,' Fleming said. 'I'm expecting my sergeant to arrive soon, but in the meantime, I want to have a look round while I'm waiting for him. Better get local CID and scene of crime guys to come and give the place a thorough check.'

'Okay, sir.' The officer hesitated. 'Only I'm not sure...'

'Don't worry, I've got protective clothing in the boot of my car. I'll go and get kitted out.'

The man looked relieved. 'Ah, right. I'll wait here for you, then get the SOCOs round.'

Fleming was getting into the protective clothing when Logan arrived. 'Guess I missed the fun, boss. Naomi got me on the phone and told me you didn't get Rimmer.'

'Missed him by about two hours it seems,' Fleming confirmed, pulling on latex gloves. 'I've asked Naomi to update the PNC and alert all ports and airports. She's also going to get CCTV footage at all London mainline train stations checked.'

Logan was getting himself kitted out while Fleming was talking. A few minutes later they were climbing the stairs back up to Rimmer's flat. The uniformed officers were ready to leave and the one Fleming had spoken to nodded as they departed. 'I've been on the phone. SOCOs shouldn't be long.'

Fleming thanked him and entered the flat with Logan behind.

'What are we looking for?' Logan asked.

'Anything which might give us a clue where he's gone.'

Logan went to look in a cupboard while Fleming searched round the living room.

'Smashed up laptop in here,' Logan shouted.

'Leave it for the SOCOs. They'll take it to the computer forensics people to see if they can do anything with it.'

'Okay,' came Logan's muffled voice.

Fleming noticed a bookcase and walked over. Rimmer had stacked all his books to line them up neatly, but there was one protruding out from the rest. It was a guide on moving to Sydney. Fleming pulled it out and flicked through the pages. There was one page with a corner turned over and Fleming saw it had a section on accommodation.

Logan appeared brushing dust off his protective overalls. 'Bloody dusty in the cupboard,' he complained. 'What have you got there, boss?' he asked, looking over Fleming's shoulder.

'Guide on moving to Sydney. There's a page marked on finding somewhere to live.'

'Bit careless of Rimmer to leave that lying around, wasn't it?'

'Hmm. Or he left it sticking out slightly in the bookcase to make sure we found it to throw us off his trail.'

Logan scratched his chin. 'You mean he's no intention of trying to get there?'

'Could be.'

'Or... he left it for us, thinking we would see it as an obvious ploy and disregard it, but in fact that is exactly where he's heading for.'

Fleming turned to look at Logan and smiled. 'Your mind works in mysterious ways, Harry. It must make your brain hurt trying to work out whether a clue is left intentionally or by mistake.'

'Just thinking of every angle, boss.'

'It's what good cops should do.' Fleming laughed, patting Logan on the back.

Fleming had decided there was nothing more they could do there when he heard the sound of voices outside. 'Sounds like the SOCOs have arrived.'

Leaving the SOCOs to do their work, Fleming wondered if Logan had a point about the book. *Was Rimmer really that devious?*

66

The train from Reading to London Paddington was due to leave in two minutes. Rimmer found a seat at the end of a carriage so he could see everyone in front of him. He threw his bag up on the luggage rack and jammed his red anorak on top. Taking his seat, Rimmer was trying to control his breathing which had become short and shallow. He closed his eyes and tried to take deep breaths.

The carriage was beginning to fill up and Rimmer's heart thumped when he saw two policemen wandering up the platform in his direction. *Calm down*, he told himself. *They can't be onto me already.* Rimmer watched in horror as they climbed into the carriage he was sitting in. *Fuck! Do I make a run for it?*

Before Rimmer did anything to attract attention to himself, the two policemen had approached a young unkempt man sitting on his own a few seats in front of Rimmer. The youth had glanced around looking a bit furtive when he slumped into his seat and Rimmer had wondered what was going on.

'All right, be a good lad and come with us,' one of the officers said.

'I didn't do nothing,' the youth pleaded.

'That's not what the man in the stationery shop told us. He reckons you took a book and left without paying for it.'

'I didn't!'

'Care to show us what you've got in the plastic bag then?'

The youth shrugged and handed it over. The constable pulled out a paperback. 'So what's this then?'

'A book,' the youth admitted. 'But I did pay for it.'

'Got a receipt?'

'No. I had to dash to get onboard.'

'There's CCTV in the shop. Think it'll show you at the till, or just slipping out the door?'

'Bastards,' the youth muttered.

'Okay, come quietly with us. We'll have a word with the shopkeeper and see if he wants to press charges if you offer to pay him. Otherwise, I'll arrest you for theft. Up to you.'

Rimmer's pulse had slowed down and he pulled the newspaper he'd bought in front of his face. Despite taking his anorak off, he was sweating as the two policemen escorted the young man out of the carriage. A minute later he felt a lurch as the train eased away from the platform.

Outside the station, rain trickled down the window. Rimmer had started to relax. He'd known the day would come when he would have to go on the run. Inwardly, he felt satisfied that at long last he'd killed the fourth disciple after a long wait. Finally, he'd fulfilled the promise he made to himself to avenge his father's death.

Thinking about his little ploy with the book on Sydney made him smile. Would the police fall for it and think that's where he was planning to run to? Maybe it would work, maybe it wouldn't. It was of no real consequence. Little details could sometimes make a big difference. You never knew. One thing did bother him. Fleming. It was a shame he was on the case. Rimmer actually liked the man and hoped he wouldn't face a situation where Fleming got in the way of his escape. If that happened, he would have to use the Browning.

Rimmer's thoughts were interrupted as they pulled into London Paddington. Pulling his coat off the luggage rack, Rimmer slipped it on and grabbed his bag. Three minutes later, he was through the turnstiles and heading for the underground to catch a tube to Victoria on the Circle line. Although the morning rush had subsided, it was still busy.

Rimmer made a point of lingering where he could see CCTV cameras. The time had not yet come to disappear. Until that time came, he would remain uneasy. Adrenalin was pumping through his body and his stomach was churning. The muscles in his neck and shoulders were tightening.

The rush of warm air coming through the tunnel indicated the imminent arrival of a train. Passengers stood precariously near the edge of the platform, taking their lives in their hands to make sure they got on first. It arrived with screeching brakes and the doors slid open. Rimmer climbed on and stayed next to the doors.

About sixteen minutes later, he was going up the escalator to the mainline station in Victoria where he made his way to the ticket office. His heart rate was increasing and sweat ran down his back as he waited in the queue. Looking anxiously around, he saw armed police patrolling, but they weren't paying any attention to him. He bought a ticket for Dover and made his way to platform two.

Five minutes later, the train pulled out of Victoria Station with Rimmer safely onboard. He picked a seat near to a toilet, put his mobile phone in his anorak pocket, threw it up onto the luggage rack and placed his bag on top.

So far, so good. Rimmer was planning ahead to his next crucial move which could be the start of his passage to freedom.

67

They were using the computer in the small incident room to go through all the CCTV footage Anderson had acquired. Jeff Miller had popped in to see what progress Fleming and his team were making.

'See you're all busy so won't hold you up,' Miller said, looking at the whiteboard on the wall. 'Seems things are developing fast. Croft and Kauffman dead, and Dan Rimmer on the run as the number one suspect in the Stroud killing, plus two others in addition to Croft. Have to hand it to you, Alex. Quite a result.'

'Only thing is... we haven't caught him,' Fleming said.

'Question of time, Alex.'

'This guy is pretty clever. It might not be that easy.'

Miller looked thoughtful. 'What about Kauffman? You think Rimmer killed him as well?'

'I'm not sure. It's possible, but we do have another suspect whose alibi doesn't check out.'

Miller nodded and made to leave. 'Impressive work, Alex. Younger will have you in my job at this rate.'

Fleming looked at Miller's glum face. 'Don't worry, Jeff. I've no intention of taking on cold cases full time. The only reason Younger bypassed you was he believed there was a potential conflict of interest because you and Frank Ingham were friends.'

'I told you before, Alex, Younger has never liked or rated me. He'll sing your praises if you catch Rimmer and have me out of the door.'

'I'm sure you would have done as good a job as we have, Jeff. Not your fault you weren't given the opportunity.'

Miller took a final look at the whiteboard. 'Well... whatever. Best of luck, Alex.'

Miller left the incident room and Fleming turned to Anderson. 'Talking about Kauffman, did you manage to get in touch with Emerson about prints and DNA?'

'Yes, sir. He's been in, but so far no matches to the Kauffman crime scene.'

'I suppose it was a long shot,' Fleming admitted. 'He'd more than likely have worn gloves and both Kauffman and his car were incinerated.'

'The SOCOs conducted an inch-by-inch search of the industrial site and found some fibres of clothing which they're checking. Trouble is, some of it may be from the boys who broke in and discovered the body.'

'What about CCTV footage around Kauffman's flat and the industrial site?' Fleming asked.

'Still going through it all, but no sign of Emerson's car so far,' Anderson said.

'Taxis?'

'Same, still checking. There're a lot of taxi operators and a very long list of drivers. It'll take some time to check them all out.'

Logan had been quiet, studying CCTV footage on the computer. He looked up for a second. 'Should we arrest Emerson?'

'Not yet, Harry,' Fleming said. 'If we do, we'll need to either charge or release him within twenty-four hours. We haven't got enough evidence yet. If we get a positive sighting on his car, or can get a taxi driver to put him at, or near, the crime scene, we'll get a search warrant and get the SOCOs to check his house to see if there's any match to the clothing fibres they found. But only after they've eliminated any link to the three boys who discovered Kauffman. We'll arrest him if we get positive evidence.'

'As regards Rimmer,' Anderson announced, 'I've updated the PNC. He's flagged up as wanted and there's an alert out to all forces at UK ports and airports.'

'Thanks, Naomi,' Fleming said.

Logan looked up at Anderson. 'Yes, well done indeed. You've been a right busy bee. I think you deserve a coffee break. Mine's a milk and one sugar. I'm trying to cut down,' he added with a smile.

Anderson made a face behind Logan's back. 'Last time you complained there wasn't enough sugar in your coffee. Don't you go complaining again if I only put one in.'

'Promise.' Logan pulled out a pack of chocolate biscuits from the desk drawer. 'I got these specially for you.'

Anderson pulled the biscuits out of Logan's hand. 'You're so kind, Sarge. If you're cutting back on sugar you shouldn't be having any of these.'

Logan laughed. 'Only one... please?'

Anderson relented, handed the biscuits back to Logan and went off to get the coffees.

Fleming looked at Logan who was staring at the computer screen. 'Got anything, Harry?'

'That's him, there,' Logan said, pointing to the man with a beard and wearing a red anorak. 'Outside Reading station. And here again at the ticket office.' Logan sped the video forward to show Rimmer getting on a train. The departure board showed it was destined for London Paddington. A few more clicks on the mouse and Logan was speeding through the film again. 'Underground at Victoria station,' Logan announced. 'He's here again climbing the escalators, then coming out onto the main concourse.'

Anderson arrived with three coffees and put them on the desk. 'Is that him?' she asked looking over Logan's shoulder at the monitor. The red anorak stood out in the crowd.

'It's him,' Logan confirmed. 'At London Victoria.'

'So he's not trying to get on Eurostar then?'

Logan sped the film on and the final glimpse of Rimmer was of him boarding a train for Dover.

Fleming took a sip of his drink. 'Better remind Dover port police about the alert and tell them we're certain he's heading their way.'

'Okay, sir,' Anderson confirmed. 'By the way, I saw Superintendent Temple and told her what was happening. She said she would let Eathan Younger know.'

'Thanks, Naomi.' Fleming rubbed at the growing stubble on his chin. 'Let's get Rimmer's uncle in for questioning.'

68

The train picked up speed as it left Victoria Station, lurching from side to side as it crossed the points at rail junctions. Rimmer had climbed into a carriage that didn't have many people in it. There were a couple of men in suits talking loudly and Rimmer heard snippets of chat about picking the low-hanging fruit, going forward, and taking things to the next level. Rimmer shook his head from behind his newspaper and wondered where all this jargon came from. 'We need to work smarter, not harder,' he heard one of the men say with great conviction.

Thank fuck I'm not going all the way to Dover, Rimmer thought.

Further back, two young men sat eating freshly baked hot pasties. The smell wafted down towards Rimmer reminding him he was hungry. Three girls giggled and laughed at the opposite end of the carriage and a woman with two children sat in seats in front of the two men in suits.

No one seemed to notice Rimmer, but he still kept his face hidden behind his paper. He felt nauseous and sweat broke out on his forehead. He glanced across and saw no one was using the toilet. It was seventeen minutes to Bromley South, but Rimmer didn't want to wait too long in case someone else needed to use it.

He looked up at the luggage rack and decided it was as good a time as any. Getting up when no one was looking in his direction, he took the spirit gum remover from his bag. Rimmer had one last glance down the carriage. No one was looking. One of the men in suits was now talking about how they mustn't lose sight of the bottom line. Rimmer shook his head in disbelief as he opened the toilet door and entered.

Looking in the mirror, Rimmer used a piece of toilet paper to soak up some spirit gum remover. While carefully peeling off the false beard and moustache, he worked the remover underneath to loosen the adhesive. After a few minutes, he'd managed to completely remove the beard and moustache. Rimmer then made sure he'd removed all traces of the spirit gum before washing his face with warm soapy water. His cheeks were a bit red, but he looked a different man.

Rimmer rammed the false beard and moustache into the waste bin, flushed the toilet and opened the door. No one looked his way, so he slipped back into his seat and held the newspaper in front of his face again. Five minutes later, the train was pulling into platform four at Bromley South Station with screeching brakes. When it slowly came to a halt with a final judder, Rimmer stood and grabbed his bag. He left the red anorak up on the luggage rack. Inside one of the pockets was his mobile phone which he'd switched on, but with all his contacts and social media apps deleted. With a bit of luck, the coat and phone would end up in Dover before the police got round to tracking it.

Once on the platform, Rimmer thought through his options while looking for a toilet. He could get a train back to Victoria and tube to Marylebone, take a bus, or get a taxi. The first two options had the disadvantage of CCTV cameras everywhere. He knew all London buses had CCTV fitted. Taking a taxi meant personal contact with someone. While still thinking over what to do, Rimmer found a toilet and locked himself inside a cubicle. He slipped off his blue jeans and exchanged them for a pair of brown ones from his bag. Finally, he took out a cream baseball cap and some dark glasses. He slipped them on and pulled the cap down tight over his forehead.

Rimmer reckoned the quickest option was train and tube. Worth the risk of the police spotting him on CCTV. They would be looking for a man with a beard, wearing a red anorak and blue jeans. He now had none of those things, and the baseball cap would hide his hair and eyes. His disguise was complete. There was a train back to Victoria in just five minutes. Decision made, Rimmer bought a ticket and made his way to platform one.

There were only a handful of people waiting. No police in sight. Rimmer had a thumping headache, and he was sweating despite a chill in the air. The thing that kept him going was the thought of a flight out to France on Emerson's plane in the afternoon.

Half an hour later, Rimmer was back at Victoria station underground. He was well on his way and, so far, things were looking positive.

69

The use of interview room one at Reading police station had become a regular event. Fleming and Logan sat opposite Phil Wyatt who told them he didn't need to have a solicitor present. Fleming cautioned Wyatt and went through the usual procedure before Logan started the recording machine.

'I want to ask you some questions about your nephew, Dan Rimmer,' Fleming said. 'You're not under arrest, so you're free to leave any time you wish.'

'Glad to hear it,' Wyatt said. 'I'd have been interested to know what exactly you would have arrested me for.'

'Aiding and abetting a suspected criminal. Perverting the course of justice by assisting a suspect to evade arrest – take your pick.'

Wyatt's eyes gave nothing away. He fixed them on Fleming. 'I've neither helped nor incited Dan to do anything, and it's news to me he's trying to escape. What's he supposed to have done?'

'Your nephew is suspected of killing four men... could be five.'

'What!'

'William Stroud, Owen Pearce, Vic Jackman, and Garry Croft. Possibly Bill Kauffman as well.'

'Can you prove that?'

Fleming didn't answer. 'Ever heard of the disciples, Mr Wyatt?'

'Who?'

'The four men I've mentioned. They were known as Bill Kauffman's disciples.'

'Never heard of it.'

Fleming waited for a few moments watching Wyatt carefully. 'There was a dispute at the AWE just before Stroud was murdered. Dan's father, Ian Rimmer, refused to go on strike and it didn't go down well with Kauffman and his disciples.'

'What's that got to do with Dan?'

'I know they bullied, harassed and intimidated Dan's father to try to make him join the strike. He didn't, and the hounding and abuse intensified. It became personal.'

'Sounds like someone did Dan a favour then.'

Fleming opened the folder on the table in front of him. 'It's claimed the dispute that caused the strike was settled, but Kauffman went to the management and told them he wouldn't call the strike off unless they got rid of Dan's father.'

Wyatt stared ahead without saying anything for a few seconds. Eventually, he spoke. 'I knew the company had paid Ian off. Bastards.'

'The management... or Kauffman and his men?'

Wyatt smiled. 'Both, as it happens. Doesn't mean Dan killed them though.'

'Dan had been looking for Croft for five years. Did you know that?'

'I did.'

'Did you know why?'

'Dan had a client who'd asked him to find Croft for him. It seems Croft owed the man a lot of money. Liam Doherty.'

Fleming shot a glance at Logan who was probably thinking the same thing. Either Liam Doherty did exist, or Wyatt was covering up for Rimmer. 'Croft fled to Australia, but Dan found out he was back in England to see his terminally ill mother.'

'So I believe.'

'Croft went to see his mother at a care home and the manager told Dan he was there. Croft disappeared after leaving the home and a dog walker found his body the next day. Croft was shot with the same type of gun used to kill Stroud, Pearce and Jackman. Coincidence?'

'They do happen.'

'Dan was in the army, wasn't he?'

'He was.'

'So he'd know how to use firearms.'

Wyatt glared at Fleming. 'Does being ex-army automatically make someone a suspect in every crime involving guns?'

Fleming ignored the question. 'Your sister was married to Ian Rimmer and she was unwell at the time the abuse was going on.'

Wyatt hadn't removed his gaze from Fleming and this time Fleming caught the hurt in Wyatt's eyes the moment he mentioned his sister. 'She was ill at the time, yes.'

'She died, and soon after Ian was paid off, he took his own life. It must have been hard – for you, and for Dan.'

'Yes, it was,' Wyatt mumbled.

Fleming detected the pain in his voice. 'There's quite a convincing case building up against Dan.'

'All circumstantial though. Have you any forensic evidence... any witnesses?'

'I believe Dan blamed his father's death on the four men, maybe Kauffman as well, and took out his revenge on them.'

'Believing it doesn't prove it,' Wyatt said.

'I can understand why Dan might want to kill them all, but I can't condone it. We need to question him, but he's disappeared. We searched his flat and found a smashed-up laptop. Hardly the actions of an innocent man.'

Wyatt stared blankly ahead and stayed silent.

'Do you know where he is, Mr Wyatt?'

'No.'

'Do you know where he might be going?'

'No.'

'When did Dan join you at Wyatt Investigations?'

'As soon as he left the army.'

'And that would be...'

'A month or two after his father died.'

'Were you close to your sister and brother-in-law, Mr Wyatt?'

Wyatt shot a sharp glance at Fleming. 'Don't see what that has to do with anything, but as it happens, I was.'

'Did they tell you what was going on – about the abuse, I mean?'

There was a long pause before Wyatt answered. 'Yes, they did.'

'And did they say who the men involved were.'

Again, Wyatt hesitated. It was as though he was working out that saying no wouldn't be plausible. Ian Rimmer would have known full well who was bullying him. Eventually Wyatt replied. 'Ian did, yes.'

'And the names were Stroud, Croft, Pearce and Jackman?'

Wyatt's shoulders slumped. 'Yes,' he whispered.

'And you thought it a coincidence they were all shot dead?'

Wyatt simply shrugged.

'You run a private investigator company. Did you trace the four men?'

'No.'

'Do you know whether Dan killed them?'

'No.'

'Do you own a gun?'

'No.'

Fleming glanced across at Logan. 'Give him the dates, Harry.' Fleming waited while Logan fished a piece of paper from a folder in front of him. 'For the purposes of the recorder,' Fleming said, 'DS Logan is handing Mr Wyatt the dates on which Stroud, Croft, Pearce, Jackman and Kauffman were murdered.'

Wyatt looked at the list without touching it.

'I want to know where you and Dan were on these dates.'

'You're joking, right. Apart from Croft and Kauffman, the others were murdered five years ago.'

'I'm sure a detective agency keeps detailed records and diaries.'

Wyatt took the piece of paper and glared at Fleming. 'I'll do my best.'

'Thank you. I want you to let me know immediately if Dan gets in touch with you.'

'Fine,' Wyatt said.

Fleming terminated the interview and indicated for Logan to switch the recorder off.

70

The meetings with Younger were always fraught affairs. He was never satisfied with progress. *I want an arrest and conviction, and pretty damned quick*, Younger had said at the first meeting when he'd put Fleming in charge of the Stroud case. Fleming had covered himself by going to update Temple first before going to see Younger. He didn't want to get in her bad books again for failing to keep her fully informed.

Younger's office door was open, but Fleming knocked anyway. 'You wanted to see me, sir?' Fleming said.

'Yes, come in, Fleming. I have a meeting with the chief constable in twenty minutes and I want to update him on things.' Younger closed the folder he'd been scribbling in and sat back in his chair. He took off his glasses and polished them with a cleaning cloth he extracted from his desk drawer. His right eyelid trembled. A sure sign of mounting stress or irritability. 'What's the current state of play?'

'We're still looking for Rimm–'

'The chief constable is under pressure to get this tied up and finished with,' Younger cut in. 'You've already let Croft slip through your grasp. I sincerely hope you're not going to let the same happen with Rimmer.'

'I was about to say, sir, the PNC has been updated to flag Rimmer as wanted in connection with four, possibly five, murders, and all ports and airports have been alerted.'

'So I can tell the chief constable an arrest is imminent?'

'I think it would be more advisable just to say every effort is being made to find him, sir.'

'And when you do, what are the chances of a conviction? So far, what you have to link him to at least four of the murders is purely circumstantial. You have little forensic evidence and no witnesses.'

'The evidence against him is pretty strong. He's gone on the run, and forensics have confirmed that a Browning nine-millimetre handgun was used to kill Stroud, Pearce, Jackman and Croft. When we have Rimmer in custody, he may confess under close questioning.'

'And if he doesn't.'

'We find the gun and link it to him.'

'And if you can't find it?'

'There's a good chance he'll have it with him.'

'In that case, you'll need backup with armed officers when you find him,' Younger said thoughtfully. The tremble in the eyelid had become more pronounced.

'I do have news on the search for Rimmer. We've got him on CCTV boarding a train for Dover. We've alerted port police.'

'Good. You'll have this all sewn up soon then, won't you?'

Fleming found Logan and Anderson still busy going through reams of CCTV footage from cameras near Kauffman's flat and the derelict industrial site. They'd not had any luck so far and were checking further out from the immediate areas. 'Any joy?' Fleming asked.

'Not yet, boss. It's painstaking work. Getting close to the end of all the material we have and there's no sign of Emerson's car anywhere.'

'Maybe I was wrong about him.'

'Changing the subject,' Logan said, 'how did your meeting with Younger go?'

'Pretty much as expected. He won't be satisfied until we've arrested Rimmer and got a conviction.'

Anderson suddenly thumped the top of her desk with the palm of her right hand. 'Yes!'

'What is it?' Logan asked, looking over her shoulder.

'There!' Anderson exclaimed, pointing to a car in a side street. 'It's Emerson's, parked four streets away from Kauffman's flat.'

'Good work!' Fleming exclaimed. 'Anything from the taxi companies?'

Logan switched from checking CCTV footage to scroll through emails which he hadn't checked since the previous day. 'Got a message here. A taxi driver picked up a man matching Emerson's description half a mile from the industrial site and dropped him off near Reading town centre.'

'Let's pull him in for questioning.' Fleming strode towards his office to pick up his coat.

As soon as he was through the door, his phone rang. He picked up the handset, listened intently for a few seconds, thanked the caller and hung up.

'It's all happening now,' Fleming said, returning to speak to Logan and Anderson. 'Dover police have been on. They've tracked Rimmer's mobile. Found it on a man wearing a red anorak at Dover Priory Station.'

Logan frowned. 'Why don't I think this is good news?'

'It's not Rimmer,' Fleming said. 'Clever man. Left his mobile on the Dover train knowing we would have it tracked. He's nowhere near Dover.'

Logan groaned. 'Younger will go into meltdown if he thinks we've missed him – especially after we lost Croft.'

Fleming sighed. 'Rimmer is now well on his way somewhere else.'

'Any ideas, boss?' Logan asked. 'By the way, the computer guys couldn't do anything with Rimmer's laptop. There might have been something on it to suggest where he might have been planning to run to, but he did too good a job on it.'

Fleming pulled on his coat. 'Right at this moment, I've no idea where he might have gone. Let's go and get Emerson.'

71

There was a chill in the air outside. But deep down in the underground at London Victoria it was warm and muggy. So far, things were going to plan and Rimmer had started to feel a bit more relaxed. It was still possible Fleming might think Rimmer's fictitious Liam Doherty was the man he was looking for. But he was sure as hell going to pull him in for questioning again once he found out about Rimmer's link to Stroud, Croft, Pearce and Jackman.

Rimmer could have no idea how close the police were to finding him. If they did catch up with him, he could always insist he was innocent and had nothing to do with the murders of the four men. The fact that they had driven his father to take his own life was pure coincidence, he could claim. After all, he was pretty sure they would have no forensic evidence. He'd been very careful about that. And there were no witnesses. But still, it wasn't worth taking any chances. Going on the run was his only real way of avoiding a very long prison sentence.

Looking up at the display screen, Rimmer saw the next train was due in one minute. *Soon be out of London.* But then, Rimmer saw two policemen walking up the platform towards him.

Adrenalin pumped through his body as he tensed up. Sweat was running down his back. The two officers had almost reached him when the train pulled in to the platform with screeching brakes. The officers turned and peered through the windows as it came to a stop. Rimmer breathed a sigh of relief. It looked as though they might be looking for someone on the train.

The doors opened and passengers poured out, fighting against people trying to get on while they were getting off. Rimmer waited patiently for the mad rush to subside before jumping into a carriage just before the doors closed again. The two policemen had turned to walk back along the platform as the train pulled out of the station. If they had been looking for someone, it wasn't him.

The second stop on the Victoria Line was Oxford Circus. Rimmer got off there and headed for the Bakerloo Line. Rimmer knew he needed to be cautious. He was heading for Marylebone, but decided to get off at Baker Street and walk the rest of the way. It was only a short distance and it would be better to enter Marylebone Station via the main entrance where he could survey the concourse before entering. The last thing he needed was for police to trap him coming up the escalator from the underground if they happened to be looking for him there. There would be nowhere to run.

Once out of Baker Street Station, Rimmer dodged between slow-moving traffic and crossed the road to head up to Dorset Square and Marylebone. Reaching the main entrance, he lingered there for a minute and scanned the concourse. He could see a couple of uniformed policemen, but they were patrolling around casually and didn't look as though they might be searching for a wanted man. Good so far.

Rimmer glanced up at the departure boards and saw there was a train leaving for High Wycombe in fifteen minutes. On his right was a small kiosk selling pasties and hot drinks. The smell of freshly baked food wafted across reminding him how hungry he was.

With a lamb and mint pasty and a cup of coffee in a paper bag, Rimmer made his way over to the ticket office and bought a single ticket to High Wycombe. He saw from the departure boards that the train was leaving from platform four. There was no sense in hanging around on the concourse so he made his way straight there. It was well before the afternoon commuter rush hour so he was able to climb into a near-empty carriage. Settling into a seat not far from the doors, Rimmer pulled his pasty and coffee out of the bag and wolfed them down.

Thirty minutes later, he came out of the station at High Wycombe and walked over to where he saw a free taxi. The driver slid his window down as Rimmer approached. 'Do you know where there's a static caravan park south of Wycombe Air Park?' Rimmer asked.

'Sure, jump in.'

It didn't take long to get there and Rimmer soon found number thirty-six. After three knocks, Emerson appeared at the door. 'Ah, Dan, see you made it okay. Come in and have a cup of tea. Just put the kettle on.'

Inside the caravan, sipping on his tea, Rimmer at last felt a sense of relief. He'd made it. 'Chances of flying out today?'

'I need to go and get some supplies shortly and check the plane over, then we can be on our way.'

Rimmer smiled and settled back in his seat. *Almost there.*

72

Logan switched the squad car windscreen wipers on to full speed as the steady drizzle of rain turned into a torrential downpour. Fleming was lost in thought as they sped south towards the AWE.

'I meant to ask you,' Logan said, breaking the silence, 'what happened about our special operations guys who had a warrant out for Kauffman's arrest?'

'Younger told me MI5 had him put under surveillance,' Fleming answered. 'Kauffman was suspected of subversive activity and industrial espionage. I had a word with the ops team to let them know we had two possible suspects for Kauffman's murder.'

'But they're not concerned with that, are they?'

'No, I let them know out of courtesy. They've passed the ongoing investigation into Kauffman's dealings with the Russians back to MI5. Special ops only got involved with Kauffman because MI5 don't have powers of arrest. Now that Kauffman is dead, our lot have no further interest in him.'

'Which means, so to speak, they're not in the loop in our murder enquiries?'

'No.'

Logan was about to say something else when Fleming's mobile indicated an incoming call: *Zoe Dunbar.* He picked up. 'Fleming.'

'Just wondering if there's been any developments since Younger's press briefing.'

'There have, but the investigation is at a crucial stage so I can't elaborate.'

'Can I now say you're looking for Liam Doherty in connection with the murders?'

'No.'

'Is that because you don't want it known, or because you're looking for someone else?'

'Persistent as always, eh?'

'It's my job, remember?'

'And mine is to ensure crucial information is not released which might compromise our enquiries.'

'You said you were keeping an open mind on the Kauffman killing. Anything more to say on that?'

'No.'

'Obliging as usual, Fleming. Can I say the search for a serial killer is continuing, but he has not yet been identified?'

Fleming hesitated before answering. 'I'd prefer you just reported that we're still looking for him.'

'Meaning you do know who it is?'

'We have our suspicions.'

'Can I say police *think* they know who it is?'

'You don't give up, do you?'

'Never.'

'When we have something to say, I'll let you know.' Fleming didn't wait for another question. He ended the call.

'Tenacious, isn't she?' Logan observed.

'It's her job,' Fleming replied, mimicking Dunbar.

'Phil Wyatt got back to me with his and Rimmer's whereabouts on the dates we gave him,' Logan said after a few minutes' silence. 'Not particularly helpful. He hasn't got any records for the dates Stroud, Pearce and Jackman were murdered. Says it's too far back.'

'Not surprising. What about the ones when Croft and Kauffman were killed?'

'He says they were both in the office doing paperwork.'

'As you say, not helpful.'

The pair fell into silence again for the rest of the journey. The rain had eased somewhat as they pulled into the entrance to the AWE. There were no pickets on the gate. Logan parked the car and the two detectives made their way to Ursula Nieve's office.

Fleming nodded at Nieve's secretary. 'Is she in?' he asked with a smile.

'Yes. Is she expecting you?'

'No, it's only a quick courtesy call. We're here to see someone else.'

Nieve's door opened and she stuck her head out. 'I heard your voice. Didn't know you were coming. Do you want to come in?' She stood aside to allow Fleming and Logan to enter then turned to face them. 'You were saying you were here to see someone else?'

'Yes, we'd like a word with Seth Emerson. Is he at work?' Fleming asked.

Nieve frowned. 'No, he isn't. He phoned in sick a couple of days ago. Is everything all right?'

'Just need to ask him a few questions.'

'Is this about Bill Kauffman?'

'Yes. Not to worry, we'll catch him at home.'

Nieve hesitated as though she was about to say something

else. 'I don't want to pry,' she said. 'But I know from the press briefing you're now looking for a serial killer.'

'Go on,' Fleming prompted.

'You asked me before if I'd heard of the disciples. I take it they're the four union men your killer murdered?'

'Why do you ask?'

'I was thinking... about that and Kauffman and, well...'

'Yes?'

'You told me it was Dan Rimmer, the private investigator, who gave the photographs of Kauffman to the reporter.'

'I did, yes.'

'Then you asked me to check for people who had left the AWE before Stroud's death and one of the names on my list was Ian Rimmer. Is there a connection?'

'Ian Rimmer was bullied and harassed by the disciples because he refused to strike. As you know, the company paid him off after the strike. His wife was ill and then died. He subsequently took his own life.'

'Oh my God!' Nieve exclaimed. 'And Dan Rimmer?'

'Was his son.'

'So you think he's the killer?'

'Probably. We're looking for him now,' Fleming said. 'By the way, no pickets on the gate. Is the strike off?'

'Yes. Kauffman was the driving force behind it. It's over.'

'Thanks for your time,' Fleming said. 'We'll let ourselves out.'

'Strange,' Logan said, shaking his head as they were making their way back to the car. 'Naomi always felt Nieve had a keen interest in this case, and there she is putting two and two together from snippets of information.'

'Clever woman,' Fleming agreed.

They had a search warrant for Emerson's house, but in fact they didn't need one now Fleming had decided to arrest him for the murder of Kauffman. He could always release him without charge if they didn't find enough evidence.

It was only a short drive to Tadley, and Fleming and Logan were outside Emerson's house in just over five minutes. Fleming knocked sharply on the door and waited. Emerson didn't appear.

Logan walked along to a window and peered in. 'No sign of life in there, boss.'

Fleming tried knocking again but to no avail.

'Could be in bed if he's off sick,' Logan suggested.

'I think he's gone on holiday,' a voice came from behind them.

Fleming turned to see an elderly man walking a dog. 'Are you a neighbour?'

'Yes. I don't usually see much of him. Keeps to himself. But I did see him leave with a big bag this morning. Threw it in his car and sped off without a word.'

'Thanks.' Fleming turned to Logan. 'Best get the SOCOs out to break in and search the house. Get them to check all his clothing to see if there's any match to the fibres they found at the disused industrial site.'

'And any clues he might have left behind to suggest where he might be going?'

'I think I know exactly where he's going,' Fleming said. 'I'll tell you in the car.'

73

Ursula Nieve sat in her office for a while after Fleming and Logan had gone. She was thinking about Seth Emerson, Bill Kauffman, and what Fleming had told her about Ian Rimmer. There was no love lost between Emerson and Kauffman for sure. But had Emerson killed him? Is that why Fleming wanted to see Seth? Or did Ian Rimmer's son kill him? Fleming seemed sure Dan Rimmer was the serial killer they were looking for.

There was something else on Nieve's mind. It had been troubling her for a while. It was not in her nature to be secretive and deceitful, and she was sure Fleming and his two colleagues had their suspicions over why she was taking such an interest in the Stroud case. She was beginning to question the worth of what she'd been asked to do, and after mulling it over for a few minutes, she rose from her desk and popped her head round the office door to speak to her secretary. 'I don't want to be disturbed for the next twenty minutes, okay?'

'Okay, Ursula. No problem.'

Nieve went back into her office and stared at the phone

before finally picking it up and dialling the number she kept locked in her desk drawer.

After a few rings a man's voice came on the line. 'Hello, Toby Omoko.'

'It's Falcon,' Nieve said. 'I have something for you.'

Shortly after Nieve had taken up post as HR manager at the AWE, she had received a mysterious phone call. A man calling himself Quentin Vere had contacted her claiming to be from the security services. He'd told her they needed to vet her for security reasons. Nieve had thought it all rather odd. The company hadn't told her this would be a condition of her employment. Vere had asked to meet her somewhere off site which seemed even more mysterious. Still, she was curious and had asked how she could verify who Vere was and that the approach was genuine.

Vere had given her a number which he claimed was a direct line to the headquarters of MI5. She could ring the number to check his credentials, he'd told her. Even more curious, she'd checked on the MI5 website and found the number was authentic. It was the number for the recruitment office. The person she spoke to seemed to be expecting her call and confirmed Vere was indeed an assistant director general within the organisation. Nieve had wondered if MI5 were trying to recruit her and, if so, for what purpose.

She had a clandestine meeting with Vere two days later. They met on the riverside walk by Vauxhall Bridge. They'd walked up the side of the Thames to Lambeth Bridge where Vere had left her. Nieve had taken an instant dislike to the man. He'd come across as an upper-class snob, pompous and full of self-importance. It turned out MI5 didn't need to vet her at all.

Vere had explained how they wanted her to provide them with information on union activity at the AWE. They had suspicions that, under the leadership of Bill Kauffman, the union had plans to disrupt and subvert work going on there. MI5 thought she would be in a perfect position as HR manager to keep an eye on them. Vere had warned her the Official Secrets Act would apply to anything she did and it even covered the fact that he'd approached her. She could never tell anyone what she was doing, not even her husband.

Intrigued, Nieve had agreed to help and Vere had put her under the control of an agent handler called Toby Omoko who would be her sole point of contact. They'd given her the code name Falcon.

~

'Go ahead,' Omoko said. 'It's safe to talk on this line.'

'DCI Fleming and DS Logan have been to see me. They want to question one of the men who works here in connection with Bill Kauffman.'

'Who?'

'His name's Seth Emerson.'

'Are they speaking to him now?'

'No, he's off sick. They've gone to his home address.'

'They think he killed Kauffman?'

'Maybe, but there is another possibility.'

'There is?'

'You'll no doubt be aware from Eathan Younger's press briefing that the police are looking for a serial killer.'

'Yes, we are.'

'The killer is most likely the man who killed Stroud.'

The line was quiet for a second. 'Go on,' Omoko prompted.

'It was nothing to do with him being an MI5 agent.'

'How do you know?'

'Fleming's looking for Dan Rimmer. Remember... the private investigator who took the photographs of Kauffman with the Russian?'

'I remember.'

'There were four union men at the AWE called the disciples. They bullied, harassed and intimidated a man who refused to strike five years ago. Stroud was one of them.'

'The point being?'

'The company paid the man off when the union went back to work and he subsequently committed suicide.'

'What's the connection with Dan Rimmer?'

'The man was Dan Rimmer's father.'

'I see.'

'Fleming thinks Rimmer held the so-called disciples responsible for his father's death and took out his revenge on them, possibly Kauffman as well. But he wants to speak to Emerson. He maybe sees him as a possible suspect for the Kauffman murder.'

'Why would someone recruited by us get involved in the bullying and intimidation of Rimmer's father?'

'Stroud probably felt he had to go along with it in order to maintain his cover.'

'Good point. Well... thanks for letting me know. At least no one knows Stroud was working for us.'

Nieve hesitated for a second. 'There's just one question.'

'Yes?'

'MI5 wouldn't have anything to do with Kauffman's death, would they?'

'Good God! Whatever makes you think that?'

'He was in the pocket of the Russians and the strike ended as soon as he was killed.'

Omoko drew a deep breath. 'You're seeing a conspiracy

where there isn't one.'

'You sure about that?'

'Absolutely.'

'Okay. What's happening about the Kauffman affair now he's dead?'

'Counter-intelligence are dealing with it. They'll probably expel Kauffman's contact, with a few other diplomats for good measure.'

'Right…' Nieve hesitated.

'Something else?'

Nieve hesitated for a second. 'I've decided to stop being an informant for MI5. Fleming is suspicious of me, I'm sure, and I don't think what I've been doing is of any real value to you. Now Kauffman is dead and the strike is over, I see even less need to carry on spying on the union.'

'Vere won't be best pleased.'

'Tough. Tell him not to worry. I won't let on to anyone what I've been doing. I'd better go.'

Nieve put the phone down and sighed with relief.

74

The rain had passed and a watery sun shone outside Emerson's house. Logan had been on the phone to Anderson to get her to arrange for the SOCOs to search the house and get sample fibres from Emerson's clothing.

'Where to, boss?' Logan asked, switching on the squad car ignition. 'You thought you knew where Emerson was going.'

Fleming was already typing the details into his mobile phone for directions. 'Wycombe Air Park.'

Logan looked sideways at Fleming. 'Didn't know you'd developed psychic powers, boss. How the hell do you know that's where he's headed?'

'I don't for certain. It's just a hunch.'

'Based on what?'

'He told me about a Cessna light aircraft he owns which he keeps there. What quicker way to put some distance between yourself and your pursuers if you decide to do a runner?'

'Sounds as good a guess as any. Are those the directions you've got there?' Logan pointed at Fleming's mobile.

'Yes. Head for Reading, take the M4 towards Maidenhead,

then the A404 to High Wycombe. I'll tell you the rest when we get to Wycombe.'

'Okay.' Logan slipped the car into gear and set off with wheels spinning on loose gravel on the road.

'Better stick the blues and twos on, Harry. We ought to get there as quick as we can. You never know. I might just be right about this.'

As the car sped towards Reading with blue lights flashing and siren wailing, Fleming phoned Anderson to see if there was any information on Rimmer. It was not good news. They'd lost him somewhere between London Victoria and Dover. 'Younger will go ballistic,' Fleming said. 'Rimmer's slipped through the net. He obviously got off the train long before it got to Dover, and he's more than likely now disguised. He could be anywhere.'

Logan navigated past two cars which had pulled over to let him by. 'What do you think about his uncle, boss? Reckon he knows something? Maybe he helped Rimmer.'

'We may find out if he was implicated in some way once we catch Rimmer.'

They fell silent for the rest of the journey as Logan weaved his way through traffic which was getting heavier as they approached High Wycombe. Despite the roads being busy, Logan made good time with his foot to the floor. Other drivers pulled over to let the squad car with its wailing siren and flashing blue lights past them.

As they drove into the airfield, Fleming could see across to the north side where pilots had parked their aircraft. 'Either we're in luck, or I was mistaken,' Fleming said.

'Boss?'

'Emerson's plane is here.'

'How do you know?'

'He told me about his Cessna 172 Skyhawk. They have wings that sit above the cockpit. There's only one here. Must be his!'

Logan found a parking space near the Booker Aviation operations and air traffic control offices. He switched off the blues and twos and killed the engine. Walking over towards the offices, they came across a balding man in his fifties looking at them with eyes and mouth wide open. The name badge on his white short-sleeved shirt told them his name was Barry.

'What can I do for you?' His voice trembled. It wasn't every day a police car with sirens blaring and blue lights flashing sped into the car park.

Fleming showed his warrant card. 'DCI Fleming and DS Logan. Is there a Mr Emerson here?'

'Seth? No, he's not here yet. Is there a problem?'

'We need to speak to him, that's all. You're expecting him?'

'Yes, his plane's all fuelled up and ready to go.'

'When?'

'A bit later. He said something about coming over to check the aircraft out first before he picks up his passenger.'

Fleming's eyes narrowed. 'A passenger?'

'Let me check. Come into the office.'

Inside, Barry put on his glasses and typed something on the keyboard on his desk with shaky hands. He peered at his computer screen and then looked up at Fleming. 'Yes, he's booked to fly out in an hour and a half with a Mr Dan Rimmer. I'm expecting to see Seth any time.'

Fleming eyes widened. *I don't believe it!*

Logan scratched his head. 'How the hell does Emerson know Rimmer?'

'Long story, but he used Rimmer to spy on his wife.'

Barry was looking in bewilderment between Fleming and Logan.

'You know where they're supposed to be going?' Fleming asked, looking at Barry.

'Le Touquet in northern France.'

Fleming turned to Logan. 'Better get Anderson on the phone. I think we'll need an armed response unit here, and damned quick. And ask her to alert Temple and Younger.'

Barry looked stunned and his face turned ashen as Logan made the call.

75

Emerson's static caravan was on a park about nine miles south of High Wycombe, a quarter of an hour by car to Wycombe Air Park. It was a pleasant afternoon with a light breeze blowing. Perfect conditions for the short flight to France.

The caravan was old and in need of renovation, but the site itself was neat and tidy. The entrance had double wooden gates, and a driveway led down to a large, neatly cut grass area bordered on three sides by static caravans. Rimmer was sipping on the tea Emerson had brewed. 'How long have you had the van?' he asked, trying to make light conversation.

'It was my father's. He left me this as well as the Cessna.'

Rimmer stretched his leg which was beginning to ache. 'How much leg room is there in the Cessna?'

'It's not too bad. It has adjustable seats which can move forwards and backwards as well as up and down. You'll be fine. It's only a fairly short hop over to Le Touquet.' Emerson watched Rimmer rubbing his thigh. 'Cramp?'

'Nah, old war wound. Plays up sometimes.'

'Really?'

'Shrapnel injury in Afghanistan.'

'Is that why you came out of the army?'

'More or less, yeah.' Rimmer wanted to change the subject. 'What's your wife going to do now Kauffman's dead?'

'Couldn't care less.'

'Have you spoken to her since?'

'No. Why would I want to?'

'Fair point. Think she wonders if you did it?'

'Probably. Before I threw her out, I had a bit of a spat with Kauffman on the picket line. Bastard tried to stop me going in to work and his cronies trashed my car.'

'You didn't go on strike then?'

'No. Kauffman was a militant troublemaker. I saw the newspaper article with photographs of him receiving a package from a stranger.'

'I took the photos,' Rimmer admitted.

Emerson frowned. 'How did you–'

'When I was following your wife. I took them then.'

'You didn't say.'

'No need. You were only interested in whether your other half was having an affair with him.'

'Thanks for reminding me.'

Rimmer felt sorry for the man. He recalled how his father, Ian Rimmer, had also refused to strike five years earlier and how the union men had persecuted him for it. And then there was Emerson's wife who left him for the ringleader. 'You joked about killing Kauffman. If I'd been you, I would have killed him.'

'I'd gladly have murdered them both...' Emerson blurted out.

Rimmer saw the pain in Emerson's eyes. 'So you did kill him?'

Emerson hung his head.

'Don't worry,' Rimmer said. 'I for one will not be turning you in.'

'I think DCI Fleming is onto me. I had to go in and get my fingerprints and a DNA sample taken. All they need is a match and I'm done.'

'Where do you plan to go?'

'I'll take you to Le Touquet this afternoon, then tomorrow I might fly west across Europe heading for Greece. I have an old friend there I could maybe stay with until I think of something more permanent.'

'Well, good luck, mate. I hope you make it.'

Emerson sat silent for a few seconds before speaking again. 'What about you, Dan? Are you sure you're looking for someone's daughter? You'd been looking for Croft for a long time and he ends up dead as soon as he comes back to England. Bit of a coincidence, eh?'

Rimmer laughed and slapped his thigh. 'Yeah, you're right. We're both on the run. No sense in trying to deny it now is there?'

Emerson smiled. 'And the other three they mentioned in the press briefing. You're the serial killer they're looking for?'

Rimmer held his hands up as though in surrender. 'Yes, I did kill all four men, but don't worry, I'm not a psychopath. My dad was the same as you. Refused to strike five years earlier and the four of them bullied, threatened and harassed him. Kauffman got the company to pay him off after the dispute ended and my dad took his own life. The bastards deserved to die.'

'Funny old business, isn't it?' Emerson said. 'We're classed as dangerous criminals, but all we did is administer justice against people who are evil.'

Rimmer was about to speak when he heard a familiar high-pitched buzzing sound. He dashed to the window and looked out.

'What is it?' Emerson asked, concern in his voice.

'Bloody drone.'

The noise stopped and there was a loud rapping on the door.

Rimmer rushed to his bag and pulled out his gun. 'Ask who it is,' he told Emerson.

Emerson did as Rimmer told him.

'My drone's crashed behind your caravan. Can I go and get it please?' a young voice shouted.

Rimmer nodded at Emerson. 'Open the door and tell him it's okay.' Taking no chances, he stood where he could see outside, gun at the ready.

A distraught looking teenager was standing holding the drone's controls. 'Sorry. Haven't got the hang of it yet. I thought it was going to hit your window.'

Emerson laughed. 'No worries. You go and get it.'

Rimmer sighed with relief and put the gun away.

Emerson turned to face Rimmer. 'I should go in a minute to check the Cessna out and make sure everything is okay before we go. What are your plans when we get to Le Touquet?'

'I believe you can walk into the town from the airfield so I'll do that, get a taxi to the station at Etaples le Touquet and catch a train to Brussels. Maybe less chance they'll be looking for me there than Paris.'

'Then what?'

'Direct flight to Brazil and I'm free.'

'I hope you do get away, Dan. I'll see you in about an hour,' Emerson said, turning to leave.

Rimmer looked out of the window to see Emerson driving off. *Brazil, it sounded too good to be true.*

76

Emerson drove out of the caravan park with a mixture of relief and concern. The drone incident had shaken him, and he'd blurted out he'd killed Kauffman. Still, he was sure his secret was safe with Rimmer who had his own secrets. The only thing troubling him was Rimmer had told him about his escape plans. Could he take the chance that Emerson might tell the police if they were to catch him? *Maybe he'll kill me when we get to France to make sure I can't reveal his plans*, Emerson thought for a brief moment before putting it out of his mind. He felt sure he could trust Rimmer. Maybe he had murdered four men, but as he said, he wasn't a psychopath. He had an understandable, if not moral, reason to murder the men. And, Emerson reminded himself, he too had killed a man.

Putting his thoughts to the back of his mind, Emerson joined the A404 to head up to Wycombe. Just over sixteen minutes later, he was pulling into the car park next to the operations and air traffic control offices at Wycombe Air Park.

While Logan was arranging the armed response unit, Fleming tried to reassure Barry whose hands were shaking. 'Only a precaution,' Fleming said. 'Emerson's passenger is a wanted man, and he may have a gun.'

'I... I understand. Should I try to warn everyone on the airfield?'

'Can you do that quickly and easily?'

'I can get air traffic control to tell pilots not to land here until further notice and radio all staff to keep indoors. There's not too many around. And Seth's was the only plane due to take off in the next couple of hours.'

'Do it. Do you know where Emerson is supposed to be picking up his passenger?'

Barry thought for a moment. 'He didn't say, but...'

'Go on.'

'I know Seth has a static caravan on a site near here. Mr Rimmer can't be far away if Seth was planning to fly out soon.'

Fleming was jotting down the address and directions to the site as Logan finished his call.

'All done, boss. The ARU should be here within the next hour. They'll be coming from Reading.'

'I've got the address and directions to where Rimmer may be holed up, but we can't leave here in case he's not and we miss Emerson.'

'Wherever he is,' Logan said, 'they have to come here, don't they? So why don't we wait for them?'

Fleming frowned. 'What if they have a change of mind and decide not to fly today? Younger will do his nut if he thinks we wasted time assuming they would turn up here.'

'Please don't tell me you're thinking of going after Rimmer on your own while I wait here.'

'Got a better idea?'

'You're mad, boss. Rimmer is almost certain to have a gun.

You can't possibly go looking for him on your own without backup.'

'I'll be careful. If they're there I'll call you and you can divert the ARU. Give me the car keys.'

Logan shook his head and reluctantly handed them over. 'This is not a good idea, boss.'

'Don't worry,' Fleming said, turning to leave. He opened the office door and took a sharp intake of breath. 'He's here!'

'Who, Emerson? Rimmer? Both?' Logan yelled.

'Emerson,' Fleming shouted over his shoulder as he dashed out of the door.

Coming into the car park, Emerson saw something which made him panic. It was the marked police car.

'Fuck!'

Glancing over to the offices, he saw Fleming and Logan rushing out. He put his foot down and sped out of the car park, turning up the narrow road leading to the north of the airfield. A line of parked planes came into view and Emerson swerved to cut across the grass towards them. He drove over the top end of the runway, glancing to his left to make sure there were no planes coming in to land, and skidded to a halt beside his Cessna.

Looking behind him, he saw the police car racing up the road he'd come up and turn to head straight for him. Emerson jumped out of the car and clambered up into the Cessna cockpit. He fumbled for the ignition key and rammed it in while flicking the throttle to open. Checking the idle fuel mixture was set at about twenty percent and that the propeller area was clear, Emerson flicked the master switch and flashing beacon to on.

Looking out of the window, he saw the police car was closing fast. *Maybe I've just got enough time.*

Emerson was sweating profusely and his hand shook as he turned the ignition to start. The engine coughed once and the propeller turned with a soft whine. The instrument panel lit up and Emerson advanced the fuel mixture to rich, checked the oil pressure and switched on the navigation lights.

The police car was almost on him as the plane eased forward in the direction of the airstrip with the propeller gaining speed and the noise in the cockpit increasing.

Fleming watched with dismay as the plane taxied to the runway. They were gaining fast, but there was no way they would reach the Cessna in time.

'How fast do these planes need to go before they can take off?' Logan asked breathlessly.

'Don't know,' Fleming answered, 'but I'm going to try to get in front.'

The Cessna was pointing down the airstrip and the engine noise increased as the plane taxied forwards.

Fleming cut across the grass and headed for the plane. They were only a few yards behind the Cessna which continued to pick up speed. Fleming put his foot to the floor and the car lurched forward onto the airstrip, passing the Cessna at ninety miles an hour.

Logan looked back and saw the terror on Emerson's face.

Fleming eased off the accelerator and the Cessna gained rapidly on them, but when Fleming slowed down even more, the Cessna veered off sideways to avoid the car and came to a halt on the grass verge. The propeller stopped with a shudder and Emerson climbed out, making no effort to run. The game was up. He had nowhere to go.

Fleming leapt out of the car and strode over to Emerson with Logan just behind. As Logan slapped handcuffs onto Emerson's wrists, Fleming showed his warrant card. 'Mr Emerson, I'm arresting you for the murder of Bill Kauffman. You do not have to say anything, but it may harm your defence if you do not mention when questioned something which you later rely on in court. Anything you do say may be given in evidence.'

Emerson stayed silent and hung his head in defeat.

'Is Rimmer at your caravan?' Fleming asked.

Emerson nodded.

The ARU unit had not yet arrived. 'We need to get there,' Fleming told Logan. 'Get onto the ARU and redirect them. And let Younger know.'

Logan made the calls and prayed they would get to the caravan park before them.

77

Rumour had it the director general was about to close down the small subversion unit in MI5. The only thing it had been actively engaged in recently was keeping an eye on union activity at the AWE. Now Bill Kauffman was dead and everyone had gone back to work, there seemed no pressing reason to keep the unit going. The Kauffman file had been passed to counter-intelligence who were dealing with Kauffman's Russian contact.

Toby Omoko wondered whether Quentin Vere would retire or if the DG would put him in charge of some other small unit. Omoko didn't care as long as he didn't have to put up with Vere any longer. He'd had about as much as he could take. His sick colleague had never come back and had sent his resignation in the post. Vere's secretary had resigned as well. Uncertainty about her future and the stress of working for Vere had taken its toll.

Vere himself was in a strange mood. Omoko was beginning to wonder about his state of mind. *Maybe we're all feeling the strain*, he thought as he trudged up the stairs for his weekly briefing meeting with him. A serious looking temp was in the secretary's chair typing away on the computer. She had short grey hair and large red-rimmed glasses sat on the tip of her nose. Her fingers moved rapidly over the keyboard and her eyes never left the screen.

Omoko stood for a while waiting for her to finish what she was doing, but she carried on typing. 'Go straight in,' she said without looking up. Omoko knocked and went in to face whatever mood Vere was in. He was standing at the window looking out across the river. 'I don't agree with all this change just for the sake of it,' he muttered without turning. 'What do you think, Omoko?'

'About what, sir?'

Vere spun round, anger in his eyes. 'Bloody changes!' he shouted, slumping into the chair behind his desk. 'Things would be different if I had my way,' he muttered. 'The place isn't like it used to be you know.'

'Really?' Omoko didn't know what else to say.

'People can't take the pressure. Your mate downstairs handing in his notice. My secretary resigning. What's it all about, eh?'

Omoko wasn't about to say he'd considered packing the job in himself. 'Sometimes people just want a change in direction... to do something different.'

'Don't know why people can't be satisfied with what they've got. Should be grateful they've got a job and stick to it. There's no sense of loyalty anymore.'

There was a knock on the door and the temp came in with a cup of coffee for Vere. She looked at Omoko as though to question whether he wanted one.

'He doesn't need one. He won't be here long,' Vere muttered.

The temp left without saying a word.

'She doesn't say very much,' Vere said, sipping his coffee.

Probably doesn't dare, Omoko thought.

Putting his cup down on the saucer, Vere looked up at Omoko. 'Anything new to report?'

'Falcon rang me. Remember I told you about the brawl on the picket line between Kauffman and Emerson? There was a newspaper article about it.'

'Yes. So what?'

'It seems DCI Fleming wants to talk to Emerson who believed his wife was having an affair with Kauffman. It's possible Fleming sees Emerson as a suspect.'

'Good for him. Doesn't help us find out who murdered Stroud though, does it?'

'That's the other thing Falcon told me. She thinks she knows who killed Stroud.'

Vere pulled off his glasses and squinted at Omoko. 'She does?'

'It's the private investigator, Dan Rimmer. The guy who took the photos of Kauffman and the Russian.'

Vere raised an eyebrow. 'How come she thinks he did it?'

'Four union men drove Rimmer's father to suicide because he refused to strike. Fleming believes Rimmer murdered the men in revenge. Stroud was one of them. He obviously couldn't shy away from the abuse they subjected Rimmer's father to for fear of blowing his cover.'

'So it's a simple matter of vengeance... nothing to do with the fact we placed Stroud there as an agent to spy on the activities of Kauffman and the union.'

'That seems to be the case, sir.'

'They've arrested Rimmer?'

'No, he's gone on the run.'

'If they catch him it can't become public knowledge that we've planted agents in the AWE.'

'You think Rimmer might have known and will reveal all at his trial?'

'If he did know, he wouldn't be able to say anything before because he would have given himself away as the killer. He'd have to keep quiet. But once he's in custody and has nothing to lose...'

'What would happen if it did come out?' Omoko asked.

'It's sensitive. We've been accused before of spying on trade unions and pressure groups and we've always denied it. Human rights, big brother, civil liberties, freedom of action and speech, infringement of privacy... you name it. Christ, the press would have a field day if it was to become public knowledge. Not going to happen on my shift, you hear?'

Omoko wasn't sure whether to mention this, but did. 'Something troubled me about Falcon's telephone call. She asked if we had anything to do with Kauffman's murder.'

Vere laughed. 'My dear boy, we don't go around disposing of people, for God's sake.'

'She thought it was convenient. Kauffman dead, link with the Russians broken... strike over.'

'There'll always be a conspiracy theory where MI5 is involved, Omoko. Don't even think there might be something in it.'

'No, sir. Changing the subject, have you heard anything from counter-intelligence about what they're aiming to do regarding Kauffman's Russian contact?'

'You should know by now, Omoko. Need-to-know basis. I've no idea what they have planned.'

'Is it true the DG is about to close our unit, sir?' Omoko asked suddenly.

Vere glared at Omoko. 'You'd like that, wouldn't you, Omoko? I know you've always wanted to get involved in something like counter-terrorism. Well, let me tell you, what we're doing is every bit as vital. Don't you forget it! And close the bloody door when you leave!'

'There is one more thing, sir.'

'What?'

'It's Ursula Nieve... sorry, Falcon. She no longer wants to be an informant. Thinks Fleming is suspicious of her, and she questions whether she can continue to be of any value to MI5 now the strike is over and Kauffman is dead.'

'Is that so? She wasn't much use to us anyway, was she?'

Omoko was surprised Vere hadn't lost his temper. 'I suppose not.'

'Make sure she keeps quiet, Omoko. I'll hold you responsible if she blabs about what she was doing.'

'Of course.' Omoko left Vere's office and shut the door rather more sharply than intended.

Vere stared ahead for a moment then made a decision. He buzzed through to the temp. 'Get me Assistant Chief Constable Eathan Younger on the phone. Thames Valley Police.'

'Eathan,' Vere said, hearing Younger's voice. 'How are you?'

'Fine. What can I do for you?'

'It's a delicate matter, and strictly confidential.'

'Go on.'

'I believe your DCI Fleming is after a Dan Rimmer in connection with the murder of William Stroud, and three other men.'

There was a guarded silence for a few seconds before Younger spoke again. 'He is, yes. Why?'

'I have to advise you, what I'm about to say is covered under the Official Secrets Act. Understood?'

'I understand.'

'Stroud was working for us, monitoring the activities of the union and Bill Kauffman at the AWE. It can't become public knowledge.'

'I see.'

'This is extremely delicate...'

'Go on.'

'I believe Rimmer is armed and dangerous?'

'We think so, yes.'

'There's a good chance he wouldn't hesitate to use his gun to avoid capture, so there would need to be armed officers involved in his arrest I presume?'

'That will most certainly be the case, yes.'

'It would therefore be convenient... only under certain circumstances... were he to try to shoot himself out of trouble and be eliminated in the process. Necessary to preserve the safety of others of course.'

There was a long silence. 'I think I understand you.'

78

The blues were flashing on the squad car as it sped on its way to the caravan park. Fleming had kept the siren off so as not to alert Rimmer as they drew closer. Emerson sat handcuffed in the back of the car next to Logan. They arrived in under fifteen minutes and Fleming slowed the car down and parked next to the entrance gates. There was no sign of the armed response unit.

'Where's your caravan?' Fleming asked Emerson.

There was no answer.

Logan jabbed Emerson in the ribs. 'Speak up.'

Emerson glanced across at Logan's menacing glare. 'At the top end of the road as you go round,' he grumbled.

'Got a number or name?' Fleming asked.

'Thirty-six.'

'You're not thinking of going in before the ARU get here, are you, boss?'

'I'd like to talk to him. Maybe I can get him to see sense and give himself up before they arrive.'

'I think we should wait here for them,' Logan said. 'If we

drive in and Rimmer sees a police car he could run for it. Could be a bit tricky to try to stop him if he's armed.'

'Is he?' Fleming asked Emerson.

Emerson glared at him.

Logan gave Emerson another prod. 'Maybe we should send you in to tell him there are armed police on the way,' he suggested. 'There's a good chance he might shoot you thinking you'd alerted them. But there's nothing to worry about if he hasn't got a gun. Then there's always the chance the police could shoot you both if Rimmer resists arrest. Not a good outcome either way if we send you into the caravan.'

Emerson suddenly had a change of heart. 'He has a gun.'

'Thought you'd see sense,' Logan said.

'I think I should try to talk to him,' Fleming suggested. 'He may panic if he sees armed police. I don't want to see him killed.'

Logan shook his head. 'I don't think that's a good idea. We ought to wait for the ARU. They should be here any minute.'

Fleming thought for a moment. 'He's done what he set out to do. I don't think he'll want to kill anyone else.'

'You sure about that. He's a cornered man, and dangerous.'

'If he knows we've got Emerson, he'll realise flying to France isn't an option. There's nowhere to run to. I think he'll see sense.' Fleming sat and thought for a few seconds before turning to Emerson. 'What state of mind is Rimmer in? Is he jumpy and nervous, or does he seem reasonably calm?'

'Are you asking me to be a bloody psychologist? How the hell would I know?' Emerson spat out.

'Was he talking lucidly?'

'I guess so.'

Logan shook his head. 'Boss, if you go in there before the ARU get here, what's to stop him coming out and holding us up at gunpoint while he gets us to release Emerson, getting in the car and hightailing it up to the airfield? He could be in the air on his way to France in half an hour.'

Fleming considered Logan's point. 'Okay, we wait for the ARU, then I want to try to talk to him.'

Logan exhaled a long breath. 'Glad you're seeing sense, boss.'

A few moments later three armed response vehicles sped down the road and screeched to a halt behind the squad car.

Fleming got out and spoke to the driver in the lead vehicle. 'Who's in charge?' he asked.

'I am,' stated the man sitting next to the driver.

Fleming showed his warrant card. 'DCI Fleming. Rimmer is in number thirty-six, at the top end of the road as you go round.'

'Okay, if you'd like to follow us,' the officer in charge suggested.

'When we get there,' Fleming said, 'I want to go in and talk to him.'

The man looked dubious. 'Too risky. I'd rather we just ask him to come out and give himself up.'

'Not sure he'll do that, but I think I might be able to persuade him to if I could get in to speak to him.'

'And if you can't convince him?'

'It could get interesting.'

'I don't think I can allow you to do that, sir. You may be senior in rank, but I'm in charge of any incident involving firearms. My responsibility.'

Fleming admired the man's assertiveness. 'Okay. You ask him to come out and give himself up first. If he refuses. You say I want to go in to talk to him... deal?'

The man turned to the other men in the ARV. 'For the record, I tried to dissuade DCI Fleming from going in, right?'

'Right,' the other men voiced in unison.

'Okay, let's move!' the officer in charge commanded.

The three ARVs sped up the park driveway and cut across the grass, coming to a halt in a line twenty yards from the front of Emerson's caravan. Fleming followed close behind.

Nine uniformed police carrying Glock 17 pistols and Heckler & Koch MP5 carbines jumped out of the vehicles and took up positions behind them. Three of the men carried marksman rifles with telescopic sights.

Fleming got out of his car and walked over to the officer in charge as he pulled out a megaphone from his vehicle. 'Tell him we have Emerson and there's no way he can escape,' Fleming suggested.

The officer nodded and lifted the megaphone to his mouth. The armed men had carbines and rifles trained on the door and windows, ready to open fire if Rimmer started shooting.

79

Nine policemen were leaning over the tops of the ARVs with carbines and rifles tucked tightly into their shoulders, aimed and ready to shoot if necessary. They had their eyes fixed on the door and front windows of Emerson's caravan. The officer in charge lifted the megaphone to his mouth. Fleming and Logan watched calmly from behind.

'This is the police,' the officer said into the mouthpiece. His amplified voice carried across the grassed area between the ARVs and the caravan. 'We're armed. Please come out with your hands held high over your head.'

There was no answer.

'Emerson is under arrest. There's no way you can escape. Give yourself up.'

Still no response.

The officer looked at Fleming. 'You want to try talking to him?'

Fleming took the megaphone. 'Mr Rimmer. This is DCI Fleming. I want to come in to talk to you. Okay?'

The seconds ticked by.

'Rimmer, you can't escape. I don't want to see any bloodshed. Can I come in?' Fleming asked again.

After a few moments, the door creaked open.

Fingers tightened on triggers.

'Just you, Fleming. And hands on your head where I can see them,' Rimmer called through the open door.

Fleming handed the megaphone back to the officer in charge. 'Give me ten minutes. I'm coming in, Rimmer!' he shouted, then put his hands on his head and walked towards the door taking deep breaths. Reaching the door, he started up the steps.

'Come in very slowly and keep your hands on your head,' Rimmer said.

Fleming entered to find Rimmer sitting at the far end of the caravan with his Browning aimed straight at him.

'Take a seat over there.' Rimmer pointed to the opposite side.

Fleming did as Rimmer told him. 'Can I take my hands down now?'

'Sure, but keep them where I can see them.'

'Can you also put the gun down? It makes me feel nervous.'

Rimmer smiled and placed it on the small coffee table in front of him. 'We meet again, eh? What do you want to talk about?'

'Quite a trail you left for us.'

'Almost worked. How did you find me?'

'I was actually looking for Emerson who happened to tell me a while back he had a light aircraft at Wycombe Air Park. I had a hunch he might be heading there. When we got to the airfield, we were informed he was due to fly over to France with you.'

Rimmer sighed and put his injured leg up on the coffee table. 'I could have been friends with you under different circumstances, you know.'

Fleming smiled. 'Fate has a hand to play. There is no Liam Doherty is there?'

'Best I could come up with to explain why I was looking for Croft. Did you believe it though?'

'I didn't rule it out, I must admit. I know why you killed him... and Stroud, Pearce and Jackman. I thought for a while you might have killed Kauffman as well.'

'Not guilty on that one, Fleming,' Rimmer retorted.

'I know. That's why I've arrested Seth Emerson.'

'So where do we go from here?' Rimmer asked. 'Seems I have three options. Shoot myself, give up, or I take you hostage and get the armed men outside to put their guns down while I escape.'

'There's nowhere to go, Rimmer. Your only chance was to fly over to France with Emerson. Not going to happen now. You have to give yourself up.'

Rimmer's head drooped. 'My mother was ill. She died because of the stress caused by the men I killed. My dad took his life because of them. I swore I would hold them to account.'

Fleming shifted awkwardly in his seat. 'I can understand why you did it, Rimmer. But I can't condone it.'

'No, I suppose not. So what now?'

'You should give me the gun and give up.'

Rimmer scratched his head. 'How do we get out of here without these guys outside getting trigger happy?'

'I go out first, show them your Browning, and tell them you've given yourself up.'

Rimmer took a deep breath. 'Okay. One thing. My uncle had nothing to do with any of this. All he did was tell me who it was that tormented my dad.'

'We'll have to question him, but he has nothing to worry about if he wasn't involved in any way.'

Rimmer nodded, picked up the Browning by the barrel and

hauled himself to his feet. He walked towards Fleming with his gun arm outstretched.

Younger had arrived in a speeding marked car and was talking to the ARU leader less than an hour after getting the message from Logan and the phone call from Vere. 'Why did you let Fleming go in there?'

'I tried to dissuade him, sir,' the man said. 'My men can vouch for it. Rimmer didn't respond when I asked him to give himself up so DCI Fleming persuaded Rimmer to let him in to speak to him. He's been in there for about ten minutes. Reckoned it was all the time he would need.'

Younger's right eyelid twitched. 'Right, we're not taking any chances. Rimmer has a gun, and he's dangerous. I don't want the life of a police officer put at risk. One of your marksmen should take a shot if they get the opportunity.'

'Shouldn't we wait to hear from DCI Fleming?' the officer said. 'We can't just shoot Rimmer if he shows himself. There has to be justification on the basis someone's life is in immediate danger. We don't know it is. Rimmer may be thinking–'

Younger's eyelid had gone into spasm. 'Fleming's ten minutes are up,' he cut in. 'Is there any sign Rimmer is about to give himself up?'

'No, sir.'

'Then I'm taking command.'

One of the marksmen had heard the conversation. 'I have sight of the target through a window. He has a gun in his hand.'

'Take the shot!' Younger commanded.

'I think we should wait, sir,' the officer in charge of the ARU urged as the marksman's finger tightened on the trigger.

'Take the bloody shot!' Younger screamed.

The window suddenly shattered and glass flew everywhere as a bullet hit Rimmer in the forehead, flinging him across the room against the far wall. His lifeless body slumped to the floor with the gun still in his right hand.

Fleming stared in disbelief. 'No! He was giving himself up!'

Collecting his thoughts, Fleming took out his mobile and photographed Rimmer with his right hand clutching the gun by the barrel. Having secured the evidence, he pulled open the door. 'Who gave the fucking order to shoot?'

'I did,' Younger admitted, looking red in the face.

Fleming glared at him. 'He was giving himself up!'

'A word,' Younger said, indicating for Fleming to join him. 'I had no choice. The officer in charge of the ARU told me you'd be out in ten minutes. You weren't. I feared for your safety.'

Fleming took out his mobile and waved it in front of Younger. 'I have photographs. He was holding the gun by the barrel to hand it over to me.'

'I want you to say he was going to shoot you.'

'No way, sir. That's not what happened.'

'Give me the phone, Fleming,' Younger insisted, reaching out for the mobile. The entire right side of his face was in convulsion. 'That's an order!'

'Fuck you... sir!' Fleming shouted and strode to his squad car.

80

Two weeks after the shooting of Dan Rimmer, the director general of MI5 closed the subversion unit. He'd denied claims from Eathan Younger that the instruction to eliminate Rimmer had come from them. Quentin Vere had been sacked and Toby Omoko was moved to counter-terrorism. Ursula Nieve continued as HR manager at the AWE, but no longer worked for MI5. The Russians sent the diplomat who was Kauffman's contact back to Russia where he would no doubt face the consequences for a failed mission.

It had been a hectic two weeks, but Fleming was enjoying a drink with Logan and Anderson at the Trout Inn. He clinked glasses with his two colleagues. 'Not a bad result, five murders solved, albeit two of them weren't on our patch.'

'But only one Thames Valley cold case cracked,' Logan reminded him.

'You're so negative, Sarge,' Anderson said. 'One is better than none.'

'Just saying... pity Pearce and Jackman weren't our cases.'

'If they had been, we'd be moving into the cold case review team,' Anderson observed.

'Good point, Naomi. Here's to one.' Logan raised his glass.

'No worries on that front,' Fleming said. 'The chief constable's suspended Younger pending a full enquiry over his part in Rimmer's shooting. And because he tried to get me to lie to cover up his actions. Temple will be happy.'

'Oh?' Logan queried.

'She didn't see eye to eye with him,' was all Fleming said. 'And Jeff Miller will also be pleased. He's secure as head of the cold case review team now Younger's gone.'

'You took a big risk, sir,' Anderson pointed out. 'Going into the caravan knowing Rimmer was armed.'

'I didn't see it like that, Naomi. I was sure he wouldn't try to kill me.'

Logan was looking through his empty glass. 'Ironic in a way, isn't it? Croft comes back after all this time to see his terminally ill mother. She's still alive and he's dead. By the way, whose round is it?'

'It's yours, Sarge,' Anderson reminded him.

'Really? Anyone want crisps?'

Fleming and Anderson shook their heads.

'Just me then,' Logan said.

'Surprised you're not going to order burger and chips,' Anderson quipped.

Logan's eyes lit up. 'Now there's a thought,' he replied, getting up to go to the bar.

Fleming looked at Anderson. 'They almost made it you know... Emerson and Rimmer. They were within an hour of flying over to France.'

'Despite what he did, you had a certain amount of respect for Rimmer, didn't you, sir?' Anderson asked.

Fleming knew only too well the anger you could feel towards someone who was responsible for the death of a parent. 'I did, yes. There was a part of me... for a while, that hoped he would get away.'

Silence fell on the pair until Logan returned with the drinks. 'Who's died?' he joked, looking at the glum faces.

'Bet you ordered chips,' Anderson said, trying to lift the mood.

Logan laughed. 'Had to. Your fault, Naomi. You mentioned them.'

'Knew it!'

Logan grinned and sat back at the table. 'Good result on Emerson, eh? Confession after we confronted him with the fact that fibres from his clothing at home matched ones found at the disused industrial site where Kauffman's body was discovered.'

'Strange, isn't it? He and Rimmer both killed people believing they had a right to because their victims had hurt them so badly,' Fleming observed.

'You're surely not suggesting they were justified?'

Fleming shook his head. 'No, of course not. But you can understand what drove them to it.'

'What about Rimmer's uncle, Phil Wyatt?' Anderson asked.

'Rimmer claimed his uncle didn't know anything,' Fleming said. 'We interviewed Wyatt again. There's no concrete evidence or proof to suggest he was involved in any way with the murders, or in helping Rimmer try to escape. He knew about the abuse Rimmer's father suffered, and knew the names of the men behind it, but that's all. He probably guessed Rimmer killed them, but there wasn't enough to charge him with any crime. He's a free man.'

'Your reporter friend, Zoe Dunbar,' Logan said, 'got more of a story than she bargained for, didn't she?'

Fleming laughed. 'She's not my friend. Dunbar is a pain. But that's her job... as she would say. And yes, she started off with interest in the Stroud case, but ended up with stories on five murders.'

'She'll have her hooks into you now,' Logan said. 'You're a good source of material.'

Logan's chips arrived and he covered the plate with his hands to stop Anderson diving into them.

'Just one, Sarge?' Anderson pleaded.

'Okay, Naomi, you can have two, because it's you.'

'You're all heart.'

Fleming smiled, sat back to take a sip of his beer, and wondered what he would have done if he'd been in Rimmer's shoes.

THE END

A NOTE FROM THE PUBLISHER

Thank you for reading this book. If you enjoyed it please do consider leaving a review on Amazon to help others find it too.

We hate typos. All of our books have been rigorously edited and proofread, but sometimes mistakes do slip through. If you have spotted a typo, please do let us know and we can get it amended within hours.

info@bloodhoundbooks.com